Even as the com cut off, there was a sudden bright flash on the horizon, in the direction of the city.

"*Hold on*," Leclair snapped. "Everybody, shockwave inbound – *hit the deck.*"

The pilot matched actions to words, flipping every rotor to horizontal and driving the aircraft towards the ground. Lori was wondering just *what* Leclair was doing – and then the shockwave hit.

Leclair had managed to get the gunship into the trees, sheltered from the worst of it, and it still took every erg of power the rotors could put out to hold the tilt-rotor aircraft in one place.

Another gunship, which hadn't made it as low, was caught by the shockwave and slammed into the trees with enough force to break both several trees and the aircraft in half. The explosion of the gunship's fuel tanks and munitions was an exclamation point on the shockwave, and Lori stared at the fire that had been seven of her people in shock.

"Everybody, get down on the ground," Leclair ordered. "We'll need to double check everything before we fly again – that's going to have done a number on the rotors."

"What the *hell* was that?" Lori finally asked shockily as she reached for the com to try to raise Anthony again.

"I'm only guessing," Leclair said quietly, "but I *think* that was a kinetic strike. There's no point grabbing the com, boss – even if I'm wrong, it's only about *what* did it, not what happened.

"Karlsberg is gone."

ISBN-13: 978-1-988035-00-0

ISBN-10: 1988035007

Published in the United States of America

Hand of Mars

By Glynn Stewart

Chapter 1

Mars shrank in the window as the starship got under way. Unlike most apparent 'windows' aboard the vessel, this one actually looked out onto space, an observatory tucked away on one corner of the immense white pyramid.

If Damien Montgomery stepped right up to the glass and turned his head just right, he could see the star-white plume of reaction mass blazing out from the battleship's matter-antimatter engines. He couldn't *feel* the acceleration as the magic woven into the runes under his feet provided an artificial gravity that countered the force of the ship's thrust.

His gaze was focused on Mars. The massive peak of Olympus Mons, visible from low orbit, had just rotated over the horizon. Over the last three years, the mountain capital of the Mage-King of Mars' Protectorate had become home.

He hadn't left Olympus Mons since arriving on the terraformed world. He'd arrived not quite a prisoner, having demonstrated a rare gift with magic and an even rarer gift for causing trouble.

Now, after three years of being the Mage-King's direct student – when and if Desmond Alexander had time around his duties and responsibilities – he was leaving again.

"My Lord Envoy?" a voice said from behind him.

Damien turned around to find himself facing a young man in a navy blue uniform with narrow gold cuffs. If memory was correct, the single narrow cuff marked the man as a Lieutenant. The man didn't wear the same gold medallion at his neck as Damien, so he was not a Mage – 'just' one of the many mundane officers that kept the Navy running.

"Yes, Lieutenant...?"

"Lieutenant Keller, My Lord," the young man replied, and a slight shiver ran down Damien's spine. Keller was, at *most,* five years younger than his own not-quite-thirty. The uniform and the sidearm the man carried should have marked him as Damien's superior in most circumstances.

The fact that Damien was the only person on the fifty million ton battleship *Righteous Guardian of Liberty* not wearing a uniform said something different. The crackling parchment in the inner pocket of his perfectly tailored black suit told the rest of the story: he bore a Warrant directly from the Mage-King of Mars as His Envoy, empowered to speak on His behalf for a specific mission.

"Mage-Captain Adamant requests your presence for dinner with the senior officers in her quarters this evening," the Lieutenant told him quickly.

Damien smiled, trying to put the younger man at ease. He quickly realized that, faced with a man who spoke with his King's Voice, clad all in black with skin-tight gloves, the young Lieutenant was *never* going to be at ease.

"Let Captain Adamant know I will be there," he finally told the Lieutenant. "Thank you."

With a perfectly crisp salute that Damien wasn't entirely sure even his current status required, Lieutenant Keller all-but fled the observatory.

Damien waited until the youth had left, and rested his gloved hand on the pocket of his suit jacket. The archaic parchment of his Warrant crinkled under his fingers and he sighed.

How had he gone from wanting to jump starships between the stars to this?

#

He was early for dinner, and only Mage-Captain Janet Adamant was in her dining room when he arrived. The room was easily large enough to seat all of Adamant's officers, with a table made from an Old Earth oak tree.

Despite living in the Sol system for three years, the table was still a luxury to Damien's eyes: he'd been raised on the MidWorld of Sherwood, almost a month's travel from Earth. At home, *anything* from Earth had been a barely affordable luxury for even the wealthy.

"Welcome, My Lord Envoy," Adamant greeted him. She was a tall woman, with the slightly Asian features of a Martian native.

"Please, call me Damien," he told her. "The 'My Lord's are confusing – I keep looking around for the *actual* important person."

"The third adult Rune Wright in the galaxy, personally trained in politics, magic and law by the Mage-King himself, and the man who brought down the Blue Star Syndicate," Adamant replied calmly. "Unimportant, huh?"

"I didn't bring down the Syndicate," Damien pointed out. "I killed Azure – a lot of hard work by people wearing *your* uniform finished the job."

Mikhail Azure, onetime leader of the largest crime syndicate in the Protectorate, had chased Damien to the end of the galaxy. Eventually Damien had been forced to carve a dangerous rune into his own flesh, allowing him to destroy the crime lord's personal warship and save his own friends.

His 'reward' for that had been to be drafted by the Mage-King.

"Most people would kill for three years of training under the Mage-King," the Captain pointed out, responding to what he hadn't said as much as what he had.

Damien shrugged.

"It wasn't a reward," he pointed out. "As you said, I'm one of three adult Rune Wrights in the galaxy. Given that our very existence is classified enough we couldn't have this conversation with your staff in the room, they couldn't exactly let me roam free."

Adamant chuckled and shook her head at him.

"Fair enough," she admitted. "Have a seat. Wine? The food should be ready shortly."

Damien gratefully took a glass of wine and a seat, nodding gracefully as each of Adamant's senior officers entered and was introduced. He wouldn't be aboard the warship long, so he only peripherally registered the names and faces.

"I can't believe they pulled a freaking *battleship* to play courier for the pipsqueak," someone muttered halfway through the soup.

Looking up, Damien met the focused gaze of the Commander who served as the *Righteous Guardian*'s tactical officer, in charge of all of the many and varied weaponry she carried. The man was easily ten years his senior, but had the grace to look embarrassed when he realized he'd been overheard.

"I'm quite grateful that the *Righteous Guardian* was going my way, actually," Damien told him. "As you say, I'm not a very large package, and I suspect they'd have found me a box on a mail courier if you'd been heading a different way!"

That got a laugh from everyone, including the tactical officer. Damien was a small man, easily the shortest person in the room and definitely the lightest. Spending three years studying magic, law, and politics had left him little time to bulk up.

"What's it like studying in Olympus Mons?" another officer, this one wearing the gold medallion marking him as a Mage along with his Commander's uniform.

"Intimidating," Damien said dryly. "Believe me, when Desmond Michael Alexander assigns you homework, you find the time to do it!"

"What's bringing you to Tau Ceti, Envoy?" another officer asked, and Damien realized that he was going to be the center of attention tonight.

"I'm joining Hand of the Mage-King Alaura Stealey for a mission," he replied. "More than that I can't say."

That put enough of a damper on the questions that he could, at least, finish eating. It also helped avoid mentioning that even Damien himself wasn't entirely sure what he was heading to Tau Ceti for.

Chapter 2

Tau Ceti had been the second target of the colonization expeditions launched in the mid-Twenty-Third century. From the not-quite-secret history archives contained in Olympus Mons, Damien was certain the reaction of the Mages leading the first expeditions to find habitable planets in the system had been outright sighs of relief.

The Compact, the deal between Mages and the rest of humanity that had ended the Eugenics Wars of the Twenty-Second and Twenty-Third centuries, had offered transport to the stars as the bribe for humanity accepting the Mage-King. Given that the Mages were the product of the very Eugenicists a century-long war had been fought to overthrow, the first Mage-King had needed a giant carrot.

Tau Ceti's two habitable worlds had been among the first part of that carrot. Their biospheres crushed by once-a-century meteor bombardments, they had nonetheless had *some* life and hence atmospheres capable of supporting humanity.

Now, over two hundred years later, Tau Ceti *f* was a chilly, but heavily populated world. A massive space station orbited ahead of it, clearing a path through the system's field of meteors and comets with an array of lasers that put even *Righteous Guardian's* armament to shame.

A similar station shielded Tau Ceti *e*, though that planet's sheer mass had limited its habitability. The station at Tau Ceti *e*, however, also shielded the third largest ship-building complex in the Protectorate. Only the yards above Earth and Mars were larger, and outside the Sol system only Legatus came close.

Holding pride of place in the center of the complex was a skeleton of girders and plates the size of the *Righteous Guardian of Liberty*. Eventually, that shell would become the thirteenth battleship of the Royal Martian Navy.

For now, the *Guardian* would slot in beside her to undergo a refit that would bring her own systems up to the same specifications as the new vessel. As Damien had reminded the senior officers, he and the mighty warship had simply been going the same way.

He'd spent most of the three day voyage in either his quarters or the observatory, and the final approach to the Tau Ceti Yard Complex found him in the observatory, stretching his eyes – with a few tricks even most Mages wouldn't know – to pick out the ship he was meeting.

"Captain Adamant," he said quietly into a communicator. "Please have a shuttle prepared for me. I will meet it in the bay."

"Of course, Envoy Montgomery," she confirmed. "What destination should I give the pilot?"

"I'm not certain what slip number," Damien admitted, "but the *Tides of Justice* is finishing up her refit about five slips up from the new battleship. I will meet Hand Stealey aboard her vessel.

"I appreciate the ride, Captain," he finished. "It has been far more pleasant than the last time I rode aboard a Royal Navy warship."

That last time had been aboard the *Tides of Justice* – and it had been an open question whether the rogue Rune Wright that Hand Stealey was bringing in was a guest or a prisoner.

#

Even the Warrant in his breast pocket was a frail shield against Damien's nervousness as the shuttle docked with the *Tides of Justice*. While the piece of parchment gave him an authority that was mind-boggling to the vast majority of the human race, Alaura Stealey was a *Hand*.

He held the Mage-King's Voice for this one mission to the planet of Ardennes. Stealey held His Voice, and every other aspect of the Mage-King's authority, permanently.

With a final thud, the shuttle connected. "We have a solid seal," the co-pilot announced, and the pilot turned in his seat to face Damien.

"Good luck, My Lord," the young officer told him.

"Thank you, Lieutenant," Damien replied. "It was a smoother flight than I expected for how busy the Yards are. Well done."

"Traffic Control has everything pinned down to the nines," the pilot admitted. "I can't take the credit."

Damien inclined his head in acknowledgement. He'd trained as a pilot as part of his Jump Mage training, and he knew that no matter *how* neatly the Yards' Traffic Control had set up their lanes and routes, *that* smooth a ride took skill.

Behind him, the shuttle airlock slowly hissed open. With a final nod to the shuttle crew, Damien Montgomery grabbed the handle bar over the lock and rotated into it. Even the Navy didn't bother with magical gravity on shuttles, and a prosaic yellow caution line marked where the swirling silver patterns of runes started.

Beyond that line was the main shuttle bay of Alaura Stealey's personal destroyer. Rather than risk making a fool of himself in front of his new boss, he pulled a tiny of bit of power into himself. A moment of focus, and a localized gravity field oriented his 'down'.

His feet settled on the steel plates out of sight of whatever welcoming committee an Envoy rated, and he calmly stepped forward across the yellow line and into the bay.

Glynn Stewart

"ATTEN-HUT!" a parade ground voice bellowed, and a double file of Royal Marines snapped to attention.

Swallowing hard, Damien stepped out between the two ruler-straight lines of armed soldiers. At the end of the corridor they formed, he spotted Alaura Stealey waiting, flanked by two men in the uniform of the Royal Martian Navy.

Alaura looked much the same as he remembered her, a slim gray-haired woman with ice blue eyes and a perpetually even expression. Like Damien, she was dressed in a plain black suit and wore skin-tight gloves over her hands.

"Envoy Damien Montgomery," she greeted him warmly. "Welcome back aboard the *Tides of Justice*. I don't believe you know Mage-Lieutenant Silversmith, the *Tides'* new executive officer, but I know you've met her Captain, Mage-Commander Harmon."

She gestured to the man on her left first, a dark-skinned and dark-eyed heavyset man with at least a foot on Damien, and then to the man on her right, who Damien *did* recognize.

Mage-Commander Harmon, then a Mage-Lieutenant, had been Hand Stealey's personal aide when she'd chased Damien halfway across the galaxy. For his sins, and the coincidence of being Damien's age, the then executive officer of the *Tides of Justice* had spent a portion of his precious free time helping maintain Damien's sanity.

Like Silversmith, Harmon was taller and broader than Damien, though his new executive officer still overtopped him by several inches.

"Mage-Commander, huh?" Damien asked as he shook the *Tides'* Captain's hand. "Congratulations!"

"It's recent, but thank you," Harmon replied calmly. "Mage-Captain Barnett earned herself a shiny new cruiser, and Her Ladyship here," he indicated Alaura with his chin, "decided she'd rather keep me than break in a new captain."

"I was feeling lazy *and* charitable that day," Alaura allowed. She held out a hand to Damien. "May I see your Warrant, Envoy?" she asked, her voice suddenly formal.

He swallowed hard and then removed the single piece of parchment from his suit-jacket pocket and passed it to her.

Slowly, carefully, Alaura unfolded the archaic document and read it over. Then she handed it back to him.

"Everything is in order, Envoy," she concluded aloud. "It's good to see you again, Damien. Commander Harmon – you may dismiss the honor guard.

"We have a great deal to discuss."

#

Glynn Stewart

Chapter 3

Lori Armstrong, onetime member of Ardennes' Planetary Parliament, tightened the cinch on her body armor vest. Whoever had designed the military-grade gear that had ended up on Ardennes hadn't really sized the armor for a woman who had freely used sex appeal to try and overturn the assumption that the opposition couldn't win seats on Ardennes.

She'd won her seat in the end, only to discover that Mage-Governor Michael Vaughn's Prosperity Party had locked up the government in more ways than one. The six seats her Ardennes' Freedom Party had managed to sneak in had been a tiny and ignored voice in a two hundred seat legislature.

Which was a story that ended here – with an ex-politician in body armor carrying a battle carbine strapped into the back of a stealth gunship smuggled in from offworld.

"How long?" she asked, pitching her voice to carry over the noise of the paired tilt-rotors carrying the little aircraft on its tree-skimming course around the planet.

"Thirty minutes, boss," the pilot replied. "Couldn't we have kicked the pot over somewhere closer to home?"

Lori shook her head wordlessly at the pilot. The woman, commander of one their two priceless squadrons of Legatus-built military aircraft, knew perfectly well that this hadn't been planned.

She grabbed a communicator and checked the tell-tales on its encryption. Like the gunship, the high-tech encrypted communicators had been manufactured on Legatus and smuggled in via false manifests and hidden cargo drops.

"Hotel, come in," she said into the device after punching in one of the twenty-six or so codes it could take.

"Please tell me you're almost here," the familiar voice of Anthony Hellet, codename Hotel, the head of the Karlsberg Miners' Union, another ex-member of the Freedom Party, answered. "The Scorpions have retreated to their barracks, but we've got *no* heavy weapons here, boss."

"We're thirty minutes out," she told him. "What were you *thinking*?" she demanded. "We're not ready, Hotel."

"It was just a strike," her old friend told her. "Shaft Six's air circulators were down, and the mine boss was ordering people in with just respirators. The crew refused.

"Then the Scorpions rolled in, and I couldn't have stopped my people from interfering if I'd *wanted* to," he finished bluntly.

The Scorpions – the Ardennes Special Security Service – were *technically* an elite paramilitary police force. In practice, Mage-Governor Vaughn used them as his personal bullies and leg-breakers across the planet.

"When the dust settled, an entire company of the thugs were dead, and Karlsberg was rising," Anthony finished. "Between our boys and the locals, they probably lost two *more* companies before they realized they'd lost the city," he said with a cold satisfaction. "But that's still two companies – four *hundred* Scorpions – in the barracks. We're trying to hack their heavy weapon auth codes, but no luck so far."

Lori nodded slowly. Scorpion small arms were much the same as the imported gear many of her own people used – to the point where the cartridges were identical Protectorate-standard rounds. Scorpion *heavy* arms, however, were locked down with authorization codes and ident-locks to prevent them falling into the hands of people who might use them to take out armored personnel carriers and reinforced barracks.

"Keep them pinned down," she ordered. "A few rockets from the gunships should clear them out."

"Then Karlsberg will be free," Anthony promised. "Let Vaughn suck on *that*."

A light started blinking on her comm.

"Hold on Hotel," Lori told him, then switched. "Alpha," she answered the channel. Many of her people knew *exactly* who she was, but she still insisted on solid com discipline.

"Boss, you have a problem," the voice of one of her cell leaders told her. "It took a few hours to make it up the chain, but the Scorps have called in the Army."

Lori's heart skipped a beat, and she glanced around the gunship. Each of the six vessels was carrying five soldiers – thirty fully equipped light infantry. Combined with the gunships' weapons and Anthony's rebel miners that would be enough to take down the shattered remnants of a Scorpion security battalion.

"How many?" she asked.

"Looks like General Keller has managed to get the entire Ninth Armored rolling," her agent said grimly. "That's almost sixty tanks, boss. No idea how many infantry. They're already out of the Montagne Noir base and heading your way through the pass."

Lori pulled up a map on the computer on her wrist and considered it. Montagne Noir was on the other side of the Rocher d'Or mountain range from Karlsberg. They wouldn't get there as fast as her gunships, but they'd roll over anything she could put into Karlsberg.

That said, there was only one route *through* the Rocher d'Or that would fit a tank battalion – and Governor Vaughn didn't know about their imports.

"We'll deal with it, Iota," she told her cell leader. "Well done."

She flipped back to Anthony's channel.

"We're going to be delayed," she told him. "See if you can take out that barracks yourself – we're going to have to deal with the Army."

Anthony was silent for a long moment.

"Good luck, boss," he said finally. "We're both going to need it!"

Shutting down the channel, Lori leaned forward next to the pilot.

"You heard," she said plainly. She could have shunted the communicator into her helmet for privacy, but she trusted everyone on the gunship with her life.

"There's only one pass," she replied. "Re-routing the squadron now."

"Can you take them?" Lori asked, as quietly as she could with the rotors running around them.

The woman looked back at the nominal leader of the resistance and grinned.

"They'll never even see us coming."

#

By the time they were half a kilometer into the pass through the Rocher d'Or mountains, Lori was convinced her pilot – also her squadron commander – was insane.

Like the gunships themselves, Alissa Leclair was an import from the Legatus system. Unlike the gunships, she'd voluntarily emigrated from the Core World regarded as the first UnArcana World, looking for work.

Unsafe flying conditions and one accident too many had driven the helicopter pilot into the arms of Lori's resistance.

Fortunately, Leclair had been trained as an emergency services pilot. She was capable of flying a nape-of-the-earth course that, combined with the stealth coating and ECM of the gunships, made them invisible to orbital platforms.

Those courses were utterly terrifying to her unfortunate passengers.

The pass through the mountains rapidly shrank to a river valley less than four hundred meters wide, with a wide road blasted into the cliffs along one side. Leclair led her six gunships screaming down the road – with ten meters of clearance from the cliffs – at two hundred kilometers per hour.

"There we go," the Legatan said with a cold flatness to her voice. "Sensors show them ten kay ahead. All pilots – arm weapons systems."

"They've *got* to know we're coming," Lori said aloud. "If we can see them, they can see us."

"Stealth is relative, boss," Leclair replied. "We're stealthy as gunships go, but..." she shrugged. "You're right. We won't be able to do this again – but since they have no clue these babies are on the planet, we can do it this time." The pilot patted the cockpit next to her affectionately.

"Sensors are showing Manticore Deuces," another pilot reported. "Those are going to be a handful."

"Could be worse," Leclair told her crews. "I'm reading M2 tanks and Basilisk transports. No flak, no rockets, only onboard anti-air. Arm your cluster bombs and rockets, then follow my lead."

It turned out Lori had only *thought* Leclair's previous flying was terrifying. The moment she ordered the other gunships to follow her lead, the Legatan pilot took the stealth gunship into a sharp dive and blasted along the middle of the mountain highway.

Lori swallowed, hanging on to her shoulder straps with whitening fingers, and then stopped breathing outright as the aircraft tore around a corner, less than a meter from the rock face, into the face of the Ardennes Army Ninth Armored Battalion.

"*Mine,*" Leclair snarled and pulled the triggers on her joystick.

Four smart rockets blasted away from the gunship, each seeking its own target. Lori watched them with her breath held, and all of them slammed into their targets. The entire front platoon of the armored column erupted into flames, and Lori realized, at last, that they could actually *do* this.

While she was overcoming her crisis of confidence, Leclair had been continuing on her lethal way. The nose-mounted auto-cannon chewed its way through a trio of APCs, leaving behind piles of burning wreckage.

Finally, in a maneuver that almost made Lori lose her lunch, Leclair stopped the gunship in midair and blasted it a hundred meters straight up. From *there*, she fired two sets of heavy cluster munitions, and then twisted the gunship over the cliff face as the first, belated, return fire tried to chase her.

Behind her, the other five gunships of her squadron began firing their own rockets.

The armored column had never stood a chance.

#

Mage-Commodore Adrianna Cor, commander of the Royal Martian Navy's Seventh Cruiser Squadron, was not a patient woman. She tolerated fools poorly and incompetents not at all.

She had no choice but to tolerate the man on her viewscreen, however, regardless of her opinion of Mage-Governor Michael Vaughn. He was the elected leader of the planet beneath her – and if his theoretically legitimate authority wasn't enough, he also had evidence that would put Mage-Commodore Cor in jail for a long time – and he *also* had a *lot* of money.

"I thought your soldiers were supposed to be well-trained and well-equipped," she said dryly. "Now, you're telling me they got their heads handed to them by *miners*?"

"In the end," Vaughn allowed. He was a bulky blond man, with muscles only beginning to fade into fat now after twenty years as a politician. "But it *started* when a company was ambushed by terrorists – terrorists with very clearly *offworld* training and weapons. The type the Protectorate is supposed to *stop* filtering through to my planet."

Cor raised an eyebrow at the Governor. Customs and import control, as he very well knew, were the responsibility of local authorities – in this case, the fifteen Tau Ceti-built 'export' destroyers of the Ardennes System Defense Force.

"If the town is in open rebellion, as you say," she told him, "then roll in your Army and be done with them. A few dozen rebels, however well trained or well equipped, can't stand off a battalion or two of tanks. Even if the entire town has gone over, which I doubt."

Instead of answering, Vaughn switched the camera to show an orbital shot from one of Ardennes' many surveillance satellites. She noted absently that the resolution on the gear was fantastic even as she unconsciously leaned closer to the screen. The screen showed the wreckage of some kind of convoy – dozens of vehicles strewn across a mountain road in pieces. Sections of the road itself were on fire, and the survivors were focusing on saving people, not materiel.

"*This* was my Ninth Armored Battalion," Vaughn said bluntly. "I don't know where the fuckers *got* them, but they have attack aircraft of some kind – attack aircraft that my surveillance satellites do *not* pick up."

Cor sighed.

"What do you need, Michael?"

"I need you to suppress the rebellion, Mage-Commodore," he said bluntly. "Bring down fire on Karlsberg, and end this infection before it can spread."

She glanced at a set of tell-tales, making sure that the conversation wasn't being recorded. So far as her flagship's computers were concerned, she wasn't in communication with *anyone*.

"That's one *hell* of a line you want me to cross," Cor told him. "There's what, fifty thousand people in Karlsberg?"

Even *she* felt a twinge of conscience over that, and she had no sympathy for mundane drones that didn't know their place.

"Fifty thousand *rebels*," Vaughn spat. "And if they have air support, I don't know if we'll be able to take the town back before the Hand arrives. Do *you* want to be the one explaining to one of Alexander's ivory tower judges the realities of maintaining an economic boom in times like these?"

Cor snorted. What Mars' representatives tended to think of the world, versus what the world actually *was*, tended to be very, very, separate in her experience. He was right though. When the Hand of Desmond Michael Alexander the Third arrived, things would get *very* bad if there was a significant open rebellion underway.

God – she'd probably want to *talk* to the rebels, instead of just dealing with them.

"I can't drop rocks from orbit on my own," she told Vaughn instead.

"Tell your staff I'll add another zero to their special comp packages," the Governor said flatly, and Cor shivered. If he was willing to throw *that* much money at it, he truly was scared of what would happen when the Hand arrived.

"You know I'm good for it," Vaughn said after a moment of silence.

Cor also knew Vaughn wouldn't go down without handing certain files to the Hand, so the money would have to be enough.

"Fine," she said flatly, then cut the connection.

#

"Turns out I shouldn't underestimate miners, Alpha," Anthony told Lori over the com. "Or you, for that matter. Seriously? The Army ain't coming?"

"Any of them that are left are busy pulling bodies from the wreckage," Lori told him quietly. "The Scorpions?"

"Turns out one of the miners had built himself a trebuchet as a hobby," Anthony replied. "Mounted it on a rooftop and used to drop a hundred kilos of mining explosives on top of the barracks. Leveled the place," he finished cheerfully.

"All right," she said. "We're en route. Between your cells and the folks I've got on the squadron, we should be able to get some order in place – and then we'll bring in some transmission gear."

"'We hold these truths to be self-evident'?" Anthony replied.

"Something like that," Lori told him, a moment of amusement managing to penetrate her veneer of shock after the sheer violence of the pass.

"Well, the miners are ready to stand behind you," he told her. "They remember your fa—"

Silence. Even as the com cut off, there was a sudden bright flash on the horizon, in the direction of Karlsberg.

"*Hold on*," Leclair snapped. "Everybody, shockwave inbound – *hit the deck.*"

The pilot matched actions to words, flipping every rotor to horizontal and driving the aircraft towards the ground. Lori was wondering just *what* Leclair was doing – and then the shockwave hit.

Leclair had managed to get the gunship into the trees, sheltered from the worst of it, and it still took every erg of power the rotors could put out to hold the tilt-rotor aircraft in one place.

Another gunship, which hadn't made it as low, was caught by the shockwave and slammed into the trees with enough force to break both several trees and the aircraft in half. The explosion of the gunship's fuel tanks and munitions was an exclamation point on the shockwave, and Lori stared at the fire that had been seven of her people in shock.

"Everybody, get down on the ground," Leclair ordered. "We'll need to double check everything before we fly again – that's going to have done a number on the rotors."

"What the *hell* was that?" Lori finally asked shockily as she reached for the com to try to raise Anthony again.

"I'm only guessing," Leclair said quietly, "but I *think* that was a kinetic strike. There's no point grabbing the com, boss – even if I'm wrong, it's only about *what* did it, not what happened.

"Karlsberg is gone."

#

Chapter 4

Several hours after arriving aboard *Tides of Justice* found Damien joining Alaura in the office attached to her quarters. The Hand poured herself a glass of wine and offered the bottle to Damien.

"Drink?"

"Coffee, please," he replied. "It's a little early in the day for those of us without iron stomachs."

She raised her glass in silent acceptance and produced a carafe and a cup out of the collection of silverware and glasses on the small table next to her desk. Presumably, some minion from Harmon's crew kept the table stocked – Damien knew from experience that the Hand's cybernetic stomach allowed her to drink alcohol without getting drunk, and the woman tended to abuse that over drinking coffee.

"How's Olympus Mons?" she asked after filling his cup.

"It's winter," Damien replied dryly. "Everyone who can't get to the southern hemisphere has locked themselves in the mountain and is pretending there isn't three feet of snow outside."

While the mountain wasn't *that* far north, the section of it that housed what was currently the Mage-King's palace was high up. Three feet of snow wasn't an exaggeration – but you didn't have to leave the hemisphere to avoid it, just travel to the foot of the mountain.

"Ah, so *that's* why you were so eager to join me on this mission," Alaura concluded. The gray-haired woman perched on the edge of her desk, watching him carefully over the rim of her glass. "I don't expect Ardennes to get that exciting."

"When His Majesty hints that it's time for one of his pupils to get real world experience, said pupil obeys," Damien observed dryly. "Also, Kiera is now thirteen, and in the throes of the worst teenage crush I've ever seen."

It took Alaura a long moment to realize how that related to Damien leaving Mars.

"On you," she finally realized aloud. "The girl second in line to the Throne has a crush on you, and your response is to flee the planet?"

Damien glared at her for a moment, then corrected her.

"System, Alaura," he pointed out. "My response to a teenage crush by the daughter of the most powerful man alive was to flee the *system*."

The Hand, one of the thirteen most powerful men and women alive, laughed at him.

"That seems surprisingly legitimate," she replied. With a shrug and a hand gesture, she flipped the data on her wrist computer's display onto a wallscreen.

"Moving on to our actual job," she continued, "this is Ardennes."

Damien studied the oddly colored planet on the screen carefully. The pale purple native trees were extremely hardy and had managed to spread across easily seventy percent of the planet's surface. Massive deposits of heavy metals and rare earths, combined with those trees, had made the planet an attractive target for colonization. A massive fault line, clearly visible even in the zoomed out holo, rendered one of the three continents not-quite-uninhabitable, but the other two were temperate and resource-rich.

"MidWorld with a Navy refueling station," he said aloud. The MidWorlds were the thirty-three systems that were fully self-sufficient, but didn't have the massive industrial complexes of the original Core Worlds. "His Majesty said that would be our destination, but I think he believed you would have more up-to-date details."

"I do, but not as many as I'd like," Alaura told him. "One of the – many – warning signs that something isn't quite right on Ardennes is that the Runic Transceiver Array on the planet is restricted to government use. I'm getting reports, but they're coming in by more roundabout routes than usual."

Damien leaned back in his seat, gesturing for her to continue. One of his many lessons on Mars had been that learning usually required simply listening.

"Mage-Governor Vaughn has been in charge of Ardennes for thirty years now. That's unusual, but not unheard of," she allowed. "In that time, Ardennes has undergone an explosion of industry and resource extraction. Again, this isn't unheard of, but there are rumors."

"We've learned the hard way not to ignore those kinds of rumors," she continued grimly, and Damien nodded. He'd visited a world once where the locals had eventually been forced to overthrow a corporate occupation by force. They'd ended up becoming one of the most rabid UnArcana worlds, blaming the Mages of the Protectorate for not saving them.

"We began asking questions and slipping agents in a year ago," Alaura explained. "Shortly *before* that, small campaigns of violence began to pop up. Nothing really major – a couple of strikes turning into riots, a few bombings. Enough to draw our attention, but nobody died."

"That changed about six months ago. Someone began launching a very well organized, very well equipped guerilla war. It lasted a month, maybe two. Then it quieted down – as if someone had made a very specific point.

"More recently, a series of cruder, more vicious attacks has been launched," she finished quietly. "Civilians have died – very different modus operandi, but still operating against Vaughn."

"With the civilian deaths, Mage-Governor Vaughn has formally requested our assistance. I think something stinks," she concluded, "but he has that right."

Damien slowly nodded, processing as best as he could.

"So what do we do?" he asked carefully.

"Three steps," Alaura replied. "First, we stop the fighting – by whatever means necessary. There is a Navy cruiser squadron in system we can call on for heavy support, but I'd rather negotiate a cease fire."

"Second, we identify whatever grievances are triggering this revolt. If they're legitimate, we arbitrate negotiations to find a compromise acceptable to everyone," she shook her head. "It's *usually* possible, especially when backed by a Hand."

"And third?" Damien asked.

"Third, we punish the criminals," she said flatly. "Murderers on both sides – rebels who blew up civilians, cops who gunned down innocents. The torturers, the killers – all of them spend a good long while in prison."

"Where there are legitimate grievances, we will *correct* them," Alaura continued calmly. "But no-one kills or tortures the innocent and walks away."

Her words hung in the silent air as Damien considered them. While he knew Hands usually did attempt to find workable compromises, they were more known for the first and third of her steps than the second.

A ping on Alaura's computer attracted both of their attentions, and Alaura slowly read whatever showed up on her screen.

"Interesting," she murmured slowly.

"My lady?"

"I don't normally like to jump to the interstellars' bidding," she told him. "But the CEO of MagnaCorp Interstellar just asked me to meet with him. And offered to break free *any* two hour stretch that worked for me."

"And?" Damien asked.

"MagnaCorp operates in thirty-six systems and employs just over fifteen million people," Alaura told him. "Rickard's time is booked in five minute chunks – six months in advance."

"He'll also have the resources to know I'm heading to Ardennes – and one of their big operations is there."

She checked her schedule and glanced back up at Damien with a thin smile.

"Feel up to a shuttle flight, My Lord Envoy?"

Damien returned the smile.

"Only if I get to fly, My Lady Hand," he told her.

Despite having kept up his simulator time while secluded in Olympus Mons, Damien let out a sigh of relief as he settled the agile Navy shuttle on the landing pad outside MagnaCorp's headquarters on Tau Ceti *f*. Chilly and damp, the planet had decided to show them an unfriendly face with a vicious storm taking shape over the southern continent as they were landing.

Despite his rustiness, he'd managed to take the shuttle through the rain and gale-force winds without any issues. No-one else needed to know how white his knuckles had been through the process!

The rain continued to hammer down around the shuttle, make a hissing sound as the drops hit and evaporated from the shuttle's hull, still heated from entry.

"We'll meet Mister Rickard inside," Alaura told him, unstrapping herself from the co-pilots seat. "I don't blame him for not wanting to come out in this to greet us," she gestured at the rain.

Damien nodded and gestured for her to lead the way. They stepped out into the rain, but none of the drops hit them. He glanced at Alaura and realized she was holding a shield of kinetic energy over their heads. It seemed a waste of energy to him, but he had been trained in a tradition that avoided the open use of magic as a sign of humility.

"It would never do for a Hand or an Envoy to appear looking like soaked rats," she murmured to him as they approached the main doors for the central sky scraper of MagnaCorp Interstellar's corporate campus. The campus was about five kilometers outside Tau Ceti *f*'s largest city, but the central tower rivaled any of the skyscrapers of the official downtown to their west.

The skyscraper was barely five minutes' walk away from the landing pad – probably closer than Damien would have been comfortable putting it, but convenient.

He followed Alaura as she walked through the main doors of the skyscraper like she owned the place, walking up to the front desk as if walking in out of the storm was a normal thing.

"I am here to meet Tomas Rickard," she told the receptionist before the elegantly coiffed blond young man finished gawking at her. "We are expected."

"So you are," an amused voice interrupted before the receptionist found his voice. "Space Traffic Control called ahead – I apologize for the weather."

"Whatever worlds we travel to, Mother Nature still does not respond to our every whim, Mister Rickard," Alaura replied, giving the speaker a small nod. "Envoy Montgomery, this is Tomas Rickard,

Chief Executive Officer of MagnaCorp Interstellar. Mister Rickard, this is..."

"Envoy Damien Montgomery," Rickard interrupted, closing the space and offering his hand to Damien. MagnaCorp's CEO was an immense man, with skin and hair so fair as to be almost pure white and ice blue eyes. "It is a pleasure to meet the man who ended the Blue Star Syndicate's depredations upon our galaxy."

Damien shook his hand.

"Many others played a part in breaking apart Blue Star," he admitted. "You are very well informed – I was not aware my Warrant had been announced in Tau Ceti."

"It is... a job requirement," Rickard said grimly. "I am aware of your Warrant, and also that you and Lady Stealey are headed to Ardennes." The CEO glanced at the receptionist, then jerked his head towards an elevator.

"Let's discuss this in my office," he continued. "I don't think what either of us has to say is for everyone's ears."

#

Rickard's office was large, as expected of the head of an interstellar corporation, occupying the entire north-western quarter of the top floor of the building. The windows on the two exterior walls gave the CEO and his guests a spectacular view of the vicious storm pounding the complex outside.

Inside, the office was surprisingly austere for its scale. A significant chunk of it had been re-purposed to a conference room with absolute top-of-the-line communication equipment, but the rest was almost empty beyond a large but simple desk and a collection of more comfortable chairs by an auto-bar.

He gestured them to the chairs and stepped over to the auto-bar.

"Drinks? The bar makes a fantastic fortified hot chocolate."

A minute later, all three of them settled into the sinfully comfortable chairs with their hot chocolates, watching the lightning outside.

"I must admit, Mister Rickard, I was surprised by your request," Alaura told him. "It's rare that the head of an interstellar corporation is willing to put that much effort into meeting with a Hand."

"And it always means we need a favor," Rickard admitted cheerfully. "In this case, I'm hoping to be able to *do* you a favor as well."

"Oh?" Alaura answered, uncommittedly.

The CEO sighed and then gestured to the window next to them. An image that Damien guessed had been preloaded for activation loaded onto a video screen concealed in the glass.

It had been, at some point, a huge industrial complex. Now, a third of the complex was lost to a crater that started outside the image, and many of the remaining buildings were knocked down. Any fires had clearly been put out by the time the photograph was taken, but the complex was probably a complete write off.

"This *was* the fusion reactor manufacturing plant on Ardennes," Rickard said quietly. "We built and tested fusion cores from one megawatt toys to one gigawatt mass-production plants here, then exported them across the Protectorate. This shot was as of two weeks ago, the latest news I have from Ardennes."

"What happened?" Damien asked, leaning forward to get a closer look.

"Our plant ended up as the center point of a mid-sized industrial district just outside one of Ardenes' larger cities. The factory next door was a chemical processing plant. Something went wrong and it blew the hell up.

"We were on track for a zero fatal accident fiscal year," Rickard continued quietly. "On the scale we operate, that is something to be *damned* proud of. And then these idiots killed two hundred and fifty-six of my people."

"There was an investigation. Their conclusion was that our neighbors, an Ardennes native corporation, had failed to comply with basic safety standards for the processes they were following."

He held up a hand before Alaura or Damien could speak, taking a moment to breathe deeply.

"We were *then* informed by Ardennes' court system that the corporation in question had been granted an exemption from the legal safety code to 'encourage their investment'. Therefore, under Ardennes law, they were *not* legally liable for death benefits to their *own* people's families, let alone *my* people."

"We will be paying for the benefits ourselves, obviously," he concluded. "But I have already told my Board that we will *not* be rebuilding on Ardennes."

"They gave an exemption to the *safety codes*?" Damien asked incredulously.

"When we move into a system, we ask for a lot of exemptions and special cases," Rickard admitted. "Usually, it's to try to make sure our operations only have to meet Protectorate-wide standards instead of more stringent local ones, and we rarely get many of them. In this case, my understanding is that several of the major shareholders are friends of the Governor."

"I see," Alaura said slowly. "You can prove this?"

"The details of the court files my local president was provided weren't supposed to leave the Ardennes system," Rickard told them. "They've been forwarded to your ship, along with all of our local research and information."

"That... could be immensely valuable," Alaura replied. "Thank you."

"It's worse than you think, my Lady Hand," Rickard warned her. "However bad you think it is, its worse.

"Vaughn has been determined to drive a major industrial revolution on Ardennes, at any cost. A lot of the money from that has poured into the hands of his friends and allies – and more has gone into funding the security service to keep a lid on protest."

"If it was really that bad, he'd have been voted out," Damien pointed out. "Everything I see shows his party continuing to dominate the planetary legislature."

Rickard sighed, looking embarrassed for the first time since they'd arrived.

"I *know*, for a fact, that Vaughn has fixed at least the last two Governor elections, and has been heavily restricting who can run for the Legislature," he admitted. "I know we have an obligation to report that," he continued, "but I only had two facilities of the size of the one on Ardennes. I couldn't risk him shutting us down."

"Now," he shrugged. "I've paid for every surviving one of my people, and their families and the families of the dead, to be relocated to Sherwood. I'd rather start again from bare rock than touch Ardennes again."

#

Chapter 5

Damien and Alaura were barely out of the shuttle when Mage-Commander Harmon intercepted them.

"You need to come with me," the *Tides of Justice*'s commanding officer told them. "I've ordered the ship prepared to travel ASAP, but the decision is yours and you need to be fully informed."

Alaura wordlessly gestured for the Commander to lead the way, and Damien followed the pair deeper into the ship.

Harmon didn't say anything further as he led them to a chamber in the ship that the Envoy hadn't seen on either of two his times aboard.

"Where is this?" he asked aloud.

"Communications Central," Harmon replied. "We get a lot of transmissions directed at us on a day-to-day basis and, well," he shrugged, "we also eavesdrop on everything going on around us. It's the job of the folks down here to sort it all and let myself and you two know what's important."

The Mage officer led his way into the room. Despite the impression Damien had got from Harmon's description, the room was empty. Viewscreens covered the walls, surrounding the half-dozen empty consoles to provide an ability to view dozens of streams simultaneously.

"It's also, for a variety of reasons, one of the most secure rooms on the ship," Harmon continued. "Take a seat, both of you."

Without waiting to see if the Hand or the Envoy obeyed, he fiddled with the controls and brought up a recording.

"This was forwarded us to by the Tau Ceti Runic Transceiver Array while you were meeting Rickard," he said quietly. "The recording is audio only, obviously."

The Runic Transceiver Arrays were massive constructs, networks of runes that filled *large* domes with a complexity that rivaled the core sections of a jump or amplifier matrix. All of that focus and energy, however, was targeted on a single room slightly less than three meters square.

From that room, a Mage could throw his voice to a single, specific, other RTA anywhere in the galaxy. He had to know where the other RTA was to within a few planetary diameters, so an RTA station also included a giant array of computers, and the message was audio only, so everything in that room was recorded.

The recording started playing.

"Tau Ceti RTA, this message is for Hand Alaura Stealey, Priority One."

The audio was distorted, static and other noises running under it. The inability to provide a clear audio signal prevented the RTAs being used for any kind of data transmission – only voice was useful, which also prevented any security except locking down the RTA itself. Despite the distortion, Damien recognized the voice instantly: it was Desmond Alexander himself.

"We have received further updates from Mage-Governor Vaughn on Ardennes," the recording continued. "He has requested that we accelerate your arrival, as the situation has drastically escalated.

"Twelve hours prior to the transmission of this message, unknown terrorists managed to drop a crude kinetic weapon on the town of Karlsberg. Shortly thereafter, a military relief column intended to deliver medical supplies and desperately needed heavy machinery was destroyed in an ambush using heavy anti-tank weapons."

"You are directed to proceed as soon as reasonably possible to the Ardennes system," Alexander continued. "Beyond that, I leave to your discretion – but the son of a bitch who just blew away fifty thousand people *must* be brought to justice.

"Olympus Mons, ending transmission."

The room was silent for a long moment.

"The *Tides of Justice* is prepared to move on your order, Lady Hand," Harmon said quietly.

"Make it so, Mage-Commander," Alaura replied flatly. "You can let your communication team have their center back, too."

Damien glanced over at her. A few things in what he was hearing didn't add up, and from Alaura's sour expression, she was thinking much the same.

"Your office?" he queried aloud.

#

Alaura threw herself into the chair in her office, turning back to face Damien with a determined expression on her face. A gesture snapped up a holographic screen from the personal computer wrapped around her arm, and she studied for a long moment before sighing.

"We have the data from Rickard," she told him. "I'm less convinced of its value now, though."

Damien leaned back against the wall next to the door, considering the situation.

"We still need to deal with the Governor if he's fixing elections," he pointed out. "We can't let that stand."

Alaura made a throw away gesture, shutting down her PC screen.

"Yes, but that just dropped off the priority list," she admitted. "From my own research and Rickard's information, I'm reasonably sure Vaughn is a good chunk of the *problem* on Ardennes. If things had stayed at the urban guerilla level, we had options.

"But," she said grimly, "someone just blew up a town. *Fifty thousand people*, Damien."

He'd been trying not to think about it.

"What use is His Protectorate if we do not protect people?" he whispered, and she nodded.

"Regardless of what Mage-Governor Michael Vaughn may or may not have done to provoke it, we cannot – we *will not* – permit that to stand unchallenged and unavenged."

A shiver ran through the ship as the engines engaged. The runes on the floor flared slightly to Damien's eyes, their magic counter-acting the acceleration to provide a consistent gravity.

Silently, he opened his own PC and pulled up the data on Karlsberg. A mining town with a population of fifty thousand, one hundred and sixty-two as per the last census. What little information he had hardly suggested a stronghold of the planetary government or a strategic target.

"I don't trust Vaughn," he said quietly, looking at an image of a rundown town with some kind of military barracks on the outskirts.

"You shouldn't," the Hand replied. "Everything I've seen suggests he's slime, the worst kind of Governor we have. If it wasn't for the Karlsberg attack, I'd happily roll in and remove him. That has to wait, now, until we deal with whatever bastard killed a town."

"Fifteen destroyers," Damien murmured, reviewing the stats on the Ardennes' Self Defense Force. "Looks like they're mostly in orbit."

Alaura stopped glaring at her desk and looked at him. "What are you getting at, Damien?"

"The ASDF should have spotted anyone getting into position to drop an improvised kinetic," he said quietly. "And if I was going to risk that, I'd have gone for a more important target than a back-country mining town.

"If I shouldn't trust Vaughn on anything else, why are we trusting him when he says his enemies blew up a town?"

#

Chapter 6

Julia Amiri studied the device sitting on her tiny writing desk with a sigh. Technically, there was nothing illegal about a civilian on Ardennes owning even the frequency hopping high-powered communicator, though the military-grade encryption programming was certainly questionable.

In practice, if the Ardennes Special Security Service learned that one of the many immigrants sharing apartments in Nouveau Versailles south-eastern quarter possessed the communicator, she'd be lucky if she lived long enough to be disappeared. They would assume, correctly, that the ex-bounty hunter was an offworld spy.

So the real question was whether carrying the device was more likely to get her in trouble than leaving it in her room.

The room in question was tiny, less than eight feet on a side and one of five single bedrooms around a central kitchen. The entire building was like that – shared tiny spaces for people living on the pittance that the Ardennes government required people to work for instead of receiving welfare.

The tall, black-haired woman smiled grimly. There was no official reward for turning in offworld spies – after all, Ardennes' government would insist they had nothing to hide from the Protectorate! – but that didn't mean her roommates wouldn't figure they would be paid for turning her in.

They would be right, after all. She couldn't risk it. She scooped the communicator into her purse with the small high velocity pistol. Unlike the communicator, the pistol *was* illegal, but would get her in much less trouble if found.

Leaving the tiny room, Amiri quickly descended the fourteen flights of stairs to the ground – she wasn't sure if the elevator had *ever* worked in this building. Certainly no-one was fixing it, and the stairs were hardly a burden for her.

Trying not to openly show her disgust for the situation around her, Amiri joined the crowd outside. There were no vehicles on the streets here – the immigrants and other poor bastards swept up in the euphemistically named 'Work Placement Program' barely earned enough at their government set wage to pay their government set rent.

The only people who benefited from Ardennes' 'social safety net' were the corporations who played nicely with the government.

With so many people moving on foot, even a tall woman with dark hair and spacer-pale skin didn't attract much notice. Amiri reached her destination without interruption and silently slipped through the side door of the rundown bar.

She trusted the kitchen in the bar to be cleaner than the one she shared. The beer, on the other hand, would have been happier poured back into the horse.

Amiri ordered it anyway as she took a seat at a side table, her eye on the dais used for various performances – sometimes comedians, sometimes strippers. Tonight, the dais held a simple podium and microphone. No fancy banners, no dancing pole, just a completely anonymous speaker.

The room was rapidly filling. The grapevine had carried the buzz about tonight's speaker to a lot of ears. No details of *who* he was – but the rumor was that he had news about the Karlsberg Massacre.

She was halfway through the sandwich of tofu pretending to be steak when the growing noise level of the bar suddenly cut off. A man had emerged from the shadows to stand in front of the microphone. He was a blandly dressed, mousy man with faded brown hair and eyes.

"I ain't giving a name," he said bluntly into the microphone, his amplified voice reaching across the room. "I ain't asking for 'em, either. I'm from the Freedom Wing, and I'm here to bring you The Truth!"

Amiri could *hear* the capitals and classified the speaker as a shill. He was an ancillary member of the Wing – the main rebel group, so far as she had learned in six months – and hugely enthused with the risk and drama of his position.

"The news tells you *we* blew up Karlsberg," the speaker said bluntly. "That, somehow, we dropped a rock from a sky the government owns to kill a town full of our friends and allies."

From the muttering around the room, Amiri hadn't been the only one to disbelieve that. She'd once been a bounty hunter and seen some of the worst humanity had to offer – but people stupid enough to try stunts like that tended not to succeed at them.

"My brothers, my sisters," he gestured around the room. "Karlsberg *revolted*. The miners, driven by one demand too many, rose up in righteous fury and drove out the Scorpions! Standing shoulder to shoulder, they showed that we will *not* be slaves!"

The muttering was a rumble now – an angry rumble, but one in support of the speaker.

"Freedom Wing Alpha was heading there to raise the banner of planetwide rebellion when Vaughn struck." The speaker's voice was soft now, and Amiri strained with the rest of the room to hear. "Never forget, my brothers – Vaughn and his cronies own our skies.

"His minions cast down fire from on high, and Karlsberg burned. Alpha was saved only because they were delayed by Vaughn's attempt to use the Army to suppress the rebellion.

Glynn Stewart

"Mage-Governor Vaughn destroyed Karlsberg," the Freedom Wing member suddenly bellowed, his words echoing around the bar as its occupants quailed. To outright accuse the governor of mass murder was a line even this friendly crowd were uncomfortable with.

"He *murdered* fifty thousand of our brothers and sisters – and the Martian ships stood by and did *nothing!*"

Now the crowd was turning ugly, and it *wasn't* directed at the speaker. It was directed at the government. If they weren't careful, there was going to be a riot here – and Amiri doubted that was what the Freedom Wing wanted. Seizing a small mining town with a surprise revolt was one thing – Nouveau Versailles wouldn't fall to anything impromptu.

"Alpha has a plan," the speaker told them. "We *will* bring Vaughn down – in the time of our choosing. We know, now, that we can't expect *Mars* to save us – we must save *ourselves!*"

That, of course, was when the Scorpions kicked the door down.

#

The bouncer at the door reeled back – first from the shock of the door bursting open, and then from the stun batons the first red and black uniformed thugs employed gleefully. Amiri slid her chair away from the table, right up against the wall to both keep her out of view and clear her to move.

Six Scorpions with stun batons cleared a space around the door, followed by six more carrying the familiar shape of modern stunguns. Equipped with advanced SmartDarts, the stunguns were *much* less likely to do permanent injury than the batons.

Which, of course, said everything one needed to know about the Ardennes Special Security Service.

The crowd was still angry, and Amiri doubted she was the only one in the bar with a weapon. Unlike most people, however, she was still paying just as much attention to the speaker from the Freedom Wing.

He was trying to slip off the stage towards the back door – but didn't make it before the last Scorpion entered.

The officer was a blonde woman who approached Amiri's own intimidating height, and she surveyed the room with eagle eyes. The Scorpion knew *exactly* who she was looking for, and her gaze settled on the Freedom speaker.

"Mikael Riordan, you are under arrest for treason," she snapped. "The rest of you will disperse."

As the crowd grumbled and started to shuffle, Amiri cursed silently. Apparently the speaker *hadn't* just been a shill – Riordan was on the list of potential contacts she'd scraped from Ardennes' planetary databases when she'd arrived. Her research suggested he reported directly to Alpha – the mysterious leader of the Wing – himself.

The crowd clearly didn't move fast enough for the Scorpions, who started pushing their way forward. Amiri watched in fascination as the workers responded by being less and less willing to move, the very effort by the Scorpions to force their way through making their progress harder.

Riordan took advantage of the confusion to dash for the back door – but the Scorpion officer had been expecting something. The rebel made it four steps before the *crack* of a stungun echoed across the bar, and the Freedom Wing speaker collapsed to the ground twitching.

"Clear the room!" the officer snapped to her men. "Use whatever force is necessary!"

The men with the stun batons grinned evilly and stepped forward, the 'less-than-lethal' weapons swinging freely.

Amiri didn't see who threw the first beer bottle. She did, from her hiding spot on the edge of the room, get a very clear view of one of the Scorpions being disarmed by a five-foot-nothing redheaded girl who proceeded to feed the thug his own weapon – on full power.

It went downhill from there.

The bounty hunter had no illusions how the brawl was going to end. The dozen Scorpions were outnumbered four to one, but had support outside and firearms. It would rapidly degrade to bullets, but many of the workers were armed and it wouldn't be a clean win for the Scorpions.

Riordan, on the other hand, was already down, disabled by the automatically tailored electronic charge of the smartdart.

The situation was a nightmare – and her best chance to make contact with the resistance.

A second wave of troopers – this bunch with more stunguns – charged through the door, and Amiri made up her mind. Hiding behind the chaos, she slipped along the wall to the door Riordan had *almost* reached.

The rebel was heavier than he looked, but still light enough for the tall and muscular woman to easily drag him out the unlocked door into the alley. Practice in bringing in bounties unobtrusively helped her do so without attracting notice from anyone who'd care.

"Stop right there!"

Of course, there were Scorpions in the alley.

She let Riordan fall to the dirty floor as she faced the pair of red and black uniformed men. They held stunguns and had uneasy looks in their eyes – probably the ones in the platoon the officer didn't trust to really get it 'stuck in.'

"Please, sirs," she simpered. "I'm just trying to get my husband home – we weren't involved in any of this, we were just out for dinner!"

The two 'cops' approached, eyeing her carefully. She was taller than either of them, though her current pose was 'non-threatening and terrified.'

"Sorry, miss," one of them said gently. "New orders, no-one is allowed to leave the area until they've been questioned. If all's as you say, you'll be fine."

"Wait," the other interrupted as he saw Riordan, "that's…"

Amiri moved. The Scorpion who'd recognized the rebel didn't finish his sentence, a perfectly delivered jab to the throat half-crushing his larynx. He collapsed backwards in a struggle for breath that would kill him without medical aid.

The other Scorpion had barely begun to react when she turned to him. She smashed her hand into the side of his head, throwing him off balance and hopefully breaking the sensitive electronics of his helmet. As he recoiled back, she hooked an ankle behind him and sent him crashing to the floor.

She was on the ground next to him before he could rise, pinning him to the ground with a hand in the hollow of his throat while her other hand plunged home a tiny needle ejected from the bracelet she was wearing.

For a moment, Amiri didn't think the drug was going to work, then the man relaxed into unconsciousness. The other man was unconscious, the damage to his larynx likely to kill him in minutes.

Sighing, Amiri knelt by his side. She'd hit him harder than she'd meant to. Twenty seconds of quick and dirty first aid rectified the worst of it, enough that he'd live long enough for his team to find him.

Twenty seconds it looked like she'd had to spare. She hoisted the still unconscious Riordan into a fireman's carry and took off down the alley at a fast lope.

He'd *better* be useful. Unconscious or not, at least one of the Scorpions' helmets would have uploaded video of her to its backup.

#

It took Riordan an unusually long time to sleep off the effects of the stun-darts. The smart weapons delivered an electric shock designed to disable; they weren't generally very effective at knocking someone unconscious. Extended periods of unconsciousness usually meant the darts had missed a pre-existing condition.

By the time the rebel awoke, Amiri had booked them into a small and dirty room in a rundown motel and stretched him out on the bed.

She was about to boot up the medical routines on her personal computer – far too expensive a program for a 'poor immigrant' to own – when Riordan finally woke up.

He jerked upright, cursing and looking around wildly.

"Where am I?" he demanded.

"Motel, about twenty blocks from where you were speaking," Amiri replied. "You were out for a long time after they stunned you!"

The Freedom Wing speaker looked at her in confusion.

"I have a neuro-electric condition," he said slowly, clearly buying himself time to think. "It doesn't interact well with electric shocks. I was stunned?" He paused, thinking. "Shit, Scorpions! What happened?"

"You went down, I dragged you out. Had to scuffle with a couple of the Scorpions myself, then brought you here."

"Is this place safe? They may call the cops!"

"Mister Riordan," Amiri said quietly, "the rooms look like this, they don't have video cameras, and they rent by the hour. No-one in this motel is calling the police."

Riordan finally sort of relaxed, rising to a sitting position and regarding Amiri.

"Thanks," he said quietly. "I doubt the Scorpions wanted a pleasant discussion on the relative merits of free market capitalism versus concealed oligopolies. What's your name?"

"Jewel," Julia Amiri replied instantly. "And from our red and black friends' shouting, you're Mikael Riordan?"

"Yeah," Riordan confirmed. "One time economics professor, one time Freedom Party member of parliament. Now public speaker for the Wing."

"You got a place to go, Mister Riordan?" Amiri asked. "I may have ended up on the Scorpions helmet cams."

"Damn," he said softly. "I'm sorry. You can't go back to wherever you were staying then – not if you're on the WPP?"

She nodded.

"Damn," he repeated. "Look, I've got a ride coming – soon as I signal, there'll be a car coming, but they won't have room for any extras."

He considered for a moment and then pulled a pad of old-fashioned paper from inside his scuffed-up suit blazer. Scrawling an address on it, Riordan handed it to Amiri.

"That's the address of a much nicer hotel than this one," he told her. "Go there, tell them Lambda said to give you a room and a tab. They'll take care of you."

"I don't just want to hide," Amiri replied with only partially falsified eagerness. Everything she'd seen on Ardennes was pissing her off. The reports she'd sent in would probably be far more valuable to fixing the planet than anything she could do with the resistance, but she still wanted her hands in it.

Plus, a line of sight into the resistance would *not* hurt when Stealey arrived to sort things out.

Riordan hesitated for a long moment, and Amiri couldn't shake the suspicion it was as much being an attractive woman as having saved him that made up his mind. He grabbed the pad back and noted down a code.

"You can call that number," he said quietly. "We'll sort out something from there, and if I need a hand with anything... I'll contact the hotel. They'll find you for me."

#

Chapter 7

Ardennes was, despite the ugliness Damien now knew was going on under the surface, an astonishingly pretty planet. Its heavy metal-rich crust and ripe-for-energy-extraction tectonic activity were what had brought the Protectorate's attention to the world, but its indomitable ecosystem had won over its colonists' hearts.

Even from space, where most planets in the Protectorate were green with imported Terran life, Ardennes was a pale purple. Its trees and natural life had resisted Terran imports with a success that had surprised the biochemists charged with setting up farms.

Thankfully, Ardennes's ecosystem was also edible to humans. Even when the local flora choked out farms, there was still plenty to eat.

Tides of Justice was slowly approaching the planet, still several light seconds away, and Damien stood on the destroyer's bridge next to Mage-Commander Harmon. Harmon stood next to the silver simulacrum of the *Tides* that any jump ship carried at its center, his hand gently nestled on the icon that, in a strange way, *was* the million ton warship.

"What is *that?*" one of the sensor techs breathed. On the screens that surrounded the bridge with the view from thousands of cameras on the exterior of the vessel, Ardennes had rotated enough to show a thin red line.

"That's the reason the colony only occupies two of three continents," Damien murmured. He'd seen pictures of the massive crack in the planet's crust while researching Ardennes, but it was still awe-inspiring to realize you were looking at a volcano visible from orbit. "It's the Zeller Fault – a single lava field that, well, can be seen from orbit."

"Our orbital slot is dropping us in above the Fault," another tech reported.

"That's the opposite side of the planet from Nouveau Versailles," Harmon objected. "Did they give a reason?"

"Mage-Commodore Cor's squadron are occupying the geostationary orbits above the colony," the tech replied. "Apparently, the Governor started to get nervous after the strike."

Mention of the squadron drew Damien's gaze to the data overlay on the visual of the planet ahead of them. A pair of cruisers, behemoths ten times the *Tides'* size, hovered on the same side of the planet they were being directed to. Four more, as Ardennes Control was advising, were settled in over the capital.

Next to the ten million ton cruisers, it took Damien a moment to sort out the Ardennes Self Defense Force ships. Tau Ceti-built export destroyers, they lacked the magical amplifiers of the Martian Navy ships, but still carried all of their regular weaponry.

"How far is our orbit from Karlsberg?" Damien asked quietly.

"Almost the exact opposite side of the planet, My Lord," Harmon replied. "Seems odd."

"Stinks to me," the Envoy replied. "Do me a favor?"

"What do you need?"

"Pull as much from the sensors as you can, and route our shuttle flights over the Karlsberg crater," Damien ordered. "Run every analysis you can on every piece of data you can get. I don't expect to get raw data from Ardennes, and I want to *know* what took out that town."

Harmon glanced away from the screens and met Damien's eyes. The Mage-Commander clearly wanted to ask something, but finally shook his head.

"We don't trust Vaughn," he said quietly. It wasn't a question.

"No," Damien agreed. "I'm not disbelieving him about what happened yet, either," he pointed out. "But I want to validate every damn thing the man says."

"As you command, Envoy."

#

Mage-Governor Michael Vaughn watched the ship settle into orbit on his wallscreen with mixed emotions. He was *proud* of what he'd achieved on Ardennes, damn it! When he'd risen to power, the planet had been in the middle of one of the worst economic depressions the Protectorate had ever seen.

He'd single-handedly dragged his world out of recession, got the unemployed working, brought in the interstellars, and re-birthed local industry from its own ashes.

There had been sacrifices. He didn't pretend otherwise – but they had been necessary. Some of them remained necessary, but he couldn't bring himself to regret rigging the elections. His opponents – like Armstrong – would have undone everything! They didn't see how fragile the edifice that supported Ardennes' economy was, how easily their populist reforms would bring it down.

So Vaughn had done what he had to do. And when the ingrates refused to recognize the necessity of sacrifice, when they rioted or raised arms against his government... well, he did what he had to do.

He didn't expect the kind of men and women he knew Desmond Alexander selected as his Hands to agree with him. Vaughn knew their reputation – Alexander preferred compromise to imposition, negotiation to suppression.

It was weakness – a weakness enabled by the iron fist of the Martian Navy and made easier by the Hands simply flitting away once they were done. They didn't have to live with the compromises they made – but those they left behind did.

"My Lord Governor," a voice said quietly behind him, and Vaughn turned to find a small and unimposing man in the red and black uniform of the Ardennes Special Security Service.

"General," Vaughn greeted his guest with a slight nod. General James Montoya commanded the Scorpions and was one of the few Vaughn would call 'friend'.

"We've put together the package," Montoya reported, stepping up next to Vaughn and eyeing the image of the *Tides of Justice*. "Our crypto-geeks swear that even a Navy computer won't show it as altered."

"But?" Vaughn asked. He knew Montoya, after all.

"They did their best to support the actual impact craters," the General said slowly. "But we couldn't justify claiming the terrorists got their hands on naval munitions. If the Hand's people really dig into the analysis of the site, they'll realize the cheap rocks our video shows couldn't have done it."

"We'll need to make sure they don't," Vaughn replied. "I will keep her distracted, focused on other matters."

He considered the Martian warship for a long moment, and then a cold smile spread across his face.

"I want you to prep one of our 'special' teams," he told the General. "*Very* carefully – they absolutely *cannot* be traced back to us."

"What target?"

"The Hand," Vaughn told him. "I'm sure we can arrange for her to visit one of our hotbeds of terrorist activity, and it would only make sense for them to take a shot at the symbol of the *true* oppressor, after all!"

"Risky," Montoya said quietly. "Hands are tough – I don't know *what* the King does to them, but I've seen video of them in action."

"They're powerful Mages, yes, but not gods," Vaughn replied with a wave of his hand. "But to be clear, my dear James, I don't *expect* our team to succeed. I'll be hardly heart-broken if they do," he admitted, "but I want them to fail. I want them to come close and die trying – I want to make this Stealey understand the true depth of our danger."

He felt as much as saw Montoya's nod of understanding and matching grin, and the other emotion fighting with pride and fear rippled through him: anticipation.

After all, keeping the engine of Ardennes' ticking had become routine. But out-gaming a Hand who *had* to be suspicious of him? Bringing her in on his side and unleashing the full force of the Protectorate on his enemies?

That was a challenge he would enjoy.

#

The shuttle was much more crowded than it had been when they'd visited MagnaCorp Interstellar. For *this* trip, Alaura was bringing a staff of six and a squad of Marine bodyguards. The Marine squad leader, a grizzled Sergeant who reminded Damien of an old shipmate now dead, rode with Damien as the co-pilot.

"You and the Hand are armed, right?" the Sergeant grumbled as Damien carefully tweaked his course to sweep near Karlsberg.

He glanced over at the Sergeant.

"We're not exactly helpless unarmed," he pointed out. The Marine, one of Alaura's regular bodyguards, had to know what was under Damien's and Alaura's elbow-length black gloves.

"I've seen Mages fight," the other man grunted. "You get tired – guns don't. You *can* shoot, right?"

Damien shook his head with an intentionally audible sigh, then flipped his suit jacket open while keeping one hand on the controls.

"Martian IronWorks Arms ST-7. Caseless rounds, ceramic chassis, defeats most weapon detection systems," he told the Sergeant, then twitched his jacket closed again over the slim, deadly pistol.

The Marine chuckled humorlessly. "Well, at least *one* of you is intelligent about it," he said. "Sergeant Cam Mitchell, Lord Envoy," he introduced himself. "We met when we were shipping you to Mars, but I don't expect you to remember one grunt of many."

"That was a stressful trip," Damien admitted. "Still, I think I do – you were the senior Corporal under Sergeant Ames, right?"

"That was me," Mitchell confirmed with a sad sigh. "Still miss Ames. He caught a bullet for Stealey about two years back, I inherited the squad."

There wasn't much Damien could say to that. He kept an eye on his scanners as he swept over the horizon, the sensor package straining to pick up anything it could from Karlsberg as he made his way to Nouveau Versailles.

"What happened?" he finally asked. "To Ames, I mean."

Mitchell grunted again.

"Was *supposed* to be a simple arbitration of a trade dispute," he said finally. "Just Ames and I went with the Lady. Got to the meeting point, and one delegation was dead to the man, and the other had us surrounded.

"They got off one shot," Mitchell said grimly. "Went clean through Ames' eye, killed him before he hit the floor. 'Course, by the time he hit the floor, most o' *them* were dead too."

The Sergeant glanced quickly at Damien's gloved arms, then away. He'd seen the motion before, from men and women who'd seen Hands in action and knew that Damien also bore a Rune of Power.

"I don't know what they thought they'd gain," he finished. "Stealey tracked them down. It wasn't even the trade company that had sent the delegation – it was some kind of death cult out of the UnArcana Worlds. Killed or got killed sixty men and women, just to get a shot at a Hand."

"Even the UnArcana worlds will act on that," Damien said softly. "Not much left of that cult now, huh?"

"*Nothing*," Mitchell replied with grim satisfaction. "Stealey likes to negotiate. Would rather convince rebels to lay down arms, make a compromise. But she is a *Hand*, Lord Montgomery. She knows when it's time to draw the sword."

Damien swallowed. As an Envoy, he didn't have the authority to order executions or judgments. He did, however, have enough power to make sure that someone *with* said authority took a close look at affairs.

The city of Nouveau Versailles finally came into view, and Damien opened up a channel with the spaceport. He was glad for the distraction, pulling his mind away from thoughts of the harsher duties of those who spoke for Mars.

#

Chapter 8

By the time Damien had rejoined Alaura and her staff and watched the Marines shake themselves out into an honor guard under Sergeant Mitchell, the landing pad had cooled sufficiently for them to exit the Navy shuttle.

The Marines exited first, marching out in two neat files to link up with the Governor's honor guard of Ardennes Special Security Service troopers in their black and red body armor. Alaura waited on the edge of the shuttle for a calm thirty seconds as the two sets of soldiers matched their lines and formed a corridor for Mars' representatives to pass down.

With that complete, she released her gentle grip on Damien's forearm and stepped forward. He waited another handful of seconds, then followed the Hand an appropriate meter or so behind her.

Mage-Governor Vaughn waited for them at the other end of the lines of soldiers, the heavyset blond man towering over both Damien and Alaura – by easily thirty centimeters in Damien's case. He wore a red and black suit, clearly stylized to resemble the uniforms of the Security troopers around him.

"Welcome to Ardennes, My Lady Stealey, My Lord Montgomery," Vaughn greeted them, taking Alaura's hands in his and bowing over them. He gave Damien a firm nod, respectful but much more perfunctory than his greeting to Alaura.

"We came as soon as we learned of Karlsberg, Governor Vaughn," Stealey told him. "A tragedy of this scale requires response. His Majesty sends his condolences."

"A response is needed indeed," the Governor replied. "Come, we have food and drink ready for you in the terminal. I find the shuttle trip from orbit the most draining part of any journey!"

"Envoy Montgomery will accompany us, of course," Stealey said. "Do you have someone to take care of our things and my staff?"

"Of course!" Vaughn snapped his fingers and gestured. One of the security men approached, and Damien saw the uniform bore the icon of a scorpion embroidered onto the collar and shoulder.

"Lieutenant, please see that the Hand's staff and things are taken to Government House. Master El-Hashem should have rooms prepared for them all."

Mitchell materialized out of nowhere behind Damien. "Corporal Wu and I will accompany you and the Envoy, Lady Hand."

It wasn't a suggestion or a request, but Alaura accepted it with a smile and a calm gesture.

"Lead the way, Governor Vaughn," she instructed.

Vaughn led them in to a luxury waiting lounge, likely usually reserved for wealthy travelers waiting for the shuttles to their liners or personal yachts. The pair of red and black uniformed security troopers guarding the entrance, however, made it clear the lounge was closed.

A server materialized as they entered and gently ushered the Marines to a set of seats near the door. Another young man quickly uncovered a small buffet table of still-warm food for the Governor's guests and disappeared.

Damien followed Alaura's lead carefully, taking a plate of food and then claiming one of the comfortable seats.

"We appreciate the welcome, My Lord Governor," the Hand said after a few bites. "It's warmer than a Hand often sees, let me assure you!"

"You are here to help find the people who murdered thousands of my citizens," Vaughn said grimly. "Any aid I can provide, any resources or personnel, is yours for the asking. We *must* bring these murderers to justice."

Either Damien's suspicions of the man were misplaced, or Vaughn was one of the best liars he'd ever encountered. With everything he'd learned so far, he wasn't prepared to take bets! The Envoy carefully tucked into the food, leaning back in his chair as he watched Alaura maneuver.

"We will need *all* of the information your defense force recorded about the attack," she told the Governor. "I will need to inspect the site, both from the ground and the air."

"All of our files are open to you, My Lady Hand," Vaughn agreed instantly. "You may also want to contact Mage-Commodore Cor. Several of her cruisers were in orbit at the time, and their sensors are superior to the ADF's destroyers."

"Of course. And access to the site, Governor?"

"That may take some time," the Governor said slowly. "The area was a uranium mine, Lady Hand. While the impactor itself appears to have been a purely kinetic weapon, the nature of the region has rendered the impact zone highly radioactive. Atmospheric heavy metal counts are dangerously high. I've ordered the entire area under a no-fly and no-entry zone until the dust settles."

"The attack was enough of a tragedy," he continued, "and since we've confirmed that all the survivors have been rescued, I hesitate to add more injury and death to the toll!"

"My people are well trained and equipped," Alaura replied. "We will be perfectly safe."

"I'm told that a storm is expected to sweep through the region for the next several days," Vaughn countered. "The storm both makes it less safe to visit now, and safer to visit once it has passed. I beg you, Lady Hand, please wait until the storm clears the area – I could not bear to report any injury to yourself to the Mage-King."

Damien eyed the Governor carefully, wondering. He didn't think there was much that you could conceal at the impact site of a kinetic weapon, not with only a few days.

"Very well," the Hand allowed slowly. "In that case, I will need to visit Nouveau Normandy tomorrow. If I must wait to see the latest atrocity, then I wish to review the files of those incidents and visit the aftermath."

"The Normandy attacks were six months ago," Vaughn objected. "We have all of those details in our files here."

"I find context important, Governor," Alaura replied. "Visiting the location of the attacks is important, as will be speaking to the people there. I do not doubt that all of these attacks are tied together – I *will* find the common link, Governor. And I will use it to drag Karlsberg's murderers to justice."

Vaughn's impressive calm slipped a bit, his eyes dark for a moment that left Damien wondering if he'd imagined it.

"Of course," he concluded softly. "As I said, all of our files, all of our resources, are at your disposal. I can have a plane ready to transport you to Normandy in the morning?"

"That will be sufficient. If you can make all of those files available to myself and Envoy Montgomery by the time we reach Government House, we can begin our background research."

Michael Vaughn, Mage-Governor of an entire system of three billion souls, bowed as he rose to his feet.

"It shall be as you command, My Lady Hand."

#

An entire floor of the eastern wing of Government House, the residence of Ardennes' planetary Governor, had been turned over to Alaura Stealey and her party.

Mitchell and his men had already set up when Damien and Alaura arrived, and directed them into the rooms on the end of the wing, furthest away from the staircase up.

"Two guards on the staircase at all times," he told them calmly. "Two more at this end," he gestured toward the doors to their rooms. "None of the staff leave this section without an escort – neither of *you* leaves without at least two Marines."

Damien smiled at the determined soldier and glanced over at Alaura.

"Who is in charge of this little party again?" he asked.

"I thought I was, but I see I have to reconsider this assumption," she replied.

Mitchell had the grace to look somewhat abashed, but he didn't waver.

"My job is to make sure you both survive, ma'am, sir," he told them. "I won't tell you how to do your jobs, but I will insist you do them escorted."

"It's fine, Sergeant," Damien replied, still smiling. "You've swept for bugs?"

"The place was *crawling*," Mitchell replied. "We've cleaned them out, but expect the terminals to be tapped. Keep anything confidential on your PCs."

"Let's not assume we're clear yet," the Envoy told him. "I'll sweep for runic artifacts. The Governor would *expect* us to clear the technical bugs, but magical ones are rare and hard to find."

"I've never heard of such a thing," the Marine in charge of their bodyguards admitted. He didn't sound like he disbelieved Damien; he sounded more frustrated that there was a threat he hadn't been aware of.

"They're still rare," Damien replied. "We've *tried* to keep the matrix designs under wraps, but I tend to assume we fail at such things."

He open the door to his room and glanced in. A king-sized canopy bed held pride of place amidst a cushioned display of luxury that made him uncomfortable just *looking* at it.

"I'll sweep for them," he concluded. "Then we can talk."

#

Wandering through the plushly carpeted halls of the rooms they'd been provided, Damien kept his eyes open for the energy flow of magic. Finding something like this wasn't something that Alaura could do – while the Hands had runes tattooed into their flesh to make them stronger than other Mages, they still lacked the ability to see the flow of magic that separated Rune Wrights from the rest of the Mage population.

There were a few technological ways to detect runic artifacts – usually looking for heat signatures – but a cleverly designed rune matrix could avoid those. No matrix Damien had yet encountered could hide from him or the Mage-King; nor had any of them proven impossible to understand.

In the end, he found four 'decorative' ivory rods, each tucked into a flower vase in the corner of a room. He laid them out on the table, studying the meticulous hand-carved silver etchings on each of them.

"This is impressive work," he told Mitchell. "It's almost a shame."

He removed the skintight glove on his right hand and held his palm out over the ivory rods. Before the Marine could ask what he was doing, energy flashed from the silver runes inlaid into his palm. Each of the ivory rods glittered with lightning for half a second and then a faint scent of burning enamel, reminiscent of a dentist's visit, wafted into the air.

"Why can *you* see them and Alaura can't?" Mitchell asked quietly, watching the smoke of burning ivory float through the air.

"Because exactly five people in the galaxy can," Damien told him. "Two are minors."

Mitchell, he knew, was cleared to know about the existence of Rune Wrights. His squad had been filled in before the mission – briefed from necessity, seeing as how protecting a Rune Wright was now part of their job.

"So that's going to be a rude awakening for the Governor," the Sergeant gestured at the ivory rods, now marked with a surprisingly attractive pattern of ash and silver.

"Indeed," Damien glanced up as Alaura entered and waved her over. "We're clear now, no eavesdroppers of any kind."

"Good," she said briskly. "What was your impression of Vaughn?"

"He's hiding something at the impact site," the Envoy replied instantly. "Not sure what he can expect to hide in a handful of days, but there's *something* there he's hoping will be gone by the time that storm passes."

"I've checked the weather report," Alaura explained grimly. "The impactor messed up the weather in the region badly – the 'storm' he mentioned is looking to be a full-blown hurricane. It may just obliterate any evidence we could hope to find."

"Damn."

"The good news," Mitchell pointed out, "is that we *did* sweep pretty close to the impact site on our way down. Combined with the data Harmon can pick up from *Tides*, he should be able to at least confirm the Governor's data."

"Or suggest that it's fake," Alaura agreed. "Damien, I want you on everything we can pull on the impact, the video from both ADF and Commodore Cor – and everything you can find in local files on Vaughn.'

"Whatever you do, *don't* link your PC into the local 'net'," Mitchell warned. "I *really* don't trust this network."

"Should we complain to the Governor about the bugs?" Damien asked. That fell under the category of 'etiquette he hadn't thought about'.

"No," Alaura replied. "That we wiped them all out – and will continue to – is enough." She glanced around the room. "Mitchell, I want you to stay in Nouveaux Versailles with Damien tomorrow. Pick your best Corporal and section to send with me to Normandy."

The Sergeant sighed. "Are you hanging yourself out as bait, ma'am?"

"Not intentionally," she told him. "Doesn't mean no-one will take a shot at me. I need to get a feel for the locals – I'm not sure how big of a time bomb we're sitting on here."

"What do you need me to do while you're in Normandy?" Damien asked.

"Sit on Vaughn," she said bluntly. "Get through those files and get out into the city. We *know* Nouveaux Normandy had a rebel campaign. Nouveaux Versailles is the capital – if the pressure is building here, Vaughn has more problems than he thinks."

#

Chapter 9

Paranoid as she was feeling, Alaura hadn't been able to come up with a reason not to let Governor Vaughn's staff arrange her transportation. The young lady who'd booked the flight and the vehicle at the other end had been competent, if flustered by the pair of armored Marines looming behind the Hand.

Landing at the Nouveau Normandy Regional Airport, a six-strong security detail from the Ardennes Special Security Service was waiting to augment the four marines Mitchell had insisted accompany her.

The pale and young-looking Lieutenant saluted as he stepped forward.

"Lieutenant Avison, my lady," he greeted her. "We've been assigned as your security detail in Normandy – while things are quiet, we don't think we caught all of the rebels and a Hand is a massive target of opportunity for them."

"I can understand that, Lieutenant," she said calmly. "The Governor's office arranged transportation?"

"Of course, ma'am," he replied. "Regional Governor Fok asked me to extend his invitation for you to join him for lunch if your business allowed."

Alaura nodded without speaking, gesturing for Avison to precede her. Fok had been Regional *Vice*-Governor until the elected Regional Governor had taken a sniper round through the center of her forehead. What intelligence she had suggested that Fok had done a good job cleaning up the mess of corruption his predecessor had left behind – quite likely part of the reason he hadn't shared the woman's fate.

"First, I wish to see where Marguerite Anderson died," she told the Scorpion as they emerged into the light. A second team of six more security troopers was waiting outside, standing guard over a trio of locally built armored personnel carriers.

"I'm... not sure that's wise, ma'am," Avison said slowly. "It's not in a good area of town."

Alaura gestured at the sixteen armed men and women surrounding them and the three APCs.

"I somehow suspect we'll be fine," she replied dryly. "Given the precision and symbolism used by the rebels leading up to Anderson's assassination, I suspect that *where* she died was as important as how and why. I need to see it with my own eyes to understand the context."

From his conflicted expression, someone had told Avison that she wasn't supposed to go there. Unfortunately for said someone, Avison was *maybe* a year out of college, and had no idea how to stop a Hand with the power to have him summarily arrested from going anywhere she wanted.

"Yes, ma'am," he finally said helplessly.

#

It was a church. Technically, though Alaura would admit she wasn't *entirely* clear on the distinction, it was probably a cathedral.

Certainly, it was a massive edifice of stone and glass, likely built when the first French and Quebecois settlers were laying the groundwork of the capital city of the province of Nouveaux Normandy. At some point in the two hundred years since, the glitter of the stained glass had been muted somewhat by what appeared to be a layer of transparent anti-ballistic armor.

The area around the cathedral was rundown, old houses giving way to row upon row of newer blocky gray concrete towers, the homes of the poor caught up in Vaughn's Worker's Placement Program.

The grounds of the old church itself, however, were clean. Simple grasses, tinged with the reddish hue of local plant life, marked neatly maintained lawns. The garbage and debris strewn through the streets of this, Normandy's poorest neighborhood, were noticeably missing here.

Waving Avison and his Scorpions back, Alaura walked forward across the flagstone path leading to the gates. She'd seen video of the shooting, but the backdrop of plain concrete hadn't revealed the nature of where Anderson had died.

Judging from her memory of the videos, though, Alaura stopped and studied the ground. *There.* The sniper round had been fired from high up and aimed down. A high caliber, high velocity bullet, it had left a visible wound even in the heavy stones that had been beneath the regional governor's feet.

A single shot, as the reports said. There were no other damaged flagstones. Someone had tried to fill this one in with cement, but it still showed the crater where the bullet had hit.

"Why was she *here*?" Alaura muttered to herself.

"*Excusez-mois, ma fille,*" a soft voice interrupted. "*Puis-je vous aider?*"

"*Non,*" she replied without looking at the speaker. "*Merci beacoup, mais je suis à la recherché.*"

She didn't need anyone helping her today. The speaker chuckled, however, and she looked up to see a white-haired man with pitch-black skin, clad in the uncomfortable looking frock of a Catholic priest.

"I am not blind, my daughter," he said kindly, his English as unaccented as his French. "Nor deaf. You are wondering about our dear departed governor's fate."

"Pardon me, Monsieur...?"

"I am Father Eli Pelletier," the old man said calmly. "I am the priest of this church, and it is my repair that you are examining so closely."

"Surely an edifice of this scale has more than one priest," Alaura objected.

Pelletier smiled, a tiny twinkle in his eyes.

"Such it does," he admitted, "but I keep my hand in on the small things as much as the large. But, my child, you had a question – and since I am not blind, I know that amulet you wear means the answer may be important."

Alaura hadn't realized that the gold hand she wore around her neck had fallen out of her shirt while she was investigating the flagstone. With a subdued sigh, she slipped it back inside her clothes.

"I was wondering why Regional Governor Anderson was even here," she admitted. "The neighborhood is not..." she gestured around, "where I would expect to find the Governor."

"It is about... context," Pelletier admitted. "History is why she was here. History is why the rebels chose this place, this day, to deliver their message."

"A very pointed message," Alaura replied.

"Miss Anderson *was* the message, not its recipient," the priest told her. "You see, she was here to celebrate the twentieth anniversary of the Worker's Placement Program. Twenty years before that exact day, Miss Anderson was selected from the ranks of the Prosperity Party's Youth Wing to cut the ribbon on the first of a new complex of affordable housing towers." He gestured to the blocks of concrete buildings behind him.

"Since, well, affordable housing towers are rarely photogenic, they had the pretty young thing cut the ribbon in front of the church – ably assisted by the mastermind of the program, Mage-Governor Michael Vaughn."

Alaura looked at the patched over hole and traced its vector back in her mind. The shot had come from the roof of one of the WPP residential towers. She stepped over to line herself up with those buildings, and then looked out over the lawns of the cathedral.

"There's only one spot on this lawn you can give a speech from, isn't there?" she said quietly.

"The timing was exact," Pelletier told her. "That was Anderson's plan – and apparently, the rebels'. Twenty years to the minute from Vaughn's announcement of the WPP, she was giving a speech celebrating the anniversary standing *right* where he did."

"And then she died."

"And then she died," the priest confirmed.

Walking back to the APCs, Alaura noticed that Lieutenant Avison was on the radio, talking to someone. As she approached, however, he put the radio back into the vehicle and came to meet her. He stopped after several steps, staring in surprise at the priest she'd been speaking to.

"What's Archbishop Pelletier doing out here?" he asked in surprise.

The Hand turned sharply to spot the priest she'd been speaking to standing just outside the doors to the cathedral. The old man bowed deeply to her, then disappeared into the building.

Apparently the 'simple priest' she'd been speaking to was the head of the Quebec Reformation Roman Catholic Church on Ardennes.

"I didn't recognize the name," she admitted aloud. "He was telling me about Madame Anderson."

Avison nodded, but was silent for a moment afterwards. It seemed the young Scorpion was unwilling to speak about the Governor – likely due to the realization that speaking ill of the dead was unlikely to do his career any favors.

"Anything I should be aware of?" she finally asked, nodding towards the radio in the vehicle.

"What? Oh!" he responded, flustered. "Governor Fok was asking if I knew if you would be available to meet with him for lunch. He just finished an event not too far from here."

Alaura checked her personal computer. She had a few more stops she wanted to make – locations of attacks both during the campaign that ended with Anderson's death and the later, cruder, campaign – but she was also curious what kind of man had replaced Marguerite Anderson.

"I will have more sites to visit afterwards," she warned the youth, "but yes, I believe I will be able to meet with the Regional Governor."

Avison bowed slightly and gestured for her to get into the vehicle.

"I will let him know we're on our way."

It said many things about the life experience of Hands that Alaura Stealey was *intimately* familiar with how it felt when an electromagnetic pulse mine was used to disable an armored vehicle. First, there was the thump as the mine launched itself from the street, latching itself onto the bottom of the vehicle.

Then there was the sensation of every hair on your body standing up as the air filled with electrical energy, and the sparking, burning sound and smell as every system in the armored personnel carrier overloaded its EMP hardening and died.

Safety systems on the passenger compartment spared them, but the slight tinge of pork to the burning smell told her the driver and gunner, exposed to their own systems by necessity, had not been so lucky.

"We're under fire!" she snapped. "Evac!"

"Ma'am, the vehicle is armor..."

"And a sitting target for people with heavy weapons," Alaura overrode her Marine. Avison was still looking at her in shock. "*Move!*"

The Marines obeyed. As her Corporal pulled the APC's emergency lever, blasting the exit hatch off with explosive bolts, Avison finally got past his own shock.

"Cover the Hand," he ordered his men. "Us first," he then told the Marines. "We're more expendable."

Even as Alaura wondered where Fok had found an *honest* man in a Scorpion uniform, two of Avison's men charged out of the APC, followed by Avison himself. Alaura's Marines followed the last of the Scorpions out, and then *finally* the Hand herself escaped.

The street was deserted. Sixteen-story concrete towers surrounded them, but they were ghost-like in their emptiness. The handful of storefronts were either boarded up or had metal shutters closed.

The armored personnel carrier was alone and obviously trashed: frozen in the middle of the street like some giant metallic bug. The lead vehicle was around the corner and gone, already out of sight.

The third APC was rolling up beside them, its gunner behind the pintle-mounted machine gun, sweeping the rooftops for threats.

"Into the buildings," Avison ordered, clearly assessing the threat much as Alaura did. In the middle of the street they were in danger from snipers and rocket teams – and she didn't expect whoever had set up an EMP mine in the street not to have a second wave waiting.

"Sir, what's your—" the gunner on the third APC never finished his sentence. A rocket blasted down from a third story window and slammed into the vehicle, directly beneath the gunner's seat. The entire vehicle vanished in a fireball of high-powered explosives.

"*Cover!*" Avison yelled, gesturing for Alaura to run for the building. The young Lieutenant had acquired an assault rifle on his way out of the APC and used it to return fire at the window the rocket had launched from.

Gunfire responded, and a second rocket slammed into the now-vacated stalled APC. Alaura's Marines hustled towards a storefront, the Scorpions following while maintaining covering fire.

Two of the Ardennes Special Security Service troopers went down, one missing a significant chunk of his head.

Alaura's Marines reached the nearest storefront, one with heavy metal shutters.

"Clear!" one of them yelled, slamming chunks of a pale purple putty on the shutter locks, then stepping back.

The thermite paste flashed blindingly bright, and then the Marines flung the shutters up to clear the way into the store. It was, Alaura noted absently, the kind of corner convenience store that showed up in poor neighborhoods across the Protectorate.

Shelves clattered to the floor as the soldiers threw together an impromptu barricade. The fire from the street had slackened off, but the attackers *would* follow up.

"I can't reach anyone," Avison told her as he rejoined them, panting and looking shaky. The young officer's gaze kept slipping out to the street, to the wrecked APCs and the bodies of his men. "I'm being jammed."

"It won't matter," Alaura told him grimly. "As soon as my PC's transmitter went off the air, Mage-Commander Harmon got an alert. If Governor Vaughn does not act, *he* will."

Avison started to object to her assumption that Vaughn wouldn't act, but before the first words were out he interrupted himself.

"Look out!" he snapped and threw himself forward. He pushed Alaura out of the way as three black-clad men in face masks emerged from the back of the store and opened fire.

The Scorpion officer succeeded at getting Alaura out of the line of fire – and himself into it. Bullets punched clean through his body armor and threw him to the ground at the Hand's feet. He met her gaze for a seemingly eternal moment, then slumped to the cheap tile.

Alaura ran out of patience. There was always a danger of collateral damage when Hands acted – but it seemed that this building was already empty.

Fire flared along her skin, searing away the skintight black gloves she wore. The silver runes inlaid into her palms and right forearms flashed with warmth as she channeled energy. The fire gathered on her for a moment, and then she *flung* it out.

The three men in the store barely had time to realize just *what* they'd cornered before they died. Bolts of fire hammered into their skulls, incinerating their brains in a moment.

Rising from the wreckage of the store, Alaura gestured for her Marines and the two surviving Scorpions to stay down. There was no-one else in the store, but a second trio of black-clad men emerged from the building across the street.

They saw her first and were started to raise their weapons when she flung her hand out towards them. Lightning crackled from her outstretched fingers, her magic ripping open vacuum channels to deliver the overwhelming electrical charge to her targets.

One managed to scream. Just one.

She walked out into the street, watching for the original snipers and rocket launchers. A single shot rang through the air as one of the snipers panicked and revealed his location, the heavy high velocity bullet missing her by inches.

Her eyes cold, Alaura filled the room the shot had come from with fire. The rockets stored there ignited, the explosion ripping a massive crater in the side of the building. A twinge of fear ran through her, and she hoped that the building had truly been evacuated, and that there had been no-one simply hiding from the thugs upstairs.

"Ma'am!" a voice shouted, and she turned at the warning from the Scorpions carefully following her out. A second rocket launcher had been brought up to the window – but she found it as it fired.

The rocket traveled less than a meter before hitting a wall of force in midair and exploding. Fire flayed the exterior facing of the building, and then Alaura ripped away the wall of the apartment with a gesture.

Two men were standing there, looking outwards in shock as their cover disappeared. Alaura pulled their feet from beneath them with her magic, bringing them down to the street with a gentleness that had nothing to do with mercy.

"Tell me who sent you," she demanded, standing over them. One of them was panicking, hyperventilating as he stared up at the bogey man of all who opposed the Protectorate.

The other spat in her face.

"*Enculez-vous, porc*," he snarled. Before she could respond, he produced a small pistol from inside his clothes – but rather than firing at *Alaura*, he shot his friend in the head. Alaura ripped the gun from his hand and flung it away.

He smiled coldly.

"The boy lacked conviction, *putain*," he told her. "*I* do not."

The assassin bit down on something in his mouth, then spasmed, his head lurching back as the poison hit his system.

He collapsed next to his friend in the ruined street, leaving Alaura alone with her dead.

"Shit."

#

Chapter 10

Mage-Governor Michael Vaughn waited for the earnest Ardennes' Planetary Army Colonel briefing him on the Nouveaux Normandy incident to leave, the door to his richly decorated office clicking quietly shut behind the woman, before allowing himself a massive grin.

It couldn't have gone better if he'd choreographed every second of the encounter himself! The men on the ground had honestly believed they were part of a rebel organization, so he knew they would have said the right things for the moments Alaura had them captured.

And Avison! He suspected General Montoya had selected the overly earnest young man himself. Officers like Avison concerned Montoya, Vaughn knew, as men who hid their vices that well were difficult to control or predict. Nonetheless, the apparently squeaky-clean officer had given the *exactly* right impression of the Ardennes Special Security Service – and then died saving the Hand's life!

With all of the assassins dead, there was no way Stealey could link the attack back to Vaughn. She *knew*, now, how dangerous his rebels were. It shouldn't take much to swing her completely on side for a forceful, permanent, solution – one with all of the resources of the Protectorate behind her.

He smoothed his face to an appropriate expression of concern as his secretary paged him. He brought her image up and regarded the young woman – as beautiful as only the finest surgeons could make her, and an extremely pleasant armful in bed – calmly.

"What is it, Rita?"

"General Montoya is here to see you, sir."

"Send him in, Rita. With everything going on, this is important," he instructed.

While he waited for Montoya, Vaughn crossed to a hutch on the wall of his office and pulled out two crystal glasses and a decanter of whiskey. The whiskey was from Scotland on Earth and cost easily several months of the fixed wage a member of the Worker Placement Program received.

The crystal was from a set made in England in the early Twentieth Century. The decanter and six glasses had cost as much as some of the *apartment buildings* Vaughn had seen constructed for those same workers.

"Get in here," he ordered when Montoya opened the door. The small man looked worried, but then, Montoya always looked worried. "Have a drink!"

He forced the glass of whiskey into the General's hand, then clinked glasses with him.

"*Santé!*" he toasted, then took a swallow of the whiskey.

"It's still early to celebrate, Governor," Montoya replied, but only *after* drinking.

"We're not done yet, no," Vaughn agreed. "But the escapade your men pulled today? And poor, poor, Lieutenant Avison's heroic death? I think we are well on our way to opening Miss Stealey's eyes."

"Do *not* underestimate the Hand, Michael," Montoya said very quietly. His use of Vaughn's first name stopped the Governor in his tracks – while Vaughn regarded the man as a friend and had tried several times to insist he use his first name, the General almost never did.

"This isn't the first time someone's tried to kill her, nor even the closest anyone has come to succeeding," Montoya continued. He took a sip of the whiskey, shaking his head. "Hell, in one incident I've managed to acquire details of, Alaura Stealey was the direct target of a *regimental assault*. An assault that left three hundred men protecting her dead – along with *every single attacker*."

"We were counting on the sheer destructive power of an enraged Hand," Vaughn pointed out. "The weapons and intelligence you provided may have convinced our tame rebels they had a chance, but *we* knew better."

"Yet you still underestimate her," Montoya replied. "She does not trust you – and she has very capable people."

Before Vaughn could ask what the other man meant, Montoya slid a chip into the reader on the Governor's desk and triggered it. A hologram of Ardennes sprung into existence over the desk, and a highlighted flight path appeared on it.

"That left her destroyer," Vaughn quickly realized. "Why wasn't I advised of this?"

"It's a Navy assault shuttle," Montoya explained. "With twenty Marines aboard, launched the *minute* that the jammers engaged.

"You didn't hear about it because they didn't file a flight path or even tell us they were coming. They launched without permission, using full stealth systems. My people learned they were coming when the fuckers landed an assault shuttle in the middle of Nouveaux Normandy."

"Dammit," Vaughn exhaled.

"It's worse. We backtracked their course through the surveillance satellites and some help from our friend Cor. They flew *directly* over Karlsberg."

"The storm rolled in already," the Governor objected. "They can't have seen much."

"It depends on what sensors they installed on the bird," Montoya said grimly. "It will take them some time, but if they get any useful data, it could invalidate our whole video footage."

"We have to take the risk," Vaughn told him after a moment's consideration. "The storm will break up the impact craters, clear away any evidence. It's nice when this planet's weather co-operates."

Montoya shook his head.

"You're right, boss, in that this went about as well as it could," he concluded. "But we *need* to remember that Stealey doesn't trust us as far as she could throw us. Anything we hand her, anything we set up, has to be *iron* tight."

Vaughn finished his whiskey in one gulp, staring at the globe of his planet. He was going to play this bitch like a fiddle, one way or another. But Montoya was right, too. He had to be careful.

"Your bag-man with the rebels," he said quietly. "Keep him in Normandy. Assign him some dipshit administrative command, something to keep him out of Stealey's sight. Make sure anything about your Special Operations Directorate is locked down, too. My seal."

Montoya nodded wordlessly, finishing his own whiskey.

"We need to keep her off balance, guessing," Vaughn continued. "When the dust settles, I don't need her to trust me or even *like* me – I just need her to do what I want."

#

"My understanding," Lori Armstrong said icily into the conference call connecting her to the other leaders of the Freedom Wing, "was that we were leaving Normandy alone to see if Governor Fok lived up to his potential."

"For that matter," the ex-leader of the Freedom Party and now rebel leader continued, "I recall agreeing to suspend operations *entirely* after Karlsberg, until we came up with a better strategy."

"So *who the fuck attacked the Hand*?" she snarled.

The line, linked to all twenty of her top cell leaders, was silent for a long moment.

Then someone sighed, and the smooth, well-aged voice of Agent Papa spoke.

"None of us did, Alpha," he said softly. "I've checked in with every cell leader in Normandy, and they've checked down. We've accounted for all of our people – and the Hand left a stack of bodies of the people who came after her."

"And innocents," Lori reminded them all grimly. Twenty-three people – including three *children* – had died when the attackers' rockets had exploded.

"Which is why *we* didn't go after the Hand," Papa replied bluntly. "Their reputation is pretty clear – anyone who attacks them dies. And if you kill one…" she could see the older man's shrug in her mind. "If a Hand falls, another rises. She'd be replaced, and her replacement would come in with a vengeance.

"And let's be honest – with Vaughn prepared to flatten towns, the Hand may be our best chance at really stopping him."

A number of the other cell leaders grumbled at that, though no-one said anything specific. Most of Lori's people wouldn't trust the Protectorate now – and she didn't blame them. But if her people hadn't taken a stab at the Hand…

"Do we have another movement forming?" she asked. "One we don't know about?"

"*Non*," a soft voice replied. "*Dupe-moi une fois, honte à toi. Dupe-moi deux fois, honte à moi.* It wasn't rebels the *last* time someone blew up a building, was it?"

"November has a point," Papa agreed. "Not just Karlsberg, but that spate of attacks two months ago in Normandy – those weren't us."

"We know who those were, in the end," November confirmed, her voice heavily accented. "One of my girls pulled flight records. Colonel Brockson arrived in Nouveaux Normandy the evening before Hand Stealey."

"Are you sure?" Lori demanded. Colonel Brockson had been the mastermind behind a series of bloody 'terrorist' attacks in Normandy after they'd pulled in their own horns.

"He's been given new resources, ordered to expand his dirty tricks team into a whole battalion," Iota, her main agent in the government's military, told them. "They call it the Special Operations Directorate, and it makes the rest of the Scorpions look like cuddly kittens."

"Damn," Lori whispered. "How widespread are they?"

"I'm not certain," Iota admitted. "I suspect he's been assembling cells of people who *think* they're rebels across the planet. As November said, though, he was in Normandy. And he's been ordered *not* to return to Nouveaux Versailles."

"If there was a goddamn red and black uniformed bastard I'd like to have a long chat with, that's the one," Papa said softly. "Oath of pacifism be *damned*."

"Is there any way we can get that information to the Hand?" Lori asked.

Her people were silent for a long moment, then November spoke again.

"*Magnifique*," she whispered softly. "I have an idea."

#

"News reports are rolling in from Nouveaux Normandy of massive civilian casualties after a failed attempt by the so-called 'Freedom Wing' to assassinate Alaura Stealey, Hand of the Mage-King of Mars.

"Current estimates are that in excess of forty people are dead, including ten members of the Ardennes Special Security Service who were escorting the Hand.

"Hand Stealey is on Ardennes on the direct orders of the Mage-King, seeking the murderers behind the destruction of the city Karlsberg. It seems the 'Freedom Wing' has no interest in…"

The video news in the corner of the staff break room of the Versailles Arms cut off, and Amiri quickly looked over to see who had interrupted her viewing. Riordan's name had got her a relatively decent room in the Arms – a mid-range hotel near the spaceport – and a tab that seemed unlimited so long as she didn't abuse it.

In exchange, she'd been quietly helping out around the hotel – mostly as muscle in the case of matters the hotel owners wanted dealt with before the police were involved. She kept out of sight otherwise, either in her room or down here in the staff break room when she needed company.

She hadn't actually *heard* anything from Riordan since she'd arrived here, however, so she was surprised to see the Freedom Wing demagogue holding the remote behind her.

"We didn't do it," he said bluntly.

Amiri eyed him carefully. If Riordan knew who she *actually* was, she doubted he would try to use her as a conduit to Stealey. The rebels would almost certainly see her as a threat, not an opportunity.

"I'm not exactly inclined to believe government news, if that's what you mean," she said slowly.

He sighed.

"Sorry, Jewel," he said quietly. "I just know that's going to be an argument I'll need to have a *lot* over the next few days. I'm not on the same page as the folks who think Mars is going to swoop in and save the day, but taking potshots at Hands is a bad way to promote our cause."

"The bar's empty," he continued. "Grab you a drink?"

So this was a social call – from a man with few friends he could trust. Amiri could play that game.

"Sure."

The bar was empty, though not closed as she'd half-expected. Riordan gestured to the bartender as they walked in and then took a

Hand of Mars   61

dark-paneled booth near a back corner. The bartender showed up a moment later with two whiskeys on the rocks.

"Why are you so convinced Mars isn't going to help?" she asked after taking a sip of the liquor. "Everywhere else I've been, the Protectorate really does try to, well, protect people."

"Mars never *has* helped here," Riordan said bitterly. "Twenty *years*, that's how long Vaughn has been in power. He buys the interstellars, accepts bribes from the local corporations – he grows fat, the corporations grow rich, and the rest of Ardennes gets turned to slaves.

"And what has Mars done? They built their fuelling station here – there's an entire *squadron* of cruisers in this system, their crews coming through on shore leave.

"What are we supposed to believe? That none of what's going on here makes it back to Mars? That Mars is somehow oblivious and Mage-Commodore Cor is blind?"

He shook his head and downed the whiskey.

"The truth is that Mars doesn't care," he told Amiri. "So long as Vaughn's tame Councilor shows up to the meetings and tells His Majesty everything is going swimmingly, the economy is improving, everything is shiny... why would Alexander care?"

There was clearly nothing that Amiri could say, so the pair drank in silence for a while.

Then Amiri made her excuses and headed back to the room where her expensive frequency-hopping communicator was hidden. Today, that level of reach was unnecessary. Today, she would simply be posting on a forum, in a code only Alaura Stealey could read.

It was time for Julia Amiri, Special Agent of the Martian Protectorate Secret Service, to report in.

Hopefully before *everything* blew up.

#

Chapter 11

The assault shuttle swept in to land on a pad completely cleared of any locals. Cam Mitchell and the other seven Marines who hadn't accompanied Stealey to Normandy had swept *everybody* else away from the landing zone, and now stood sentinel in black body armor carrying battle carbines.

Mitchell had at least made the token gesture of asking Damien for *permission* to do so. Damien suspected that had been more to give him a stick to beat complainers with than any intention of allowing people to stay if the Envoy refused.

Damien waited until the ground around the shuttle had cooled and the landing ramp began to slide open before walking, quickly, out onto the landing pad. Four Marines, part of the contingent Harmon had sent down, exited the shuttle first.

They greeted him with crisp salutes and stood aside. Next out was a pair of Marines clad in Exosuit Battle Armor. Towering a head or more above their more conventionally armored compatriots, the two soldiers in the powered armor swept out of the shuttle wordlessly, nodding to Damien as they took up sentry positions.

Then, finally, Alaura exited the little ship. The Hand looked tired and met Damien's gaze with a small nod.

"We're all alive," she said quietly as more Marines stepped out of the shuttle behind her. "Some good men aren't – and neither are the innocents who were caught in the crossfire."

"I saw the report," Damien told her, his voice equally quiet. "It wasn't your fault, Alaura. It was the bastards who came after you."

"What's Vaughn saying?" she asked.

"Freedom Wing," he replied. "All over the news. 'The depraved terrorists have struck at the representative of our beloved Protectorate.'"

"A little *too* all over the news," Damien noted.

"Agreed," Stealey said, her voice still tired. "I need a fucking drink, Damien. Let's talk somewhere more secure."

Damien glanced around, arching an eyebrow at the twenty fully armed and armored Marines now forming a perimeter around the pair of them.

"More concerned about ears than guns, Damien," she told him sharply, but it got a small smile from her.

"I know," he allowed, returning the smile. "We've kept our rooms clear."

#

"This planet," Alaura announced between sips of whiskey, "is fucked up."

Damien said nothing, nursing a cup of coffee as he waited for the Hand to get to her point. The Marines were busy settling in the new squad and the two senior Martian representatives were alone.

"The entire legal system has become a series of special case exemptions," she continued, "and a good *third* of the population is in indentured servitude. I'm honestly surprised nobody is *starving*. I can't *blame* the Freedom Wing for rebelling!

"But they've also crossed about half a dozen lines I *can't* let them cross," she finished, staring morosely into her glass. "Assassinating governors? That's arguably a legitimate target. *Blowing up a city*? Attacking *me*?"

"Assuming they did it," Damien quietly pointed out. "*Vaughn* blames them. But Vaughn is a corrupt crook who's been using this planet as his own personal factory.

"Look at the pattern," he continued. "Anderson's death was the end of a clean, precise, urban guerilla campaign. Evidence suggests a well-trained, well-equipped group with a solid plan. With their objective complete, they disappeared – only to reappear three months later, with a hack-job of a terrorist campaign.

"The two campaigns are completely different levels of accuracy, planning, and precision. Perhaps most importantly," he reminded her, "the first campaign represents a group we'd negotiate with – and the second does *not*!

"Desmond hammered a point home a few times over the years – *always* ask who benefits.

"Who benefits from us thinking the Freedom Wing is the worst kind of terrorist group? The kind of group that would level cities and attack Hands?"

Alaura looked at him in silence for a long moment and then swallowed the tumbler of whiskey.

"There's also the possibility of multiple factions in the same movement, or even them just growing desperate," she pointed out. "But you're right – we need to know *exactly* what happened. Both in Karlsberg and in Nouveaux Normandy."

"You've got a plan," Damien said. It wasn't a question – he'd sparked her thought process, and he could see the wheels turning in his boss' head.

"Not so much a plan as a division of labor," she warned. "Sorry, Damien, but you don't have the oomph to pressure Vaughn. You've the technical authority, but he won't buy it. Even from me, I'm probably going to have to lean on the implicit threat of Mage-Commodore Cor's squadron.

"So I'll ride our dear Governor, and dig into their files on Karlsberg," she continued. "I think I'm going to break out the Hand itself, too. See what those overrides get me out of some of their locked files."

One of the very high level secrets Damien had been briefed on was that the golden amulet the Hands wore was not merely a symbol of office – it was also an override chip, capable of accessing any government system in the Protectorate at the highest levels of security.

"But first," Alaura paused, crossing to the door and leaning out. "Maria, I need you."

A moment later, Maria Wong – Alaura's personal chief of staff – entered the room. The dark-skinned and red-haired woman glanced at Damien for a long moment, then turned her attention to her boss.

"Yes, My Lady?"

"Maria, I want you to find the names of every trooper and civilian who died today," Alaura told her grimly. "Then find their family and dependents. Whatever happens, I want a note adding *all* of their survivors to the Martian General Pension fund added our records. The soldiers died defending me, and those civilians got caught in the crossfire. We owe them."

"Yes, My Lady," Maria confirmed. "Anything else?"

"Arrange a meeting with the Governor," Alaura told her, glancing at the clock. "Make it tomorrow evening, I'll need some time to dig into what's going on. Make sure the Marines get settled in, and give Mitchell a heads up that he'll be escorting Envoy Montgomery shortly."

"Of course, My Lady," the Chief of Staff agreed. With a tiny nod to Damien, she slipped out of the room, the Hand closing the door behind her.

"Where am I going?" Damien asked.

"Nouveaux Normandy," Alaura answered. "I don't think I'll be capable of being objective enough to investigate the attack cleanly. I need you to dig into it – *all* the way into it, Damien. Turn over every stone, follow every link – if you're right, if it was Vaughn's people, not the Wing, it changes *everything*. Follow me?"

Damien swallowed hard, but nodded.

"I'm sending Mitchell's entire squad with you," Alaura continued. "Anyone who decides to launch a follow-up round isn't going to last long enough to realize it's a bad idea."

"I'll find the truth," he promised.

"Don't worry, Damien, I'm not sending you off into the bush alone," the Hand told him with a smile. "Some of this is paranoia, too.

I've got an itchy feeling between my shoulder blades, and I want us in different cities.

"One of my agents checked in while I was on the flight back – coded message drop. She's linked in with the Wing, and they're telling their own people they didn't do it," she continued. "The drop included a contact code; I'm flipping it to your PC."

"She's in Normandy?"

"No, here in Versailles," Alaura replied. "I don't expect you to need to contact her, but I want to keep you in the loop – so no matter what happens, we see this through. Mars *owes* these people, Damien – and we *will* see this done."

"You're just nervous because someone tried to kill you already," Damien replied, trying to make light.

The Hand shook her head. "It's more than that," she said quietly. "Either the Freedom Wing is what Vaughn says it is, and they're very dangerous and very desperate, or *Vaughn* is behind a lot of this."

"In which case, our dear Governor is very dangerous and very desperate," he said softly.

"Exactly." Alaura began to dig into a black briefcase she'd brought to Ardennes with her and removed a small velvet box. "Catch."

"What's th—" Damien opened the box to find the golden fist of a Hand's insignia on a plain gold chain. He swallowed. "These are gene-locked," he objected. "I can't use yours."

"That isn't mine, Damien," Alaura told him gently. "We both know what His Majesty intends for you – and today, it will be *damned* useful for you to have the Hand to crack the local files in Normandy.

"I'd say you can give it back when we're done, but like you said. They're gene-locked."

"There's formalities and training still to pass, but Desmond didn't give me your Hand because he expected you to fail."

#

Damien was more than a little distracted as he left the section of Government House that their staff and Marines had completely taken over. Nonetheless, he *had* been taught to maintain some semblance of situational awareness, and was *completely* taken aback when he managed to run into one of the cleaners.

"I'm sorry," he immediately told the older woman, offering her a hand up.

"*Tout va bien*," the woman replied, taking his hand and then bowing over it when she was on her feet. "It's all right, My Lord," she

Glynn Stewart

repeated, in heavily accented English. "I wasn't watching where I was going."

Assurances and apologies exchanged, the Envoy of the Mage-King of Mars spent a minute helping re-assemble the cleaner's cart, and then continued on his way – paying more attention, now, to where he was going.

Slipping *back* into the zone secured by the Marines, he quickly sought out Sergeant Mitchell.

"You got the word from Alaura?" he asked.

"Yes, sir," the Marine replied crisply. "My squad will be ready to go in an hour, and I've checked in with the Navy pilots – they'll be fueled up and ready to fly by then."

"Thanks, Sergeant," Damien replied. He paused for a moment and met the Sergeant's gaze frankly. "I've been trained in this, but I've never led an investigation before in my life," he admitted. "Any suggestions?"

Mitchell considered.

"I'm a bodyguard, sir," he pointed out. "But... I've followed Stealey around like a heavily armed puppy on a few of these. I'll keep an ear open, let you know if anything doesn't add up to me."

"I appreciate it, Sergeant," Damien told him. "I *want* these bastards."

"Assume nothing, verify everything," Mitchell replied calmly. "This whole planet *stinks*, and I'm not talking about the air quality."

The Envoy nodded, the gold amulet in his jacket pocket a surprisingly heavy weight. Unconsciously, he touched the amulet – only to feel a layer of paper over it.

"What the...?" he muttered. His suit blazer had both a sealed interior pocket – now containing the Hand – and a mostly decorative outer pocket. Reaching into the outer pocket, he pulled out a sheet of neatly folded paper.

"I'm guessing you didn't put that in there yourself," Mitchell told him, scooping the sheet out of Damien's grasp with a gloved hand. "Better safe than sorry, sir," he said by way of apology.

"I am wearing gloves, Sergeant," Damien pointed out. Like Alaura – and most other Jump and Combat Mages for that matter – Damien wore skin-tight gloves to cover up the runes inlaid into his palm. His were the same jet-black as his suit blazer and ran all the way up to his elbows, covering runes most other Mages would *not* have.

"And if someone was being a clever bastard, they'd have accounted for that," the Marine pointed out. "I'm expendable, My Lord. You aren't."

"Fuck that, give me the note," Damien ordered.

With a long-suffering sigh, Mitchell quickly unfolded the note – presumably to trigger any trap concealed in the infinitesimal space between the halves of the sheet – and handed it back to the Envoy after a moment.

"Thank you," Damien said dryly as he glanced at the handful of lines on the sheet.

If you seek answers on the Special Operations Directorate, find Colonel Elijah Brockson.

- *A friend*

"That's… rather un-useful," Mitchell noted, reading over Damien's shoulder. "The note could be from *anyone*. How can we trust it?"

Damien looked at the paper carefully.

"It was planted on me by a member of the staff," he concluded aloud. "I think we can safely say it's from the Freedom Wing."

"From the rebels? So why would you trust it?"

"I don't," the Envoy replied dryly. "It is, however, one more starting place than I had *before* they planted it on me. I think that I have some research to do on our way to Normandy.

"And in the meantime," he continued, turning back to Mitchell, "I believe we have some preparation to do. And Sergeant?"

"Yes, My Lord?"

"I suggest you pack for arrest and interrogation."

#

Chapter 12

The shuttle was in Nouveaux Versailles for less than twenty hours. It was eight in the morning, local time, when Damien and Mitchell boarded the Navy ship for the trip back to Nouveaux Normandy.

Several of the Marines promptly went back to sleep after strapping themselves in. Damien and Mitchell passed them, entering the semi-private 'officers' compartment' between the main cargo bay and the cockpit.

The assault shuttle was designed to carry an entire platoon of Marines, either in exosuit battle armor or accompanied by a light tank. Mitchell's single ten man squad were dwarfed by the cargo bay, but the officers' compartment had the advantage of a computer setup designed for tactical deployments and strategic communications.

The Marine Sergeant blandly took up a position blocking the door to allow Damien to work in privacy. Something about the way he did it made Damien very sure the soldier knew that Alaura had given him the Hand and was making sure he could use it without interruption.

"Lieutenant," Damien asked the pilot over the intercom, "can you hook me up with a direct link into the government network?" He paused. "For that matter, can we keep that completely separated from the shuttle's systems?"

The Navy officer laughed.

"I'd appreciate the last, yeah," he admitted. "The tactical setup back there has a fully separated computer network for just that reason. Should be linked in to the global-net already."

"Thanks, Lieutenant."

Damien spent a few moments familiarizing himself with the computer system. The setup was designed primarily for communication and co-ordination, but was capable of handling a complex data search if you found the right tools.

He linked into the Ardennes planetary government's databases, pulled up personnel files for the Ardennes Special Security Service and, after a short moment of hesitation, typed in "Colonel Elijah Brockson."

The database churned for a moment, then flipped up an 'Access Denied, Record Restricted' message.

That was strange. Apparently, even Brockson's very *existence* was classified?

Damien typed in the access code the locals had provided him. Supposedly, he'd been provided full access to their systems, but the same message flashed up. Now it had an extra line – "Gubernatorial Seal."

Most likely, if he hadn't been typing in the exact name, the record would never have shown up in his search. Since he was looking directly for the man, however, he'd bounced up against a hard seal – one Vaughn had either implemented himself or had been done under his direct orders.

Glancing at both doors of the compartment and swallowing hard, Damien reached into the inner pocket of his suit jacket and pulled out the Hand. The golden icon was light, no more than forty or fifty grams, but it seemed to hold the weight of worlds.

He turned it over in his hands. The Hand was a closed fist cast in gold, and he didn't see any way to connect it to the computer at all.

"It needs to touch your palm. Warmest part of the body and the easiest spot for the gene scan," Mitchell told him from the door. The Sergeant was eyeing the amulet with awed eyes. Somehow, despite the fact that Damien *knew* the Sergeant had seen Alaura's Hand dozens of times, the icon was still awe-inspiring to the Marine.

It was *terrifying* to Damien.

Following Mitchell's advice, he stripped off the skintight glove from his right hand. He stretched his fingers for a moment afterwards, watching the silver inlaid on his palm and forearms ripple gently. Finally, he placed the Hand in his palm and watched.

For several seconds, nothing happened. Then, as the tiny golden symbol warmed from his hand, it shivered slightly and he felt a momentary prickle – and a connector port slid out of the thumb.

Damien wasn't sure if he'd been expecting something more dramatic – or just nothing, the Hand not actually being his.

He took a deep breath and slipped the connector into the computer. It beeped, and 'OVERRIDDEN' flashed up on his screen across the 'Access Denied' message.

Even unlocked, Brockson had a very bland record – though interesting in its blandness. Up until five years ago, he had a normal-looking progression through the ranks, up to Captain at age thirty.

Then the first 'Special Assignment – SOD' entry popped up. Three months, no details, followed by a promotion. Several more 'Special Assignments' followed, until a year ago, accompanying his promotion to Colonel, was the note "Assignment – Commander, Special Operations Directorate."

That was the last note in the file until very recently, when Brockson had been assigned as 'Logistics Coordinator, Nouveaux Normandy Province'.

It looked like a lot of information had never made it into the files, but the latest position looked odd. Damien pulled it up. With the Hand overriding all security measures in the government system, the

Glynn Stewart

database happily informed him that while the posting was *backdated* to a week ago, it had been entered last night.

A few keystrokes brought up another database, this one the government records tracking official and civilian travel. Brockson had arrived in Nouveaux Normandy ten hours before Alaura had, accompanied by several cases of cargo under a Special Operations Directorate seal instructing that they were to be handled with care and not opened or exposed to heat.

Another, more local database, told Damien that Brockson had only *just* signed in at the Nouveaux Normandy Logistics Center this morning. He'd been in town for a full day before checking in at his supposed assignment – an assignment that hadn't existed until *after* the attack on Alaura.

None of Damien's briefing files had mentioned anything about a Special Operations Directorate, either. Searching for the Directorate in the government 'net, however, returned nothing except a list of personnel.

Any further files on missions or tasking was clearly not kept connected to the net. A list of personnel, however, combined with the passenger tracking system for air traffic and a paramilitary force's general preference for locating its people, gave Damien a starting point.

The Directorate's personnel were scattered across the planet, usually in singletons. Running his track into the past he found clusters, times and places where anything from five to twenty SOD officers and personnel had met up for several days or weeks.

Some of the dates and times looked familiar, and Damien pulled up one of his briefing files – and promptly swore.

"Sir?" Mitchell asked, surprising by the sudden exclamation.

"Vaughn is a murderous fucking son of a bitch," the Envoy said bluntly, gesturing towards the screen. "We *thought* it looked like there were two terrorist groups – one precise urban guerilla movement, one wanton terrorist faction."

"It looks like we were right," he continued grimly, "except that the wanton terrorists work for the Governor."

#

The sight of the red and black uniforms of the Scorpions waiting when Damien exited the shuttle sent a shiver down his spine. The Special Operations Directorate was a unique group with its own crimes, but he had to wonder about *any* organization that contained something like the SOD.

For that matter, he had his suspicions about just how Vaughn had kept the peace as he quietly choked every last penny out of his planet – and the Ardennes Special Security Service was high on his mental list of suspects.

A squad of the Scorpions were providing security for the pad Nouveaux Normandy Air Control had directed them to, and a trio of officers were waiting at the edge of the pad.

The pad was still too hot for them to step onto, but Damien wasn't feeling overly patient. Despite Mitchell's uncomfortable look at Damien heading out of the shuttle, the shield he was holding protected him completely.

He'd also extended it around the two Marines Sergeant Mitchell had sent out immediately after him, though their exosuit battle armor meant it was likely redundant.

The expression of the lead Scorpion officer as Damien walked calmly across the still steaming concrete surface, accompanied by the two-meter-plus hulks containing his bodyguard, was worth every erg of energy the shield took to maintain.

"My Lord Envoy," the large black man, apparently unused to being the one intimidated, greeted Damien with a slow salute. "I am Major Ken Leblanc, commanding officer of the Thirty-Seventh Special Security Battalion."

"A pleasure, Major, though I'll admit the circumstances could be better," Damien told him, returning the salute. The 37th, according to his research, was one of the two Security Battalions actually housed in Nouveaux Normandy.

Damien kept walking, forcing the Scorpion officer to fall in at his side. The two junior officers were brushed aside by the bulk of the exosuited Marines, falling in at the end of the little procession.

"How can the Ardennes Special Security Service help you, My Lord?" Leblanc finally asked.

"Two of the men who were with Hand Stealey survived, correct?" Damien replied, stepping out into the streets of the city and glancing around. Nouveaux Normandy's nicer areas rivaled even Mars for glitz and glass, but he could see the concrete blocks of the apartments built for the Work Placement Program even from here.

"That's right," Leblanc confirmed. "Lieutenant Avison and his squad were from my battalion."

"I'll need to speak to those men, immediately if possible."

"They're in protective custody," Leblanc said slowly. "I'll need to get confirma…"

"No, you won't," Damien told him flatly. "I *will* speak to them. Now."

"I…" Leblanc trailed off as Damien turned to face him.

There was no way the man had risen to the rank of Major without getting his hands dirty on this planet. Damien held that thought in his mind as he met the gaze of the much larger, more physically intimidating man, and removed his Warrant from his pocket.

"Do you need to see my Warrant, Major?" he asked quietly. "Or do you accept my authority as your Governor has?"

Leblanc finally shook his head.

"No, My Lord Envoy," he admitted. "We have a vehicle waiting for you, this way, sir."

#

The armored limousine Leblanc provided was subtler than the armored personnel carriers they'd ferried Alaura around in. That subtlety was somewhat ruined by the pair of exosuited Marines jogging on either side of it.

By the time they reached the Ardennes Special Security Service's main Normandy base, Mitchell and his Marines had 'borrowed' the vehicle Leblanc's security detail had arrived in and caught up to them. The big Major looked unimpressed when the transport truck pulled up and disgorged Marine black and gold uniforms, not Scorpion red and black ones.

"Sergeant, have your men wait here and prep for an arrest," Damien murmured. "Make sure that Colonel Brockson does *not* leave the base while I'm here."

"Of course, sir," Mitchell agreed. "You *are* taking an escort in, correct?"

"*Not* Braid and Coral," the Envoy told him, glancing at those two worthies in their two meter suits of battle armor. "It would be a little much," he finished dryly.

"I'll accompany you myself, My Lord," Mitchell told him.

"Just make sure about Brockson," Damien ordered.

The Sergeant nodded and gestured his two section leaders over to him.

There were a few minutes of quiet muttering, while Leblanc was looking more and more uncomfortable, and then Mitchell and two Marines joined Damien.

"Let's go, Major," Damien told Leblanc.

"Your men will have to leave their weapons at the front security desk," the Major said as they headed towards the entrance to one of the several mid-sized office buildings that anchored the Scorpion base.

"No, they won't," Damien told him affably. "Please make sure of it before there are any misunderstandings."

The Major looked like he'd been chewing on lemons, but when they reached the security desk he bluntly ordered his people to issue Mitchell and his Marines passes for their weapons.

"This way," he said once they were through, and led the way down into the bowels of the building, finally passing through an – open – heavy security door into what was unquestionably a prison.

"I thought they were in protective custody, not a dungeon," Damien observed.

"There is nowhere safer on the planet than down here, My Lord," Leblanc replied. "I assure you, they are being made as comfortable as possible."

Finally reaching the section of the empty underground prison the two soldiers were in, Damien conceded at least that point. Someone had made an effort to re-calibrate the lights from their harsh institutional brightness to something more tolerable, and the rough prison cots had been replaced with comfortable looking beds and couches. Several cells, behind a secondary security door, had been converted into an apartment.

That secondary security door was still sealed with both mechanical and electrical locks and guarded by four men in medium body armor.

"The Envoy is here to speak with Riley and Pierre," Leblanc told the men. "Open it up."

"Thank you, Major," Damien said. "Now, once the door is open, my men will provide security until I'm done speaking with them. We will advise when I am done."

"That's not..." Leblanc trailed off on his own accord this time. "As you command, My Lord Envoy."

"Thank you," Damien told him quietly.

With a small, somewhat pained looking, nod, Leblanc opened the door and led his men back down the corridor.

"You have some kind of jammer for the bugs, Sergeant?" Damien asked quietly once Leblanc was far enough away.

"Of course," Mitchell replied.

"Then let's find out what Riley and Pierre have to say."

#

Chapter 13

With the asexualizing body armor off, Riley turned out to be a slender woman with dark, buzzed-short hair. Pierre, on the other hand, was a completely bald man barely an inch taller than Damien's own five-foot-nothing.

When Damien entered their 'suite', Riley was settled in watching something on a display screen, and Pierre was pacing the length of the cell block in a bounding, nervous pace.

"Riley Beaumont and Pierre Winslow?" he asked softly, making sure they could both hear him. With Leblanc gone, and the necessity to maintain a facade gone with the Major, Damien allowed himself to relax. He did not need to intimidate these people.

"Yeah," Riley replied, glancing up at him. "Well, it looks like a suit, walks like a suit and quacks like a suit, so I'm guessing you're from Mars?"

Damien was pretty sure he *wasn't* supposed to have heard the muffled chuckle from the Marines behind him, but he was also glad to see the pair still had spirit. Leaving her comment hanging for a moment, he pulled up a chair and gestured for Pierre to sit.

After a moment, the nervously pacing soldier did so, but continued to nervously fidget.

"I am Envoy Damien Montgomery," he told them. The title felt pretentious as hell to him still, but the pair needed to know how deep the waters they were swimming in were. "The rest of your squad died protecting Hand Stealey – that will *not* be forgotten."

"Vaughn will wave their bloody shirts all over the place, that's for sure," Riley said bluntly. "Every ounce of mileage he can get from Mars out of Avison's body is profit to him, I'm sure."

"Beaumont!" Pierre snapped, the soldier's face worried.

"Before we continue," Damien interrupted before the Scorpion could continue, "I should probably mention that that I am recording this conversation. And, thanks to the wonderfully complex toys of the Royal Martian Marine Corps, I can guarantee that nobody *else* is."

Pierre's fidgeting stopped. Riley's lackadaisical, somewhat lazy, pose vanished into an instant sitting form of attention. Unlike the moment before, Damien had no problems believing the pair were real soldiers now.

"Playing the real game now are we?" Pierre asked. "You might get us in deep shit, even covering us like that you know."

"You fought and your friends died to protect Hand Stealey," Damien reminded them. "Olympus Mons does *not* forget its debts. You need protection? Money? A ticket offworld? Name it."

The room was silent for ten seconds. Twenty.

"You're serious," Riley finally said into the quiet.

"I am the Voice of the Mage-King of Mars," Damien Montgomery told them, the words falling like tombstones in the quiet underground cell. "My word binds Olympus Mons. And I *need* to know who tried to kill Alaura Stealey."

Pierre sighed, leaning back in his chair.

"We don't know anything," he replied. He held up a hand when Damien was about to reply, and repeated himself. "We don't *know* anything.

"But we can guess, and we can draw conclusions," he continued. "Look, people don't call us Scorpions because it's a really cool badge. They call us Scorpions because we're nasty, we're sneaky, and we stab folk when they're not looking."

He gestured at Riley. "Beaumont here? She's squeaky-clean, three months out of school and assigned to Avison's squad. Me? Not so much," he admitted, meeting Damien's gaze. "Avison was like her. Ten months out of the Academy, idealistic as hell. I think Leblanc was trying to shield him from some of the harsher realities, but I *also* think it meant someone marked him as expendable.

"As someone who'd look good dying for the Hand," he concluded bluntly. "The rest of us? Just collateral damage – like the fucking kids.

"I can't say anything for sure – like I said, we don't know shit," Pierre repeated quietly. "But they didn't throw us down here until *after* we'd been interviewed by Colonel Brockson."

"Special Operations Directorate," Damien said quietly. He left the words hanging in the air, but both Pierre and Riley nodded fiercely.

"Scary fucker," Riley observed. "I swear he was trying to make sure we *couldn't* identify anything – but hell, the only thing I can say for sure is that those were *our* guns."

"Our guns?"

"The rocket launchers," she said grimly. "I picked up the signature pattern on my scanners – Martian Ironworks Arms Shrike Five Anti-Armor rockets. Ardennes Army doesn't have 'em – they use the Seven, it's got a rotary magazine. Only force on the planet with the Shrike Five is the Scorpions."

"Soon as he was done interviewing us, Brockson said we were in protective custody and threw us down here," Pierre told Damien with a shrug. "Don't know if it was Riley mentioning the Shrikes, or just wanting to be sure we didn't say anything to the wrong people, but they locked us up good."

"You want out?" Damien asked.

"Hell yeah," Riley snapped. "I'll take that ticket offworld, too. *Yesterday.*"

Pierre took a second to think about it, but nodded slowly.

"Yeah, I'm with Beaumont," he said quietly. "I hear Martian summers are ten months long. I'd like to find out."

Damien stood and gestured for them to follow him.

"I still have business here," he admitted, "but I'll make sure you're spaceport-bound first, I think. You've been more helpful than you suspect."

#

On his way to Brockson's office, Damien began to have an inkling of why the Mage-King selected his Hands with such care. Having been connected to the chip inside the golden amulet, his personal computer was now capable of locating Colonel Elijah Brockson's personal computer in the military facility.

Personal computers included everything from birth certificates to bank account details and were among the most heavily encrypted civilian electronics in the Protectorate. Accessing one without permission was legally a form of assault, and government access to a PC required a warrant.

As a Hand, Alaura's word counted as a legal warrant. To enable that, the Hand itself was loaded with the encryption keys to override the security on most PCs. Combining the Hand with Alaura's orders, Damien effectively had a blank warrant to lay open many of the deepest secrets of those around him.

The three years of training and a planned year-long apprenticeship – all of which followed doing something spectacular enough to attract Desmond's attention – seemed a frail shield against that much authority and power.

"You'll want to lock his PC," Mitchell told him quietly as they exited the stairs onto the seventh level of the office tower. No-one had challenged them since they'd left the dungeons. Damien had sent the two junior Marines – with an order signed in his Voice – to take Riley and Pierre to the spaceport, leaving only the Sergeant guarding him.

"I can *do* that?" Damien asked.

"Security lockdown," Mitchell confirmed. "Theoretically, it's a defense against theft, but that little gold toy of yours gives you the ability to lock it down remotely. If he's busy, he might not even notice."

Brockson technically had a job to be doing in Normandy, and Damien doubted he would be interfacing his personal computer with the general base network to help do it. That PC likely contained enough evidence to allow Damien to ask some *very* pointed questions of the Governor.

They paused outside the Special Operations Directorate Colonel's office for a few minutes while Damien found the command he needed. Like all computer commands, it was perfectly innocuous looking. With a deep breath, Damien squared his shoulders and touched the key.

He could not afford weakness now and, with a firm nod to Sergeant Mitchell, Envoy Damien Montgomery, Voice of the Mage-King of Mars, entered the office.

#

Colonel Brockson clearly hadn't expected to be interrupted. He looked up from the desk screen he was working on in annoyance, glaring at the intruders into the plain, completely undecorated, office he'd apparently inherited.

"Who the fuck are you?" he snapped. "This is a private office."

"Colonel Elijah Brockson?" Damien said.

"What?" he demanded.

"You are Colonel Elijah Brockson, Ardennes Special Security Service? Currently assigned as Logistics Coordinator, Nouveaux Normandy Province?"

"I am. Now get out of my office before I call security," Brockson snapped.

"They wouldn't obey your orders over mine, Colonel," Damien told him. He wasn't, he had to admit internally, entirely certain on that point. Legal authority didn't always translate into actual power. "I am Envoy Damien Montgomery. I'm investigating the assassination attempt on Hand Stealey, and I have some questions."

Brockson stared at Damien in shock for a moment, almost immediately absorbed in a sharp laugh.

"I guess I can't stop you if you're really an Envoy, kid," he replied. "Don't know what you think *I* know about it!"

Damien smiled thinly.

"I have to admit," he said genially, "I found it interesting that you left Nouveaux Versailles, what, ninety minutes after the Hand informed the Governor's people she was coming here? Now, if that had been a previously booked flight, I might have understood it, but you had to have a military flight held for you and your cargo."

"I take it you've never been military?" Brockson told him. "Hurry up and wait – or in this case, wait for the cargo, then hurry up."

"Indeed," Damien allowed. "What happened to your cargo, though, Colonel? You loaded eight crates – cargo labeled as explosive, but locked under a Special Operations Directorate seal – onto that transport plane. No such crates have been checked in at either base in this city."

This time, Brockson was *definitely* caught off-guard. He took a moment to answer, and spoke slowly when he did.

"I'm afraid you must be mistaken, Envoy," he told Damien. "I don't know what the Special Operations Directorate is, and I checked my cargo in when I arrived – but given that it was mostly paper notebooks and new data chips, I doubt it stood out to whatever search you did."

"That's funny," Damien told him softly. "Your file has you assigned as the commanding officer of the Special Operations Directorate, so I'm *very* sure you know exactly what it is. Would you care to elaborate?"

"I'm sorry, I really don't know what you're talking about," Brockson said finally. "For that matter, accessing my file is a violation of my rights. I will have to raise this with the JAG."

"Colonel, I speak for the Mage-King of Mars," Damien reminded him. "If you've lost track, he is your ultimate boss. I have full authority to access your file. Full authority to override the Governor's seal on said file.

"I *know* you head the SOD," he continued. "I even have a damned good idea just what you've been up to. But I still have one question, Colonel?"

"Entertaining as this has been," Brockson snapped, "I think the joke has worn thin. I don't know who you actually are, but I'm pretty sure the Mage-King's Envoys have better things to be doing with their time than this!"

"Did the poor bastards you set up know who you work for?" Damien asked softly. "Or did they think you were another rebel like them?"

"You have no proof of these insane allegations," Brockson told him. "I'm calling security." He went for his personal computer, only for it to refuse to respond.

"I suspect your personal computer contains more than sufficient proof," the Envoy said quietly. "I secured it before we entered – to prevent you doing anything stupid.

"Sergeant Mitchell – arrest Mister Brockson, please."

Despite the entire conversation, Brockson was frozen in place for a moment by sheer shock. Then he made a dive for the door. His palm caught Mitchell's grasping arm, deflecting the Marine Sergeant into the wall.

The Scorpion made it all the way to the door before Damien stripped the glove from his right hand. As Brockson tried to dodge out of the office, he ran into a wall of force that bounced him back to the floor.

He sprang back to his feet, then froze in place as Damien wrapped him in bonds of pure force with a gesture.

"We'll want his PC too, Sergeant," Damien ordered blandly. "I'll be intrigued to see what answers Mister Brockson gives us – one way or another."

#

Glynn Stewart

Chapter 14

Mage-Commodore Adrianna Cor watched the assault shuttle take off from Nouveaux Normandy with thinly veiled disgust. The evidence suggested that Vaughn's people were incapable of even the most rudimentary track-covering – the Hand's lapdog Montgomery had found the head of the Governor's precious 'Special Operations Directorate' in under a day.

She had to admit – to herself, if not to her bridge crew, at least – that blowing the shuttle out of the sky was tempting. Unfortunately, there was no way she could justify a weapons malfunction *that* precise. Montgomery was going to deliver Brockson, wrapped in a neat bow, to the Hand.

Cor was not aware of anyone ever managing to keep secrets from a Hand. And since she suspected that Brockson knew of at least *some* of the deal between her and Vaughn that meant that she was going to be strung up right next to the Governor.

Her bridge crew was silent around her. Their gazes were locked on the shuttle as well – they all suspected what she had done, and they'd all been present when they'd decided to take the Governor's money and blow away a city.

"I wish I knew what they were thinking," she muttered aloud.

Her tactical officer cleared his throat hesitantly, and Cor leveled a steely glare on him.

"You have something, Trevor?" she asked calmly.

Lieutenant Trevor Hamilton nodded, looking somewhat abashed.

"I… figured we'd want to keep an eye on what the *Tides of Justice* was up to," he admitted. "Since we have the squadron flagship codes, I, um, used them to hack into the internal security feeds. I don't have access to Stealey or Montgomery, but I can give you the *Tides'* bridge feed."

"Do it," Cor ordered. "Feed it to my station."

The mundanes on *her* crew, at least, knew their place. Hamilton was about as useful as a non-Mage could be, she reflected. If they made it through the next few days, she'd have to see about getting him bumped to Lieutenant-Commander.

A moment later, the image of the bridge of Alaura Stealey's personal transport popped up on her screen, an audio feed linking in from the speakers in her chair.

"It's about fifteen seconds delayed," Trevor warned her. "I'm pulling it from their backups, not directly from the camera feed."

Cor nodded absently, her attention now focused on the scene in front of her. She recognized Mage-Commander Harmon – he had a solid reputation, though he'd spent the last few years as Stealey's pet.

"All right people," Harmon was saying. "Right now, I've got a Hand about to meet with the Governor and an Envoy holding evidence of high treason on his way to meet them both.

"But we didn't *come* here to arrest a corrupt Governor, folks. So, tell me, before we risk losing the thread, are our games worth it? Can you tell me what happened to Karlsberg?"

"The system is just running an analysis of everything we've pulled now," another officer, a Mage-Lieutenant unknown to Cor, reported. "It should take another... that's odd."

"What?"

"It came back almost immediately," the Mage-Lieutenant told him. "This doesn't make sense, sir. The system recognized the impact pattern."

Cor froze. That thought had never crossed her mind. Of *course* a Navy computer would recognize the impact pattern, even from less than complete data.

"The system is telling me it was a Talon Seven Orbital Impactor. But..."

"But what, Evan?"

"They pulled *our* orbital impactor rounds when we were seconded to Hand Stealey," Evan said helplessly. "The Navy watches them like hawks. There's no way rebels got their hands on them. Hell, even the ASDF couldn't get them."

The Mage-Lieutenant swallowed, squared his shoulders, and said the words Cor was dreading.

"Sir, the only people in the system with Talon Sevens are the Seventh Cruiser Squadron."

The bridge of Cor's flagship was deathly silent. Everyone around her knew what they'd done. They knew that what they'd just heard from the hacked video feed was their death.

Cor was not going to accept that.

"Ma'am, they're activating their engines – and transmitting to the surface," Trevor snapped. Suddenly, the fifteen second lag in the video they were watching was critical – possibly fatal.

Because Adrianna Cor had to make a decision – and had to make it without knowing what Harmon was telling the Hand.

"Battle Stations," Harmon snapped. "Clear for emergency jump – get me a channel to Montgomery and Stealey."

Before that channel opened, the screen cut to black.

"What happened?" Cor demanded.

"Battle Stations severed all non-critical external communications," Trevor reported. "Ma'am, they're clearing the planet and preparing to jump. What do we do?!"

Suddenly, everything was very, very, clear.

Adrianna Cor was not going to hang for fifty thousand mundane rebels.

Vaughn had to have a plan for the Hand – the woman was unlikely to live out the day, especially with Brockson under arrest. If the Governor wanted to live, Alaura Stealey and her people had to die.

All of that would be wasted if the *Tides* reported.

"Mage-Captain Ishtar," Cor said calmly to the woman standing next to the simulacrum at the heart of the bridge – the heart of the ship. At the sound of the Commodore's voice, Ishtar instinctively laid her runed palms on the tiny magically perfect model.

"Yes, Commodore?" the Captain of the *Unchained Glory* asked quietly.

"Destroy that ship."

The cruiser shuddered as the Mage-Captain closed her eyes. A moment later, the sky lit with fire as magic reached across the empty void to the *Tides of Justice*.

With her crew focused on trying to jump away, the destroyer never had a chance.

#

While Adrianna Cor had been watching Damien's shuttle leave Nouveaux Normandy, Alaura Stealey was wondering when Mage-Governor Vaughn was going to let her get to the point of the evening.

He'd insisted on a dinner meeting and then had his staff put on an incredibly impressive spread. They'd met in a small dining room, not one of the grandiose halls Government House possessed, but the room was still decorated in wood and velvet from Terra.

The meal had started with escargot – actually imported from France on Earth, of all things! – and progressed through several courses. If this was how Vaughn normally ate, she was surprised it had taken him this long to start to go fat.

Alaura was, despite her cybernetic stomach, hardly immune to good food. The quality and delight of the spread Vaughn had put on had put her in a good mood – but so had the sure knowledge that tonight she would finally get to arrest the bastard.

"I presume," she finally said firmly as the servers carted away laid-out whiskey and disappeared from the room, "that you've heard about Montgomery's arrest."

"Yes," Vaughn said slowly. "I must admit, Lady Stealey, I am somewhat disappointed. My understanding was that you would at least give me some heads up before you started arresting my citizens – *especially* my officers. I must register a protest over Envoy Montgomery's high-handed…"

"Montgomery was entirely within his authority," Stealey interrupted him flatly. "And even if he wasn't, I fully support his actions. You forget your place, Mage-Governor Vaughn."

"My place?" Vaughn demanded haughtily. "Do not forget whose planet you stand upon, My Lady Hand."

"This world belongs to the people of Ardennes," the Hand told him quietly. "And they long ago bent their knee to Mars. In exchange, I believe, for the enforcement of a uniform code of laws upon even the most mighty.

"You swore an oath, Governor, to honor those laws – and those laws charge the Mage-King of Mars to stand as the court of last resort and the voice of the silent. You answer to Desmond Michael Alexander – and he has sent His Hand and His Voice to Ardennes, Governor."

"Do you have a point to this egotistical rant, My Lady?" Vaughn asked pointedly. "You have the authority to make arrests on Ardennes, I do not dispute that. I ask for the courtesy of fair warning as, last I checked, I still ruled this world."

Alaura opened her mouth to change that simple fact, and her personal computer squawked an emergency signal. A moment after the raucous alarm silenced her words, Mage-Commander Harmon's voice echoed through the dining room.

"Stealey, Montgomery," he snapped. "Karlsberg was destroyed by a *Navy* weapon – Mage-Commodore Cor has betrayed us. I am maneuvering for emergency ju—"

Alaura closed her eyes in a moment of grief. She'd heard that sharp cutoff in a transmission before – enough times to know exactly what it was. Harmon was dead, and his ship with him.

If Vaughn's face had betrayed any hint of whether or not Cor was working for him, it had passed while her eyes were closed. Nonetheless, the gaze she leveled on him was even and cold. The *best* case she could see for Mage-Governor Michael Vaughn was if Cor was threatening or blackmailing him.

"I think," Vaughn told her, his voice soft and slow as he fiddled with a control under the dining table in front of him, "that whatever you meant to discuss tonight should be put aside in the face of this new information. My Defense Force is hardly capable of protecting us from an entire squadron of rogue cruisers!"

Alaura smiled thinly, her gaze still leveled on Vaughn.

"Wrong choice, Michael," she said conversationally. "You could, I suppose, have thrown yourself on my mercy. Claimed the 'big bad evil Commodore' had threatened you, murdered your people to keep you in line. I don't think I'd have believed you, but it would have bought you time."

Shoving her chair back and rising to her feet, Alaura looked down at the seated Governor. She knew there wasn't much intimidating to her – many mistook her age and iron-gray hair as more grandmotherly than threatening – but there were times.

Vaughn shivered away from her.

"Michael Vaughn," she said formally, "you are under arrest for High Treason against the Protectorate.

"Don't worry, Cor will get hers, but I need to remove the *distraction* first."

The Governor sighed and laid what he'd been fiddling with on the table. It was a diffuser – now spraying something into the air.

"I was afraid it would come to this," he said conversationally. "Desmond's Hands have always been ivory tower intellectuals, unable to see the realities of what needs to be done to build economies and keep the peace.

"I cannot – I *will* not let you destroy all I've built," Vaughn told her fiercely. "I have struggled for decades. Sacrificed – and demanded sacrifices of my people. We've made something of Ardennes, and you would throw all that away on the words of a few malcontents who fail to understand the necessity of their sacrifice!"

"I arrived on this planet with enough evidence to arrest you, Vaughn," Alaura told him bluntly. "Rigged elections. Murdered protestors. Now, we know that the entire terrorist campaign you asked for help with was staged – to bring us in to quell your enemies.

"You should have known better," she warned him. "Now, I think it's time we got going."

"I don't," Vaughn replied. "You see, Hand Stealey, I expected this – or something like it. Most of the food you've been served contained components of a binary poison. One innocuous enough that even your cybernetics allowed you to ingest it. This is the other half," he gestured at the diffuser, "and you've been breathing it for a good minute."

She'd been feeling it for at least ten seconds, but she'd been so angry she hadn't noticed it. Alaura's fingers were slightly numb. Her chest was starting to ache and her throat was scratchy. The bastard had managed to poison her *despite* her advantages.

With a snarl, Alaura gathered power. She might die – Vaughn might succeed at that – but Ardennes would be free either way. Her hands flashed with fire, destroying her gloves, and then she lashed out at Vaughn.

Her fire hammered into a shield of force – one of the strongest she'd ever encountered. Fire splattered across the room, lighting the priceless drapes on fire.

"You may have the Mage-King's gift, Hand," Vaughn told her, finally rising to his feet, his face eerily shadowed by the flames and the darkness growing across Alaura's vision. "But I am no weakling. Plus, the poison was chosen to rapidly degrade your access to your magic.

"I am sorry, My Lady Hand. But I will not see all I have built destroyed! Yours is but one more necessary sacrifice."

Alaura struggled, raising energy for a strike that would destroy them both, but Vaughn beat her to it.

Silver fire flashed from the Governor's fingertips, and the poison robbed Hand Alaura Stealey of the strength to defend herself.

#

Chapter 15

Brockson was not the most co-operative prisoner ever.

In the end, Damien had used magic to *drag* the Special Operations Colonel out of the Scorpion base. Sheer audacity had carried them through most of the base, and a flash of Damien's Warrant had got them out of the building.

From there, Marines in exosuits took over the prisoner. Something about the hulking suits of combat armor shut down further debate, and they commandeered a pair of APCs without further argument.

Despite his resistance, the Colonel remained silent until they reached the shuttle and locked him into the restraints in the officer's compartment with Damien and Mitchell.

As the shuttle accelerated away from Nouveaux Normandy, carrying them back towards Versailles and Brockson's fate, the Colonel leveled his gaze on Damien and smiled thinly.

"You're going to find out damn quickly how limited your authority really is, kid," he said calmly. "Governor's gonna rip you a new one."

Damien ignored him, focusing on downloading all of the data from Brockson's personal computer into the shuttles computer – and his own PC. Just in case.

"That shiny paper may *say* you can do whatever you want, but this is *Vaughn*'s planet," the Scorpion continued after a minute or so. "What the paper says and what you can actually do ain't the same thing, kid. They should have taught you that before they let you off Mars."

"Can't even let me go and walk away now," Brockson told him with a satisfied smirk. "This one's gonna go all the way up to the *Council*, and the Mage-King will kick you loose, just you *watch*."

The Council of the Protectorate, the collection of representatives sent to Mars to speak for the worlds the Mage-King ruled, could ask the King to review a decision made by one of his Voices or Hands. Such a review went against the representative in question about a quarter of the time – but if it did, that was the end of that person's authority. The Mage-King could not trust people with his authority who he'd had to counter-act in the past.

Damien checked that the download was running smoothly and looked up at Brockson. He met the Ardennes Security man with a small smile of his own.

"Vaughn won't be in a position to save you, I'm afraid," he said quietly. "We had enough evidence to arrest him for treason when we arrived. Even if we didn't," he gestured towards the computer they'd cut off Brockson's wrist, "a Hand's authority is sufficient warrant to make all of your personal files and notes permissible evidence. Can you really tell me there's nothing in there that could send even a Governor to the gallows?"

That at least gave Brockson pause. Even from his casual skim while initiating the download, Damien knew the man had recordings of his orders for the attack on Alaura. While Vaughn could probably *try* to pin that one on General Montoya, combined with everything else they already had...

Vaughn was going to hang. Damien didn't even need Brockson to turn Mountain's Evidence – the Colonel was likely going to hang right next to his boss. The Protectorate didn't use capital punishment often, but their crimes fell into the category.

It seemed Brockson realized that as well, as the man was finally, blessedly, silent.

That silence was rudely interrupted an emergency signal from Damien's personal computer, which automatically played the override signal.

"Stealey, Montgomery," Mage-Commander Harmon's voice exclaimed into the shuttle. "Karlsberg was destroyed by a *Navy* weapon – Mage-Commodore Cor has betrayed us. I am maneuvering for emergency ju—"

Silence returned to the compartment and Damien stared at the computer on his wrist in horror.

"Get him back on the line," he ordered Mitchell.

The Marine dove into the computer system for a moment, and then looked back up, shaking his head.

"They're *gone*, sir," he said quietly. "Cor... blew them to pieces."

That took Damien a moment to process. The *Tides of Justice* had a crew of four hundred and twenty – and they were all dead.

"Get me Alaura," he snapped. She was supposed to be meeting with the Governor, but that now *needed* to be interrupted.

"We have a problem, boss," another voice interrupted – over the intercom from the cockpit.

"What *now*?" Damien demanded.

"We have radar contacts at fifty klicks and closing fast," the pilot informed him grimly. "Warbook is calling them F-60 high-altitude interceptors, but we're not getting *any* IFF codes." She paused. "If they've got the load-out we sell to the system governments, they'll range on us in barely a minute."

"Can we defend ourselves?" Damien asked, considering the situation.

Glynn Stewart

"We weren't loaded with any missiles when we left the *Tides*, sir," the pilot admitted. "All I have is the cannon, and if the buggers have missiles we're outranged four to one."

Damien exhaled, slowly. "All right," he told her. "Pipe a detailed visual feed to my compartment. Use any defenses or evasions you need."

"Sir?" the pilot replied questioningly.

"I will deal with them," he said quietly. "Trust me."

Gesturing for Mitchell to watch Brockson, Damien pulled up the screen with the visual feed. Quickly, carefully, he oriented himself and the screen so that what he was seeing was in the direction he was facing.

Zooming in on the two jet fighters, the Envoy stripped off his elbow-length gloves and suit jacket. Silver glimmered in the light from the screen as the silver polymer inlay on his skin rippled with his movements, the slight chill of the air cooling the metal.

"I see your compatriots are weak on the concept of loyalty," he told Brockson coolly, his gaze focused on the distorted, heavily zoomed, image of the aircraft.

"I would call these rebels, not my 'compatriots'," the prisoner replied.

"Sorry, Colonel, I don't buy that *any* rebellion could acquire F-60s," Damien told him dryly. "There's a limit to my credulity."

"Why not?" the Scorpion replied. "They got their hands on stealth attack gunships, after all."

"The difference, my dear Colonel, is that the data we have on that attack suggests *those* were from Legatus," the Envoy said softly. He didn't explain why that made a difference, but Brockson sighed and shrugged.

"They won't know I'm aboard," he allowed. "Montoya won't have told them. Makes it easier on everyone.

"Don't think sending them video of me will make a difference, either," he continued. "They're loyal to the *Governor*. You should have just left well enough alone."

"That, Colonel Brockson, would not be doing my job."

"*Vampire!*" the pilot shouted over the intercom. "Missiles detected, four inbound. ETA two minutes."

Damien sighed and slowly stretched his neck.

"We have that on record?" he asked quietly.

"Everything aboard is recorded," Mitchell replied.

"Thank you, Sergeant," Damien told him, and then focused on the growing dots of the missiles, rushing towards the frail-feeling assault shuttle at four times the speed of sound.

Warmth flared through the runes wrapped around his torso and arms, power surging and circling in his body as he reached out across the intervening space, judging distances and speed with trained practice.

The screen lit up brightly the first set of missiles ran into a wall of force that appeared directly in their path and detonated, convinced they'd hit their targets.

As he turned his focus to the second pair of missiles, everything went to hell.

"Look out!" Mitchell bellowed, but, focused on his magic, Damien didn't react in time.

Brockson slammed into him full-force, the Scorpion latching his hands around Damien's neck with brutal force. Half-formed old memories paralyzed Damien for a moment, the Mage struggling helplessly against Brockson's iron grip.

The moment passed faster than his attacker would have wanted, and Damien *flung* Brockson away with a blast of magic.

"Deal with the missiles," Mitchell snapped at him and charged Brockson. Somehow, the Scorpion Colonel had managed to escape the cuffs that bound him, and he met the Marine in the middle of the tiny compartment, struggling to get past him to attack Damien.

Damien tried to turn his attention back to the missiles rapidly closing on the shuttle, but the life or death struggle mere meters away from him threw off his attention. Focusing hard, he threw another shield of force at the missiles.

One exploded. The other wobbled on an evasion pattern and clipped the edge of the shield, spiraling through the air wildly before smoothing out its flight towards them.

Then a gunshot echoed through the tiny compartment, and his attention was brought back to the moment. Damien spun back towards the struggling pair in the aircraft to realize that Brockson had got his hands on Mitchell's sidearm.

Despite being shot, the Marine grabbed onto Brockson's arm, struggling to regain control of the weapon.

He failed.

Before Damien could act to intervene, the pistol fired again. And again. Four times, the sharp report echoed in the tiny room, and Cam Mitchell collapsed. Brockson shoved him aside, the dying Marine unable to resist, and then fired twice more – into the door controls for the main compartment.

"Time to die, kid," he said harshly, raising the weapon towards Damien.

The immediate threat triggered reactions programmed into him with years of harsh training. The momentary shock at Mitchell's death fueled a sharp gesture and surge of power. A blade of pure magical force slashed across the compartment, removing Brockson's hand and the gun with it.

The Ardennes Special Security Service, for all its many flaws, produced tough, *tough* men. Even missing a hand, his life's blood pumping out onto the shuttle's metal floor, Brockson *charged* Damien.

Damien's gun was in his hand without him thinking. His instructors on Mars had spent *weeks* drilling that tiny teleport into him until it was an unthinking action.

He fired.

The ST-7 wasn't a high-caliber weapon and Brockson was a big man. He fired five times, and the Scorpion lurched back with each impact. A blast of magic followed the last bullet, flinging the dying man against the opposite wall from Mitchell.

"I'm evading, everyone *hold on*," the pilot yelled over the speakers, and Damien yanked his attention back to the missile.

It was almost on them, and he threw magic at it, trying to stop it before it hit them.

At the same time, the pilot dove for the ground, trying to generate a miss.

They both failed. The missile slammed into the back of the shuttle and exploded. The entire spacecraft lurched, spinning through the air as the engines failed and shrapnel filled the main compartment.

Standing next to the screen, unstrapped in and unprepared, Damien was thrown across the room. He threw out magic, slowing himself before he slammed into the wall.

Then the shuttle spun again, nosediving downwards as the pilot lost control.

Damien tried to shield himself again, but the corkscrewing fall threw off his angle and he saw the wall coming straight for him.

Blackness.

#

Chapter 16

The building was on fire, and everything was proceeding exactly according to plan.

Mage-Governor Michael Vaughn stood in the situation room buried deep beneath Nouveaux Versailles and watched the center of his government burn. The rebel attack he'd arranged was being as dramatic and destructive as he'd hoped.

As he watched, part of the west wing of the House exploded outwards, a Mage from Hand Stealey's party blasting their way out to escape the attack. Two rebel Mages countered, dragging the Martian bureaucrat to the ground and burning her alive.

Missiles responded from the sky. Ardennes' Army gunships swept through the air, targeting the rebel Mages and heavy weapons. Grounded by 'inconveniently' timed maintenance, the gunships had been too late to save Government House – or any of Stealey's staff.

Ever since the Freedom Party had staged its mass resignation and walk-out, becoming the Freedom Wing and openly declaring rebellion against him, Vaughn had known he would need a stalking horse eventually. So he had set Montoya and the Special Operations Directorate the task of creating it – the 'Action Wing'.

He watched on the screens around him as the Action Wing's rebels died. With the Scorpions and the Army moving in, most would not escape. But enough would. With the destruction they'd wreaked, the bodies of the security guards and Army troops responsible for protecting Government House, and their escape, Vaughn would be able to justify much.

With Stealey's body burnt in the fire, and nature having had its way with Karlsberg, whoever was sent to resume her investigation would have evidence of nothing except an armed and virulent revolution. One guilty of atrocities the Protectorate would not forgive or forget.

Even if there were prisoners taken tonight, which Vaughn doubted his men would even try for, it wouldn't matter. The Action Wing believed that they were members of the Freedom Wing, and the same cellular organization that had frustrated his attempts to break open Armstrong's organization meant that even the Freedom Wing couldn't be sure they weren't!

"My Lord Governor," a surprisingly calm voice interrupted. Vaughn turned from the monitors to find a gray-uniformed older man standing behind him. General Caleb Zu was the senior-most officer of the Ardennes Army. He bowed slowly, his white hair shimmering in the light from the screens.

"I must apologize for our failures," Zu said stiffly. "We – *I* did not anticipate such a violent attack from the rebels. And now we have lost Hand Stealey."

"A tragedy, my old friend," Vaughn said quietly. Zu was *not* in his confidence about the Action Wing. "I don't blame you or your people," he continued. "*None* of us foresaw the Wing launching so blatant an attack."

"Or in such strength, and with such knowledge of our routine and positions," Zu replied bluntly. "They had heavy weapons and perfect knowledge of our guard posts. They knew where to hit and when – we lost fifty people before we even knew we were under attack!"

"Governor, General!" one of the many sensor technicians interrupted. "We just got confirmation from Commodore Cor – the *Tides of Justice* was destroyed by sabotage! There were no survivors."

Zu grunted as if struck, closing his eyes in pain. Vaughn himself winced – he'd presumed from Mage-Commander Harmon's transmission that Cor had acted to preserve them, but he hoped she had *something* to back up that story!

"What about Envoy Montgomery?" he asked aloud. "Have we managed to find his shuttle yet?"

"No, Governor," the tech replied. "I can query Cor's ships – they may have been in position to see what we missed."

"Do so," Vaughn ordered. The disadvantage of arranging for Montoya's 'dark' interceptors to take down the shuttle when none of the satellites could see it was that he didn't know what had happened himself! With the Navy scans, he could still hold up the rebels having advanced tech to draw help from Mars, without having the interceptors in a position where he had to actually *catch* them.

"They're sending us the feed now," the tech reported, throwing it up on one of the screens.

Vaughn turned to watch the recording. Even to Navy sensors, the F-60s hadn't shown up until they'd gone to active targeting. He watched, impassively, as the two fighters closed with and fired on the shuttle. He heard Zu make a hopeful noise beside him when the first set of missiles exploded – clearly taken down by a Mage – and tried not to look disappointed.

What followed was... unclear, from such a high level perspective. One missile was knocked out, but the other made it through. The shuttle wasn't instantly destroyed – the Martian Navy built its craft *tough* – but it was clearly crippled, falling rapidly from the sky.

"Cor's people report they couldn't track the interceptors once they went back to stealth," the tech reported. "I'm sorry, sirs, we lost them."

"Gunships at the Rocher d'Or," Zu whispered. "Interceptors now. Rocket launchers, sniper rifles, perfect intelligence. Who *are* these people?"

"Aided by inside agents," Vaughn told him bluntly, an instant decision made. "It appears that we put too much trust in some of our people."

"Who?!" Zu demanded. "If they're mine I'll..."

"He was a Scorpion, Zu," Vaughn told him. "Montgomery arrested Colonel Elijah Brockson earlier today. He... had the information, and the authority to help cover up importing weapons. I fear many of tonight's deaths and tragedies can be laid at his feet."

After all, the man was most likely dead.

"Damn," Zu whispered, eyeing the burning half-ruin of Government House on one set of monitors, and the smoke where the Navy shuttle had gone down on the other. "There may be survivors from the shuttle crash," he said suddenly, sharply. "I'll send my people."

"I need your people cleaning up Nouveaux Versailles, Caleb," Vaughn told him swiftly. "People *trust* your troops, we need that right now to keep the peace!"

The Ardennes Special Security Service could keep the peace in Versailles. A few more heads might get broken, a few more idiots end up in jail. It wasn't anything Vaughn would weep over. But pulling the Army into Versailles meant that they couldn't check on Montgomery's crash.

"I'll have Montoya send choppers to check for survivors," the Governor assured. "If anyone has survived, we'll find them."

And because Montoya would send the *right* pilots and crews, take care of them.

#

Lori Armstrong stared at the news in horror. It hardly made her stand out – everyone in the hotel lounge who was staring at the screens showing the images of Government House burning, was doing the same thing.

"Reports continue of street fighting in Nouveaux Versailles as Ardennes Army ground troops track down the remnants of the Freedom Wing forces that struck at Government House this evening," the reporter told her fixated audience. "Reports are that hundreds of security officers and civilian staff are dead, though we have confirmed that Governor Vaughn is still alive.

"We have no evidence as to why the Freedom Wing launched this well-equipped attack, or even where a group of ex-politicians acquired the weapons and people to launch such an attack."

Not least, Lori knew, because the Freedom Wing hadn't *launched* the attack. It was *possible* a rogue cell had launched the assassination attempt in Nouveaux Normandy, though unlikely. An assault of this magnitude would have taken *every* cell – and even then, she suspected that the attackers had had better weapons and intelligence than she would have had!

"Analysts suggest —" the perfectly-coiffed talking head stopped as someone off-screen spoke to her. A moment later, with her teleprompter reset, the woman swallowed hard – the first sign of humanity Lori had seen from the woman in five years of her presenting the news.

"We have breaking news," she said slowly, regaining her composure. "Reports from Government House now confirm that the primary target of the attack was Alaura Stealey, Hand of the Mage-King of Mars."

"First responders have identified Hand Stealey among the dead already removed from the House's wreckage," the anchor continued, and Lori sucked in a breath, feeling like she'd been punched in the gut. They were fucked. They were *so* fucked.

"Other reports suggest that her second, Damien Montgomery, Envoy of the Mage-King of Mars, was also killed in a high-altitude assassination carried out with military-grade attack aircraft. While Montgomery's body has not been recovered, his shuttle was shot down some seventy kilometers short of Nouveaux Versailles."

"This attack constitutes the single most devastating direct attack on Protectorate officials on Ardennes... ever."

Lori finished her drink in a single swallow, glancing around the lounge. The rest of the guests fell into rapid gossiping, all trying to dissect how this bombshell was going to affect their businesses and lives, or just morbidly going over the details of the violence.

None of them were paying enough attention to notice her leave.

#

Lori made her way through the guest portions of the third-best hotel in Ardennes' second-best mountain resort town with practiced ease. She'd grown up in this building – her father had built it, a long time ago.

Now, technically, she didn't own it. There was no financial connection between her and the building to be found – but everyone from the new owners to the kitchen staff knew who she was. Both aspects had their advantages.

Today, they let her slip into an unused conference room and activate the security shielding. The door locked, and security screens would prevent any eavesdropping or electronic bugging of the room.

She still swept the room quickly with a scanner designed to pick up any electronic bugs before bringing out the encrypted military com and turning it on.

"I need everybody online," she said into it calmly. "Emergency link-up, find somewhere private where you can at least listen in the next five minutes."

She waited. Leader of a planetwide resistance or not, she'd had to learn patience as a politician on Ardennes, and again as a rebel. Five minutes notice was nowhere *near* enough time to get everyone on the line, but those who couldn't would get the recorded message later.

A few verbal acknowledges and a lot more text notifications came in over those five minutes. Lori had more of her core cell leaders than she expected, probably because *everyone* was watching the news.

"You've all seen the news out of Nouveaux Versailles," she said bluntly when the five minutes were up. "I doubt I need to tell any of *you* that it wasn't us. The Governor has found a spectacular use for his stalking horse rebels."

"I don't know what his plan was, but I doubt its coincidence that the Hand died," Lori told her cell leaders. "I think that Montgomery and Stealey had found out what was really going on and were about to act on it."

"That should work for us then, shouldn't it?" Riordan asked. "They say when a Hand falls, another rises. Whoever comes in next will know…"

"How, Lambda?" Kappa, their senior agent in the Ardennes Self Defense Force, demanded. "It hasn't hit the news yet, but Stealey's destroyer is *gone*. Cor is claiming sabotage by the Wing that no-one detected in time, but most likely *she* killed them. If both Stealey and Montgomery are dead, and their staff and notes gone in the fire… who's left to tell the King the truth?"

"No-one," Lori said flatly. "Vaughn will spin it to Desmond's people any way he likes. In the end, I can't help but think his house of cards is going to come tumbling down, but that doesn't change what it's going to mean to us in the short-term."

"Which is?" Riordan asked.

"A Hand falls, another rises," the Freedom Wing's leader repeated Lambda's words. "Another Hand – or several! – will follow in Stealey's footsteps, with cruiser squadrons instead of a destroyer, and Marine battalions instead of a platoon. They will arrive with authority and firepower that Vaughn cannot even dream of, and they will rip this planet apart until they have dismantled the rebellion that killed Alaura Stealey."

"But that wasn't us!" another cell leader complained.

"They won't care," Lori warned. "This is the single worst direct attack on the Hands in years, if not ever. The Hands and the Mage-King must be *seen* to act. They will discover the truth eventually – but not in time to save any of *us* if we aren't very, very careful."

"Which is what we need to do, because I *don't* want to be collateral damage before the Mage-King's people work out who *really* killed Alaura Stealey."

"We're going dark," she ordered. "Shut down everything. Training camps, ammunition manufacture, recruiting, even *speechifying* – shut it all down."

"We can't completely shut down the bases," came Sierra, the Legatan woman now running their gunship squadrons. "Even if we don't *fly* them, the gunships require regular maintenance."

"Fine. But bury them deep," Lori ordered. "No emissions, as little traffic as possible. We intentionally put the airbases close to settlements to hide the traffic, so let's make damn sure the traffic stays hidden."

"We can't afford any slip-ups now," she reminded them all. "When the Hands come hunting, the only rebels I want them to find are Vaughn's people!"

#

Chapter 17

It took Damien a moment to identify the beeping sound that slowly penetrated the black fog. It wasn't a sound he'd heard outside of training videos, so it took longer to identify than it would have – though his slowly fading unconsciousness didn't help.

When the 'Critical Damage' alarm of a Navy assault shuttle finally registered, his eyes snapped open fast enough to leave his skull pounding.

He was lying on the roof of the assault shuttle's officer compartment, the screens with their flashing alerts two meters and more above him.

Struggling to his feet, a wave of dizziness and nausea swept over him. Concussion. He'd hit his head.

That realization brought everything back, and he looked over the compartment, hoping to somehow find Mitchell alive.

He hoped in vain. The Marine Sergeant's body had fallen from the floor to the roof during the crash and was broken in ways that made it very clear he was *not* getting back up.

A quick glance confirmed that Brockson was also thoroughly dead. Damien was alone in the compartment and struggled against the concussion to think.

If the Critical Damage alarm was going, but the shuttle was still mostly intact, the fail-safes must have succeeded in ejecting the fuel tanks prior to impact. That meant he had time.

Forcing himself slowly to his feet, he also knew he didn't have *much* time. Someone had shot down a shuttle carrying an Envoy of Mars. Unless they were terminally stupid, they *would* come back to finish the job.

The door to the cockpit refused to open, the electronic access panel completely dead. Hammering his battered brain into co-operation, Damien managed to remember and find the manual override. Locked down while the door had power, it allowed it to be opened if power failed.

He cranked the wheel. Ten seconds. Twenty. Finally, the hatch slid sufficiently open for Damien to squeeze into the cockpit.

Any hope of finding help vanished immediately. The pilot's head hung at an impossible angle, and while the unbreakable transparent shield at the front of the ship had lived up to its marketing, the *consoles* had not. Shrapnel from the impact had torn the co-pilot apart. The man had died of blood loss before Damien had regained consciousness.

He had at least made it to the cockpit first aid kit, which allowed Damien to find it without having to strain his memory. His head already hurt badly enough.

Once he'd got some painkillers into his system, he realized he was bleeding. Nothing major, but he carefully dealt with the scrapes and cuts that had ruined his expensive suit.

With his wounds bandaged and his head starting to feel slightly better, Damien checked the emergency cabinet the first aid kit had come from. While the pistol stored there was less powerful than his own and the ammunition wasn't compatible, there was also a pair of battle carbines and an armored vest.

Throwing the vest over the remnants of his dress shirt – and the lighter armor vest he wore under the shirt – he filled its pockets with clips and picked up one of the carbines. The missile had hit the compartment the Marines had been in, which meant he was almost certainly alone.

Finally, he linked his personal computer into the shuttle's systems. It didn't tell him anything he hadn't expected – the shuttle was running out of power, had ejected its fuel, and wasn't going *anywhere*.

Nonetheless, it had enough transmission power to link him into the planetary datanet. The contact code Alaura had given him was a single use code, one he hoped was still being checked.

His PC obligingly gave him the encryption algorithm to use, and he fired a message off to the code.

If anyone was eavesdropping on the 'net – as he was sure Vaughn's people were – it would look like a 'first touch' message from a dating site.

The contact, hopefully, would be able to interpret it into co-ordinates and a desperate plea for help.

Battered and concussed, Damien wasn't sure how far he could make it on his own.

#

From the moment the news of the attack on Government House had broken, a rock had settled in Julia Amiri's stomach.

The confirmation, an hour or so later, that Alaura Stealey had died in the attack turned that rock into spikes and lava. She'd made what excuses she could to the kitchen staff she was helping out, and fled back to her room.

'Jewel', immigrant to Ardennes who'd got herself tied up in someone else's revolution, had no connection to one of the chosen trouble-shooters of the Mage-King of Mars.

Julia Amiri, on the other hand, had been directly working with Alaura Stealey for three years. She hadn't intended to allow herself to become attached – the Protectorate Secret Service was a job, after all, a glorified counter-espionage organization.

But losing the boss who'd pulled you out of one scrape after another for years... hit hard.

It was Alaura Stealey who'd chosen to believe the random bounty hunter who had offered to help trace Mikhail Azure in his pursuit of Damien Montgomery. Stealey had believed that she could help, and that she *wanted* to help.

They'd saved Montgomery – who had, it must be admitted, done a decent job of saving himself – together. They'd brought peace to four worlds together, and Amiri had figured that Ardennes would be world number five. The planet needed it, after all!

The announcement on the news that Montgomery's shuttle had been shot down was the icing on the cake. Both their first and last missions together were now wasted efforts, blood and tears shed for nothing.

On her own, there was nothing Amiri could do for Ardennes. She had a damn good idea of who had *actually* killed Alaura Stealey though – and as a senior agent of the Secret Service, she could make the Hands who would follow listen.

For now, though, she had to get off Ardennes. Disappearing would likely confuse Riordan and his friends, but the biggest favor she could do their revolution at this point was get what truth she knew into the hands of Desmond Michael Alexander and his Hands.

She grabbed her PC to pull up the details she needed for one of her emergency escape plans and stopped. A blinking 'new message' icon had appeared – attached to a specific one-time account. The account she'd given Alaura Stealey.

For a moment, she allowed herself hope. It was possible, after all, that the media Vaughn was controlling was lying about her death.

The message dashed her hopes. It took her a moment to translate it, but the co-ordinates were clear. Seventy-five kilometers outside of Nouveaux Versailles, in the massive forest between the city and the mountains – on the route from Nouveaux Normandy.

Only one other person than Stealey might have had that code, and that person's shuttle had gone down in about that area.

For a moment, Amiri seriously considered just running. She didn't know Montgomery well. Didn't owe him what she owed Alaura. He would be alone, injured, and hunted. No-one would ever know if she left him and went to Mars – many would even say that was her duty, to make sure the truth reached Mars.

But, a long time ago, Damien Montgomery had killed the man who'd murdered her brother and their crew. Regardless of duty, she owed him.

With a sigh, she programmed in the code Riordan had given her.

"What?" he answered.

"Riordan, this is Jewel," she said quietly. "I need a favor."

"This is not a good time," Riordan told her. "You've seen the news. It wasn't us, but we've got to react – got to deal with the consequences."

Amiri sighed and then let 'Jewel' go.

"Mikael, listen to me," she continued sharply. "If you believe anything you've told me – if you believe in the cause you convinced so many to follow, understand this:

"What I need to ask may make a bigger difference to your cause than anything you've done before or could ever do again. I am not exaggerating when I tell you that the fate of Ardennes rides on the next few hours – and rides on you helping me."

There was silence on the line for a long moment.

"Who are you?" he asked. "You're not who you say you are."

That was true enough.

"I am the only hope you have to stave off the vengeance of the Hands," Amiri told him.

Silence again.

"What do you need?"

#

Modern medicine could do many things, but it couldn't cure even a mild concussion with a few pills. The drugs from the shuttle's first aid kit were sufficient to allow Damien to stand without dizziness or nausea, but only so long as he didn't move very quickly.

It would have to be enough. Standing in the emergency exit from the cockpit, he could see the fire starting to spread from where the fuel tanks had landed – several kilometers away, but the sticky scent of Ardennes' pale purple trees burning was reaching him anyway. The wind was *not* on his side.

Everyone else on the shuttle was dead. Magic and more than a little bit of luck had spared him, but he was alone and injured. Worse, if Vaughn had come after *him*, he was pretty sure that he had to have moved on Alaura.

Unless he was wrong in his estimates, Damien was potentially the last member of the team that had accompanied Alaura Stealey to Ardennes. If Vaughn had gone this far, he wasn't going to do anything as foolish as retrieve any survivors alive.

With a glance at his PC to orient himself on the map, he set off for the nearest road. Thankfully, that road was *away* from the fire starting to slowly spread through the forest behind him. He hoped that the purple and wet foliage would at least slow the flames.

He estimated it at two hours after the attack when he heard the rotors for the first time. He took cover and watched the helicopter gunships pass overhead. A twist of magic zoomed in on the nearest of the three aircraft and confirmed what he'd feared: the icon painted on the doors was the stylized scorpion of the Ardennes Special Security Service, not the crossed rifles of the Ardennes Planetary Army.

The Scorpions wouldn't have been sent to bring in survivors.

Grimly focusing through the fog from the drugs and the concussion, Damien moved forward once more. Behind him, the sound of the rotors slowly faded as the gunships approached the crash site. One set quieted further and then went silent – presumably landing at the wrecked shuttle.

Keeping one ear on the Scorpion aircraft behind him, he focused on putting one foot in front of another. It would take them time to confirm he wasn't on board or near the shuttle. His path wasn't well hidden, but looking for it would buy him more time – potentially even enough time that the fire would overtake the wreck before they'd found it.

Ten minutes later, he was struggling to keep moving while maintaining a spell that allowed him to still hear the rotors behind him. The third set switched back on suddenly, going from silent to full power in moments – *far* faster than the aircraft had to be rated for.

He couldn't see to confirm, but he suspected that they'd just made an emergency ascent, dodging away from the fire that would now incinerate the bodies of Cam Mitchell and his men.

"Sorry Cam," he whispered into the gathering twilight. "Best I can do."

Trying to judge distances based on the rotors of aircraft now kilometers behind him was proving difficult. If the Scorpions followed normal search and rescue – or search and destroy – doctrine for Protectorate forces, the three would now split up, each taking a segment of the compass away from the fire and sweeping for thermal signatures.

Damien tried to wrap a shield around himself to cover his body heat, but with the fog in his brain he was only half-sure he'd succeeded. Stumbling over a tree root, he realized he'd lost his direction. He wasn't sure which way the road was now.

Now would be a good time for Alaura's agent to show up. He allowed himself a hopeful moment, and then brought the map back up on his computer. The electronic signature *might* be detected – but wandering in circles in the forest with a concussion could kill him almost as easily as Vaughn's soldiers. It would just take longer.

It took a moment for the Planetary Positioning System to find his location, a moment Damien spent carefully scanning the sky for aircraft. Finally, it brought up his location on the map. He hadn't gone as far off-course as he'd been afraid of – he was only a half-kilometer from the road.

Shutting down the network connection, he set off once again. A moment of dizziness struck him and he wavered. Despite not nearly long enough having passed for it to be safe, he paused and took more of the medications.

He could get his liver fixed later if he lived through today. For now, the extra stability and reduced nausea was enough to allow him to make his way through the trees towards the road.

The drugs carried him onto the road, a four-lane expressway that cut a laser-straight line between Nouveaux Versailles and the province of Nouveaux Bordeaux on the other side of the immense forest occupying the center of the continent.

The expressway was empty. That was not what Damien had been expecting – he'd figured that once he'd reached the road he would have enough witnesses to be safe until Alaura's agent got there.

If they'd closed the road, however, he was in trouble. He was panting, half-out of breath. He couldn't go much further, not sustained by anti-nausea meds and painkillers. He could hear rotors again, and *knew* the gunship was closing behind him – either by chance, or because they'd picked up his PPS signal.

Damien ran his fingers over the gold medallion at his throat with a sigh. Carved into the precious metal was the quill feather of a trained Rune Scribe, and the three stars of a Jump Mage. *Not* carved into it were any of the qualifications he'd earned over the last few years – qualifications that would have made his pursuers far more hesitant.

Too exhausted to run, he breathed deeply and turned to face the sound of the helicopters. They'd killed his co-workers, killed his boss – killed his *friends*.

Let them come.

#

Riordan couldn't have been far. He arrived quickly after Amiri got off the line with him, pulling up in front of the hotel in a boxy stylized utility vehicle – she recognized the chassis as having started as the last generation of the Marine's all-terrain vehicle.

This one was black, and lacking the pintle-mounted machine gun. As she slipped into the passenger seat, she also noted the leather seats and high quality electronics.

"Nice car," she noted.

"It's mine," Riordan told her. "Buried through a few shell corps at this point, but still mine. This better be worth it," he warned. "Things are... worrisome right now.

"It will be," Amiri promised. So long as Montgomery was still alive when they got there. "You brought weapons?"

"Cases in the backseat," he replied. "Wait till we're out of town. Now, tell me you at least know where we're going?"

Nodding, she leaned over and plugged the co-ordinates into the PPS system. It threw up a map, a guide, and a timeline.

"That's quite a ways," Riordan told her as he pulled the truck out onto the main roads. "What's that way?"

"I know you were watching the news," she said quietly.

"Shit. The shuttle?"

"Someone lived," she told him. "I got an SOS message, and I have no transport of my own. You were my only choice."

"Don't I feel privileged," the Freedom Wing cell leader muttered. "Why the hell were *you* getting SOS's? What's going on?"

"Wait till we're out of town," Amiri repeated back to him.

With a curse, Riordan apparently accepted that, throwing the vehicle into gear and sweeping them down onto the highway. The next few minutes passed in silence, a mental clock running in the agent's head. She really wasn't sure they had enough time – they may have already taken too long.

"All right, Jewel," Riordan said quietly as the city lights started to fade behind them. "I'll be honest – I'm going on faith here because a dead Hand means we are *so* fucked I'm willing to grasp at straws. I'd love some clue of what sort of straw I'm grasping for, though."

"My name isn't Jewel," she replied.

"No shit."

"My name is Julia Amiri, Special Agent for the Protectorate Secret Service," she continued, ignoring his outburst. "Alaura Stealey assigned me to Ardennes as a forward operative. My mission was to infiltrate the Freedom Wing and establish lines of communication for once Vaughn had been arrested.

"Once Stealey arrived on planet, I provided her with a onetime drop code to establish further communications or use as an emergency SOS.

"After the crash, I received an SOS code and these co-ordinates," Amiri concluded. "Since I know Hand Stealey wasn't on the shuttle, I presume she provided the code to Envoy Montgomery, and that he survived the crash."

Her companion was speechless. Leaving him to process, the agent checked the cases in the back for weapons. Two of the cases were bog-standard assault rifles, made to the same pattern across the Protectorate. This pair had been manufactured on Amber, a world with notoriously lax laws on, well, everything.

The third case made her eyes light up. "Can you even use this?" she demanded of Riordan as she ran her eyes over the bulky lines of one of Legatus Arms newest and most dangerous toys.

"I have a rough idea," he admitted.

"I'm fully qualified," she told him. "I'll handle it."

She smiled, running her fingers over the Legatus Arms Tactical Battle Laser, Mod Five. It was one of very few energy weapons manufactured in the Protectorate, and one of the best she was aware of.

"Remind me why the hell I'm driving a Protectorate special agent into the middle of the country to rescue a Protectorate Envoy?" Riordan finally asked. "Last I checked, I was technically a traitor."

"No, you're a rebel," Amiri corrected him. "It's a fine distinction, but when a planetary government gets as down in the muck as Mage-Governor Vaughn's has, it's a hair we're perfectly willing to split.

"The real answer to your question, though, is that Damien Montgomery is the only person on the planet with the authority to charge Governor Vaughn with Hand Stealey's murder. If *he* lives, Vaughn falls. If he *dies*... your rebellion will probably be collateral damage of the inevitable fallout to Stealey's death.

"Things are worrisome right now. Everything is teetering on the edge – and Montgomery might be able to salvage the situation. You have to pick a side, Mikael."

"It's not *my* side I'm worried about," the rebel told her. "It's *yours.*"

"I work for the Protectorate of the Mage-King of Mars," Amiri said quietly. "Our job is to protect people – even, when necessary, from their own governments."

Silence filled the car for a moment.

"There's a roadblock ahead," Riordan suddenly told her. "What do you want to do?"

"We can't stop," she replied. "Even if Montgomery was somehow uninjured from the crash, he won't have much time before the Scorpions move in. Hell, if there's a roadblock..."

"The Scorpions have probably already moved in," he agreed grimly. "The car has the armor of the military version. I suggest you hold on."

With a small smile, the first sign of anything except anger or despair Amiri had seen out of the man since he'd picked her up, Riordan gunned the engine.

The blockade consisted of a handful of plywood barriers and two highway patrol cars. The three women and one man directing traffic back probably had no idea why the road was closed – and likely would have been furious if they knew they were being used to reduce potential witnesses to murder.

They were *not* expecting the big armored truck to ignore the flashing lights directing people off to the side and slam forward at full speed. The plywood barrier splintered under the impact, and Amiri got a perfectly clear glimpse of the senior officer's utterly stunned face as they plowed past.

She still half-expected gunfire, or *some* kind of response, but whatever the highway patrol had been told was going on, they were clearly willing to write off some idiots as evolution in action.

The barrier cleared, she took a deep breath and pulled the battle laser from the back seat. If they were lucky, they'd find Montgomery, stick him in the car, and disappear before the Scorpions arrived.

Given the day so far, she didn't expect to get that lucky.

#

If the gunship had picked up Damien's Planetary Positioning System signal, the pilot hadn't regarded it as enough reason to call for backup. The single aircraft swept over the forest, bare meters above the trees as a spotlight played over the ground below.

Damien, too tired to keep running, stood on the edge of the expressway watching it come. Injured and exhausted, he couldn't reach out far enough to bring the helicopter down from a distance – plus, technically he remained an agent of the law. He wasn't supposed to strike first.

The gunship crew were clearly focused on the forest beneath them, since they'd emerged into the cleared zone around the highway before they noticed Damien standing there watching them.

As soon as they *did* notice him, the spotlight immediately settled on him. The light hammered spikes into his concussion, and Damien reeled away, covering his eyes from the light with his hand.

"Put your hands over your head and freeze where you are!" an amplified voice bellowed. "This is an interdicted area. Identify yourself immediately!"

Blinking away the dizziness, Damien straightened and faced them, keeping his hands exposed though not raising them as ordered.

"I am Envoy Damien Montgomery," he shouted back to them. "I am in need of transport and am commandeering your craft under my Warrant. Land immediately!"

Any chance that they were actually there to rescue him vanished as the gunship immediately *jumped* away, the pilots engaging in the standard anti-Mage maneuver of 'create distance'.

Damien was saved from having to decide if that was enough aggression for him to act by the aircraft's gunner opening fire moments later. Two missiles detached from the sides of the helicopter gunship, and a nose-mounted mini-gun opened up half a second later.

There were limits to a Mage's power and reaction time, and if he hadn't been expecting *exactly* that it might have been enough.

As it was, he'd raised a shield before he'd even seen the attack craft. The missiles exploded in the air ten meters away from him, and the stream of fire from the mini-gun ended in the same place. The explosions and gunfire lit an invisible sphere in the night.

Damien winced, his attention wavering as his concussion screamed against the strain of the spell. Bullets tore through the momentarily vanishing shield, tearing up to the dirt to his left before he restored the shield – but he couldn't keep this up for long.

A second salvo of missiles screamed through the night, hammering into his shield and driving him to the ground. His concussion sent spikes of pain stabbing into his skull, and he struggled back to his feet, forcing himself to both hold the shield and locate the helicopter.

They'd left the spotlight on. It might have helped them target him – but it also helped *him* find *them*.

Another stab of pain ripped through his head and then, for a moment, his head was clear and he could see the spotlight, though not the gunship itself.

The wall of force he conjured didn't need to be that accurate. It crashed down on the attack gunship like the fist of an angry god and yanked the Scorpion aircraft out of the sky.

It slammed into the asphalt with enough force to make the ground tremble under Damien's feet, and then promptly exploded as munitions met fuel and sparks.

The explosion hammered into his shield, which came apart into fragile wisps under the blow – but still sheltered Damien from its force.

Silence fell over the twilit road. The acrid scent of burnt plastic and metal wafted towards Damien from the crash, accompanied by the popping sound of the burning remnants of the aircraft.

Wavering against the concussion and the energy drain of so much magic, Damien trembled, trying to find the momentum to keep moving.

Glynn Stewart

He struggled through his pockets, finally finding another set of the anti-nausea meds and slugging them back. He clearly hadn't grabbed enough of anything – he didn't have the food or water for an extended hike, and he probably wasn't going to have the time.

As if summoned by his thought, he began to hear the faint sound of rotors again. Two pairs, most likely the other two aircraft from the search squadron. They'd know where the other gunship died, and he didn't think he could fight two ships through his concussion.

Nonetheless, it wasn't as if *running* was an option. He turned to face the rotors, hoping the drugs were enough to keep him standing.

Focused on the oncoming aircraft, he missed the engine of the approaching vehicle until the big utility vehicle came to a sharp stop behind him and a familiar voice shouted at him.

"Hey, Montgomery," Julia Amiri told him. "As pretty a fire as you've made, I get the feeling being elsewhere is a better idea, right?"

He turned towards her, blinking in surprise as her presence completely failed to process. She wasn't registering as a threat – she just wasn't really registering at *all*.

"Shit, he's been hit hard," another voice, one he didn't recognize, told Amiri. "Quick, let's get him in the car – we don't have much time."

He was... conscious enough to get halfway into the car with Amiri's help. He fell the rest of the way as the driver gunned the engine.

"We do *not* want to be here," the strange man announced calmly as the door slammed shut behind the sprawled Mage.

Damien was unconscious before he could agree aloud.

#

Chapter 18

The fires were starting to burn out.

There wasn't much left of Government House. The fires, the explosions, and general devastation had turned the seat of a planetary government into a shattered ruin. Rebuilding would be expensive if it was even possible. It might be necessary to simply write off the old structure and build a new mansion.

If Vaughn's plan came even close to working, it would be a more than acceptable cost.

He'd relocated to a small conference room, still buried in the command center barely a kilometer from the smoldering ruins of his home. A pair of Scorpions, both of them fully trained Enforcer Mages and members of the Presidential Security Detail, kept most of the staff and media from bothering him.

Montoya, of course, simply walked right past his men. The Governor waited for the door to close behind the commander of the Scorpions before speaking.

"Well?" he demanded. He knew that the backdrop of the burning city on the wallscreen behind him would be unsettling, even to a hardened man like Montoya. Perhaps *especially* to Montoya, who knew damned well who'd ordered the disaster still taking shape above them.

"The SDF has confirmed what Cor's people said," Montoya replied. "There were no survivors from the *Tides of Justice*. Of course, our brave men and women thought they *wanted* to find survivors, so they were looking hard."

Vaughn nodded silently, considering. That was one mess neatly cleared out of the way. The crew of the *Tides* had clearly realized *something* in their final moments, but with their deaths it would go to the only safe place for secrets: the grave.

"And the House?" he demanded, gesturing at the fire on the screen behind him.

"We have a clean sweep," Montoya confirmed. "Planted Alaura's body in the middle for the rescue crews to find, and every member of her staff is confirmed dead.

"Two of them were Mages no-one had bothered to mention to us," he continued. "Recruiting Mages for the Action Wing was a good idea, though I made *damned* sure neither of them survived the pursuit."

"Good," Vaughn grunted. "The rest of the Wing?"

"Over-extended and shattered," Montoya said calmly. "Between my boys and Caleb's, we killed over eighty percent of the teams deployed for the attack. No-one's going to be surprised when the remnants are hard to find and disconnected from the rest of the rebellion."

That had been a concern when they'd set up the Action Wing – its actions were intended to draw the attention of Protectorate law enforcement away from other things, and to tarnish the overall Freedom Wing. But, necessarily, the Action Wing had only the most tenuous of links to the Freedom Wing.

The Action Wing having been smashed to pieces alongside its greatest 'triumph' would make that lack of links seem perfectly reasonable.

"What about the contact points?" he asked.

"Three of our contact officers died in the attack," Montoya replied with a shrug. "Brockson was with Montgomery, so he's probably dead. The others are making sure the members of the Wing who know them... don't survive the pursuit."

"And Montgomery?" Vaughn asked.

The commander of his special forces sighed.

"The shuttle was shot down, and the jet escaped without being identified," he confirmed. "But..."

"But what, Montoya?"

"Our ground sweep got caught up in the forest fire triggered by the crash. But they did manage to confirm that Montgomery was not among the dead," the General said quietly. "We lost contact with one of the aircraft ten minutes ago. The other pair are moving to support, but they'd spread pretty far out."

"You lost contact with..."

"With a forty-five million Martian dollar imported helicopter attack gunship, yes," Montoya said bluntly. "I'd *like* to assume they're having communication difficulties. Unfortunately, I suspect..."

He cut off as his wrist computer buzzed. Tapping a key, he opened a holographic window.

"Report, Lieutenant," he said sharply. "I'm with the Governor, connect me to your video feed."

A moment later, one of the views of the wreckage of Government House was replaced with a moonlit highway and a burning wreck.

"Not entirely sure what we're looking at, General, but I'm pretty sure that's Hussar Two," the pilot reported. "They look... flattened."

"Is there anyone in the area?" Vaughn demanded. "Any thermal signatures?"

He could *hear* the pilot swallow hard when he realized who was talking.

"We've run scans," the pilot reported. "The entire forest west of here is going up in flames, but if he followed the road or went east, we'd be able to pick him up. If he was on foot, we'd have found him by now, sirs."

"What are you suggesting, Lieutenant?" Montoya asked.

"Someone picked him up, General," the Lieutenant reported. "Probably *after* he killed Hussar Two. We can't pick out the tracks of a single vehicle, too many have passed in even the last few hours."

"I'm sorry, Sir, Governor – he could have gone either way, and with a vehicle he's long gone. We've lost him."

Montoya held a hand up to forestall Vaughn speaking.

"Thank you Lieutenant," he said calmly. "Return to base and organize a medical unit for Hussar Two."

"Thank you, sir."

The voice channel cut out, and the video link froze on the last picture of the wrecked gunship.

"Yelling at the pilot won't help us, sir," Montoya told Vaughn as the Governor glared at him.

"Two people needed to die, James," Vaughn said harshly. "Two people – with the authority to hang us both. *Everything* was about making sure Alaura Stealey and Damien Montgomery died. And now you're telling me Montgomery lives, and you have no idea where he is?"

"We'll find him," the Scorpion replied calmly. "He has no resources, no contacts, and no allies. He may have found a ride on the highway, but he still has to find somewhere to sleep. Every method of payment the man has is a government card, and we can track those."

"And if he meets up with the rebellion?"

"The Wing is going to go into deep hiding, the kind only the Hands will drag them out of," Montoya pointed out. "Without that kind of authority and resources, Montgomery won't be able to find them."

"He doesn't need to find the Wing to find allies," Vaughn pointed out. "We have other 'friends' out there. What happens if he hooks up with the fucking Greens?"

Montoya shrugged.

"They know perfectly well their seats in the Parliament are on sufferance," he pointed out. "Would they really back him?"

"To bring us down?" Vaughn demanded. "Hell yes. We both know they've skirted the edge too many times to ignore, and would *happily* put Montgomery in touch with the Wing. Hell – one Hand falls, another rises to replace them. Just keeping Montgomery alive until the next Hand shows up could screw us."

The leader of the Scorpions eyed his Governor. Vaughn turned a determined gaze and a cold smile on his most reliable subordinate.

"You get your wish, James," he said bluntly. "I don't trust the Greens, they're a vulnerable point with the Envoy on the loose, and we know where they are."

"If you don't have evidence, manufacture it," the Governor of Ardennes ordered. "And then lock up their whole 'Annual Convention'."

#

Chapter 19

Hauling an unconscious man into a hotel gave Amiri a strong sense of déjà vu. From the quirk on his lips, Riordan was drawing the same connection as he and a hotel staff member held a side door open for her.

"Where are we?" she asked as they proceeded as delicately as possible down a staff corridor.

"High Ardennes," he told her. "Second-best mountain resort town on the planet, closest ski resort to Nouveaux Versailles."

"Ah," Amiri acknowledged, though she guessed it didn't really matter. "Own this hotel too?" she asked.

"Like the car it's buried under a bunch of shell corps, but yeah," Riordan admitted. "Old Man Riordan built quite the hospitality empire, but didn't want anyone to know he was rich. Strange old bastard, he was."

The staff member led them into a public corridor, then swiped them into a room.

"Best ground floor suite, sir," the suited clerk told Riordan. "We'll cycle the booking, make it look like you aren't here."

"Thank you, Hedley," Riordan told the young man.

While Riordan was playing 'good manager', Amiri promptly charged into the 'room'. Suite was a more accurate descriptor as the 'room' had two separate bedrooms off a central seating area.

"Best suite indeed," she muttered, carrying Montgomery into one of the rooms and dumping the bloodied Envoy on the expensive duvet.

"Second best hotel in town," Riordan told her, dumping his coat and following her into the suite. "Dad made a point of never owning the best – attracted too much attention."

Ignoring the rebel's reminisces about his father, Amiri began quickly checking Montgomery over.

"He's been hurt pretty bad," she said quietly. "Lots of minor trauma, at least one blunt impact to the head."

"They shot his shuttle down, Julia," Riordan replied, suddenly serious. Weird – she hadn't thought hearing the Freedom Wing speaker use her real name would have given her shivers.

"He's lucky to be alive," he continued. "He *should* be going straight to a hospital."

"And what would happen to him there, Mikael?" Amiri demanded.

Riordan straightened and shook his head.

"Nothing good," he admitted. "I'm assuming you have first aid training of some kind, but this is beyond a first aid kit and good intentions. We need a doctor."

"It's your hotel!" she snapped. "Find us one."

A sigh and a shake of a head transmuted into a roguish smile.

"It is my hotel," he murmured. "I can't be found anymore than he can," he continued, gesturing towards Montgomery on the bed, "but I have people here. I'll see what I can do," he promised, glancing down at the very small man on the bed.

"Keep him alive until I get back," he asked, then left the room to find help.

Amiri watched him go, then turned her attention back to Montgomery. At this point, her first duty as a Protectorate Secret Service Agent was to make sure he stayed *alive.*

She slowly and carefully peeled off the shredded remnants of his suit jacket, wincing as she realized that his rough bandages were coming off with the clothes and leaving raw skin behind. Slowly, grateful that the young man was unconscious, she got his shirt and blazer off and looked at him.

It took Amiri a moment to even process his injuries once she got a good look at his torso. Alaura had once shown the ex-bounty hunter the strange swirling runic inlay that ran up her arm, a rune carved by the Mage-King himself that increased the Hand's power tenfold.

Montgomery's *entire torso* was covered. From the standard Jump Mage runes inlaid into his palms to what looked like two separate runes covering his chest, swirling characters of silver polymer had been carved into his skin in patterns that tried to shed the eye. The runes covered both of his arms, wrapping onto his torso and looping around his chest and back.

Between, over, and around the runes were the inevitable bruises and scrapes of surviving a crash. He'd roughly bandaged the one really bad gouge across his ribs, and she carefully replaced the bandage with clean gauze and tape from the hotel room kit.

With his wounds at least somewhat bound, she tucked a sheet over the Envoy. He wasn't as young as he looked, she knew – short as he was, it was easy to forget that Montgomery was almost thirty, and only five years younger than her.

His clothes were going to need to be destroyed, and she started going through his pockets to make sure they kept anything of value. The Warrant had somehow survived undamaged, its traditional parchment crinkled but untorn. As she removed it from the blazer, she felt a hard lump she wasn't expecting to find.

The pockets had been shredded, so it took only a moment to extract the object from the jacket and let it fall into her hand.

It lay there, unresponsive and impossible.

Glynn Stewart

Montgomery was an Envoy, not a Hand. Amiri had been fully briefed on the young man accompanying Alaura to Ardennes. If he'd been a Hand, Alaura would have *told* her.

Yet the icon she held in her fist was a Hand's symbol of authority.

"When you wake up, I have a lot of questions," she told the unconscious man.

But she'd need them answered before she let Riordan know there was anything to question. Tucking the Warrant and Montgomery's wallet into a folio she found in the closet, she slid the Hand into her own pocket.

Part of the job of the *Secret* Service, after all, was to keep the Mage-King's secrets.

#

When Riordan finally logged back into the net, Lori was furious with him.

"Where the hell did you go, Lambda?" she demanded. "We're in the middle of organizing an evacuation, and the man who arranged half our safe-houses ups and disappears! Where are you?"

"Breathe, Alpha," her wayward cell leader told her. "You have a list of most of the safe-houses for a reason. But I was given what I thought was an opportunity to change *everything* – I had to take it, Alpha. Even if I was wrong, I judged it worth the risk."

"I'm in High Ardennes now," he continued. "And I need your help."

Lori blinked. When he'd gone dark earlier in the day, Riordan had been in Nouveaux Versailles. Now he was in the same town as her – and he was one of the people who knew where she was.

She touched a command on the military encryption coms, opening a direct channel to Lambda and activating a different encryption algorithm.

"What's going on, Mikael?" she asked quietly.

"Envoy Montgomery survived his shuttle crash," Riordan told her. "I've got him and a Protectorate Secret Service agent holed up in the Silver Lion Hotel, but the Envoy is hurt – flesh wounds and a concussion that I can identify, but I'm no doctor and I don't know what I can't see!"

Lori was stunned into silence.

He was right – this could change everything. If they managed to get the Envoy on their side, then when the next wave of the Mage-King's servants arrived with their righteous rage, Montgomery could direct them at the *right* target. Envoy Montgomery's survival could end Vaughn's entire scheme – his entire *government*.

"Damn," she whispered.

"Yeah."

"Can we trust him?"

"I don't know," Riordan admitted. "He passed out about when I arrived. The Secret Service agent though... she says they were planning on arresting Vaughn sooner or later. Only their uncertainty around the destruction of Karlsberg had protected him this long."

"So he might work with us," Lori said aloud.

"He's an Envoy, Alpha," Riordan reminded her. "Saving his life won't hurt, but you need to remember – it'll be us working with *him*, not the other way around. The man speaks for Mars."

"I guess we'll find out the hard way," she told him, making her decision. "Dr. Staite is in High Ardennes – he owes me some favors and he's sympathetic to the cause. I'll see if I can talk him into a house call."

"I'll keep my eyes open," Riordan promised. "I'm linked back in for the evacuation, too. Even if this works out, we want our people buried deep. Envoy or no Envoy, right now Montgomery's only resources are his own bare hands."

#

With Dr. Staite on his way to the Silver Lion, Lori turned her attention back to co-ordinating the quiet dissolution of her rebellion into small and hideable components. The biggest problem, as Sierra had pointed out when they first realized how deep a hole they'd been dropped in, were the airbases.

It had taken a lot of effort, money, and favors to sneak in their two squadrons of Legatus-built stealth gunships. Even sitting in a bunker though, the aircraft required regular maintenance, which left the Freedom Wing running two complete airbases on opposite sides of the planet. They *couldn't* fully shut those down, not without risking losing the gunships.

Thankfully, both of the airbases were literally bunkers – quietly blasted into mountains with expensive, radiation-blocking, shielded launch doors. Mage-Governor Vaughn had spent a lot of money over the years on his surveillance satellites, and the Wing had learned to stay hidden.

As she finished directing one of their direct action cells – high on the Scorpions' list due to recent operations – to take shelter in the airbase on the south continent, an urgent alert light flashed up on her com. One of her cell leaders was requesting a private channel.

"Alpha," she answered crisply.

"Boss, it's Iota. You have a problem." Iota was their source in the Ardennes Military – a mid-ranked officer who commanded the day shift on the busiest communication center on the planet.

"No shit," she replied. "But I take it you mean a *new* problem."

"They're keeping mission specifics *damn* close to their chest, but a full battalion of Scorpions just rolled out High Ardennes-way," Iota told her. "Mage-Colonel Travere has taken operational command, and brought his Enforcers with him."

"Well, shit," Lori repeated. Mage-Colonel Travere was the most senior of the handful of combat Mages in the Scorpions. He headed the glorified 'platoon' made up of the Enforcers who worked for Montoya. Perhaps thankfully, finding Mages sadistic enough to fulfill the kind of missions Vaughn and Montoya had for Scorpion Enforcers apparently wasn't easy, but…

"How many is he bringing?" she asked. The Wing had Mages in its ranks, but none of the hundred or so Guild-trained combat Mages on Ardennes had joined them.

"They're not saying," Iota replied. "I did some digging, and it looks like he's got his entire Bravo Squad. Ten Mages, plus Travere himself."

"Any idea what they're after up here?"

"They're not saying on channels," Iota told her. "I think they know whatever Hand replaces Stealey will crack open government communications like a rotten nut when they arrive. Scuttlebutt on the air is Travere's orders were on *paper*."

"I can tell you one thing, though," he continued. "They didn't borrow any gear from the Army. No heavy tanks, no exosuits, no anti-aircraft. All they rolled was APCs and light armor."

Lori considered the resources they had at the airbase near High Ardennes and hidden in half a dozen warehouses around town. Even with just the personnel she had in town, she could guarantee that battalion would never come home. If she rolled the gunships and weapons hidden at the bunker in the mountains nearby, the Scorpions would never make it to High Ardennes at all.

Of course, at this point, that would kill everyone involved.

"They're not after us," she murmured. If nothing else, Montoya and Travere were smart enough to know they'd run into the gunships if they came after the Wing – and bring the AA units to deal with them.

"I don't think so," Iota confirmed. "But they'll be running by you. Keep your head *way* down."

"*Merci, mes amis*," Lori told him. "We'll be careful. Thank you."

"*Bonne chance*, boss," he replied.

Cutting the channel, Lori turned back to her immediate concern. Suddenly, concealing everyone in High Ardennes had moved up the priority list!

#

Glynn Stewart

Chapter 20

Damien woke up out of a black fog for the second time in what he hoped was the same day. The feeling was familiar enough that he half-expected to find himself surrounded by a wrecked shuttle, which made no sense to him for several seconds.

Then his memory of the last few hours rushed back in, and his eyes snapped open and he tried to rise.

"Whoa there, sonny," an unfamiliar voice told him. "Give a man a chance to see how well you're ticking before you run off half-cocked!"

Blinking against the dim light, Damien slowly looked around. He had been stripped down to his underwear and lay on the bed in what looked like a hotel room. The bed was huge, but he'd been laid on one edge of it and a tall, heavyset, gray-haired man was standing over him.

The man wore a plain black suit and held a medical scanner.

"Who are you?" Damien coughed out. The last thing he remembered was a car pulling up behind him after he'd taken down one of the Scorpion gunships – a car with Amiri in it!

Glancing around again, he spotted the ex-bounty hunter. The tall, broad-shouldered woman stood just inside the door of the hotel room, her gaze flickering between whatever was outside the room and Damien himself.

"I am Doctor Adrian Staite," the old man told him calmly. "Now, I understand you have had a difficult day. Please lie back down so I can finish examining you. It is important, young man."

He met Amiri's eyes. He hadn't seen the woman in well over two years, but he knew she'd been working for Alaura. Presumably, she was the agent the Hand's code had reached. Her timing, in that case, had been impeccable.

The ex-hunter nodded her head slightly. She, at least, thought the doctor could be trusted.

"Can someone brief me?" he asked as he lay back.

"Once I'm done, no earlier," Staite said bluntly. "You'll do none of us any good if that head wound is worse than it looks, will you?"

Sighing, Damien gestured for the doctor to continue. Staite proceeded to poke and prod, both with the oblong scanner he was holding and his hands and fingers. After several minutes of that, he flashed a light in Damien's eyes that made the Envoy blink and recoil.

"Hrm," he muttered aloud.

"I don't think I'm dying, Doctor, so where am I at?" Damien demanded.

"You're right, you'll live," Staite said dryly. "You'll also be pleased to note that none of the abrasions or cuts you picked up have damaged the integrity of your runes – the polymer withstood the impact without damage."

"It had better," Damien muttered. The polymer was supposed to withstand anything an armored starship hull could withstand – it should take impacts *better* than his skin.

"You'd lost a lot of skin, and a good bit of blood despite your bandaging job," the doctor continued. "I've sprayed down the worst injuries with plasti-skin and run a liter of blood into you while you were still asleep."

He shrugged.

"Otherwise, you have a mild concussion," he continued. "My recommendation is that you go back to sleep. I've a couple of medications that if you take and then sleep about eight hours, you'll be back to a hundred percent."

"Of course, if you let anything *else* smash you upside the head, it'll be worse now," he warned. "So, take the meds I'll grab you, sleep till morning, and then be careful."

Damien looked at the doctor levelly.

"I'll try," he promised.

"I've met your type, son," Staite told him. "That's the best I'm getting, isn't it? I'll grab those meds – *don't* leave the bed."

The doctor walked away from the side of the bed, but was swiftly replaced by Amiri.

"You heard all that," Damien said.

"Yeah," she replied. "Try not to die on me – we've still got a lot to do."

"How bad?"

"Alaura's dead," Amiri said bluntly. Damien nodded – he'd been pretty sure of that. "Vaughn staged a fake 'rebel' attack on Government House. The entire delegation was wiped out. He's also claiming sabotage took out the *Tides of Justice*."

"No," Damien said quietly. "That was Cor."

"*Mage-Commodore* Cor?" Amiri demanded. She looked shocked. Apparently, neither she nor the rebels she'd made contact with had managed *that* connection yet.

"Cor took out Karlsberg," Damien told her. "Harmon worked it out – it was a Navy orbital kinetic weapon. The Mage-Commodore has betrayed Mars."

"That reduces our options a lot, Damien," she said quietly. "I'd been writing her off anyway – clearly Vaughn had *something* over her – but I didn't think she'd be actively against us." She glanced back over her shoulder to be sure they were alone.

"I have escape plans in place, Montgomery," she whispered. "I can get us both off-planet and en route back to Mars inside forty-eight hours."

He shook his head, wincing against the pain.

"Not yet," he whispered. "Not ruling it out, but not yet." He glanced down at his undressed form. "Where is...?"

Staite returned as he was speaking, and he met Amiri's eyes, hoping the woman could guess what he meant.

"Your Warrant is in the folio on the dresser over there," Amiri told him, gesturing towards the dresser with her right hand. Her *left* hand, however, opened her jacket slightly, allowing him to see a handful of links of gold chain hanging over the edge of the inner pocket. She quickly scooped those back into the pocket, but he'd seen what he needed to.

She had the Hand, and had kept the rebels from knowing about it.

"So we're on our own," he finally said, considering what she'd said. "You have contacts?"

"One with the Wing, yes," Amiri admitted. "He found us Doctor Staite, but the Wing is... busy."

"Going to ground," Damien concluded. It made sense. Anything else would be damned stupid right now.

"Everyone's waiting to see which way Vaughn jumps now," Amiri told him. "So what do we do?"

"Our young friend here takes these pills and sleeps," Staite interrupted, gesturing for Damien to rise and passing him a glass of water and two small blue pills. "They'll clear the bruising and get your head working again by morning."

"Things are falling apart," he continued quietly, "but the center will hold until you wake up, Mister Montgomery. You can't save the world if you can't stand."

Damien took the pills and shook his head at the doctor.

"I hope you're right," he told Staite. "That things will hold together till morning."

Amiri smiled and patted a long black object leaned against the wall next to the door. It took him a second to recognize the military battle laser – a squad support weapon, usually.

"I'll guarantee you this, Montgomery," she said with a small smile. "*You'll* still be here come morning."

The medications were already kicking in, and Damien returned the smile as he laid back down. Everything might be coming apart – but at least he had someone to watch his back.

#

Riordan returned in the morning, before Staite's drugs had worn off. Amiri had cat-napped through the night, being willing to give the hotel's security *some* credit, and was sitting in a chair she'd moved over in front of Montgomery's door when the rebel returned, the battle laser across her lap like a pet cat.

"How is he?" the rebel asked.

"Sleeping," Amiri told him pointedly. At this point, she was ranking 'keep the Envoy alive' high on her list of priorities. She liked Riordan, but there were limits.

He simply nodded and threw himself into the couch. His hair was mussed and his suit rumpled; he looked like he hadn't slept at all.

"Hell of a night," he said aloud. "We got everyone in High Ardennes buried three layers deep. Hopefully it will be enough."

"Against what?" Amiri asked.

"Whole fucking *battalion* of Scorps, headed up by General Montoya's favorite pet Mage sadist, is heading this way," Riordan said grimly. "We've got eyes on them, don't think they're coming for us, but we don't know who they *are* coming for."

"I didn't think the Guild *liked* sadists," Amiri pointed out.

"Yeah, but the Testers get *real* snarky if they put too many obstacles in the way of Mages by Right."

She winced.

The Royal Testers were, in general, a hugely necessary and positive part of the Protectorate's structure. They traveled from world to world, school to school, testing every child of the Protectorate's far-flung stars for the gift of magic. For those born to the families of Mages, with the privilege and history those clans inevitably gathered, it was almost a formality – Mages married Mages, so their children were almost always Mages.

For the rest of humanity, it was even more of a formality – Mages found in the general population, those who would become Mages by Right like Montgomery, were roughly one in a million. Since they didn't have the family connections of Mages by Blood, the Testers stepped into a similar place in their lives.

And, if a Mage by Right was a sadist, it might well get swept under the rug in the Protectorate's unending appetite for new Mages for everything from antimatter production to the Navy.

"Just the fact that Mage-Colonel Travere is in command makes me nervous," Riordan admitted to her. "He brought a bunch of combat trained Mages with him, but we don't *have* any Mages here in High Ardennes. If he's coming for us, he hasn't brought enough heavy weapons for the job – but he's brought too many Mages for anything else we can think of."

Something buzzed in Riordan's jacket and he pulled out what Amiri recognized as a military-grade encrypted communicator. Like a lot of the gear she'd been seeing so far, it had been made on Legatus. If the rebellion's equipment was being smuggled in from offworld, she would have expected more of it to be from different places – or mostly from Amber, known for not asking questions of its exports.

Riordan held the com to his ear, triggering a privacy field while he spoke into it. Halfway through the conversation, he blanched, his face turning pale and staying that way.

Finally, he lay it aside and looked back at Amiri. He looked even more tired than he had before.

"They bypassed High Ardennes," he said quietly. "Nobody's sure, but we think they're headed for the Sunshine Resort."

"Which is?"

He shook his head.

"I *know* who you work for, and I still forget you're not from here," he told her. "Sunshine is way up in the mountains, the best ski slope and hotel near High Ardennes. We... aren't entirely sure why they're headed there, but they've already cut off all communication from the resort."

"Whatever's going to happen out there, they don't want anyone to see it."

#

It was another twenty minutes, with no further news, before Montgomery woke up. Amiri heard him moving around and stepped back into the hotel room where the Envoy was slowly getting dressed.

She hadn't found him a new suit, and his body armor had been *shredded*, but she'd at least dug up a pair of slacks and a dress shirt that fit him. As she entered, he was buttoning the shirt up, closing the collar overtop of the leather band wrapped around his neck and its gold medallion.

As soon as the door closed behind her, he turned and held out his hand wordlessly.

Amiri didn't ask what he was after. She dropped the tiny and intimidating weight of the Hand into his palm. It sat there for a long, long moment. Then it buzzed slightly as it warmed against his skin and popped out its access port. Gently, he closed it back up and then hung it around his neck, under the shirt.

"It is mine," he said quietly. "That's what I spent the last three years training for, but I wasn't ready yet. Alaura was supposed to teach me."

"Not anymore," Amiri told him.

"Not anymore," he agreed.

"Have you thought about my suggestion?" she asked. "Honestly, just getting you out alive will bring Vaughn down and finish the mission."

"I know," he said quietly. "But what do you think will happen here if we run, Amiri?" he asked, gesturing around them. "Vaughn has blamed the death of a Hand on the rebels. He likely believes he can get away with anything in 'the pursuit of Stealey's killers'."

Montgomery paused, looking away from Amiri and at the wall.

"If he succeeded in fooling the Hands, he would be right," he admitted. "A Hand falls. Another rises, and they rise for vengeance as much as justice. With Cor working for Vaughn, too… we can't leave, Amiri," he concluded. "Whether or not I'm supposed to have this yet," he touched the amulet under his shirt, "I *have* it. And I'm here. I have to do *something*."

Amiri let disappointment run through her for a moment. Part of her wanted to knock out Montgomery and Riordan, package them up and ship them off-planet with her. The two *idiots* who'd fallen into her care were going to get her killed.

"I guess I work for you now," she said with a sigh. Alaura would have come to the same conclusion. He might not *think* he was supposed to have the Hand yet, but he certainly seemed to be *thinking* like one of the overly noble twits Desmond picked for the job. "What do we do?"

"Vaughn has most of the planet on his side," Montgomery observed. "The pair of us are a little outnumbered. We need to talk to the Freedom Wing. We're going to need them."

"Conveniently, there's a gentleman just outside with an encrypted military-grade com to the rest of their leadership," Amiri told him. "Should I introduce you?"

#

Glynn Stewart

Chapter 21

Dawn was rising over the pristine snow of autumn in the mountains. The pale golden rays of Ardennes' sun shone across the fresh fall, and were obliterated as metal tracks smashed into the scant inches of white.

Four light tanks led the way up the mountain, their treads spraying the snow off the road and across the cleared ditches around them.

Behind them, five armored personnel carriers preceded ten heavy transport trucks, followed by five more APCs and a final pair of light tanks to close off the column.

The image flipped to another camera, and the room around Lori was dead silent. Sunshine was a low slung chalet-style hotel with only one road in and out. A car trying to leave had just run into the tanks. The cameras planted along the road the previous night couldn't pick up sound, but the gesturing of the officer sitting on top of the lead tank was unmistakeable.

The driver's response clearly wasn't acceptable. With a gesture, the officer *ripped* the door off of the car and gestured troops forward. The driver and passengers were dragged from the vehicle and off to the side. Once they were out, the officer – the Mage – gestured again, throwing the entire car off the road.

"I know who they're after," the smooth voice of Agent Papa said quietly in Lori's ear. She had her com feeding to an ear bud right now – everyone's gaze was focused on the image being fed to a projector screen in the conference room beneath High Ardennes' third-best hotel.

"Who?" she demanded quietly. She hadn't heard from Papa since everything had started to come apart – the man was in Nouveaux Normandy, so the clocks were ahead of them, and he'd been busy with his own affairs.

"I was asked not to tell you," he continued. "I work with them in... my other capacities, but they do know I work with you as well. Now," he sighed. "I do not think even the seal of the confessional should bind me now."

"Who, Papa?" she repeated.

"The Green Party was holding its annual conference in Sunshine," Papa said quietly. "They kept it quiet – for all that they're allowed to hold their seats, they don't want to draw *too* much attention to themselves."

Lori nodded slowly. When her Freedom Party had abandoned Ardennes' farce of a democracy, the Ardennes Green Party – latest in a long legacy of environmentally focused political groups stretching back to Old Earth – had become the only opposing voice in the Ardennes Planetary Parliament.

The presence of an opposition bloc – even if it was only five seats out of two hundred – helped legitimize Vaughn's election victories. So he tolerated them, even as they attempted to be a voice of conscience with regards to the rapacious environmental policies his government followed.

Apparently, that tolerance had run out.

"They can't be the only people up there," she whispered.

"They sent Travere, Alpha," Papa said quietly. "That tells us what we need to know. For their sakes, I pray they surrender without a fight."

Lori turned her attention back to the image on the screen. The armored personnel carriers had formed a solid wall of metal across the only way down the mountain, then disgorged their troops. The Scorpions formed a loose skirmish line surrounding the building, while Mage-Colonel Travere and the tanks went right up to the main doors.

With a flippant gesture, Travere's magic ripped the main hotel doors off. The tanks leveled their main guns on the gaping hole, and the Scorpions charged in.

Like the rest of the cell in the room with her, Lori Armstrong watched in silence. Her enemy couldn't reach her – the Wing was buried deep now. So instead, Vaughn was lashing out at whoever he *could* reach.

And she couldn't do anything. To stop a battalion of Scorpions would take enough force to be all-too-visible – and she didn't trust the Navy not to annihilate High Ardennes from space to kill them.

"Alpha, its Lambda," another voice interrupted her thoughts. "I need to talk to you. Private channel."

#

Damien was doing his best to pretend to be patient. After Riordan had disappeared to 'consult with his superiors', the young Mage had taken a seat on the luxurious couch in the suite's sitting area and started reading a book on his personal computer.

He wasn't sure he'd progressed more than a single page in the hour he'd been waiting, and he doubted that Amiri was fooled in the slightest. The woman hadn't survived as a bounty hunter before meeting Alaura Stealey by being unobservant.

Finally, Riordan returned to the suite, carefully shutting the door and locking it behind him before grabbing a chair and facing Damien.

"Well?" Damien demanded. "Did you set a meeting?"

He knew immediately that the rebel had done nothing of the sort as the man shifted uneasily in the chair.

"Everything is going to hell," he finally said. "Alpha isn't sure we can trust you – or that it's worth the risk for us to even consider working with you. After all," he shrugged hesitantly, "at this point, your goals are our goals. We don't lose by leaving you to go back to Mars on your own."

"Right, so we're on plan 'get the fuck out' then, are we?" Amiri asked.

Damien held up a hand to forestall her enthusiasm.

"You're not done," he told Riordan. "What else?"

Riordan glanced at where Amiri had risen to her feet, the Legatan battle laser in her hands, and swallowed hard.

"We *do* have a problem," he admitted. "One we can't safely address ourselves, but if you were to intervene, Alpha might reconsider the value of an alliance."

"Of course. What do you want?" Damien demanded.

"The Scorpion battalion that bypassed High Ardennes has seized the resort at Sunshine," Riordan told him. "That was, apparently, where the Green Party was holding their annual convention. Vaughn has arrested the entirety of the opposition in Parliament."

"He thinks that the death of a Hand will cover many sins," the Envoy said quietly. "If he succeeds in convincing Mars that you killed Stealey, he will be right."

"We can't rescue the Greens," Riordan admitted. "We'd attract too much attention, and we're not sure Vaughn and Cor would hesitate to blow High Ardennes away from orbit if we do rescue them."

"Whereas if I do something, it can be chalked up to a desperate search for allies," Damien replied thoughtfully. It made sense, though it was dangerous. An entire *battalion*? "What sort of force did they take the resort with?"

"Mechanized infantry," the rebel replied immediately. "Six tanks, dozen or so APCs. At least half a dozen Mages under Mage-Colonel Travere."

"Half a dozen Mages," Amiri said quietly. "Damien, I don't like that math."

Damien considered the odds. Amiri had to have at least some clue what the runes inlaid across his torso were – she'd worked with Alaura long enough to have seen the Hand's Rune of Power. Six Mages, plus a battalion of conventional troops...

"We'll have to be very clever," he responded. "A direct assault would be suicide."

Both Riordan and Amiri stared at him like he was insane. Apparently, a direct assault hadn't crossed anyone else's mind.

"I don't suppose you can give us any help?" Damien asked Riordan.

"Alpha didn't say one way or another, and I want to save those people," he replied. "I've got footage of the attack, maps of the complex, and a vehicle. I don't think I can put up manpower, but..."

"How about explosives?" the younger Mage asked. "And I'll need active links to any cameras you have around the site. For that matter, I'll want cameras that we can set up – I'll need surveillance around the entire exterior."

"I can get some mining explosives pretty quickly," Riordan told him. "Rockets or grenades... would take a couple of days."

"Mining explosives will do," Damien told him. "I'll need proper winter gear," he gestured at the slacks and shirt he wore. He glanced over at Amiri. "So will Julia, though I don't think she'll need any more weapons. You seem fond of that laser."

"It's a handy toy," she replied, eyeing him carefully. "You have a plan?"

"Like I said," Damien Montgomery told his team – such as it was. "We're going to have to be very clever."

#

Chapter 22

It might not have been winter yet in Ardennes' northern hemisphere, but it was still bitterly cold on the mountains above the Sunshine resort. Despite the effective – and expensive – winter gear that Riordan had managed to procure in short order, Julia Amiri shivered against the chill.

If pressed, she might have admitted that the flashing red "POTENTIAL AVALANCHE" warning on the bottom of her snow goggles made her nervous. The super-modern 'glasses' contained a suite of sensors that were scanning the snow around her, and linked in to the weather satellites and other tools.

The snow beneath her was old, leftover from last winter and crusted over. Amiri wasn't hugely experienced with snow, but she had no reason to mistrust the snow goggles' warning.

Beneath her, down the slope of the mountain, she could see the main entrance to Sunshine and the row of tanks and APCs blocking anyone trying to leave or enter the resort. There weren't many Scorpions visible on the grounds – most were inside the hotel and other buildings.

This was the last of the eight charges she'd put together from the mining explosives, and she sighed as she *very* carefully made her way off the slope. The warning on her glasses slowly faded to a dull orange, still strongly suggesting that she should be somewhere – *anywhere* – else.

"Charges set," she said softly into her microphone. "Moving to a safe zone and setting up the laser."

"We're not ready down here yet," Riordan told her. The Freedom Wing cell leader's voice was strained, but then he and Damien were climbing up the side of the mountain. Automated equipment had got Amiri onto the top of the mountain, but the men were going to be too close to any sensors the Scorpions might have set up.

"Let me know," she said shortly. She'd spotted a rock outcrop rising out of the snow earlier, and that was her new destination. Hopefully the snow would hold her weight until she got there…

#

The wind whipping across the face of the mountain made the climb bitterly cold. Damien had scoffed at the number of layers that Riordan had acquired from the sporting goods store, but now he was glad for every scrap of fabric wrapped around his all-too-vulnerable skin.

"Why are these lines even *here?*" he asked the Ardennes native as he pulled himself up the cable. The pair, neither very experienced with climbing, had attached harnesses and automatic ascenders to heavy metal cables fixed into the mountain, running from the cliff at the back of the Sunshine resort to a winding mountain road two hundred meters below.

Two thirds of the way up said lines, the sheer icy face of the cliff was making Damien uncomfortable. They'd pulled the cables out of the snow, but even through his gloves the twisted metal fiber felt brittle.

"During the summer, idiot tourists – and local teenagers! – rappel down the side of the mountain, and then use ascenders like these to get back up," Riordan replied. "Since it's unhealthy for the rock to keep hammering in new pitons, they installed fixed heavy cables lines a decade ago. The cables tend to be replaced annually though."

"In spring, I'm guessing," the Envoy replied dryly.

"Yeah," Riordan replied. "I've done the climb before," he continued. "I don't remember it sucking *quite* this much."

As if to drive home his point, a sharp gust of wind sent the rebel skittering across the icy surface, holding tight to the cable as he slid uncontrollably.

Damien took a sharp breath and pulled himself up the cable, holding himself above the ascender with a tight grip on the freezing metal. A moment later, Riordan slid across the ice beneath him, missing him by a handful of centimeters.

He thought that was the end of it and began to sigh in relief as Riordan's slippery trip began to slow.

Then Damien realized that the two cables had become wrapped around each other above his head. The pulling on his line brought his attention to the crossed metal fibers above him – just in time to see Riordan's cable, brittle from the winter cold and stressed beyond its design, *shatter* from the friction.

The end flashed past his eyes, and he saw the other man begin to fall.

Clever plans fled Damien's mind. Hanging onto the cable with his left hand, he pushed himself away from the cliff face and flung out his right hand. Fire *flashed* into existence around the runes in his flesh, incinerating the layers of fabric around his hand as he reached out with his magic.

Lines of force wrapped themselves softly around Riordan, gently slowing his fall. Once the rebel's fall had been arrested, Damien gestured upwards. His magic propelled the older, heavier man up the mountain faster than any powered ascender could have lifted him.

Moments after settling Riordan on the edge of the cliff, Damien unclipped his own ascender and rose on a gentle elevator of his own power. Settling onto the frozen ground next to Riordan, he looked down at the shaky Freedom Wing demagogue.

"You okay?"

"Why wasn't, that the, plan from the beginning?" Riordan demanded, the words coming in spurts as he gasped for breath.

"Because if Travere and his Enforcers are paying any attention, I just rang the biggest doorbell in four or five kilometers," Damien told him.

"Oh. Shit."

"Yeah." Damien turned his gaze on the resort complex. The cliff was beneath a small dip, and it appeared that their impromptu arrival hadn't attracted conventional attention at least.

"Amiri," he tapped the communicator. "Any idea where they're holding the Greens?"

"I'm showing two concentrations of thermal signatures," the Secret Service agent told him. "A big one, looks like two or three hundred people in what I *think* is the big conference hall. Then there's about thirty or forty people in the restaurant – on your end. The rest are in pockets, look like wandering guards and search parties tearing the place apart."

Damien glanced over at Riordan. "Your guess?" he asked the rebel. "You know the players better than us."

"I don't think even Travere is planning on mass murdering the guests," Riordan said quietly. "I'm guessing the forty in the restaurant are our people."

"All right." Damien glanced across the resort again. While the armored vehicles were forming a blockade across the entrance, the heavy trucks that had transported most of the Scorpions had been parked in an impromptu motor pool closer to the building. Unless he was mistaken, each of the transport vehicles should easily carry thirty or so politicians, staffers, and family members.

"We need one of those trucks," he told Riordan. "Think you can grab one? When we blow the charges, pull it over to the main entrance and be ready to pick everyone up."

"Wait, you're going in alone?" the rebel demanded.

Damien smiled sadly.

"Mikael," he said gently. "You're no soldier. No spy. No Mage. You'll just slow me down. And," he saw the side door closest to them open up, "I think our doorbell ringing got noticed. Get the truck."

Leaving Riordan in the dip, trusting in the man to go collect the truck, Damien emerged from its shelter and headed towards the door.

A single man stepped out of the hotel. He was in the Scorpions' winter uniform, a heavy black and red affair that stood out against the snow like an old bloodstain, with the gold medallion of a Mage at his throat.

For a moment, the sight of the medallion, uniform, and body armor of a fully trained Mage Enforcer half-stopped Damien in his tracks. Enforcers were only a half-step below the combat Mages trained by the Martian Marine Corps, trained by the Guild to be elite mercenaries, bodyguards – and to serve in planetary armies. They were so far beyond the Mage he'd been before going to Mars that a single Enforcer could have easily overcome that young Mage and all his friends.

Damien was no longer that young Mage.

"Hey," he hailed the Scorpion. "I need a hand here – I got lost on a ski trip and just made my way back. It's fucking *cold* out there!"

The story was atrocious, rendered even less believable by the fact that the hiking trails came down in a completely different part of the resort. But it got him closer – *much* closer.

Then the Enforcer, already looking confused by Damien's story, spotted his right hand – where the glove had been burnt away by a burst of magic to expose the silver polymer rune inlay below.

To Damien's eyes, the man suddenly lit up with an aura as he channeled power, the energy flickering down his arm to the runes on his own palms.

After three years of training under the Mage-King, Damien didn't need to gather power. As soon as the Mage began to act, his runes flared with warmth and electricity flashed from his exposed hand. The sparks slammed full-force into the Enforcer, flinging the man backwards even as fire flashed away from his own hands.

Snow melted where the Scorpion's fireball had landed, but the man lay slumped against the door, twitching as electricity surged through his body. By the time Damien reached him, the Enforcer was unconscious. A faint and ragged, but still present, pulse responded to Damien's touch, and then the Envoy dragged the other Mage into the hotel.

He hadn't thought about using a non-lethal level of force – he'd just defaulted to it. Nonetheless, since the man *was* still alive, Damien couldn't leave him in the cold to freeze to death!

#

No-one building a civilian resort deep in the mountains had put any thought into trying to shield the building from military-grade passive sensors. While the insulation built into any structure this high in the mountains limited the use of infrared, combining the fuzzy blobs of concentrations of people with the scanners picking up radio leakage gave Amiri a near-godlike view of Sunshine.

"Damien, you've got new movement heading your way," she told the Envoy. "Looks like you attracted attention."

"Damn," he replied. "All right, we needed them elsewhere anyway. Blow the charges."

"How exactly are you getting those people *out* if we block the only road?" she asked. Somehow, in all of their planning, the young Mage hadn't mentioned that part.

"Trust me," he told her. "And trust me that we don't have time," he continued grimly. "Blow the charges *now*, Amiri."

She knew *that* tone. Alaura had practiced the same one – it apparently came standard issue with the golden amulet.

Shifting to make sure she could *see* what happened through the scope of the laser, she triggered the command she'd programmed into her personal computer. For a moment, nothing happened.

Then a burst of smoke erupted from halfway down the slope. The soldiers on the APCs were observant – they noticed it and immediately dropped into their vehicles, battening hatches against an attack.

The first explosion did nothing visible. Neither did the second. By the third, though, the entire mountain was rumbling.

The fourth and fifth blew massive chunks of ice into the air, slamming into the ground and setting entire snowfields into motion. The sixth explosion directed the motion, moving it into the channels weakened by the first three.

Snow rippled down the mountain, carving a path towards the APCs in a tidal wave of snow and ice. It hammered down on the armored vehicles, their hatches shielding them against the elements.

Then the seventh and eighth charges blew. The last pair didn't release snow. Carefully positioned on a cliff her sensors had told her was more fragile than it looked, the last pair blasted a thousand tons of mountain rock free – and sent it careening down the path the snow had just carved.

Tanks and APCs half-buried by the snow couldn't dodge and were crushed as multi-ton fragments of rock crashed into them. Several of the out-buildings were ripped apart by the avalanche she'd unleashed, and only the careful design of the landscaping in the resort's valley directed the debris away from the hotel itself.

The third avalanche wasn't triggered by any of her charges. It came from even higher up the mountain, rock and snow triggered by the earlier avalanches that came sweeping down on Amiri's sheltering rock outcropping.

Her sensors gave her mere moments' warning – enough to dive into cover, abandoning her scanners but hauling her gun with her.

The rock outcropping wasn't much – but it was, hopefully, enough to shield her as the mountain loosed its wrath on the humans who'd dared to use it as a weapon.

#

It was impossible to miss that the charges had succeeded. The entire hotel building shook as the mountain came down around them, and the lights flickered around Damien as the building switched over to emergency power.

The shaking continued for longer than he'd been expecting, and he was starting to worry for the structural integrity of the building as pictures shook themselves off the wall nearby and light fixtures swung themselves into walls and shattered.

Finally, silence returned, and he touched his communicator.

"Amiri, are those troops moving away now?" he asked.

There was no response.

"Amiri?" he repeated. Only silence responded, and Damien swore. Whatever had happened to the Agent, he couldn't do anything about it – he had a building full of civilians to rescue. "Riordan, what are you seeing?" he demanded.

"The armor is *gone*, Montgomery," the rebel replied. "Crushed – but the road's gone with them. There's troops moving in from everywhere to try and dig out survivors. Transports trucks are abandoned, grabbing one right now but I have no idea how we're getting out of here."

"Leave that to me," Damien told him. "Sounds like I'm clear. Hold tight on that truck till I call you."

"Roger."

It seemed that they'd succeeded in drawing most of the soldiers out of the hotel. Despite Amiri's earlier warning, Damien saw no-one as he made his way through the battered hotel. Inside the building, it looked like an earthquake had struck – cracks had appeared in the walls, things had been knocked over or free.

The emptiness made the back of his neck itch, and he found himself raising a defensive shield unthinkingly. It made him a little more visible to other Mages, but he left it up. Either Travere and his Mages were busy rescuing their friends, or he was going to need it.

Tucking himself against a corner to stay out of sight of any remaining patrols in the building, Damien checked his location against a map of the building and Amiri's description of the clusters of people.

If he read the map correctly, he was a corner and twenty feet from the main restaurant and the smaller group of prisoners.

Taking a deep breath, Damien stepped around that corner and walked calmly towards the glass doors of the entrance. Someone had activated the metal shutters used to lock the restaurant up at night, and then attached an emergency police lock to keep the shutters locked to the ground without the proper codes.

It was a formidable obstacle to anyone without the codes, heavy welding equipment – or a Mage. There were no visible guards, the paramilitary soldiers most likely outside trying to dig their friends out of the avalanche.

The lack of defenders in a building seized by Vaughn's paramilitary troops was nerve-wracking, and it was almost a relief when the attack finally came.

A bolt of fire flickered out from an alcove he'd missed, hammering into his shields from behind. The bubble Damien had wrapped around himself was a relatively weak defense, a roughly spherical force bubble that moved with him without too much thought.

Relatively weak or not, it was designed to stop bullets and shed a mid-strength fireball with only a minor tremor of energy drain.

Damien spun, dodging sideways as a second fireball splashed through where he'd stood a moment before. He flung out one hand, sending a blast of fire flashing back towards his assailants.

He felt magic flare and his fire was knocked aside. Three men emerged from the shadows to face him, all in the heavy winter uniform of the Scorpions – and the man in the center wore the oak leaves and gold medallion of a Mage-Colonel.

"I presumed someone would try and sneak in while we were distracted," Mage-Colonel Travere said coldly. "I didn't think the rebels even had decent Mages, but here you are. It's a shame. Any Mage could do better than joining the rabble."

Damien smiled coldly and met the Mage-Colonel's gaze.

"My name," he said quietly, "is Damien Montgomery, Envoy of the Mage-King of Mars. Your Governor is guilty of treason. Work with me, and no-one else needs to die today."

Travere jerked back as if physically struck, looking Damien over carefully.

"You're supposed to be dead," he said conversationally. "Killed in a shuttle crash, shot down by the rebels. I guess," he said in a blatantly fake sad voice, "I'll have to fix that.

"Because, you see," he continued, his voice hardening, "several hundred of my men are buried under your avalanche, and likely dead. So no matter what you say, I think someone does still need to die today."

This time, the Mage-Colonel knew he was facing a Mage. His attack was focused and powerful, a tightly focused stream of fire that would cut through any defense a Mage could muster.

Damien wasn't there. He *blinked* forward, a teleportation spell putting him *behind* the three other Mages. Lightning flared out from his hand, slamming into one of Travere's two Enforcers.

This wasn't the stun spell he'd used outside, and the smell of burnt flesh filled the hallway as the Scorpion went down hard.

"*Jump Mage*," Travere cursed, spinning as he spoke and sending another perfect lance of flame flashing out at Damien. The hotel walls behind him sparked and smoldered as the Envoy was, once more, somewhere else.

"Hold him," the Mage-Colonel snapped, and his remaining minion obeyed with a will. Bars of force tried to snap onto Damien, attempting to hold him in place for the stronger Colonel to deliver the death blow.

Spell and counter-spell wove through space for a moment, then Damien redirected the whole mess into the wall. The side of the corridor disappeared, several entire hotel suites shattering into pieces that scattered across the mountainside.

Damien followed up with a fire-blast of his own, the same tightly focused beam that Travere had attacked with. The Enforcer threw up a force shield to block it – only for Damien's spell to burn clean through the defense and punch a fist-sized hole through the man's chest.

He and Travere faced each other in the corridor for a moment, the Ardennes' soldier's men dead around him. Then the second story of the building, above the rooms the struggle had blasted to splinters, collapsed.

Debris blocked the daylight that had begun to stream in from the outside, and then the damage severed a hidden power cable in the roof, plunging the entire hallway outside the restaurant into darkness.

There was silence in the hotel, any temptation to make noise on the part of the civilians locked into the restaurant buried by the clear and obvious signs of violence outside their door.

Damien listened and looked carefully. Travere was in uniform, but not wearing any sort of headgear – he wouldn't have thermal vision of any kind. Smiling to himself, the Envoy reached out with other senses – senses even another Mage wouldn't have.

Long ago, he'd learned to read the flow of magic in mankind's runes. Under the Mage-King's tutelage, the Rune Wright had learned to see *any* flow of magic – including that in the runes carved into the flesh of many Mages – and *all* combat Mages..

"I can still see you, Colonel," he said softly as he identified the shifting light of the other man's magic. "I can sense the magic in your blood.

"You challenged Mars, Travere," he continued, closing on the other Mage. "How did you *think* it was going to end?"

Travere's response was light and fire. With one hand, the Mage-Colonel threw a ball of light into the air to allow him to see, and then he filled the entire hallway where he'd heard Damien speak with fire.

The runes wrapped around Damien's torso flared to life as he drew on their strength, corralling the Scorpion's strike with a net of force – and then flinging it *back* at the man. A blast of flame intended to fill a corridor and catch someone he couldn't see was focused back to the size and position of a single man.

With his own full strength turned on himself, Travere didn't even have time to scream.

#

Chapter 23

It turned out that there *were* soldiers in with the Green Party prisoners, but when Damien tore the security shutters off the doors and stormed into the room, they had their weapons on the ground before he could even demand their surrenders.

The sergeant in charge kicked his assault rifle over to Damien with his hands in the air.

"*Je ne mourir pas pour cette*," he spat. "I won't die to arrest the harmless," he continued in English.

"You and your men over there," Damien ordered, gesturing the Scorpions away from their weapons and prisoners. Nodding and signaling for his men to follow him, the Scorpion squad leader obeyed.

Damien waited for the soldiers to back themselves into the corner, well away from their prisoners and weapons, then turned his attention to those prisoners.

They were a sad-looking collection of men and women in businesswear. They'd clearly been forced to sleep in the clothes they'd been wearing when the Scorpions had stormed the hotel, and several of them had visible bruises.

"Are you all able to move?" he asked gently.

The politicians looked around at each other for a moment, and then a gray-haired man with a neatly trimmed beard stepped forward.

"None of us are badly injured," he said grimly. "But you'll understand if I fear a scheme of some kind to damn us all? We have done *nothing* – we are not rebels, just politicians."

"That distinction is unfortunately now lost on your governor," Damien told him gently. "I am Envoy Montgomery, I'm here to help you. I won't *make* you come with me, but I wouldn't recommend staying."

The old man glanced around at his people, then sighed.

"I am Jacob Pierre," he said quietly. "Leader of the Ardennes Green Party, such as our Governor has allowed it to be. We have several handicapped individuals who travel by wheelchair. I am not certain…"

"We have a vehicle waiting," Damien cut him off. "What we do not have is *time*, Monsieur Pierre."

Pierre drew himself up for a moment, as if offended, and then released all of his tension in a single breath and a firm nod.

"Of course." He turned to his people. "Let's get moving everyone. Joe, Raul, help Lori. Everyone else – follow Montgomery."

"Thank you," Damien told him softly.

"If we live… thank *you*."

The main opposition party of the Ardennes Planetary Parliament may have been bruised and exhausted, but the chance to escape got them to move with a will. Damien led the way out of the hotel, pointedly *not* hearing the gasps from some of the more impressionable members at the shattered state of the corridor outside.

"Riordan, we're on our way," he radioed. "Please tell me you've got a truck."

"I've got a truck, but I haven't heard anything from Amiri," the rebel replied, his voice worried. "I..." he swallowed, "I don't think we've got cover fire."

"We'll deal," Damien told him. "And if we don't hear anything, I'll go back for her, Mikael. Your planet's already killed too many of my friends."

No-one barred their way, and he led the Greens to the service entrance without any issues. Riordan was waiting for them with the big armored truck, standing next to the back of the truck as he pulled down the door.

"We don't have a ramp," Riordan told the one woman in a wheelchair. For a moment, the rebel looked helpless, but the two burly men already accompanying her simply grinned.

"We made this far, monsieur," one of them said. "Clear the way *pour un moment*, we will see it done."

Damien gestured the rest of his rescuees away from the truck while he kept an eye for the rest of the Scorpions. The two big staffers picked up the wheelchair bodily and heaved it into the back of the truck, with Riordan helping guide the chair into the body of the truck.

"All right," Riordan said to the rest once the woman was aboard. "Get aboard – it's going to be cramped, but it's what we've got."

Pierre started to corral his people, the party leader showing a sense of experience at organizing this particular stampede. Glancing over at Damien and Riordan, he gestured them towards the front of the truck with a nod of his head.

"I'll get them sorted," he said softly. "Just... get us out of here. I owe you both."

Damien nodded and followed Riordan to the front of the truck. Swinging into the cab, he took stock of their resources.

"We have no guns," Riordan said quietly. "The only heavy weapon I had was the battle laser Amiri took. If they try to stop us..."

Amiri had been supposed to provide covering fire with the laser from above the resort, but she still wasn't on the radio. Damien wasn't sure what had happened to her, but the immense avalanche that had swept the mountain suggested unpleasant possibilities.

"I'll deal with it," Damien repeated. Before he could say more, Pierre swung up into the cab.

"Everyone's aboard," the politician said quietly. "I'm not sure how you're getting the truck out through the avalanche, though."

"Yeah, I was hoping I'd get some explanation of that *before* I drove into something," Riordan agreed.

"Magic," the Envoy told them drily. "I figured that was obvious?"

"So what do I *do*?" Riordan demanded, shaking his head.

"Just drive," Damien instructed. "I'll take care of the rest."

Muttering under his breath, Riordan threw the big truck into gear. The engine came to life with a roar, and the vehicle lurched into motion. They drove out of the service lane and around the hotel, allowing Damien his first look at the disaster zone they had made of the road.

There had been tanks and armored personnel carriers lined up across the entrance. He couldn't tell – there was no sign of any vehicles in the field of devastation. Two entire buildings had been ripped to pieces and scattered across the road, and rocks from the cliffside they'd collapsed filled the pass leading down the mountain.

He swallowed hard. It had been a logical, easy, plan – take out a significant chunk of Travere's troops, and distract the rest. Looking at the shattered field in front of him, with red and black uniformed soldiers digging desperately to try to find their friends, it didn't seem quite so logical or easy anymore.

"Take us over the avalanche zone," he finally ordered Riordan, drawing power to him for the spell he'd need. "I can't give you a lot of traction, so just go straight."

Even while looking at him like he was crazy, the Freedom Wing rebel obeyed. The heavy truck rumbled across the resort's grounds towards the devastated field. They were most of the way there before anyone spotted them, then people started pointing and gesturing.

Damien wasn't worried about the soldiers. He was watching for Mages, knowing that at least half a dozen more of them were around. Some of them had to be buried with the tanks, but he couldn't count on *all* of them being out of the fight.

"Hold on," he murmured as the rock-pile approached, and released the power he'd summoned. Riordan cursed in shock as his wheels left the ground, running on iron-straight rails of solidified air.

"Just *drive*," Damien ordered. The other man obeyed, while Pierre stared on in shock as they drove on air, rising to easily four or five meters over the debris field.

"Watch out!" the party leader snapped.

Holding his attention on the road he was forging in the air, Damien could barely spare enough attention to spot the soldier with the rocket launcher that Pierre was pointing out. Despite his intent, he couldn't spare the energy to counter-attack, and for a moment prepared to drop the truck to protect it.

Then the soldier's torso exploded in a puff of red, the telltale sign of an invisible military-grade laser. More explosions followed on the ground around him, ice and rock vaporizing in small explosions as the battle laser walked across the field, driving the Scorpions back.

It seemed Amiri was okay after all.

#

Amiri didn't remember anything between ducking under the rock outcropping, and waking up with a start in a dark pocket, slightly short of breath. The clock in her goggles informed her she'd only been unconscious for a few minutes, and the lump on the back of her head suggested she'd been hit by debris.

From the staleness of the air she was breathing, she was pretty sure her little pocket was running out of oxygen, and fast. As she scrabbled to her knees in the pitch-black space, though, her hands fell on the familiar metal stock of the battle laser.

The air was sparse enough she could feel herself starting to panic, and she forced the panic down. She'd been in worse spots in her years as a bounty hunter. Well, one worse spot, and her brother had saved her from that.

Montgomery was too busy to save her, which left it up to her. Taking a deep breath of the heavy air, she picked up the laser and carefully activated its screen. It appeared undamaged, which given the notoriously fragile nature of even military laser weapons was a minor miracle.

Setting it for a wide cone, she pointed it away from the rock behind her and fired. Super-heated steam filled her impromptu cave as snow vaporized and blasted away – but she only got a tiny glimpse of blue sky before more snow and rocks filled the hole again.

Swallowing, she aimed higher and set the weapon for a maximum duration beam – one that would require most of a minute of cooling before being fired again.

This time, the steam exploded outwards as she blasted a woman-high hole through the debris and snow. Unsure how long the gap would remain, she dove for it, pulling herself most of the way out before it started to collapse on her.

She almost lost her boots, but she managed to get out and onto the side of the mountain.

The mountainside beneath her was strewn with debris, a long trail of destruction stretching down and past the battered resort nestled in the valley beneath her. The landscaping had preserved the hotel itself, though it looked like *something* had collapsed an entire wall's worth of suites.

As she breathed deeply of the frigid mountain air, she spotted one of the heavy trucks rip out from behind the hotel, heading for the exit. All of the Scorpions looked to be digging for their friends, which meant it was almost certainly Montgomery and Riordan.

Checking her weapon, she realized the laser was still overheating – and it looked like they were going to need her help a lot faster than the weapon would cool on its own, even in the mountain air.

She stared at the snow in front of her for at least five seconds before the solution came to her. Laying down, she quickly packed snow over the battle laser, using the debris from her avalanche to build a rough weapon mount and cooling sleeve.

The laser was still insisting it needed to cool – and as she finished packing in the snow, she spotted the Scorpion with the rocket launcher. Regardless of what the weapon's computer thought, it was out of time.

Setting it to the lowest energy level and holding her breath, she lined up the laser and fired.

The man with the rocket launcher exploded away from the beam, a chunk of his flesh exploding into hydrostatic shock waves that couldn't possibly leave him alive.

Then she lay down a slow, low-energy suppressive fire. The Scorpions had had a really, really, bad day. If they were willing to keep their heads down, she was willing to let the rest of them live.

Finally, the flying – *seriously, Montgomery?!* – truck touched down on the road beneath the avalanche and began to trundle away to safety.

"Amiri, are you okay?" Montgomery demanded over the radio.

"Got buried, had a laser," she replied. She glanced back at her pack. "I don't think my hang glider is intact, I'm going to have to hike my way out."

"I doubt the mountain is stable enough, Agent," the Envoy said dryly. "Give me your co-ordinates."

She did. "Why?" she followed up. "What are you going to do?"

Silence answered for a moment, then Riordan replied.

"Apparently, he's going to jump out the side of the truck and use magic to land safely," the rebel told her. "I'm not entirely what his plan is from there."

Amiri barely had time to wonder what the kid was *thinking* when there was a sudden popping noise, triggering a minor slide of snow thirty feet away from her. Spinning towards the noise and drawing her sidearm, she found Montgomery standing there, delicately balanced on the debris and wreckage their plan had scattered across the mountain.

"What are you *doing*?" she demanded.

"I refuse to allow my best ally on this rock to break her fool neck trying to climb down a mountain we just demonstrated is unstable as hell, Julia," Montgomery told her bluntly, crossing the snow to her gently. He offered her his arm. "May I give you a lift?"

"Has anyone told you that you're insane?"

"My old crew called me that a few times," he replied innocently as she stepped closer to him and hooked her arm through his. "I never did understand why. Hold on."

She didn't even get a chance to ask why before the mountain disappeared, to be replaced by their hotel suite in High Ardennes.

The ex-bounty hunter, a hardened soldier, spacer, and spy... glared at Montgomery for all of ten seconds before she noisily threw up on him.

#

Chapter 24

Lori met Riordan and his passengers in a parking garage at the edge of town. The big military truck barely fit into the first floor of the concrete structure, but it was at least out of sight from any watching satellites or Navy warships.

"Please tell me you have some plan for getting us out of here," Riordan told her as he dropped out of the truck. "I... didn't fully expect Montgomery to succeed, so I didn't plan past getting here. I have places to *put* them," he continued, "but they'll track the truck here, and we can't afford for them to track us away from here."

"Maintenance tunnels," Lori told him calmly. "I used to play in them as a child, and one of our people 'borrowed' the access codes from their servers after we set this as the rendezvous point."

Jacob Pierre joined the pair, taking Lori's hands in his own and bowing over them.

"*Mademoiselle* Armstrong," he greeted her softly. "It appears I have the impetuous rebellion of yours that I have long berated to thank for my life."

"You have Envoy Montgomery to thank," she replied uncomfortably. "We... couldn't risk acting with our own resources – we would have put all High Ardennes at risk."

"Of course," Pierre agreed. "I did not expect you to save us, Lori," he admitted. "We... spent too long castigating you for having the courage to act. You were right, and I was wrong. Vaughn is too far gone to be convinced or swayed."

"One of us had to stay," Lori reminded him. "*Someone* had to try, and you had the patience for it, not me."

"We need to get these people moving, Lori," Riordan told her. "After the disaster Montgomery made of the resort and Travere's battalion, I don't think they followed us – but Montoya will be moving new troops into place as we speak, *and* asking for help from Cor."

Lori nodded and gestured for the rescues spilling out of the truck to follow her.

"It won't smell overly nice," she told them over her shoulder, "but the maintenance tunnels are supposed to be secure. Any record that we used them will be wiped too, so the trail will end here. You'll be safe."

She opened the door and gestured for the refugees to go past her. One of her Freedom Wing soldiers was waiting on the other side, and began to gently guide the Green Party politicians and staffers into the underground network.

"I thought we were safe at Sunshine," Pierre finally murmured from behind her. "I've spent years keeping us completely separate from your Wing. We've done *nothing*."

"Except oppose Vaughn," Lori told him. "That, it seems, is now enough. No resistance will be tolerated, all dissent will be crushed. He thinks he's blamed us for the death of a Hand, Jacob, and that's the fire he'll burn us all in given half a chance."

"But the Envoy is working with you," Pierre objected. "That means... Mars knows what happened."

"Montgomery knows what happened," Riordan said quietly. "I don't know what the man's plan is, but he wants our help. So..."

"I asked him to rescue you," the Freedom Wing's leader told Pierre. "To prove both that we could trust him, and that he was, well, worth the risk."

Jacob Pierre shivered at the thought.

"I saw him fight Travere," the old politician admitted. "I don't think anyone else did, but there was a gap in the shutters I could see through. He took on Travere and two of his Enforcers and killed them. A Marine Combat Mage shouldn't have been able to do that. *Nobody* could have."

"But he did," Lori said grimly.

"He did," Pierre confirmed. "And made it look easy. I don't know what Montgomery is, Lori, but I don't think he is just a Mage – or just an Envoy! He's a dangerous ally, but..." he shrugged as the last of his people made their way into the tunnels.

"If you want to know if he's worth it, he is," he finished bluntly. "If nothing else, his word alone will hang Vaughn when the next Hand arrives to avenge Alaura – a mere Governor against an Envoy?"

"So what, we should get him on side and then sit on him?" Lori asked.

Pierre laughed, a sharp bark that seemed to surprise him as well as Lori.

"It would be wise," he agreed. "But... I do not think 'sitting on' Montgomery is going to happen." The old man glanced after his people, then back at Lori.

"I don't expect I will see Montgomery again until all of this is settled," he concluded aloud. "But you will, I am sure. Give him my thanks for my life, and the lives of my people."

"I will," Lori promised.

"Stay alive, my dear," Pierre told her, then set off down the tunnels after his staff, leaving Lori and Riordan standing alone in the rapidly darkening parkade.

"How long until they find the truck?" she asked.

"I'm pretty sure it has a tracker," Riordan admitted. "An hour, maybe two."

She gestured for him to precede her into the tunnels, closing the door behind them and inputting the code that would both re-lock it and wipe any record it had ever been unlocked.

"Once you're back to the hotel, tell Montgomery I'll meet him," she told him. "I'm not sure what we can do anymore, not with Vaughn controlling the skies, but he may see a path I don't."

#

"It's confirmed. Travere didn't survive the attack."

Vaughn grunted at Montoya's words, looking at the satellite footage of the wreckage that had been the Sunshine resort.

The avalanche had triggered an alert that had sent dozens of regular emergency personnel out to the location. While they'd placed themselves under Scorpion authority when more senior Special Security Service officers arrived, their presence had definitely made any attempt to bury what had happened impossible.

Not that they had a damn clue what had happened.

"Any luck finding footage of the attack?" he demanded.

"None," Montoya replied sourly. "Travere had us rig the satellites so they weren't overhead when he was there – a safety measure, just in case. So now..."

"Now we have no idea how he died," Vaughn snapped, sweeping a glass of whiskey off the desk in the temporary office he'd commandeered in the command center. It hit the ground and shattered, and he stared at the amber liquid amidst the ice cubes and shattered glass.

Travere had been... not quite a friend, but a trusted subordinate, a Mage who understood the measures necessary to hold an entire planet together.

"Why did it take so long to identify Travere?"

"Because there was nothing *left* of him," Montoya snapped, his voice harsher than he usually addressed his Governor. Vaughn let it pass – Travere *had* been Montoya's friend.

"His body was burned to ashes," the general continued after a long moment. "The section of the building he was in was half-wrecked. I saw the pictures. It looked like... it *was* the aftermath of a Mage fight."

Vaughn's gaze snapped to Montoya, meeting his most trusted subordinate's gaze. Montoya was *not* a Mage – but he had, once, a very long time ago, been a Martian Marine. Unlike anyone else Vaughn knew, the Scorpion's commander knew what the aftermath of two Mages going head to head looked like.

"There are *no* Mages in the Green Party," he observed. "So this wasn't a case of them breaking themselves out."

"No," Montoya agreed. "And, well... so far as we can tell, there was only one Mage. He or she left Travere and six Enforcers dead behind them."

"One Mage did that."

"One Mage," Montoya confirmed. "A Marine Combat Mage *might* manage that, given time and preparation. Maybe."

"The Freedom Wing doesn't *have* any Enforcers or Combat Mages," Vaughn objected. "There are no fucking Combat Mages on the *planet*, Montoya."

"That we know of," the Scorpion pointed out. "But... there's one Mage we *don't* know the abilities of."

"Montgomery."

"I did some research on our Envoy after he killed my gunship," Montoya told him. "He has... a reputation. Do you remember the Blue Star Syndicate?"

"They're gone now," Vaughn pointed out. The Syndicate *had* been a criminal organization, with ties to everything from trafficking sex slaves to manufacturing and selling illegal weapons. Their leader had died in some conflict on the Fringe, and the Protectorate Navy had done their job for once and rolled up the remnants.

"Yes. Azure died, and that was all they wrote," his general confirmed. "But did you know *how* Azure died?"

Vaughn wasn't sure what Montoya was talking about and was about to snap at the general when it struck home.

"Montgomery?!"

"Azure was chasing a jump freighter called the *Blue Jay* that was rumored to have been upgraded with an amplifier," Montoya told him. "The old man caught up with the *Jay* somewhere out in the Fringe – and didn't come back. The *Jay* hasn't been seen since either, but the crew *has* shown up.

"And the last Jump Mage of record for the *Blue Jay* was Damien Montgomery, who next showed up on Mars, being trained by the Mage-King himself."

"You think our lost little Envoy killed one of the most powerful Mage criminals of the last twenty years?" Vaughn demanded.

"It looks... possible," Montoya told him softly. "And if it's true... I'm not sure our Envoy is lost, or little.

"And whatever Damien Montgomery is, I no longer think he's harmless!"

#

Chapter 25

Amiri had managed to clean herself up and change by the time Riordan finally returned to the hotel room. She'd even mostly managed to stop glaring at Damien for not warning her.

He'd apologized – profusely! He'd actually forgotten how bad being the carry-on in a personal teleport was, otherwise he'd have warned the Agent in advance. A ship jump didn't have the same effect, as everyone *inside* the ship basically experienced it the same way.

Personal teleports were not as accommodating.

"I see I guessed right on just where you'd disappeared to," Riordan observed as he entered, finding Damien and Amiri sitting in the suite's living room. "You both okay?"

"Despite Montgomery attempting to scare the living daylights out of me, yeah," Amiri told him, and Damien smiled to himself. The Secret Service Agent seemed to be handling getting buried alive better than he would have!

"And our rescuees?" Damien asked.

"Being hustled through tunnels and taxis to safe-houses across the town," Riordan confirmed. "Some we'll have on buses or in other vehicles heading down to the cities."

"They're safe?"

"As safe as we can make them," Riordan told him. "That isn't... perfect. With the Wing going into hiding itself..."

"We deal with the world we have, not the world we want," Damien said quietly. "Have you spoken to Alpha?"

"I have," the rebel admitted. "She wants to meet. But, bluntly, we *are* going into hiding. We now *know* Cor is working with Vaughn – and the Mage-Commodore owns the sky. Neither Alpha nor I are sure just what we can do for you."

"It depends," Damien replied. "I need to know your resources, your limitations – I need to know the strength of your will, Riordan. How far you'll go – how hard you'll fight. I can do nothing on my own," he admitted, "but I can also provide the Wing a legitimacy no-one else on Ardennes can."

"And you're apparently no slouch in a fight on your own," Amiri interjected. "Which is not, everyone should note, stopping me from coming with you to this meeting." She held up a hand as Riordan started to speak. "It's not his call," she told the rebel, and Damien silently admitted that she was right. "Right now, keeping him alive is my job, which means whether or not he gets a bodyguard is my call, not his."

"Set it up," Damien told Riordan. "My schedule is open," he continued dryly, gesturing around the hotel suite. "Whatever works for Alpha – but the sooner the better."

"It'll be tomorrow morning," the rebel replied. "I suggest you both get some rest. I certainly intend to!"

#

It felt like Lori had just fallen asleep when the emergency alert on the encrypted communicator startled her awake. It took her a moment to realize where she was and what was going on – the hotel room was hardly a familiar place to wake up.

Then she finally finished waking up and recognized the emergency alert for what it was, and hit the 'receive' command.

"Alpha here," she responded sharply.

"Alpha, it's Kilo," a flatly calm voice said over the channel. "We have a problem."

The politician Lori had once been would never have recognized that tone. The rebel leader she'd become did, as it was a tone she'd heard far too many times after Karlsberg: the calm that came from the end of all hope.

"What's happening?"

"The Scorpions hit one of our safe-houses in Allarain," Kilo continued in that same dead voice. "They must have broken someone and fast. Five more are already gone, and I don't know how the other three were missed."

Lori exhaled sharply with a gut-punch sensation. When they'd gone to ground, the Freedom Wing's safe-houses had got crowded. Six safe-houses down was easily thirty or more people arrested or dead.

"There's no way they didn't find out about the Argent Cavalier office," Kilo continued. "I'm there now and I've set up the data purge, but we kept a lot of the files on paper."

Argent Cavalier had been an 'investment holding company' on paper, dealing in the buying and selling of shares on Ardennes' planetary stock exchange. In reality, it had been a money laundering service and general financial administration center for the Freedom Wing.

No matter how much you wanted to keep things silent and hidden, some records were necessary with money. The records in Argent Cavalier's files and computers would, if nothing else, lead the Scorpions directly to the two air bases with their hidden squadrons of stealth gunships.

"Get out of there, Kilo," Lori ordered. "Set a fire, set the delete, and *go*."

"No can do," Kilo replied in that same dead voice. "That was the plan. Hell, my backup was to have you send Sierra if things were looking dire.

"But I underestimated 'dire'," she continued unflinchingly. "There's Scorpions in the building – APCs on the ground, a gunship on the roof. There's no way out. It's four in the morning, there's no-one else in the building."

Lori realized what was going on at last and swore aloud.

"Dammit, Kate, there has to be *something!*" Even as she spoke, though, her use of Kilo's real name told the truth. Kate Guérin was trapped, and she was going to die.

"We both know the answer, Alpha," Guérin said flatly. "Truth is, I never figured deleting and burning files would be enough. The office was rigged with charges months ago. Let the fuckers come."

A crash echoed through the radio channel, followed by gunfire, then a moment of silence.

"*Reddition et déposer vos armes!*" a voice shouted.

"*Venez et prend les!*" Kate spat back, and more gunfire followed.

Lori knew what was coming, but she couldn't bring herself to turn the com off. She owed her friend that.

"Hey asshole," Kate finally shouted as the gunfire slowed again. Her voice was strained. She sounded exhausted and in pain – the Scorpions had clearly hit her. "*J'ai une secret* – you were fucked as soon as you walked through the door."

Lori heard the beginnings of an explosion, and then the channel cut out.

#

"In our top news story this morning, we have mixed news out the city of Allarain this morning," a news reporter blared behind Damien as he, Amiri and Riordan took a seat in the restaurant of one of High Ardennes' many hotels. This seemed to be an even higher class than the one they were staying at, and the waiters had clearly been expecting them. They were seated in a booth tucked away into a corner so unobtrusive as to almost be a separate room.

The booth also had its own TV, playing the news story that was slowly attracting Damien's attention away from the excellent coffee he'd been served.

"Despite a breakthrough by the Ardennes Special Security Force that allowed elite counter-terrorism teams to arrest dozens of the Freedom Wing rebels, the terrorists managed to plant and detonate a bomb in an office building in downtown Allarain. While no civilian casualties have been confirmed yet, at least twenty Security Service personnel were killed in a valiant attempt to disarm the bomb to protect Allarain.

"Investigations and raids continue this morning, as our brave security forces sweep up the remainder of the rebel network in…"

The screen cut out as two women slid into the booth across from them. One was a gangly brunette woman with short-cropped hair and soft brown eyes. The other was shorter, though still taller than Damien himself, with blonde hair and an attractive physique.

The blonde woman's eyes said everything. They were a light blue, and might once have been warm and caring. Today, they were red from crying and the temperature of ice.

"Alpha," Damien greeted her softly. "I appreciate you meeting with me. I know you have a lot going on and more on your mind."

Carefully studying the woman, he recognized her from the briefing notes on Ardennes. Six years before, Lori Armstrong had challenged Mage-Governor's Vaughn's Prosperity Party in the planetary election. She'd succeeded, but the Freedom Party had dissolved before the next election – sheer frustration, from what Damien could tell, shattering any attempt at peaceful change.

From those ashes, the Freedom Wing had been born. He wasn't surprised to see Armstrong at the center of it all. The other woman hadn't been in any of his briefings – she was a stranger, but held herself like a soldier. A bodyguard, though likely no more *just* a bodyguard than Amiri was.

"As you saw on the news, we have not been as successful as we hoped," Armstrong told him grimly. "Now we are in the process of moving anyone we believe may have been compromised by the Allarain raids.

"To be blunt, Envoy Montgomery, I am not sure how we can help you."

"Right now, you are burying your people and your resources as deeply as you can, so that Alaura's replacement won't find you when they come looking for Alaura's killer," Damien said quietly. "If I can make contact with Mars that will no longer be necessary. With only Vaughn's people to worry about, who you have more practice in avoiding, I hope to use your resources to short-circuit any attempt by Vaughn to do something stupid."

"Going openly against an entire planetary government qualifies as 'something stupid' on *our* end," the other woman interjected. "If our resources were sufficient for that, we'd be having a very different conversation."

From the way Armstrong looked at the other woman, Damien added 'military advisor' to her classification. Armstrong might head the Freedom Wing, but this other woman seemed to know more about their military force. Interestingly, she also spoke with a clear Legatan accent.

"What would be necessary depends very much on what sort of 'something stupid' Vaughn attempts," Damien admitted. "But the first step, before anything else, is that I need to get in contact with Mars. We all know if a Hand falls, another rises to replace them. My word and my evidence is sufficient to make sure that Hand will come for the right person when they come for Alaura's killer."

"Which is of value to us, but hardly infinite value, Envoy," Armstrong replied. "I do not believe the Hands are stupid. I expect Vaughn's folly to come apart at the seams once the new Hand arrives – especially so long as you're alive to communicate with them."

"Miss Alpha," Damien said softly, "do you honestly believe that Mage-Commodore Cor will stand by while Mars destroys Vaughn?"

The rebel leader was silent, clearly thinking hard.

"I do not know why Cor has thrown in with the Governor," he continued. "But I do know that she ordered the weapon dropped that destroyed Karlsberg. But the Hands, the *King*, do not know this. They will assume that they can call on Cor for military force in this system – and they will *not* bring a force capable of defeating Cor's squadron.

"If no-one is warned, the next Hand to arrive will walk straight into a trap. It will end with Vaughn and Cor in open rebellion against Mars – and once he's gone that far, how patient do you think he'll be with your rebellion? What limits do you think he will put on his men then, with no outside eyes to fool?"

The little side room was silent for a full minute, and then second woman spoke quietly.

"We lost a lot of our firepower in Allarain," she admitted. "What even Alpha doesn't know yet," she glanced sideways at Armstrong, "is that most of our pilots for our southern squadron were among those captured. We don't have backups. We barely managed to train enough people to field our aircraft as-is."

Damien nodded slowly, and the beginnings of a plan began to come together in his mind.

"You need those pilots," he said aloud. "I need access to the Runic Transceiver Array in downtown Nouveau Versailles – a task for which a distraction would be helpful."

"All the prisoners from Allarain are held in the Versailles Bastille, about fifteen kilometers outside the city," Armstrong objected. "The place is a fortress – automated anti-aircraft guns, robot sentinels, tracking turrets."

"All automatic?" Damien asked.

"What else would they be?" Armstrong demanded.

"If I can give you a way into the Versailles Bastille, can you get me into the RTA?"

Armstrong glanced at her companion, then back to Damien.

"I'd say there's no way, but you managed to get the Greens out of Sunshine. Can you really open a path into the Bastille?"

The golden hand inside Damien's jacket, the one containing override codes that would work on any computer in the Protectorate, suddenly felt very, very heavy.

"Yes," he said simply.

Armstrong nodded sharply.

"Then I think we can get you to the Array."

#

Chapter 26

"I know I'm just the bodyguard around here," Amiri said bluntly as she stepped into Montgomery's hotel room, "but having *some* idea what the hell you're planning would be helpful."

The Envoy had covered what he was doing when the door had opened, but once he glanced up and saw it was her he slipped his personal computer out from under the blankets. He was sitting cross-legged on the bed, and flicked the door shut behind Amiri with a small hand gesture.

"You're not just the bodyguard," he told her mildly. "I'd be dead without you – or lost, without a clue where to find the rebels. Have a seat," he gestured to the chair and tiny desk on one side of the room.

"The only thing we have that can get into the Bastille is that little golden toy of yours," she reminded him. "Last time I checked, that would mean *you* have to go there. But I can't speak to Desmond, I'll get stuck with flunkies."

"Correct on all points but one," the Envoy told her dryly, then held up his wrist with the personal computer. The Hand was slotted into one of the data access ports and a regular data key was in one of the others.

Every time she saw the Hand, Amiri started to get nervous. Damien was… young, polite, and, with the Runes of Power carved into his body, an extraordinarily powerful Mage. She also knew, unlike most, that he already had a body count to make serial killers blush.

He also seemed to be under the illusion it was possible to *have* the Hand without *being* a Hand. No-one in the galaxy would question the right of someone bearing that icon to give any order they wished, to wield the full power of the Mage-King. However, it had ended up in his hands, it was *his* Hand. Which meant that, regardless of what the earnest young man sitting on the bed thought, he *was* a Hand of the Mage-King of Mars.

Montgomery was a small man, looking almost like a child as he sat cross-legged on the bed. He was young and earnest, and more than a little attractive – and she was terrified of him.

"Which point am I wrong on?" she finally asked.

"The Hand is not the only tool we can break the Bastille's defenses with," he told her. "While the icon itself can override any of our computers, anywhere, anytime, it can also generate onetime override codes that can be used separately from it."

He pulled the data key from his PC and handed it to Amiri. She took it, staring down at it in shock. It felt far too light for what was arguably one of the more powerful cyber-weapons in the galaxy.

"That data key carries a code that will disable the Bastille's defenses under a Royal Override," Montgomery continued. "In theory, it should only work once. In practice..." he shrugged. "It's quite possible it could be re-used repeatedly on different systems."

"That's... dangerous to give the Wing," she said slowly. "We're working with them for now, but..."

"They may still turn against the Protectorate," Montgomery agreed. "That's why I'm not giving it to them. I'm giving it to you. You'll have to accompany the Bastille strike, de-activate the defenses for them."

She stared down at the key for a long moment.

"And how am I supposed to keep *you* alive if I'm a hundred kilometers away while you assault one of the most fortified locations on the planet?" she asked.

"When not concussed, I am generally capable of taking care of myself," he said dryly. "Perhaps more to the point, my understanding is that Alpha's plan is more of an infiltration than an outright assault.

"Also, I need you at the Bastille," he finished softly. "While Vaughn may have chosen to shove his Freedom Wing prisoners in there, it *is* a maximum security prison. The kind of people who end up in those places... I don't want them out by accident."

There was a tinge of what might have been... guilt? in his words. Amiri wasn't sure what that was about – but she also knew that she didn't have Montgomery's whole story. She wasn't sure if anyone who *hadn't* been on his old ship did, who was alive at least. Stealey had to have known it all.

"All right," she allowed. "But if you get yourself killed, I will find a way to bring you back so I can kill you again myself. Understood?"

#

Lori wasn't expecting to interrupt much of anything when she barged into Sierra's room – the Legatan woman was a quiet sort, with no hobbies the rebel leader was aware of. What she found forced her to a sudden standstill, and she began slowly shuffling back.

"You may as well stay," the other woman told her. Sierra was kneeling on the ground, an open book laying on the ground before her. Returning to the book, she continued to read, softly.

"He trains my hands for battle, so that my arms can bend a bow of bronze. You have also given me the shield of Your salvation, And Your right hand upholds me; And Your gentleness makes me great."

Closing the Bible, Sierra crossed herself and rose smoothly to her feet.

"How may I help you, Alpha?"

Lori studied the Legatan soldier carefully. Religion was not uncommon in the Protectorate – most of Ardennes' people were Quebec Reformation Catholics – but it was generally regarded as something private. While she *recognized* the Psalm Sierra had been reading, it caused her to look at the woman in a new light.

"I'm sorry for interrupting," she said finally. "I should have waited."

"We are effectively at war," Sierra told her with a small smile. "God will understand."

"I should still at least *knock*, Alissa," Lori acknowledged, and Alissa Leclair bowed slightly.

"Apology accepted, then," the Legatan woman told her. "And I repeat myself: how may I help?"

"What did you think of Montgomery?" Lori asked. She'd asked the other woman to accompany her as much as a bodyguard as anything else, though having now met the unassuming man who bore the Mage-King's Warrant, she wasn't sure she'd ever been in danger.

"He's... not what I expected," Leclair allowed. "But I think that makes him more dangerous, not less. He would not bear the paper he bears were he weak."

"Do you think he can do what he promises?"

Access to the Bastille and the liberation of Leclair's pilots would be a game-changer – one that would enable them to do *something*, even though Lori wasn't yet sure what that something would be yet.

"Yes," the Legatan said flatly. "But I worry about hitching ourselves to him, Alpha. We look to Mars to save us from Versailles – but Versailles *answers* to Mars. How blind can they have been?"

"You think we shouldn't work with him?"

Leclair glanced away and sighed.

"No, I think we have to work with him," she admitted. "Or Vaughn will burn us all down with him – Montgomery offers a chance to stop him. But watch your step," the pilot told Lori. "He won't be here next year. He doesn't have to live with the consequences – and he *won't* share your vision of Ardennes."

"Except of an Ardennes that no longer has Michael Vaughn as Governor."

"Yeah," Leclair snorted. "That vision he shares. Vaughn killed a Hand. A Hand falls. Another rises. Mars will burn him to ash. It's the world *after* Vaughn where you may have problems."

"Sufficient unto today are the sins thereof," Lori told her quietly. "Without him we have nothing."

"I'm here to help, boss," the Legatan woman who'd trained and commanded Lori's handful of aircraft pilots told her. "What do you need me to do?"

"Pick someone else to lead the Bastille op," Lori instructed. "I've got a plan to get Montgomery into and out of the Transceiver Array, but I want a fall-back if everything falls apart. You're it – you'll fly him in and out in one of the gunships."

"I'll have *some* kind of ID for this stunt, right?" Leclair asked. "We are talking the Array in the middle of the Nouveaux Versailles government district, after all. Security is going to be damned tight."

"You'll have an ID, even an official flight plan," the Freedom Wing's leader promised. "If everything goes according to plan, no-one will ever know you were there."

Leclair shook her head. "I think I've heard that one before," she replied dryly. "I don't remember it ending well."

#

Chapter 27

The Freedom Wing's underground airbase was impressive to Damien. They'd clearly spent a lot of time and resources blasting the secret facility into the mountain, and then covering up what they'd done to anyone looking from outside or above.

It reminded him, in many ways, of Olympus Mons. Of course, the Mountain had been dug out to protect against a world with an atmosphere – then, at least – hostile to human life. Freedom Wing's Airbase Alpha had been designed to hide.

He and Amiri had entered the base through a natural-appearing cave he would have completely dismissed had Riordan not led them directly to it. The rebel had used a flashlight to guide their way through the rough terrain, until the cave had smoothed out and met a large metal hatch, still with no lighting.

Once inside the security hatch and past the armed guards, the complex turned into machine-smoothed stone walls and floors familiar to any resident of Olympus Mons. It lacked the runes that turned Olympus Mons into a giant amplifier, but those were unique. They had been carved to allow the Olympus Project to identify even the tiniest sparks of magical gift and judge the successes of their eugenics program.

The failures of said program had covered large swathes of Olympus Mons in small, unmarked, graves.

Damien shivered. For all that his home was now under a mountain, cave complexes made him claustrophobic.

They had, at least, now entered the main hangar area. From the size of the space, he assumed it had started as a natural cavern – there was no way they could have excavated the immense open space the helicopter gunships sat in without attracting *some* attention.

The gunships themselves held most of Damien's attention. They were impressive craft, twenty meters from the tip of the nose to the end of the tail rotor. Instead of the single rotor assembly of a less stealthy aircraft, they had an assembly on either side of the main craft, with casings wrapped around the rotors to muffle the sound. The entire chassis was coated in a dark gray ceramic coating he recognized from one of the many intelligence briefings on Mars – a radar absorbing material developed by the Legatus Armed Forces.

Looking over the aircraft again, he realized he recognized them from that same briefing.

"Last time I checked, the Phantom V wasn't supposed to leave Legatus," he said mildly to Riordan. "Something about Charter restrictions on top-line military hardware."

The Wing had acquired more than just the gunships, too. There were crates of munitions along one wall – enough to supply the single squadron here for a dozen battles. Fueling stations, reloading robots, maintenance gear – someone had delivered a complete mobile airbase to Ardennes, under the nose of both Vaughn's government and the Martian Navy. It fell to Mars, after all, to enforce the Charter restrictions on top-line military hardware.

A planet could *develop* whatever they wanted for their own forces, but military hardware had to be approved for inter-planet sale by Mars. It was a rule often winked at, but rarely to the extent of entire top-of-the-line aircraft squadrons ending up in the hands of rebel groups.

"I... have no idea," Riordan told him, the speaker and rabble-rouser looking confused. "I wasn't involved in acquiring them."

"Oh, he's right," Sierra interjected, the Legatan pilot joining them as they stood at the edge of the underground airfield, eyeing the dangerous looking vehicles. "They're the current generation of stealth gunship, I don't think the LAF has even finished rolling them out to all of their own ground support units. I have *no* clue how the hell the smuggler we bought them from got them – and I didn't ask," she finished cheerfully.

"Today, I'm glad you've got them," Damien admitted, eyeing the formidable war machines. "*How* you got them concerns me, but today I'm glad you have them."

Shaking his head, he turned his attention from the gunships to the woman who commanded them.

"This is your operation, Sierra," he told her. "Amiri has the virus to disable the Bastille's defenses. She'll be able to transmit it via any short-range radio once you're close enough – *should* be from outside any active kill zone."

"'Should' isn't a reassuring word, Envoy," Sierra said dryly. "But I get it. Hey, Brute!" she bellowed, gesturing for a small man, barely taller than Damien's own underwhelming height but blond to the Envoy's brunette, to join them.

"This is Brute," she introduced him as he approached. "He's my second-in-command, and will be in charge of the Bastille strike force. He'll have five gunships and thirty guys and gals with the best gear we've got."

"*Bonjour*," Brute greeted them all, bowing slightly at Sierra's introductions. "I've friends in the Bastille," he told them in thickly accented English. "But those turrets and kill-bots..." he shivered.

"Will all be shut down," Damien promised. "And there's almost no human presence on the site, so once the computerized weaponry shuts down, you should have a clean shot at your people."

Automated prisons were common in the Protectorate – highly secured facilities that would feed the prisoners, clean the cells, and prevent escapes with almost no human involvement whatsoever. It reduced the concern about objects being smuggled in, and the use of SmartDarts in at least the innermost layers of security really did allow the robots to shoot first and leave the questions for the humans.

Of course, computer security was *the* top priority for prisons like the Bastille. The one thing they hadn't counted on was someone from Mars showing up with the override codes. Since the facilities needed to be controlled by humans, there had to be override codes – and every government computer in the Protectorate could be accessed and overridden by a Hand.

The rebels didn't know Damien had a Hand, and that was how he planned to keep it. Even this small use of it made him feel like a fraud – he'd only had the icon for one mission, and he certainly didn't have the authority to use it to break open a high security prison!

But regardless of whether he was *supposed* to have it, he did. And he was too short on tools and allies to ignore his most powerful weapon just because he felt like a fraud.

#

Chapter 28

There was something lately about small men being utterly terrifying.

Amiri held onto the straps holding her into the gunship with white fingers as they tore over the treetops with a meter or so to spare. Brute clearly knew the *exact* capabilities of the aircraft he flew, and he brought them in towards the Bastille at a speed and margin that put Royal Martian Marine Corps assault pilots she'd known to shame.

The other four gunships followed behind at a more sedate pace, leaving it to Brute and Amiri to test – and hopefully disable – the Nouveaux Versailles Bastille's defenses.

"We're clearing the forest in about thirty seconds," the pilot informed her. "There's only about twenty kay of plains before the Bastille and we're running at full power, not stealth – we'll be challenged before we're fifteen kay out and the systems will fire at ten."

That didn't take much translating. Amiri slotted the data key Damien had given her into the aircraft's communication system and accessed the files. A few keystrokes later, and she was looking up as they passed out from over the forest and into the plains near the city of Nouveau Versailles.

A light blinked to life on the console – an incoming communication.

"Unidentified aircraft, this is Nouveaux Versailles Bastille," a male voice announced in a bored tone. "You appear to be on course for our facility. Please either identify yourself or change course as you are about to enter a no-fly zone that will be enforced with lethal force."

Amiri smiled coldly and hit the transmit key. Seconds passed.

"Unidentified aircraft, this is the Bastille," the voice said again, now starting to sound less bored. "I repeat, you are entering a no-fly zone enforced by automated anti-aircraft weaponry. Identify yourself or break off."

"Did they get the transmission?" Brute asked, his voice concerned.

She checked the system. A blinking icon informed her she'd received a text-only message from the system.

"We're in and their security system is down," she told him. "I don't know how long till he," she gestured at the speaker, "realizes that."

"What the hell are you *doing*?" the voice demanded. "I cannot stand down the system; if you do not identify yourself in the next thirty seconds, the guns *will* fire!"

"Wish me luck," Brute told Amiri, his hands on the controls as white as hers. "This could be very, very messy."

They crossed the ten kilometer mark and none of the threat indicators lit up. Amiri held her breath until they hit five kilometers and Brute began slowing the aircraft.

"Your wonder boy delivered," the pilot said, his voice surprised. "I'll call in the rest of the squadron – you want to talk to cranky voice?"

Amiri nodded and pulled up the communication system.

"Bastille, this is the Freedom Wing," she told them calmly. "We are now in control of your defenses. Surrender now, and no-one will be harmed."

The channel was silent, and Brute slowed the gunship to a halt, rotating it over the main courtyard and looking for defenders. No-one reacted for a moment, and Amiri saw the icons of the other four gunships appear on Brute's screen.

"You're insane," the Bastille controller finally replied. "You'll never get away with this!"

"That's tomorrow's problem," Amiri told him sweetly. "We're here for our people. Any of yours who get in the way die. Your call."

She killed the channel and turned to Brute.

"Take us down," she ordered.

#

At some point, Vaughn was sure, the woman in charge of the emergency command center was going to work up the nerve to tell her planet's leader to get *out* of the center's main operating theater. Depending on what was going on at that moment in time, he might even listen to her.

Until she did, however, this was the best place to keep an eye on the events rapidly sweeping Ardennes. Allarain had been their biggest – if most mixed – success, but operations were being carried out across the planet.

So far, most successes had been minor. Given time, however, he was sure they'd find another loose thread that would lead them to either the Wing – or perhaps even more importantly, to Montgomery. The last thing Vaughn needed was someone with *authority* to counter his tale of what had happened.

The various techs and officers were quiet, trying carefully *not* to attract the Mage-Governor's attention. When one of them started tapping keys with a concerned face, their muttering caught his ear.

"What is it, son?" Vaughn asked, the surprise of his arrival causing the young man to swallow his gum and choke.

Glynn Stewart

A glass of water and a chance to regain his equilibrium later, the officer – a lanky blond youth barely old enough for his Lieutenant's bars, checked his screens again then looked up at the Governor.

"The Nouveaux Versailles Bastille has gone off the air," he admitted aloud.

"That's not possible," the Colonel commanding the center objected. The woman had clearly seen Vaughn descend on her staff officer and rushed over to either save his ass or throw him under the bus – the Governor wasn't sure which.

"Why not?" Vaughn asked quietly. "We've over thirty Freedom Wing terrorists locked up there. If there's anywhere the rebels would try and attack, it would be that Bastille. It *should* be suicide," he agreed, "but they may still manage to disable the communications."

"The Bastilles aren't radio stations that can just 'go off the air'," the Colonel replied, a strained patience in her voice that Vaughn noted for later. "They're the highest security prisons on the planet. They have hard lines and dedicated communication satellites; there is no way for them to be jammed or cut off."

"I'd agree with you ma'am," the Lieutenant told her, with a panicked glance at Vaughn. "Except that we're getting *no* communication from them. I've tested the channels – the satellite and cable are still intact. There's just... nothing *coming* from the Bastille."

"Get me satellite overhead," Vaughn demanded. "If we have a dedicated coms satellite, please tell me it has a fucking camera?"

"It should, sir," the junior officer told him, busying himself with his console as Vaughn turned a wary eye on the Colonel.

"What do we have as a rapid reaction force?" he demanded.

"... not much," she admitted. "Most of the Scorpions are tied up in the global sweep for the terrorists. We could leverage Army units, but..."

"I'd rather not have the Army in one of the Bastilles," Vaughn agreed, considering.

"I've got visual on Versailles Bastille, sir, ma'am," the Lieutenant interjected. Without asking for further instruction, he threw the satellite image up on the screen where his two superiors could see.

Two helicopter gunships, their forms vague and blurry as their mottled gray color closely matched the concrete below them, orbited the central courtyard. Three *more* were on the ground. It was hard to tell at the level of detail on the image, but it looked like they were unloading people.

"That's not *possible*," the Colonel objected. "The anti-air would have shot down anyone trying to assault the facility!"

"It has *happened*, Colonel," Vaughn told her sharply. He turned back to the junior officer. "What is your name, son?"

"Lieutenant Romain Duval, sir," the youth replied.

"Well, *Captain* Duval, get me Generals Montoya and Zu on the line on the double," Vaughn ordered the freshly promoted officer. Proving his worth almost immediately, Duval promptly grabbed the nearest three techs and began placing calls.

Vaughn turned back to the Colonel in charge of the center.

"My aversion to Army units is weakening, Colonel," he admitted. "But please tell me we have something else."

"We have a battalion running air and ground security on the Central District itself," she told him, consulting her personal computer as she spoke. "If we strip them down to the exterior barricades – leave the RTA to regular security guards and a few patrols, we should be able to load two companies – four hundred men – into transports in the next half an hour."

Vaughn considered. He didn't *like* leaving the Central District vulnerable – while he'd organized the only actual attack to hit there himself, there was a risk the attack had emboldened groups that didn't realize that.

The alternative was to watch the only prisoners they'd taken be whisked out of his highest security prison like it was a *daycare*.

"Do it," he ordered, then turned to Captain Duval. "Do you have them?"

"Both General Zu and General Montoya are on the line and waiting in your office, sir," the young man replied.

"Thank you, Captain."

#

Amiri transferred the link to the Bastille's systems to her personal computer and dropped out of the back of the gunship. The Wing had provided her with a set of body armor, and no-one had yet tried to take the battle laser back.

Landing in the middle of the courtyard, she waved Brute back into the air as she ducked over to the short platoon of troopers the Wing had sent along.

"Keep an eye on us from above," she told the pilot. "We're not *trying* to be sneaky, so it's not a question of *if* help is coming, you get me?"

"I got you," Brute replied. "Good luck!"

Turning to the troops around here, Amiri gave them a wintry smile.

"Looks like the Scorpions are keeping their heads down," she said loudly. "Unfortunately for them, we need the command center – I can apparently shut down their guns more easily than I can get cell numbers!"

That got a chuckle from the rebels, though it was also completely true. The codes Montgomery had provided had allowed her to assume direct control of the Bastille's weapons systems and shut down their communications, but it didn't actually give her access to the Bastille's internal databases.

At least some of the rebels knew the rough layout of the facility, though, and the assault team quickly sorted themselves out into order as they charged deeper into the massive concrete fortress.

The first few floors passed with no resistance. Amiri spotted the hatches and rails of layer upon layer of automated defenses that would have killed them all in the first few steps, but the codes Montgomery had given her had shut everything down.

Two floors down, they ran into a heavy security gate. The automated turrets on either side were slumped in uselessness, but the heavy steel barricade itself remained in place.

"Should we blast it?" one of the troopers, carrying a similar laser to Amiri's own, asked.

"Give me a moment," she replied. There was a keypad next to the door. She crossed to it and checked it against her personal computer. The data key Montgomery had given her hummed softly for less than a second and then threw up an eight digit code.

Waving for the rebels to take up positions, she punched in the code. The lights on the pad flashed several times, then the door slowly ground upwards.

The Scorpions on the other side had clearly been expecting a more violent breach. It took them a moment to process the door opening from behind their impromptu barricade – a moment the rebels took full advantage of to grab whatever cover they could.

Amiri pressed herself against the wall next to the keypad, taking cover against the disabled turret as a fusillade of bullets passed her in both directions.

Then the distinctive 'hiss-*crack*' of a weapons grade laser hitting skin and vaporizing chunks of flesh interrupted the gunfire, followed almost immediately by the rapid coughing sound of an automatic grenade launcher.

Six explosions later, the gunfire from inside the hatch ceased. It took a moment more for the rebels to stop shooting – their trigger discipline was better than she'd expected, but still worse than real soldiers or even the bounty hunters she'd worked with before.

Two of the Freedom Wing rebels were wounded. Stepping through the hatchway, Amiri counted six... possibly seven, it was hard to be sure, Scorpions. The prison guards had carried light weapons and no body armor, versus the heavy weapons and combat body armor the Freedom Wing had equipped their people with.

It hadn't been a fair fight.

"This way, we're still four floors up from the command center," the rebel leading the way said grimly.

"How many guards are there?" Amiri asked, falling into step beside him.

"Not many," he told her. "When the ASPF" – Ardennes System Police Force, the star system level police force that the Scorpions tended to walk all over now – "ran the Bastilles, we had twenty people in each. They couldn't add many more without turning cells into barracks."

"Let's hope they didn't," she replied, glancing back at the two soldiers they were leaving behind with one of their pair of medics. "I don't know if we can handle being outnumbered."

#

Every step forward and down from the first ambush left Amiri waiting for the second shoe to drop. Half a dozen guys with light gear were a lot less resistance than she'd been expecting. Despite the assurances that the Bastille's relied almost entirely on automated security, she hadn't really believed that shutting everything down with Montgomery's codes would really see them through.

The first ambush remained the only ambush, however, as they descended ten floors to the underground levels of the Bastille and approached the heavy security hatch sealing the Bastille's currently impotent command center away from the rest of the fortress prison.

"No explosives," she ordered. Glancing at the array of weapons the rebels were carrying, she sighed. "No bullets, either. Gas grenades first, then lasers – *carefully*," she warned the other two gunners carrying battle lasers.

Once she was sure the rebels – not a group known for being disciplined troops at the best of times – were going to follow her orders, she punched the code Montgomery's data key had given her into the pad. The heavy hatch groaned and slowly began to move.

The grenadiers didn't *quite* follow her orders, she noted. Of the grenades thrown through as the door began to open, at least two were smoke grenades, not gas grenades.

Given the thermal optics on the lasers, that worked out quite well.

Amiri dove through the hatch once it was open enough for her, relying on the smoke to cover her arrival. Flashes on the thermal scope marked weapons fire aimed at her, and she returned fire. Invisible pulses of lased light burned paths through the smoke and vaporized flesh.

Other thermal signatures hit the ground, Scorpions giving up the fight. A few seconds of smoke-filled chaos, and then silence reigned as the air exchange labored mightily to clear the air.

As the smoke faded, Amiri leveled her laser on one of the men who'd hit the floor. He blinked away the smoke, his eyes red and wide he stared at the business end of the crystalline lasing chamber.

"Play nice, now," she instructed. Glancing around the room, she saw that the rebels were efficiently cuffing the wounded and uninjured alike. It didn't look like any of the Freedom Wing fighters had been injured, but four more Scorpions were dead, with six prisoners.

The Scorpions apparently had *reduced* the manpower at the prison from when the police had run it.

"You look like you're in charge here," she addressed the prisoner at the end of her weapon. His collar bore the insignia of a Captain, which meant he was the shift commander if not the base commander; with less than twenty men on site, she wasn't ruling out the latter.

"You're *insane*," he told her. "What do you want?"

"I answer to a higher authority than you," Julia Amiri, Protectorate Secret Service Agent, told the paramilitary officer bluntly. "What I want from *you* is the locations of the Freedom Wing prisoners that were brought here over the last few days. Can I trust you to pull that out of the system without doing something stupid?"

The Scorpion officer nodded slowly, rising and returning to his chair at a gesture from her laser. As he began to work, she linked into the system from her personal computer and began to see what information she could access.

Ah! That was the external sensors.

Oh.

She hit the communicator.

"Brute, you have incoming," she told the pilot. "I'm only *seeing* transports, but I'm guessing they'll be jets or helicopters of some kind to keep you busy."

"Oh, what a lovely day," he replied with a laugh. "I was starting to get bored."

"You're nuts," Amiri told him. "Pass it on to the Envoy as well," she reminded him. "If they've pulled that many troops out of Versailles, he should be clear all the way in!"

#

Chapter 29

Among the many talents of the Legatus Phantom V, it turned out, was the ability to tune its stealth coating to produce a completely false radar return. A pointless trick in daylight, it definitely had its uses on a foggy evening like the one wrapping Nouveaux Versailles.

Damien sat in the co-pilot's seat next to Sierra, watching in silence as the Legatan woman deftly negotiated her way through the fog and the late evening air traffic towards the spherical marble dome of the Ardennes Runic Transceiver Array.

They were close enough now that he could begin to feel the thrum of the power of the Array's runes. The hemispherical dome was identical to others he'd seen pictures of, though the one at Olympus Mons was buried underground with the rest of the Mountain's runes and infrastructure.

Underneath that dome were layers of silver runes, each inlaid into one of sixty-four separate hemispheres, each smaller than the one outside it and linked to the layer beneath.

Building an Array was a project of years, dozens of highly trained Mages, and massive amounts of money. Necessary as they were for interstellar communication, most of the Fringe worlds didn't have one.

Ardennes, so far as most of its people were concerned, might as well not. The marble dome was inside a ten foot tall concrete wall, broken at even intervals with guard towers. A ring of anti-aircraft turrets sat inside that wall, one of the guns tracking the helicopter as they approached.

"ARTA Control, this is flight F-451," Sierra said into the communicator. "We are en route to the ARTA Landing Pad, I have Mister Brad Jolie aboard for his scheduled thirty minute usage window."

She turned to Damien.

"Jolie is a mid-level executive and Mage with StellarCharm Interstellar," she told him. "He *could* use the RTA to talk to his headquarters, but never has. We borrowed his authorization codes – and nobody at the Array should know what he looks like."

"Flight F-451," the radio crackled. "You are cleared to approach and land at pad two. The RTA schedule is clear, the coordinator will meet Mister Jolie at the main entrance. Welcome to ARTA, F-451."

"We're in," Sierra whispered. "I'll get us on the pad. After that, it's up to you, Mister Montgomery."

"It's a glorified phone call," Damien reminded her. "I think I'll be fine."

The helicopter settled onto the pad, and Sierra gestured toward the exit.

#

The coordinator was a slim woman dressed in a plain black suit. She greeted Damien with a perfunctory handshake and gestured for him to follow her.

Her cold shoulder was perfectly fine with him. Despite all the effort that had gone into this trip, they hadn't had the time or luck to acquire a civilian helicopter for the visit. The Phantom V was a stealthy, capable craft – but it couldn't disguise that it was an attack aircraft to anyone actually *looking* at the thing.

The coordinator's perfunctory greetings meant she didn't have the time to realize what the vehicle he'd arrived on was before leading him into the massive marble dome. A massive pair of security hatches slid aside at a handprint from the woman, and he was inside.

He tried not to inhale obviously as the wave of power hit him. Very few people, even among Mages, could sense the surrounding energy the way he could. Even among those Mages, only Rune Wrights like himself and the Mage-King could read the runes around him at a glance.

The flow of energy around him was all directed towards one place. The suited woman led the way deep into the maze of layers, past a small set of offices and through several more security doors.

Finally, the last security door opened into the polished black innermost hemisphere. Silver runes glittered across the onyx room, all of them slowly spiraling into a single black plinth at the exact center of the hemisphere.

Another suited woman, this one wearing the gold medallion of a Mage, was standing next to the plinth, waiting for any inbound communication. At the sight of Damien and the RTA coordinator, she nodded slightly and stepped past them, heading for the office suite.

"My communication is confidential," Damien told the coordinator. "I'm going to have to ask for privacy, and for the recording devices to be disabled."

Normally, every sound in an RTA chamber was recorded, as the same chamber that transmitted also received. The Mage who'd been in the room when they arrived would have responded to any unscheduled communication and the recordings would have been forwarded to those who needed to know.

"With the planetwide security situation, we're under orders from the Governor's Office not to shut down the recording devices, sir," the coordinator told him, the first words she'd said to him since his arrival.

"I was not informed of this when I booked my window," Damien told her, doing his best to imitate the coldly arrogant tones and posture of a senior corporate executive. "My information is time-sensitive and must be transmitted to my head office tonight. I am not prepared to have it recorded for the paranoia of a backwater governor who can't deal with some raggedy-assed terrorists."

"You are welcome to reschedule your window," the coordinator told him. "I don't know when the restrictions on recordings will be lifted, though."

Despite the prissy, bored, tone of her voice as she rejected his request, she stretched out her hand to him, palm open in a universal gesture.

With a sigh, Damien dropped a credit chip – one of several anonymized chips he'd carried to Ardennes in various denominations – into her hand. He'd expected to have to bribe his way in, and the amount on the chip was likely several months salary for the woman.

She glanced at it, checking the number on her PC, then tapped a command on the computer.

"Recorders are off," she told him in the same prissy, bored tone. "No-one is scheduled to be in until morning. Let Mage Trudeau know you're done when you leave."

Damien waited patiently while the woman left, looking around to try to identify the recorders she'd disabled. Thanks to a briefing from the Protectorate Secret Service, intended for *exactly* this circumstance, he quickly identified all twelve of the microphones. With a tiny burst of magic, he burned them all out.

Since they were turned off, it would take a while for anyone to notice – and tonight, he needed to be sure.

With a deep breath he stepped forward to the plinth and removed his elbow-length gloves. Laying his bare hands on the plinth, he channeled energy through the runes in his skin and into the massive assemblage of runes and power around him.

The Array didn't know where to send the energy, but *he* did. He'd checked the calculations again on the helicopter flight and knew exactly where to send it. The catchment area of a Runic Transceiver Array wasn't much smaller than the planet it was built on, but from thirty-some light years away even that was a tiny target.

He hit it perfectly.

"This is an Alpha One Priority Communication," he said aloud, the magic whisking his words across the light years. "Authentication Lima Victor Romeo Seven Seven Sierra Six Five Romeo Alpha Lima. I repeat, this is an Alpha One Priority Communication."

He took a breath.

"I need to speak to Desmond Alexander immediately."

The tiny room was silent for a moment, and then a sleepy voice suddenly echoed into it.

"This is Mars RTA Control, we are receiving you," the Mage on the other end told him. "It's past midnight here, we're not waking the Mage-King up. We'll record your message and have it added to his morning queue."

"What part of Alpha One Priority did you not get?" Damien demanded. "Confirm the authentication."

"We authenticated the code, we'll have it added to his priority queue. Please transmit for recording."

Damien paused, taking a deep breath as he considered the relatively quiet life of the bureaucratic Mage on the other end, and then ran out of patience.

"This is Envoy Damien Montgomery, and you have confirmed this is an authenticated Alpha One request," he said harshly. "Every second this channel is open risks being bought with blood. Unless that is a bill you wish me to levy on *you* when I return, I suggest you wake Desmond Alexander the fuck up."

A long moment of silence followed.

"My apologies, Envoy," the voice, no longer sleepy, finally answered. "I will contact the King's staff immediately, please hold the channel."

#

With the Freedom Wing fighters scattered throughout the Bastille, opening cells and rescuing their friends, the command center rapidly got very quiet around Amiri. Two of the rebels had stayed to keep an eye on their Scorpion prisoners, but for some reason no-one in the room seemed inclined to strike up a conversation.

The controls for the various screens and systems of the fortress prison were hardly intuitive, but she'd at least managed to access the facility's radar and automatic warbook and throw up the approaching air transports on a large screen.

The Bastille's new 'defenders' had gone to full stealth mode on the Phantom V's, leaving plain transport helicopters the only aircraft on the scanners. Twenty of the big aircraft had lifted off from Nouveaux Versailles Central District and headed her way.

That meant roughly four hundred soldiers. While that was a *lot* more people than she had in the fortress, she trusted Brute to even the odds.

She was starting to wonder where the *Scorpions'* escorts were when the screen suddenly flashed up new threat warnings. High-powered radar sweeps hammered across the sky as six jet fighters came dropping in from high altitude at Mach Two.

In theory, the radar sweeps from the jet fighters' high-powered arrays should have picked up even stealthed craft. In practice, the Phantom Vs were almost forty years newer than the fighters available to the Ardennes Special Security Service.

Amiri wasn't sure what the detection threshold for the Phantoms was, but they weren't showing up on the Bastille's huge radar dishes. There was no way the jet fighters saw anything.

That is, until Brute's team opened fire. Each of the five gunships fired a pair of anti-radiation missiles, blasting high into the air towards the jet fighters.

The Scorpion aircraft went into evasive maneuvers – but kept their radars on, trying desperately to locate the Freedom Wing helicopters. It was exactly the wrong thing to do, as the ARMs homed in on the radar emissions with deadly precision.

Sixty seconds after the jet fighters fired up their radar, they were descending fireballs, leaving the transport helicopters wide open to Brute's squadron.

The *smart* pilots realized it. The neat formation of transports came apart into swirling chaos – some pilots diving for the ground, others turning to run.

Six of the transport helicopters kept grimly on. A hundred and twenty Scorpions died moments later as heat-seeking missiles flashed through the air, scattering the aircraft and their passengers across the sky.

It took Amiri a moment to understand what she was seeing on the radar after that. Then she pulled up the view from a camera on top of the fortress.

White specks were beginning to fill the sky under the transports. Troops, crew and pilots recognized the futility of trying to take on the deadly aircraft Legatus had given the rebels and bailed out.

Her sensors didn't have enough resolution to say how many *people* escaped. From how long it took Brute's team to destroy the remaining helicopters, it looked like he gave those bailing out the time to do so; it was likely more of the troops escaped than she thought.

Not one of the helicopters survived to land or flee.

#

Mage-Commodore Adrianna Cor watched the destruction of the assault force in a state of not quite shock. The jet fighters had taken the exactly correct approach to knowing the enemy had stealth craft, and all it had done was seal their fates.

That was *military* technology – *real* military, not Ardennes' glorified backwater militia. Martian Marines could duplicate the stunt the rebels had just pulled, but a ragtag bunch of revolutionaries *shouldn't have* that tech.

"Any ID on those aircraft?" she demanded of her CIC staff.

"Nothing yet," the Mage-Commander running the shift reported. "But from the quality of the stealth tech... they're Core World-built. Probably either ours or Legatan."

"Could *we* detect them?"

"Not from space," the officer admitted. "But our assault shuttles should be able to from atmosphere."

Cor considered for a moment, glancing at the communications station. Even regardless of their unofficial agreements, this was a situation where the Governor could request the Navy's aid. She wouldn't normally *offer* it, but...

"Have Major Morales prepare three assault shuttles for a combat landing," she instructed. "Get me an ETA as soon as you can." She couldn't trust the Marines for *everything*, even if Corral and the other officers were mostly on side. He would know to send the... less reliable units for this. Those losses would be less inconvenient than others.

She stood and turned back to the communications station. "Please contact Mage-Governor Vaughn and direct the channel to my office. I'll be there by the time you have the channel up."

The young officer there barely had time to acknowledge her order before she swept out of the Simulacrum Chamber that acted as *Unchained Glory*'s bridge. Her office was barely ten meters down the corridor, and she had time to reach her desk and pour herself a glass of wine before the channel with Vaughn opened up.

"What do you want, Adrianna?" the Governor demanded. He looked frazzled – the chaos he'd created was starting to wear on him. "We have a bit of a situation down here."

"I'm aware of the situation at the Bastille," she told him. "I wanted to inform you that under Article Seventeen of the Protectorate Charter, we stand ready to assist in any way we can."

Vaughn winced. Article Seventeen covered situations of outside interference – but it also covered 'complete failure to maintain law and order by local forces'. Tucked away in the sub-clauses of Seventeen was the authority of a Hand to relieve a Governor – but also the clauses obligating the Navy to assist when rebels with offworld tech attacked a prison.

"Can you destroy the prison?" he finally asked. "I'm not going to miss a bunch of murderers and rebels."

Cor checked the figures on the Bastilles on her side screen and shook her head.

"We *could* destroy the Bastille with a kinetic bombardment," she told him. "However, you built them well. They're hardened against that kind of attack – the sustained sequence necessary to guarantee its destruction would cause major collateral damage to Nouveau Versailles itself."

"That is... not acceptable," he agreed after a moment. "What *can* you do?"

"My staff assures me that whatever stealth craft the rebels are in possession of will not be sufficient to defeat the sensors on our Marine assault shuttles," she told him calmly. "I can have three platoons of exosuited Marines and their assault shuttles on their way shortly. I think we can agree that a hundred and twenty exosuits should be able to neutralize our terrorists."

Vaughn looked like a drowning man thrown a rope.

"I agree completely," he told her. "I... always appreciate the willingness of the Royal Martian Navy to assist with our little problems."

"We'll see if we can make this one go away," she replied with a smile.

And unlike some *other* problems she'd dealt with for Vaughn, this one wouldn't be haunting her dreams.

#

Chapter 30

"Damien. You're alive."

He didn't have to ask who was speaking. After three years at Olympus Mons, Damien could recognize the voice of Desmond Michael Alexander the Third, Mage-King of Mars, in almost any circumstance.

Hearing it now, in the polished ebony heart of Ardennes' Runic Transceiver Array, caused him to sag in relief.

"My liege," he greeted Alexander, his voice thrown across the light years by magic. "I am. I don't know what you have been told about what happened here?"

"Vaughn reported a rebel attack and sabotage," Desmond said slowly, his voice heavy with emotion of some kind. "He told us that Alaura and all of her people were dead and the *Tides of Justice* destroyed by Freedom Wing saboteurs and attacks."

"He lied."

The two words landed in the hemispherical room like tombstones, and silence was his only answer for several moments.

"I'd guessed," Alexander said finally. "I am preparing a task force, but none of my Hands are available yet. What happened?"

"He used a secret team inside his Special Security Service to assemble and equip a 'rebel' faction that he controlled," Damien told his King quietly. "I believe he killed Alaura himself, but his tame rebels killed the rest of the team – and his own people shot down my shuttle, killing everyone aboard but myself.

"I'm sorry, my liege, but I am the only one left."

"I was afraid of that," Alexander replied. There was a long pause. "There is something else," he continued. "Vaughn's betrayal was expected. Sabotage would have been insufficient to destroy the *Tides*. Your Warrant alone should have sufficed for the local naval squadron to enact his removal."

"Mage-Commodore Cor has broken your Protectorate and betrayed Mars," Damien said quietly. "The *Tides of Justice* was destroyed by close-range fire from ships we thought were her sisters."

"Damn."

"I have made contact with the rebellion," Damien told his King. "They are helping me get access to the Transceiver Array, and I have helped them short-circuit some of Vaughn's excesses. Their resources are impressive; co-opting them has proven valuable."

"I trust the judgment of the man on the scene, Damien," Alexander said softly. "You bear my Warrant, you speak in my Voice – any promises you made in my name will be honored. You know this."

"I do," Damien acknowledged, swallowing hard.

"Vaughn must be removed," the Mage-King continued. "Too much blood has already been shed. What do you need?"

"Warships," Damien answered. "With Cor's betrayal, we need sufficient space-borne firepower to neutralize her squadron and the Ardennes Self Defense Force. I suspect every warship in the Ardennes system will obey either Vaughn or Cor, and will fight to defend them."

"I will arrange it," Alexander said flatly. "There should be sufficient ships in Tau Ceti, even if we have to borrow from the system fleet. Three days, Damien, and you will have your warships. Their commander will place herself at your command – do what you must."

"My command?" Damien asked. "I… cannot command warships." An Envoy did not hold what ancient Rome had called *imperium* – the right to command military force. A *Hand* did.

"Did Alaura give you the Hand?" the Mage-King of Mars asked bluntly.

The young Mage, so many light years away, swallowed hard and nodded. Realizing after a moment that his King could not see him, he spoke aloud.

"Yes."

"You stand on a world I cannot touch," Alexander told him. "You could have – you perhaps *should* have run. Have hidden, until a Hand arrived to fix the problem."

"Cor's betrayal would have destroyed them," Damien said. "It would have… betrayed the Protectorate."

"You stand on a world I cannot touch," the Mage-King repeated. "You bear my Hand, you speak with my Voice, you fight my battle – and you honor and *understand* my Protectorate.

"Damien Montgomery, regardless of the paperwork, regardless of announcements and ceremonies and grand speeches, you have *done* what I would have asked a Hand to do. So yes, the Naval forces sent to Ardennes will place themselves under your command.

"And yes, it will fall to you to remove Mage-Governor Vaughn. He will become desperate. The people of Ardennes will need a protector. It will fall to you.

"I need not send a Hand to Ardennes, for I already have one there.

"You are my Hand, Damien Montgomery," Desmond Michael Alexander said flatly. "You have bought that with blood and honor. A Hand falls. Another rises.

"The people of Ardennes, whether they know it or not, look to Mars for salvation. *I* look to *you* to answer them."

Damien swallowed hard again, but found his spine straightening at his King's words. Even though Alexander could not see him, he removed the Hand from his pocket and hung it around his neck, letting the golden symbol slip beneath his shirt and lie, cold, against his skin.

"I understand," he said slowly. "I will not fail them."

#

Chapter 31

This time when the contacts appeared on the Bastille's sensors, it took Amiri a moment to work out what was going on. She was watching for contacts inbound from Nouveau Versailles or approaching from the Army bases.

She hadn't been expecting anyone to drop from orbit.

The computers warned her there were contacts, but proved recalcitrant when it came to giving her more information. There weren't many things that could disguise themselves while dropping through atmosphere, but she knew of at least one.

Unfortunately for the Royal Martian Marine Corps, the Bastille had been equipped with extremely powerful radar arrays and the inevitable turbulence of entering atmosphere told her where to look. A few keystrokes aligned the big dishes and lit up the dropping assault shuttles with radio waves, exposing them amidst the turbulence of their descent.

Three modern RMMC assault shuttles. Depending on gear, that could be anywhere from sixty to a hundred and eighty Marines – loyal soldiers of the Protectorate, following orders from the rogue Mage-Commodore.

That… was a problem.

"Brute, this is Amiri," she said into the communicator. "We've got friends dropping from out of the sky. I think we're going to have to change plans."

"Saw the pulse," the pilot said calmly. The radar pulse would have highlighted the spacecraft to everyone for dozens of kilometers around. "We've got them outnumbered two to one."

"And each of those shuttles out-masses your entire squadron," Amiri said flatly. "They're bigger, they're better armed, and they have the altitude advantage. You can't fight them, Brute, and we always knew it was a chance we'd have to break out on the ground.

"Break off and get out of here," she ordered. "Meet us at the rendezvous point."

Silence.

"Fine," the rebel pilot told her. "You'd better have a plan," he continued.

"Go," she replied. She had at least two, but they were rapidly running out of time.

Flipping to another channel, she raised all of the Freedom Wing fighters in the building.

"All right everybody," she said briskly. "Everyone's favorite rogue Mage-Commodore has decided to play, and our flight has been canceled. Make your way to the Bastille motor pool on Level One, but keep an eye out for Marines." She paused. "If you run into them, hit them with everything you've got," she ordered quietly. "If they make it down, we're out of chances to change their minds."

Those orders given, she turned her attention back to her incoming guests. She had at least *one* shot at getting them to back down. Sighing, she grabbed the microphone for the Bastille's own communication system and hailed the incoming shuttles.

"Royal Marine Flight Group, be advised this facility is now under the jurisdiction of the Protectorate Secret Service," she told them. "Authentication Lima-Seven-Lima-Omega-Niner-Niner-Alpha-Five.

"I repeat, this facility is now under the jurisdiction of the Secret Service. Break off your approach and stand down, or I will be forced to destroy your shuttlecraft."

She waited. The automated message receipt system on the assault shuttles told her they'd got the transmission, but none of them replied. They were now a hundred kilometers up and dropping fast. She had... minutes.

"Royal Marine Flight Group, this is your final warning," she said calmly. "This facility has been seized by the Protectorate Secret Service, authentication Lima-Seven-Lima-Omega-Niner-Niner-Alpha-Five.

"If you do not break off your approach and stand down, I *will* be forced to defend this facility with all available force. This is your final warning."

As she spoke, she began to access the anti-aircraft systems. Unless she was severely mistaken, the Bastille had surface-to-air missiles designed to shoot down incoming shuttlecraft. The codes Montgomery had given her could be used to turn them on as well as off.

The problem was that it was easier to shut down *everything* than to turn on something specific. She didn't even need to activate the IFF – Brute's squadron was out of the free-fire zone. She just needed the launchers *active*.

"You're Secret Service?" the officer who'd mouthed off at her earlier said softly from where he was tied up. "That auth code... it's real?"

She glanced at the time to landing, then back at the officer and the Freedom Wing soldier guarding him.

"Let him at the console," she told the rebel. "Check it yourself," she instructed the officer, turning back to bringing the system online.

Several seconds later, she realized she was actually in the menus for the *internal* security system and had accidentally discovered how to activate individual sectors of that system. That might help once they were landed, but she would rather that *didn't* happen.

Glynn Stewart

"Authenticated," the officer said quietly, and looked over at her, straightening against his handcuffs.

"Ma'am, I am Captain Davis Hiverner," he told her. "I accept your authentication and authority. We don't have time to get these cuffs off, but I can walk you through activating the SAM turrets."

"You'll need a ride when we're done," Amiri said quietly.

"I know," he agreed. "But... I didn't sign up to beat up civilians and guard political prisoners. Let me help you."

With the Marines about to start knocking, she didn't have many alternatives. She gestured for him to begin.

#

Mage-Commodore Cor watched her shuttles drop on the screen in the center of her flag bridge with pleasure. It was always satisfying to be able to unleash the full power of the force under her command against the mundane fools who stood in the way of her goals. Watching those unable to grasp reality be swept aside at the whim of their betters was gratifying.

Major Morales had selected the men to take down as carefully as she'd hoped. While the Major himself was completely her man, many of his sub-officers and men were more... old-fashioned in their loyalties. He'd selected his force entirely from those men – they would follow orders for a mission like this, and if the Freedom Wing proved more intractable than expected, their deaths only strengthened Cor's position.

Regardless of their loyalties, they'd properly ignored the blatantly false attempt by the rebels to pretend they were Protectorate Secret Service. There were no PSS agents on the planet – as the senior military officer in the system, Cor should have been informed if any had been deployed.

The shuttles dropped below the clouds, starting to become more difficult to make out in the visual. Her flagship's sensors still highlighted them clearly. They couldn't find the stealthed aircraft that had made the assault, and Cor found herself concluding, sadly, that they were unwilling to challenge her Marines.

She missed the first warning flash from the fortress prison. Cor was more used to using her displays to track space movements and exercises than ground combat, and she didn't understand what the screen was telling her for a moment. None of the staffers on her flag bridge would have dared to try to explain it, either. They would risk far too much by assuming she *didn't* know what she was seeing.

Then five more warnings flashed, and *Unchained Glory*'s computers automatically added icons for the rising surface-to-air missiles fired from the fortress. Six missiles – two for each shuttle – blasted into the air from the Bastille, and the Mage-Commodore swore under her breath.

There was *no way* the rebels were in command of the prison's defenses – it wasn't *possible.*

But it was happening.

As she watched, all three shuttles dropped like rocks – their pilots aiming them for the fortress' courtyards and firing the engines downwards. It was risky, but it *could* save them – especially as their ECM began to hash the surrounding area, rendering it impossible for even the *Unchained Glory* to track what happened.

The explosions stood out, though. The original designers of the Bastilles had been *insane*, she realized. Not satisfied with sufficient weapons to stand off any airborne or ground-launched assault or prison revolt, they'd added weapon systems capable of engaging an orbital drop. The missiles weren't nuclear or antimatter tipped, but at their speed heavy conventional warheads were sufficient.

When the dust and ECM cleared, two of her shuttles were gone. A moment to check and she confirmed that Major Morales had *not* survived, which caused a pang of sadness.

It wasn't a very big pang. Morales hadn't been a Mage – he'd been useful, but there were others to take his place.

She hit a button, opening a channel to the surviving platoon leader.

"Lieutenant Hammond, report," she ordered.

"Hammond here," a young, breathless voice replied. "We are deploying."

A loud crashing sound, rapidly repeated, interrupted him.

"Get down," Hammond ordered. "Use the mobile shields, *suppress those guns.*"

"We're running into heavy resistance," he said to Cor. "All automated – this entire sector is firing on us. It's mostly lightly weaponry, not much of a threat to an exosuit except in quantity – but this place *has* quantity."

"We need to prevent the prisoners escaping, Lieutenant," Cor told him. "You will have to advance."

Silence answered her for a long moment.

"We'll do what we can," the young officer said flatly. "Hammond out."

She tried to raise him, but failed.

"Is he ignoring me?" she demanded of her staff. They flinched away from her, but then one of the officers finally spoke up.

"No, ma'am," he told her. "The entire Bastille just disappeared into a fog of jamming – no coms, no sensor readings."

Cor looked back to the visual representation in the center of her flag bridge, only to watch it disappear as dozens of rockets flashed into the air and exploded into smoke. The electronic jamming blocked her scanners – the smoke blocked their telescopes.

She was blind, and out of touch. Her pleasure at the assumed destruction of her foes turned to ashes in her mouth.

This wasn't supposed to happen to the Royal Martian Navy!

#

Damien emerged from the immense dome of the Runic Transceiver Array in something of a daze. He wasn't sure any more what he'd been expecting, but to have Alexander promote him to Hand and drop the entire mess of Ardennes in his lap definitely hadn't been it.

The Phantom sat alone on the helipad when he returned to it, with Sierra nowhere to be seen. There was a faint smell of cordite in the air, snapping him out of his longer-term worries. He removed his right glove and slowly drew energy into his hand as he glanced around for the pilot.

She emerged from the bushes beside the pad a moment later with a pistol in her hand, glancing at him nervously.

"A Scorpion patrol came by and recognized the Phantom for what it is," Sierra said grimly as she approached. "I don't *think* they got a message off before I killed them, but they'll be missed pretty quickly either way. Are we done here?"

"We're done here," Damien assured her, resolving not to piss the Legatan woman off. For an ex-paramedic, she seemed to take killing four or five men a little *too* calmly. There was something in her eyes that made him uncomfortable too... a familiar flatness to her pupils.

"Then let's go," she told him, gesturing to the gunship.

Moments later, they were off, Sierra weaving the aircraft between office towers with consummate skill.

Then a light started flashing on the console and she swore. Hitting a key, she accepted the call.

"Flight F-451, this is Nouveau Versailles Control," a calm voice told. "There's been an incident at the RTA. You are ordered to cease your course and return to the facility to co-operate with the investigation."

She glanced over at Damien. Her eyes were calmer now, but there was still something odd about them – something *familiar* too. Almost like her pupils were half-square, which had to just be a trick of the light.

"Can't go back," she said simply. "If I ignore them, they'll react before we're out of town, and I *can't* stealth my way past police aircraft when I'm surrounded by skyscrapers."

"Do what you have to," he ordered.

The pilot nodded grimly and engaged the throttle, driving the helicopter towards the edge of the city faster. A minute or so passed, and then the light flickered on again.

"Flight F-451, this is ground control. If you do not return to the RTA site, we will assume you were responsible for the attack on our personnel and shoot you down. You have thirty seconds to comply."

Damien watched over Sierra's shoulder as she flipped the key that enabled the gunship's weapons. Making sure he had a clean line of sight to the sensors, he removed his gloves and tucked them inside his coat. He'd prefer *not* to have to engage – it would make what was going on obvious.

But better for a Mage to have been clearly involved than for them not to make it home.

"I see they're giving up on talking to us," he said softly, spotting the two new icons on the scanners – flashing orange as 'unidentified' contacts. The contacts turned red a moment later as Sierra dialed them in and labeled them as hostile.

"And they're not playing games," she replied. "Those are jet interceptors – I think they're guessing who we are, and guessing right."

"Can you take them?"

"If we were outside the city, I'd just disappear," Sierra said grimly.

"That wasn't the question."

"It'll depend," she replied. "Ground control has an accurate guess of what we are. But if these guys trust their radar... they'll come in fat and sloppy."

Damien glanced at the icons closing – and closing in fast and high. They weren't breaking the speed of sound, but they were pushing close against it. They were at most a minute outside of range.

"Good luck," he told her, and settled his own mind – clearing his thoughts to more easily channel magic.

"And... now," Sierra whispered and hit a button. Damien felt the gunship shake as two decoys launched from the back of the aircraft, and two missiles flared out from the launchers tucked under the rotors.

At the same time, she dove down, driving the helicopter closer to the ground even as more contacts flared onto the display – four missiles launching from the jets.

Damien focused on the missiles. Those were something he could deal with without being obvious. Practice and training let him pick out the tiny dots of the weapons as they approached, and he reached out with his magic.

Force 'gently' grabbed the two lead weapons, shoving them off their course – and into each other. Fire lit up the night sky as the warheads exploded. Sheltered in the light of the destruction of the lead missiles, Damien reached out and *crushed* the trailers, leaving their damaged chassis to fall – hopefully harmlessly! – to the street below.

Without magic interrupting their flights, Sierra's missiles were more successful. One hit a decoy, adding to the fireworks in Nouveaux Versailles' sky. The other slammed into the lead jet fighter and detonated, scattering the high-tech aircraft in pieces across the city.

This was apparently more than the other interceptor's pilot was expecting. The aircraft jerked away from the fireball that had been his wingman and climbed *high*, blasting out of the Phantom's range at high speed.

"Sucker," Sierra whispered. "Missed your chance – now you get to watch me *disappear*."

Glancing away from their attacker, Damien realized they were now well clear of Nouveaux Versailles' Central District with its constraining towers. As the jet interceptor flashed away, clearly intending to prepare for another run, the Legatan woman hit a set of commands.

Suddenly, instead of imitating a civilian helicopter, the Phantom was imitating empty air.

It was hard to read body language from the tiny dot of an aircraft on a radar screen – but Damien was sure he could see the pilot's confusion nonetheless.

#

Chapter 32

Mage-Captain Jane Adamant jerked awake to the alert. Years of practice had trained her to awaken instantly, but she still could swear she'd only been asleep for a few moments as she pulled herself from her bed and tapped a key, accepting the transmission voice-only.

"Captain, it's Lieutenant Fiero," her junior communications officer, the woman currently stuck manning the station in the middle of the ship's night, greeted her. "Tau Ceti f RTA has forwarded an Alpha One priority transmission from Mars."

She shook the final dregs of sleep from her eyes. Alpha One from Mars almost certainly meant from the Mage-King himself – and even *battleship* Captains didn't receive many missives directly from the King.

"Forward it to my cabin," she ordered. "Thank you, Lieutenant."

By the time the Captain had grabbed a robe and wrapped it around her body against the slight chill of the cabin, an icon had appeared on both her cabin console and the PC discarded on her dresser. Belting the robe tightly closed, she touched the icon.

An authentication prompt appeared, demanding her personal identification and security codes. While the Transceiver Mage at the array would have heard the entire message, those individuals were among the most tightly screened and highly cleared individuals in the Protectorate for just that reason. Once the messages were recorded into the system, the security and encryption went back on.

No-one had yet worked out how to transmit anything except the voice of the speaking Mage via the Runic Transceiver Arrays. In an era of massive data transfers and computers capable of storing all mankind's knowledge that fit in a wristwatch, the only instantaneous method of interstellar communication was somewhat less capable than an early telephone.

Her codes input, the file began playing, the even voice of Mage-King Desmond Alexander filling her cabin.

"This message is for Mage-Captain Adamant aboard the *Righteous Guardian of Liberty*, from Desmond Michael Alexander. Authentication is Kilo Kilo Seven Nine Victor Charlie One Six.

"Captain Adamant, I am not certain what information has reached you with regards to the events on Ardennes. I will summarize these events as I am aware of them, as much of what has been previously disseminated has turned out to be incorrect.

"As has been announced, Hand Alaura Stealey is dead. However, new evidence has confirmed that her death was the work of Mage-Governor Michael Vaughn, *not* the rebellion.

"I have also confirmed that the destruction of the city of Karlsberg was *not* the work of the rebellion. Karlsberg was destroyed by *Navy* munitions, Captain Adamant. Munitions fired from Mage-Commodore Cor's warships."

Adamant paused the message to curse. She'd known Adrianna Cor in the Academy – the woman had been brilliant but arrogant, tied up in her own views of how the world should be. Skill had driven the other woman up the ranks faster than most, but it looked like that was coming to an end.

Sighing, she restarted the Mage-King's recording.

"Given that both the local government and Navy forces in the Ardennes system have been compromised, we need to deploy external resources to secure the system before we can attempt to fix the clusterfuck it is clear Ardennes has become.

"You're it," the Mage-King told her flatly. "Consider this message notification of your promotion to Mage-Commodore. Paperwork will follow with the appropriate physical couriers, but you'll need the authority.

"You are to assemble a task force of sufficient force to secure the Ardennes system, assuming full resistance from both the Ardennes Self Defense Force *and* Mage-Commodore Cor's Seventh Cruiser Squadron."

She paused the recording to curse again. The promotion was welcome, but enough firepower to take on an entire cruiser squadron? If she wasn't starting with a battleship, it would be impossible. As it was... she swore again, then unpaused the recording.

"If Mage-Admiral Segal does not have sufficient vessels to spare, you will commandeer combat units from the Tau Ceti System Fleet," Alexander continued, as if such things were straightforward. "Under any circumstances, you will depart Tau Ceti within twelve hours of this message.

"Once you arrive in the Ardennes system, you will neutralize *all* warships in the system and secure the orbitals. As soon as practically possible, you will place yourself under the command of Hand Damien Montgomery.

"I leave the disposition of your Marines and securing the surface to your judgment and that of Hand Montgomery," he finished. "I promised Hand Montgomery he'd have support in three days, Mage-Commodore. I trust you to honor my promises."

There was a pause in the recording.

"I am not sending you because you're all I have available, Commodore," he said quietly. "I'm sending you because you're the *best* I have available. I do not expect you to disappoint me."

The recording ended, and Adamant learned back in her chair, eyeing the innocent little icon carefully.

It was a lot to take in at once. *Hand* Damien Montgomery was a new one – it seemed hers wasn't the only promotion going around. She *should* be able to get the ships she needed out of Segal, but it could be a problem. The old man was notorious for not giving up warships once he'd got them.

But Segal also wouldn't let the Navy look bad, and if she had to commander ships from a star system government, the Navy couldn't look worse.

Sighing, Adamant stood and crossed to her closet. She was going to have to wake the old Admiral up either way, and she was damned if she was doing that in a bath-robe.

#

Either Mage-Admiral Segal *slept* in his uniform, or he was much faster at waking up and dressing than Adamant was. His staff only ran five minutes or so of delaying action before they connected the newly minted Commodore to the man.

Segal was a short man with broad shoulders and salt and pepper hair. His eyes, when he met Adamant's gaze, were dark but calm.

"Mage-Commodore Adamant," he greeted her. "Congratulations."

"Your staff is good," she said admiringly. She didn't think they would have had a chance to let the Admiral know about her promotion before connecting him.

"A presumption, Commodore, not my staff," Segal told her calmly. "You were due for that promotion. Any emergency sufficient for you to wake the system commander would be such that you were being deployed out-system, which would inevitably come with said promotion.

"Now, since you have managed to wake me up, what is the emergency?"

Adamant shook her head, not quite sure how to respond to the Admiral's entirely correct pronouncement.

"Ardennes has apparently turned into a worse disaster than we feared," she told Segal. "Stealey wasn't killed by the rebellion – she was killed by *Vaughn*."

"That should be a courier's task, Commodore, not a battleship's," the Admiral observed. "Mage-Commodore Cor possesses more than sufficient space-borne firepower and Marines to remove a recalcitrant Governor. Unless..." he trailed off, and she could *see* the realization hit him in mid-sentence.

"Mage-Commodore Cor has been compromised," she confirmed. "Information from Hand Montgomery has confirmed that it was *her* vessels that destroyed the city of Karlsberg."

Segal was silent, the excessively clever Admiral clearly processing what she'd said.

"What is your mission, Commodore?" he finally asked.

"I am to proceed to Ardennes and secure the orbitals, either by the destruction or capture of both the Ardennes System Defense Force and the Seventh Cruiser Squadron," she explained. "I will need to commandeer escorts from your forces."

"My dear, you have a *battleship*," Segal pointed out. "With your re-deployment, my most potent vessel becomes a cruiser. Cor only has cruisers, and the ASDF only has destroyers. How much additional firepower do you need?"

"Mage-Admiral, His Majesty assumes – and I concur – that we must assume that the Seventh and the ASDF will be deployed in concert. I am hesitant to face seventy-five million tons of warships with fifty, regardless of my individual advantage."

Segal nodded with a sigh, gesturing off-screen as he brought up another computer screen.

"Do you truly believe Cor's people will follow her into that depth of treason so blithely? What sort of force level are you envisaging?"

"Cor's people followed her into killing fifty thousand people with an orbital strike, Mage-Admiral," Adamant pointed out. "After that... if nothing else, she can hold that over them to force their obedience.

"I need at least two cruisers and a destroyer squadron," she continued. "A tonnage advantage will hopefully help force at least the ASDF to surrender without a fight."

"Given the area of responsibility of the Tau Ceti Station, I'm not sure I can spare that many ships, Commodore," Segal pointed out. "We are, after all, responsible for the security of the Yards, as well as the jump lanes around this system."

"His Majesty also gave me authority to commandeer units from the Tau Ceti System Fleet," Adamant told him. "My understanding is they just finished construction of a flight of four brand new cruisers – I imagine they'd be ecstatic to test them out with full Navy approval."

Segal paused for a moment, and then started laughing, a deep braying chuckle that she would never have expected to hear from the older man.

"I see that Desmond continues to have every one of his senior officers' foibles and weaknesses memorized," he admitted aloud. "I apologize for dragging my feet, Commodore. It is true that my responsibilities are extensive, but I need *hulls* more than tonnage – where your need is the complete opposite.

"I cannot spare a destroyer squadron," he continued. "But I *can* spare the Second and Third Division of the Second Cruiser Squadron. Four cruisers should be sufficient for your purposes, wouldn't you agree, Mage-Commodore?"

Adamant considered it for a moment, checking the statistics on the four cruisers she was being offered. Segal's offer was actually even better than he was implying – each of the four ships he was offering were brand new twelve million ton *Honorific* class cruisers, out-massing the older cruisers in Cor's squadron by twenty percent apiece.

"That will more than suffice, Mage-Admiral," she told him. "If you could inform the ships' captains in question as soon as possible? I will want to hold a task force meeting at," she checked the time, "ten hundred hours Olympus Mons Time.

"My orders are to be underway by fourteen hundred," she added. "My understanding is that Hand Montgomery has co-opted local rebel forces to help minimize ground-side collateral damage, but if we miss our arrival time... they could be in trouble."

"My experience, my dear Mage-Commodore, is that it is *never* wise to disappoint a Hand," Segal replied. "Your Captains will be there for your meeting."

#

Chapter 33

It was well past midnight local time when Damien returned to the airbase. He glanced around the hangar, realizing quickly that none of the other gunships had returned. The cavern was echoingly empty, with only him and Sierra – Alissa Leclair – standing in it.

"Where is everyone?" he asked aloud.

"I haven't heard anything about major losses," Leclair told him. "I think we're just the first back – they may still need to shake pursuit. I need a drink," she finished bluntly.

"Go ahead," he told her, gesturing towards the barracks with its tiny bar. "I'll wait until I hear more."

The Legatan woman regarded him levelly.

"Your loss," she finally sniffed, before wandering off deeper into the underground base.

Damien, shrugging, took a seat on one of the munitions crates to keep an eye on the big shielded doors sheltering them from the outside world.

He needed time to process what Alexander had dropped on him. He'd known relatively early on that he was being considered as a candidate for Hand – he'd caused and wandered into enough crazy shit before Alaura had brought him in for the Mage-King to have a good idea how he ticked.

The plan had been for him to spend a year shadowing Alaura, providing a level of magical support even the Hands couldn't back. The Mage-Kings had long ago learned several things about the Runes of Power inlaid into the Hands: first and foremost, that they needed to be uniquely tailored to the magic of the individual they were carved on.

Only a Rune Wright could read the layers and complexities of an individual's magic closely enough to create a Rune of Power for them. Even they had difficulties reading *another* Mage's magic, so the Mage-Kings had restricted themselves to only marking a single Rune on their Hands.

Reading their *own* magic, however, was a different matter entirely. Damien hadn't pushed too hard against the limits Alexander told him were true, but he understood that the current Mage-King's father had injured himself quite badly trying to add too many Runes of Power. Alexander the Third had settled on five.

Damien, the only non-Royal Rune Wright in the galaxy, had followed his example. Those five Runes had taken his at-best mediocre power levels and elevated him to a level with, effectively, *no* equals bar the other Rune Wrights.

So he had been sent to provide the unexpected 'muscle' that a Hand like Alaura Stealey might have needed. The plan had been a year-long apprenticeship, watching Alexander's best Hand operate – and now Alaura was dead and he had been raised to Hand within *weeks*.

It felt like the entire planet was resting on his shoulders, and he didn't see an answer – the Navy could deal with Cor, but if they had to take Nouveau Versailles from space tens of thousands would die.

He didn't *miss* Lori Armstrong entering the hangar and approaching him, but he was paying little enough attention that it was still a surprise when she spoke.

"They had to go to Plan B," the head of the Freedom Wing told him. "Cor dropped Marines – Amiri got the Bastille defenses back online, but that just gave them a headache."

"Damn," Damien whispered. He shook his head. "It's a legitimate response," he continued quietly. "She'll have sent the Marines she thought would stay loyal to Mars – the ones who might have helped us stop her."

Lori swallowed visibly. "The bitch would, wouldn't she?" she said fiercely. "Dammit, My Lord Envoy, this has to *end*!"

"Amiri and your people got out?" he asked.

"Everyone's out," she confirmed. "Several wounded, but they stole transport trucks, blew smoke, and triggered the Bastille's jammers. There's no way they were tracked, even from orbit. It's just taking them longer to get home – everyone is fine."

"I'm glad to hear," Damien replied. "No offense, Miss Armstrong, but your planet is killing a lot of good people these days."

"*Vaughn* is killing a lot of good people," she objected. "I don't think the planet has a grudge against anyone."

"Fair," he allowed, glancing back at the overhead doors.

"Did you reach the Mage-King?" Armstrong asked after a minute or so of silence.

"I did," Damien confirmed. "I'm... still processing a lot of what he said. But," he shrugged and glanced back to the rebel leader. "How long it would it take to organize a meeting of all of your leaders?" he asked.

Lori considered, glancing at the time on her wrist computer.

"I could probably pull something together by morning," she told him. "Why?"

"I have good news and bad news," Damien replied. "And I'm going to need your help – the entire Wing's help."

"You've... done everything we asked," she told him after a moment's hesitation. "I can organize it, but I fear what you may need from us. And… I don't know if I can promise the full Wing will listen. Many of the cell leaders hate Mars as much as Vaughn."

"We have failed you," Damien acknowledged. "And now we ask you to help save yourselves from our failure – it is natural. But I promise you, Lori, we will make it work. Vaughn *will* pay for his crimes."

Anything Lori might have said in response was lost in the cacophony as the overhead doors finally slid open, allowing the gunships to land, one by one.

Damien was on his feet by the time Amiri exited Brute's helicopter, and he noticed that Riordan had appeared from nowhere when the doors opened. Some instinct held him in place as the rebel stepped forward, approaching the ex-bounty hunter special agent.

Amiri looked shocked as Riordan wrapped her in a tight embrace, and Damien smiled to himself as her stiffness faded before the Ardennes' native had finished hugging her. From where he stood, it was very clear that *she* initiated the kiss that followed, and he turned his gaze back to Armstrong.

"The prisoners?" he asked.

He had to repeat himself before Armstrong shook herself free of a shocked stare at Amiri and Riordan and turned back to him.

"Most of our fighters and the prisoners are traveling by ground," she told him. "They split into small groups and scattered. We'll have the pilots to their bases by end of day tomorrow – then the Wing will be fully restored to all of what resources we have."

"We'll talk in the morning," the Hand told her quietly, glancing back at Amiri. It didn't look like he was talking to his Agent until morning either. "I think we all need to get some rest."

#

"My Marines have finished securing your prison, Governor," Cor told Vaughn over the video link. "Our losses were heavy. It seems your little rebellion has now shed Martian blood.

"How the hell did they get access to the Bastille's weapons, Vaughn?" she demanded. "I've seen the specifications for your prisons – they were designed by professional paranoids!"

"That was the point," Mage-Governor Michael Vaughn told his ally calmly, massaging his temples as he glanced around the office tucked away in the underground command center. He was starting to miss the airy top floor office he'd kept in Government House.

"They were designed so that no-one could get in, and no-one could take control," he continued. "And no, I'm not sure how the rebels took control of the weapons systems. I regret the deaths of your men, but it could have been worse."

He met Cor's eyes, and she nodded slowly. He knew damned well she'd used the attack as an excuse to purge the unreliable elements of her Marine detachments, and her comment about 'Martian blood' was more than poetic license. While it was unlikely any of the men who'd died re-taking the Bastille were Martian-born, the Mage-King didn't take the deaths of those who swore allegiance to him lightly. It was another anvil he could hang around the Wing's neck – and this one honestly!

"Have you found Captain Hiverner?" he asked. "He was in command of the prison, and should have a better idea than anyone else of just what happened."

"No," Cor said softly. "My men haven't rescued or found the body of anyone by that name. If he's missing…"

"*Tabernac*," Vaughn swore. "I guess that explains how they got in." He straightened and faced Cor. "Mage-Commodore, if one of my people committed treason, we will find the truth. The bastards who killed your Marines *will* be found and punished."

Cor nodded, once.

"Let my people know if there is any assistance that the Royal Martian Navy can provide," she told him briskly. "We will speak again soon."

The image of the Martian squadron leader disappeared from the screen, which began retracting into the desk. Vaughn looked past it to where James Montoya leaned against the wall, listening in on the conversation without contributing.

"Hiverner is yours," he said quietly.

"He is," Montoya agreed. "And he requested prison duty after getting mixed up in one of our uglier suppression ops. He did well in the op, so I granted his request – it looks like I should have looked harder into why he wanted to be in something most would call 'cleaner'."

"Especially before we handed every fucking Freedom Wing prisoner we'd taken over to him," Vaughn snapped. "Would you care to explain how *any* aspect of this is not a fucking unmitigated disaster?"

"No, because it's an unmitigated disaster," Montoya told him bluntly. "What's *worse*, boss, is that you missed the real problem."

Vaughn glared at his chief enforcer and closest friend.

"What the fuck are you talking about?" he demanded.

Montoya walked forward from the wall, his PC linking into the screen and causing it to extend from the desk again. Once fully up, the screen lit up with a view of the Nouveau Versailles Central District, focused on a collection of Fire Department vehicles clustered around the burning wreck of an aircraft.

"While we were all focused on the Bastille," Montoya said calmly, "a security patrol at the Runic Transceiver Array turned up dead. When ARTA control identified an aircraft leaving from near where they were found, they were ordered to return.

"The controller smelled a rat when the flight refused to turn around and ordered an intercept on his own authority," the Scorpion General continued. "He was entirely correct – when two F-60 interceptors tried to force the helicopter down, it turned out to be one of the rebels' damned gunships."

He gestured at the wreckage on the screen. "This *was* one of the Nouveau Versailles' Defense Squadron's interceptors. The other broke off to gain distance after this plane was shot down, and the rebels demonstrated that their gunships have a level of stealth tech that should *not* be available to them."

"You lost them," Vaughn concluded.

"Exactly. What I have confirmed," Montoya continued, "is that the gentleman whose name the appointment was booked in hasn't left the tower he lives and works in for about six days. *He* definitely wasn't in the ARTA."

"Then who was?" the Governor demanded. "Everyone who enters the Array is recorded."

"And those cameras were destroyed. Up to the point of their destruction, they recorded an empty chamber." Montoya sighed. "Most likely, at least some of that footage was faked – we *know* the ARTA administration takes bribes to allow unrecorded transmissions. We allow it as a favor to the interstellars, and now it has bitten us in the ass."

Vaughn looked at Montoya levelly, then back at the wreckage of one of his precious imported jet interceptors.

"What are you presuming, James?" he asked softly.

"The most likely person on the planet to make a secret call home is Montgomery, boss," Montoya said flatly. "And if the Envoy has called home to Mars, we're done, Michael. The Mage-King will know *everything*, and the next Hand he sends is going to show up with a fucking battle fleet."

The General made a sharp gesture with his hand and the screen shut down again, facing his Governor squarely even as Vaughn sputtered in disbelief.

"You can justify everything we've done to yourself if you want, Michael," Montoya continued sharply, "but Desmond Michael Alexander will *not* buy it. He'll hang us for what we've done – and Cor alongside us.

"It's time to think about backup plans. We've got enough loyal Mages – we can load enough money and bullion on a fast ship to live our lives out comfortably a long way from here – beyond even Alexander's reach."

Vaughn knew he was gaping at Montoya, his mouth opening and closing like a hungry goldfish. Finally, he swallowed and squared his shoulders.

"No, James," he said calmly. "Ardennes is *my* planet," he continued. "If Alexander wants to demand my head, he will have to take this world by force. Cor and the ASDF will fight, and I doubt the Mage-King will be inclined to create a precedent of the violent removal of an elected planetary Governor."

His General – his *friend* – shook his head.

"You don't know that," he pointed out. "And given that it's more likely than not Alexander can prove we rigged the election – and if he seizes Cor's ships, he can prove we destroyed Karlsberg... He can say we've crossed lines no-one else has – that we represent a unique case."

Vaughn shivered at the image of Karlsberg after the strike. It had seemed such a *logical* decision, but looking at the aftermath had made logic a frail shield.

"This is my world," he repeated. "I will *not* run. Not before the Hands have arrived and laid out ultimatums – not while there is a chance of sustaining all that I've built. We stay, my friend."

"At least let me put in some insurance policies!" Montoya demanded. "A fast ship, and bargaining chips for if push comes to shove. I don't want to hang, boss – but I also don't want to watch *you* hang."

Neither of the two men was much for emotion. That was more of a declaration of friendship than Vaughn had ever heard from the other man, and it weakened his resolve – a little.

"Fine," he allowed. "Prepare your fast ship. Make your insurance policies. I don't like it, but we may need them."

#

Chapter 34

Amiri wasn't used to waking up with someone else in her bed, and it took her a moment to remember who was there with her. Once her initial urge to leap from the bed and look for a weapon had passed, however, she rolled over on her side and looked at Mikael.

She was honest enough with herself to admit she'd mostly taken the man to bed out of sheer exultation at still being alive – the arrival of Marines at the Bastille had shaken her. She'd been more pleased with the experience than she'd have expected, but it still wasn't more than a fling.

Mikael shifted slightly in his sleep, his hand slipping up to lay gently on her hip and she caught herself smiling.

Okay – it wasn't *much* more than a fling. Yet. If they all lived…

That was a dangerous path to walk down. She took his hand in hers and pressed a kiss to his fingers, and then slipped out of the bed. The rooms Leclair had assigned to the 'important' guests at her secret airbase to were surprisingly comfortable, and the rebel slipped easily back to sleep as Amiri rose and dressed.

Somehow, the Secret Service Agent was unsurprised to find Montgomery sitting in the hallway outside, quietly reading on his personal computer.

"You didn't need to wait up for me," she said softly. "I can find my own way around."

"We need to talk," the Envoy said sharply. As she glanced back at the door behind her, he smiled and shook his head. "Not about that," he told her, but the mirth quickly fled his face.

She followed him, and he led the way into a side room – a storage room, from the looks of it. The room's main appeal was that it was empty of people, and the stacks of crates – cannon ammunition for the gunships, from the looks of it – provided easy seats.

"Did you get through to Mars?" she asked as the Envoy sat, facing her. "Is help coming?"

"Help is coming," Montgomery confirmed, his voice soft. "His Majesty promised warships sufficient to defeat both Cor and the ASDF. They're due in sixty hours and counting, and will place themselves under my command when they arrive."

Under his command…

"He confirmed you as Hand, didn't he?" she asked.

The younger man twitched, taken aback.

"Yes," he admitted. "An Envoy can't command the Martian military. A Hand can."

"You were a Hand from the moment Alaura gave you the amulet, Damien," she pointed out. "I knew that, even if you didn't. No-one would ever argue with you so long as you *held* the Hand. Everything beyond was formality."

He nodded, slowly.

"I... didn't think of it that way," he admitted. "Or if I did, it didn't sink in until His Majesty informed me in no uncertain terms that I am his Hand on Ardennes."

"Doesn't change my job," she told him. "Though I think yesterday is the last time you're getting me away from you, My Lord," she continued. "My job until this mess is resolved is to keep you alive so you can resolve it – I can't do that if I'm dozens of kilometers away when someone shoots at you!"

"You're right," Montgomery agreed after a moment. "I don't... think of myself as that important."

"Then start," she said bluntly. "Right now, you speak for Mars on Ardennes. I *know* what those runes are, too, Damien. You are the most powerful Mage on this world. The most powerful *man* on this world. Whether they know it or not, you are these people's only hope."

"That's... basically what His Majesty said," the Hand agreed. "I'm..." he swallowed words even *he* seemed to realize he couldn't say anymore.

"We're meeting with the Freedom Wing's cell leaders in an hour," he said instead. "We'll need them – if the Marines have to take Nouveau Versailles by assault, a lot of bystanders are going to die."

"Do you have a plan?" Amiri asked. So far, his plans had seemed to work out, even if they tended to be terrifying to the woman charged with keeping him alive.

"Not... yet," the Hand admitted. "Leverage the Wing's knowledge of the planet to build one. Haven't got past that point yet."

"You'd better," she warned. "You're the Hand."

"Let's keep that between us for the moment," he ordered. "There... will be a time. I don't think this morning is it. Not yet."

"You're the Hand," she sighed in acceptance.

#

Walking into a conference room of people expecting him to save their planet was the scariest thing Damien had ever done. The amulet under his shirt felt like it was made of lead, an unsupportable weight dragging him forward to a responsibility he wasn't sure he could meet.

He and Amiri entered the room last. Several of the other cell leaders had arrived overnight, and six men and women were waiting for them at a long, round black table. A wallscreen on the far wall was lit up with a number of icons, each representing a cell leader that wasn't physically present.

Twenty men and women who, between them and others now dead, had built a planetwide rebellion from nothing, waited on Damien Montgomery, Envoy of the Mage-King of Mars. He knew Lori, Leclair and Riordan – Alpha, Sierra, and Lambda.

The first of the other three was a white-haired black man he recognized from his briefings as Archbishop Eli Pelletier, head of the Quebec Reformation Catholic Church on Ardennes. The other pair, a pale-skinned woman with jet-black hair and a ruddy-complexioned bald man, he didn't know.

"That's everyone, then," Lori said quietly as the door slid shut behind them. "Envoy Montgomery, be known to the leadership of the Freedom Wing. You asked to speak to us, and after the rescue of our compatriots from the Bastille, we owed you that much."

"*Et pas plus*," another voice objected, one of the images on the screen flashing as the cell leader behind it spoke. "His *agent* rescued our people," the woman continued thickly accented English, "not him."

"And our people are saved regardless, November," Lori told the speaker. "Without Montgomery, half our pilots would be in jail, along with two dozen others. Let's hear him out."

"Mars has not helped us before!" November spat back. "Why should they help us now?!"

Damien held up a hand to forestall Lori and then leaned forward.

"Two reasons, November," he said quietly. The woman was quiet, perhaps surprised by his objection. "The first, more pragmatic reason is simple: Vaughn killed a Hand. We *cannot* let that stand – a Hand falls, another must rise, and the one responsible must pay.

"But as to why we *didn't* act, you must remember that even Hands are bound by law," he told her. "It took time for us to gather the evidence to move against Vaughn – more time than it should," he admitted, "because none of us realized that Mage-Commodore Cor had betrayed us. She arrived when we were first preparing to move against Vaughn, and reassured everyone that the situation was under control.

"We failed you," Damien said after a long moment of silence. "But we have every intention of fixing that failure. I did make contact with the Mage-King last night from the Transceiver Array, and at least the first steps have been taken."

He glanced at Lori.

"If you'll permit, Alpha," he told her, "I will explain what is being done, and what still needs to be done."

"Carry on, My Lord," she told him, sending a sharp glance at the wallscreen – presumably the cameras feeding back to the cell leaders were over there. "I think we can all be *that* patient."

Damien glanced at Amiri for support and she made a small nodding gesture – 'get on with it', he was pretty sure.

"His Majesty is now aware of Mage-Commodore Cor and Mage-Governor Vaughn's treason," he said simply. "With Cor in orbit with enough firepower to destroy any ground attack, Vaughn cannot be removed.

"Therefore, a Task Force is even now being assembled that will proceed here with the intent of neutralizing the Seventh Cruiser Squadron and either capturing or killing Mage-Commodore Cor," he told them. "The Task Force is expected to arrive in approximately sixty hours."

The room was silent for a long moment. They'd been trying for years to overthrow Vaughn, and suddenly he'd handed them their trump card on a silver platter.

"That's that, then isn't it?" Pelletier asked softly. "But it isn't, is it?" he continued. "It's never that simple, and if it were, you'd been telling us to go dark and bury our heads, wouldn't you?"

"It would be a lot safer for everyone, yes," Damien agreed. "But it depends how many people you're prepared to let die for you."

"And just *what* do you mean by that?" November demanded.

"You all saw what happened when Commodore Cor's Marines attacked the Bastille," he reminded them. "The defenses layered around Nouveaux Versailles and the other major cities are at least as powerful. Any Marine assault to remove Vaughn would run straight into those defenses, and will take heavy losses.

"To avoid those, the Navy will have to carry out significant orbital bombardment," he continued. "You've seen the aftermath of Karlsberg. The strikes would be more precise – but also more powerful. Collateral damage would be unavoidable. More would die – Marines, Ardennes Army, and civilians, when the Marines hit the cities. Urban fighting is brutal."

November was silent, but Damien could *see* the slightly ill expression on Pelletier's face. Oddly, the old priest didn't seem *surprised* by his description – it was more the expression of old memories than that of shock.

"But if we work together," Damien continued into the shocked silence, "we can hit Vaughn while the Navy is dealing with Cor. Versailles' defenses were stripped when we attacked the Bastille. The Governor *is* vulnerable."

"I... don't think we can give you an immediate answer," Lori said after a long moment of silence. She glanced around the table, taking a read of her people that Damien couldn't match. "We'll need time to discuss – in private."

"I understand," Damien allowed, inclining his head slightly, somewhat relieved to be off the immediate hook. "Amiri and I will leave you to your deliberations. Let me know when you have a decision or if I can be of assistance."

"Thank you, Lord Montgomery."

With a nod and a small bow, Damien withdrew with a feeling akin to relief.

#

Two hours after the Envoy left, Lori was feeling *anything* but relief. After about six iterations of the same circle, all of the relief and excitement of realizing the Navy was *finally* going to help out had long been ground out.

"Mars left us to *rot*," November spat at the others. "I'll be damned before I fight alongside them – let their Marines burn. We don't owe them *merde*."

"But we owe our people something," Pelletier said in his smooth voice. "It's not merely the Marines who'll die – it'll be our Army. Our civilians. Our brothers and sisters – those we set out to save."

Lori glanced around the five others at the table. Leclair looked exhausted more than anything else, but no-one had expected the Legatan to step on board with working with Mars. Her homeworld had birthed the UnArcana movement barring Mages from planets after all.

Most of the others were wavering. No-one seemed to be able to make up their minds. Lori wasn't sure herself what the best course was – even if they *could* somehow capture Vaughn, they could only hold him and the city if the Navy arrived in time.

"You can't rely on Mars," Leclair finally said, interrupting the beginning of another row. "They'll stand shoulder to shoulder with us if they're *here* – but they're not, are they?"

Silence answered the Legatan.

"We're going to count on the Navy to come riding to the rescue, on the word of one admittedly brave and honorable servant of the Mage-King?" she continued. "Do we really believe that the Mages will save us from their own? They've ignored Vaughn for years – if he hadn't been a Mage, do you think that would have happened?"

"Mars looks to their own first," she said bluntly. "They'll strike now because Vaughn killed one of their own. I call a pox on both their houses – let Mars choke on their own pet."

Lori saw Pelletier draw in a breath to speak, the old priest as tough and stubborn as old leather. She gestured him to silence and leaned forward.

"We're not getting anywhere," she said aloud, admitting what everyone had to be thinking. "Let's break for the moment – some of us I know need to make sure they're properly covered," she gestured towards the wallscreen.

"We don't need to decide this morning. Let's all think about this and re-convene in five hours," she instructed. "We have the time – and we're sure as hell not getting anywhere right now."

Maybe in five hours she'd have some idea of what she'd say to convince her compatriots – or even of what she needed to convince them of!

#

Chapter 35

Damien was reviewing the data he had on the anti-air and anti-space defenses of Nouveaux Versailles when Amiri walked into his room, the Secret Service Agent not even bothering to knock. He glanced up as she came in, and then watched the tall woman as she crossed the room, pulled a spare chair up next to the desk and took a seat, watching him.

He returned her gaze for a long moment. Her silent regard was nerve-wracking, and he finally broke the quiet.

"Did you want something, Julia, or are you just here to fuck with me?"

"I'm trying to find the Hand inside the man hiding in his quarters," she said bluntly. "I'm not Desmond Alexander. I don't know what he sees in you. I don't know your plan. And right now, the future of this planet hangs on what you're going to do.

"So I'm trying to see how hiding in here while the only force you *might* be able to commandeer runs in circles, serves your plan."

He glared at her. She was right, but it still burned to be called on it.

"I don't *have* a fucking plan," he snapped. "Is that what you want to hear, Julia? I don't have a gods-damned *clue*. The only plan that comes to mind is to mount up and attack Nouveaux Versailles on my own, and runes or no runes, that's fucking suicide.

"I need the Wing – I need their brains, and I need their knowledge – and I need them to come on-side of their own free will. Ordering them around isn't going to save anyone."

And he was terrified. He'd spent the last three years buried in the most secure fortress on the planet, learning everything he could about magic and law. He'd fought before that, and he'd fought now to survive, but it wasn't his first choice.

Even on the *Blue Jay*, he'd only been trying to save himself and his friends. Now, an entire *world* seemed to be expecting an answer.

"They're not going to 'come on-side,' Damien," Amiri said flatly. "They ran in circles for two hours and are splitting up to 'think it over'. Like you said, no-one can order them around – not even Lori. All our dear 'Alpha' can do is *lead* them, and right now, she's leading them into indecision and fear."

Damien threw up his hands, the holographic screen from his PC fading out in the air.

"And what do you want me to *do*?" he demanded.

"I don't know," she admitted. "But what I do know? These people need a Hand. They *need* someone to show them a way. Otherwise, the

Marines are going to arrive, and tens of thousands will die because they'll have no choice but to bombard the city's defenses.

"That's the kind of mess from which UnArcana worlds are born," she reminded him. "And they look at you, and they see a kid playing at war. I *know* your past. I know the Mage-King gave you that Hand for a reason. But they don't even know you're a Hand, and they can't see past your appearance.

"Telling them you're a Hand won't help – you need to prove it. You need to make them believe you can save them."

"And what if I can't?" Damien whispered, even as her words tugged at something in his mind.

"If you can't, no-one else will," his bodyguard told him.

He swallowed hard. She was right. That thought was what terrified him and had him hiding in his room. He'd *seen* what happened when Mars failed to intervene properly – he'd almost died on Chrysanthemum, a world where a lack of Protectorate intervention had led to the locals getting Legatan help and becoming an UnArcana world.

Legatan help. Like helicopter gunships, advanced weapons, veteran trainers – even Augment special forces. The kind of men and women who could, say, take down a security patrol without blinking.

"*Son of a bitch*," he swore aloud as the pieces clicked into place. A moment later, he was on his feet. "Where's that battle laser of yours, Julia?"

"In my room," she replied, clearly confused.

"Grab it," he ordered. "I may not have a plan yet, but if nothing else, I just realized there's an extra player in this twisted game – and I want to make sure whose side they're on."

#

Alissa Leclair had been living permanently at the hidden airbase for a while, and her quarters were near the command center – well away from where the various guests had been quartered.

"Would you care to explain why I'm toting a squad support weapon through the middle of a friendly base?" Amiri demanded as Damien checked to make sure the corridors were clear around them.

"Leclair is a Legatan Augment," he explained simply. "And almost certainly a Legatan *spy*. If she so much as twitches, shoot her and keep shooting until she stops moving." He stepped up to the door, grinding any fear or nervousness under foot.

"Is it likely to get that bad?" his bodyguard asked, subtly shifting her stance as she realized he was deadly serious.

"I hope not," he admitted, and knocked on the Legatan woman's door.

"What is it?"

"It's Montgomery," he told her. "Can we talk for a minute?"

"Sure."

The door slid open and Damien stepped through. Amiri followed him through a moment later, and the door slid shut behind them as Leclair turned to face them.

"What the *fuck*?" she demanded as she found herself staring down the crystalline emitter of Amiri's battle laser.

"Sit down, Miss Leclair," Damien ordered flatly. "Like I said, we need to talk, and I need your complete honesty."

"So you have your minion point a *heavy weapon* at me?"

"If I'm wrong, I will apologize, but I have the suspicion not much less would suffice if you decided to be a threat," he told her calmly. "You see, your contacts slipped in your scuffle last night. I was too distracted for it to really hit home."

The Legatan woman stared at him like he was crazy.

"What are you on about?"

"I take it you weren't briefed on my history," Damien told her conversationally. So far, there was still a chance he was off-base, but he doubted it. "Or you'd have known I once spent a month transporting an entire platoon of Legatan Augment commandos."

She froze. It wasn't even a subtle thing. Every conscious and unconscious movement completely shut down as her body slipped into an inhuman trance. Her eyes flicked to the battle laser, assessing.

"I almost didn't realize what I'd seen," he continued, certain now. "After all, who has *square* pupils? Only combat Augments. I'm surprised the Directorate didn't send a more... subtle agent."

The Legatus Military Intelligence Directorate officially didn't exist. Certainly, the Mage-King's government had never acknowledged its existence – but everyone knew it was the dirty tricks branch of the Legatan government. A branch that, at least occasionally, helped rebellions turn planets into UnArcana worlds.

"Even if I *am* an Augment," Leclair said slowly, "I'm still a private citizen, here on my own business. People off Legatus like cyborgs little enough that it's wise to keep secrets."

"I could almost buy that, Miss Leclair," Damien told her. "Except... modern stealth gunships? A pilot completely trained in the use of those aircraft? An entire *arsenal* of modern small arms and squad support weapons?" He gestured to the laser in Amiri's hands. "No. This is an LMID operation. I saw them on Chrysanthemum, and I can see the pattern. So you have a choice. You can tell me the truth, and we can perhaps come to a compromise – or I can tell Lori her entire rebellion has been funded and orchestrated by Legatus to betray the Protectorate."

The Augment, still in that inhumanly frozen combat mode, glanced at the battle laser, then at Damien's ungloved hands where the silver inlay was fully visible.

He could see the moment she made up her mind, her body slipping out of the hyper-active combat mode piece by piece, slowly returning to a normal human tone.

"Fuck," she said softly. "This whole op has been a disaster from the beginning," she told them, slowly leaning back and taking a seat on her bed. "You may as well take a seat. Keep the gun on me if you want, Amiri, but let's all be honest – I'm not one of the Mage-hunters, so I don't stand much of a chance against Montgomery here."

Damien pulled up a chair, but Amiri remained standing, the laser's emitter still trained on Leclair.

"I wasn't *supposed* to be an infiltrator," Leclair told them. "You're right – LMID doesn't send combat Augments on infiltration missions. By and large, we don't even send Augments on them, but there are a few with more expensive optics used for quiet ops.

"It was supposed to be a full-disclosure armed support mission," she continued. "The Wing was offered a deal – in exchange for putting UnArcana status to a vote in the new, properly elected, legislature, we'd provide aircraft, armor, and infantry equipment, plus trainers for all that, to wage their revolution. We were offering a lot for what we figured wasn't a big concession.

"Armstrong and her people turned us down flat. We had to scramble at the last minute – in the end, we started smuggling the gear we'd planned to *give* them into the shipments they were paying for. More than a few smugglers and arms dealers got paid twice, but we got the gear we wanted into their hands here.

"I and a few others were already en route, so we were tasked with subtler infiltration," she explained. "I was supposed to command the training team, but I was the only one who actually managed to get into the Wing – and the trust I earned was worth too much to risk it by bringing in the rest of my team.

"So yeah," she concluded, "I'm LMID. But honestly? We're here because Mars *wasn't*. At this point, we're not even getting anything out of it – but we'd planned the op and Vice-Director Rickets figured removing Vaughn was worth the money and equipment we already had in place all on its own. A moment of weakness on his part, I suppose."

"I can imagine that de-stabilizing the Protectorate and distracting Martian resources for years were also on his mind," Damien said dryly. "So what happens if I tell Armstrong and the rest this?"

She stiffened again, though this looked to be a more… human reaction than her earlier lapse into combat mode.

"Nothing of much fun for anyone," she admitted. "They need me to lead the gunship squadrons, but wouldn't trust me if they knew the truth. Armstrong might even do something… unwise."

"Like kill the spy?" Amiri asked from the door.

"Like that," Leclair agreed, glancing over to the Secret Service Agent and the bulky laser.

"I think we can probably avoid that," Damien allowed. "On two conditions."

Leclair glared at him, but he let it wash over him. He'd been glared at before – and by people more likely to kill him.

"You support me in getting the Wing to act," he told her. "And when the dust settles, and Vaughn is gone, you disappear before I have to start investigating all of the Legatan gear that got mixed up in this. You understand me, Miss Leclair?"

"I'm not your enemy, Montgomery," she pointed out.

"You were here on a mission to de-stabilize a Protectorate world and send it careening into open civil war," Damien replied flatly. "Barring Vaughn's insanity, we would never have been on the same side. Work with me, and I'll forget I saw you. Oppose me…"

"I get it," Leclair said aloud. "I'll do it," she agreed. "Regardless of our reasons and our causes, today we *are* on the same side. I, for one, want to see that son of a bitch fall. *Nobody* should nuke a city and walk away."

"On that, Miss Leclair, we are in complete agreement," Damien told her.

#

"Are you ready?"

Amiri's question interrupted Damien's pacing. For the first time ever, he wore the golden Hand of his new office outside of his clothes, but they hadn't yet left his quarters. Armstrong had re-convened the cell leaders ten minutes before, but he doubted they were getting any further.

"Yeah," he said after a moment's thought, glancing over at his bodyguard. "You?"

"All I've got to do is stand there and look pretty," she told him sweetly. "But yeah, let's go."

She led the way in front of him, clearing the corridors from his room to the hidden airbase's single conference room. What he was aiming for now was as much theater as psychology, but every piece of momentum he could leverage, he would use – and complete surprise about the Hand was the biggest piece he had.

Two Freedom Wing fighters, in street clothes under medium body armor and carrying assault rifles, barred the doors to the conference room. They both looked uncomfortable as Damien and Amiri approached, and one of them clearly saw Damien's Hand, involuntarily taking a step back.

"Let us in," Damien ordered.

"They're not to be interrupted," the less aware guard told him. "Armstrong was very clear."

Damien turned to the guard and tapped the Hand. The rebel glanced down and his faced whitened.

"Regardless of whether you let me through or not, I'm going in," Damien said quietly. "I'd rather not hurt anyone, though."

He wasn't sure which guard hit the door panel, but both were out of his way with commendable alacrity. Nodding calmly to the guards, Damien Montgomery, Hand of the Mage-King of Mars, took a deep breath – and entered the room.

Any conversation on the conference call cut off as he and Amiri barged into the room, allowing the door to close behind them as Armstrong and the others looked up in shock.

"Have you come to a decision yet?" he asked mildly.

"We have not," Lori told him, eyeing him askance. "I told you we would let you know when we did."

"And the timeline has now become ridiculous," he told her bluntly. With a subdued flourish, he tossed the Hand onto the table. Lori stared at it like it was a venomous snake, about to lash out and bite her. "What's the obstacle?"

"You're not an Envoy," Lori whispered. "You're a god-damned *Hand*."

"Yes," he confirmed aloud so that everyone on the conference call knew exactly what he'd just done. "And I repeat myself, *Alpha*, what's the obstacle? What does the Freedom Wing require?"

He glanced around those in the room – Leclair, Pelletier, Armstrong and the others.

"Do you need pardons for crimes committed to date?" he asked. "Then done. Immunity from prosecution for actions to overthrow Vaughn? Done. Access to government systems? Done. I am a Hand, but I am not Legion. I need your help – what price do you demand?"

"It is... not a matter of *price, monsieur*," November's accented voice replied.

"Isn't it?" he asked. "You are here because you swore to overthrow Vaughn. You took up the cause of your people's liberty.

Now, faced with the fulfillment of that oath, you waver. Faced with sacrifice in the name of your cause, you quibble.

"I offer you victory in the cause you fight for," he continued. "Fight by my side, and you will be remembered as heroes. Stand aside, and you will be remember as fools who betrayed your oaths and let Ardennes burn."

He met Armstrong's eyes levelly and saw the answer in them. He continued regardless.

"If you will turn me away, then turn me away," he told them. "I will storm Versailles myself. Fight by my side or get out of the way – honor your oaths or betray them. Choose. We are running out of *time*."

The conference room was silent for a long moment, and then Leclair laughed.

"'Yea, though I walk through the valley of the shadow of death, I will fear no evil'," she quoted. "You'd really do it, wouldn't you? Try and storm the city with just Amiri and your magic?"

"If I must," Damien replied.

"'The Lord is my shepherd, I shall not want'," Pelletier's voice rumbled into the room. "'He restores my soul, he leads me in the paths of righteousness for His Name's sake'. Our dear Sierra picked an appropriate Psalm," he told his fellows. "I believe the path of righteousness has been laid before us. We would betray our cause and the path on which we have laid our feet, were we to turn aside now."

The room was silent for a long moment.

"*Il est un batard, mais il est notre batard*," November finally said into the silence. "You're Martian, Hand, and I don't trust you," she told Damien. "But you're right. This is our cause, and you're our only hope."

A moment of silence passed, and Armstrong met Damien's gaze levelly.

"I think you have our answer, My Lord Hand," she told him. "Even if perhaps we needed more convincing than we should, we are with you."

"Then I come back to my first question, with a different emphasis," he replied. "What do you need? If we are to neutralize Vaughn, what do we need that we don't yet have?"

The table was silent again, but it was a far more positive silence – a thoughtful silence.

"Two things, I think," Pelletier finally said aloud. "Intelligence is necessary – we need to know where Vaughn is hiding."

"I'm guessing the Command Center," Damien replied. "From what data I have, the planetary Emergency Command Center and the Nouveaux Versailles Defense Command and based in the same underground facility – from there, Vaughn can control the planet.

We'll need to seize it either way, and it's the most likely location for the Governor."

"We've already shown we can get the Phantoms into the city without too much difficulty," Leclair reminded. "That can get sixty troops wherever we need them, and the Scorpions in Versailles are shattered."

"But the Army remains," Pelletier said calmly. "There is most of a division – eight thousand men and women – based in and around Nouveaux Versailles. Which brings me to our second need: we need the Ardennes Army to sit this out."

"That's a tall order," Damien observed. "I believe General Zu is in command?"

"Of the entire Army, but he's headquartered in Versailles," Pelletier agreed. "I believe the good General's loyalties have always lain with the *people* not the government. So long as we were rebels, he would never work with us…"

"But it's a different matter when he's speaking to a Hand," Damien finished for the priest. "While the thought of simply sneaking into his house is tempting, a meeting would be better. Can you set one up?"

"He is a good Catholic man," the Archbishop replied calmly. "His conscience has not sat easy with Vaughn's governance.

"In short, yes, I can arrange a meeting."

#

Chapter 36

When the French and Canadian national governments on Old Earth had launched the colonization expedition to Ardennes, one of their major sources of funding had been the Catholic Church. Its Quebec Reformation branch had been on good terms with both governments, and by contributing funds and personnel the Church had got a foothold on the ground floor of an entire planet.

One of the consequences had been an old European informal definition of 'city' – one that required a cathedral.

Of course, Ardennes' cathedrals had been built in the twenty-fourth century. Underneath their native stone facades and stained glass were all of the modern amenities. Their pulpits had cleverly designed acoustics and expensive electronic sound systems, designed for easy upgrading. And hidden away from the eye of the congregations were modern apartments – and modern conference rooms.

The conference room 'Papa' Pelletier had snuck Damien into was a perfect, if small, example of its type. From the personal computer on his wrist, he could activate a series of screens built into all four walls, or raise a three-dimensional display tank out of the middle of the table. With the exception of the cruciform-heavy décor, the room wouldn't have looked out of place in any corporate headquarters in the Protectorate.

Damien wasn't alone in the room for very long. Less than ten minutes after he'd been smuggled into the cathedral and set up in the conference room, the door opened again and a gray-uniformed, white-haired man stepped into the room. The Hand got a glimpse of Pelletier behind the General, but the Archbishop only bowed and then closed the door behind Zu.

"General Zu," Damien said quietly. "Thank you for meeting me."

The old General stared at him for a long moment and then exhaled in an explosive sigh.

"Envoy Montgomery," he replied. "Wait, no," he corrected himself as his gaze took in the amulet hanging on Damien's chest, starkly contrasting his dark gray suit and shirt, "*Hand* Montgomery. One falls, another rises indeed."

"I serve Mars as His Majesty requires," Damien replied, his voice still quiet. "Have a seat, General. How much did Pelletier tell you?"

"Less than you would think," Zu said dryly. "In that he told me nothing, only called in an old favor to have me meet someone without even knowing whom. To be honest, I was expecting Armstrong and considering how to get out of *that* without having to arrest her or breaking my oaths.

"I did not expect you – and I did not expect a Hand."

With a sigh and an almost visible creak, the old General took a seat across from Damien. "I promised Eli I'd hear you out, and even if I hadn't, you are a Hand."

"The Archbishop aside, I don't think you'd be here if you didn't have some idea of the truth of the events of the last week," Damien said softly. "Some suspicion, if nothing else, of who truly killed Hand Stealey."

Zu winced and leaned forward onto the table, rubbing his temples.

"I suspect many things, My Lord Hand," he said finally. "I can prove none of them. Or do you think me so lacking in honor I would let the things whispers accuse my Governor of to pass?"

"But I have no proof, and he remains my Governor," the General told Damien. "Oath and law alike command my obedience while these things are true."

"I *have* proof," the Hand replied flatly. "I can prove a dozen of his crimes or more, but let's leave it at one: I know he killed Alaura Stealey with his own power."

"And so he is judged for one and not the many," Zu whispered, and Damien shook his head.

"He is judged for them all," he said flatly. "Every protestor ridden down, every child murdered in a faked terrorist attack, every miner killed at Karlsberg – every worker in Government House sacrificed to make the attack on Stealey look good. I judge him for them all, and I judge him guilty."

Damien's words were *not* metaphorical. A Hand, above all other things, was a *judge* – the highest member of the Protectorate's judiciary short of the Mage-King himself.

The old General's face was now entirely buried in his hands, and he stayed like that for a long moment. When he straightened, however, his gaze was level, and he appeared calm.

"I do not doubt you," he said flatly. "And unless I choose to defy the Hand you wear, I am bound to obey you over even my own Governor. But understand that I cannot deliver Vaughn to you."

He held up his hand before Damien could speak, shaking his head and continuing.

"It is not that I am unwilling," he clarified. "But Vaughn has long had his finger in the promotions and assignments in the Ardennes Planetary Army. Many of my officers owe their loyalty to him. Those loyal to me or even simply to justice are insufficiently concentrated for me to assemble any kind of reliable force.

"Were I to move against Vaughn, my Army would tear itself apart – and I would achieve nothing. So tell me, My Lord Hand. What would you have me do?"

"That is about what I was expecting," Damien told him, considering the old General. Trying to build a truly professional army while Vaughn kept interfering to keep chunks of it loyal to him must have been frustrating for Zu, but the old man barely showed it.

"I have assets in place or in motion to remove both the Governor and Mage-Commodore Cor," he told Zu quietly. "But the resources I have on the surface are insufficient to overcome both the Ardennes Special Security Service forces in this city *and* the Ardennes Planetary Army forces here.

"While it would be *useful* if you could provide reliable troops, it is not necessary," Damien continued. "What I *need* is for you to make sure the Army stays in their barracks when I move."

"You're working with the Freedom Wing," Zu stated. It wasn't a question, and Damien wasn't really surprised. If he didn't need Army troops, he'd either co-opted the Wing or brought his own – and Zu would know exactly how many of the people Damien had arrived with were still alive.

"Does it matter at this point?" Damien asked. "Vaughn is guilty of treason, murder, and more besides. Can you really judge the Freedom Wing for standing against him?"

"No," Zu sighed. "No, I can't. But it's been my job for a long time to make sure they couldn't destabilize the planet."

"Hardly an unworthy goal, General," the younger man told him. "Avoiding destabilization is high on my list of priorities – but removing Governor Vaughn is at the top."

General Caleb Zu laid his hands on the table and firmly shook his head, as if shaking clear loose thoughts.

"I can make sure the Army stays in their barracks," he finally said. "That's an order both loyal and disloyal will obey – and make sure others obey. They don't want to fight their brothers in arms any more than we want them to. How am I to know timing?"

"When the Navy arrives, lock them down," Damien told him. "If you have a secure communications line, I'll take that too – I can think of too many situations where being able to reach you will be necessary."

"Then it is done," Zu said calmly. "Past time, I think, for justice to return to Ardennes."

"That, my dear General, is why Mars sent a Hand."

#

Chapter 37

Amiri sat on the mountainside watching the sun set. She wore a heavy coat against the chill, but the view was worth it.

From here, you couldn't make out the cities and conflicts of humanity, only the snow, and the forest below. A glow in the distance marked what she knew was Nouveaux Versailles. Somewhere between that glow and her, Damien was in a helicopter winging his way back to the hidden airbase.

Sixteen hours remained before the earliest time the Navy task force could arrive. The next day would see the end to her mission on Ardennes, one way or another. That mission had changed and metamorphised since she'd arrived. First, to spy and make contact with the rebellion. Then, to protect Montgomery.

Then she'd had to kick the Hand's ass into final gear – but once he got going, Montgomery had proven he had at least *some* idea of what to do. Now, she'd see the mission done – watching the Hand's back and keeping him alive.

Crunching sounds in the snow distracted her from the sunset and she glanced behind her. Somehow, she wasn't surprised to see Mikael Riordan walking across the snow towards her.

"Grab a patch of snow," she told him. They hadn't really spoken after falling into bed together, nor had it been repeated. She got the impression she'd shocked him.

"I forget how beautiful sunsets are in the mountains," he said softly as he settled into the snow next to her. "I grew up here – you get used to it, but it... means something to see it with new eyes."

"New eyes?"

"I'm not a fighter, Julia," he said softly. "I don't think I've ever gone to sleep *knowing* I'm going into battle the next day. But I can't sit this one out – none of us can."

"You could, you know," she told him. "You're a speaker, not a fighter. No-one will think less of you if you stay out of the fight. We'll need you to help rebuild, if nothing else."

He shook his head.

"Found out that I can't stand by while others go into battle," he said simply. "The other night... I'd rather fight by my people's side than wait for them to... not come back."

He was talking both generally... and specifically. With a sigh, she shifted slightly to rest her leg against his, and reached out to take his hand.

"That wasn't a mistake," she told him firmly. "Passion of the moment – of surviving? Hell yes. But not a mistake."

"Didn't think it was," Riordan replied, squeezing her hand gently. "But it helped me make up my mind, Julia. I'm going into battle beside you, I'm not staying behind. This is my planet and I'll fight for it."

"You're a better man than this rock deserves," Amiri observed, glancing back out over the stark white snow and pale purple foliage of the foothills beneath them.

"Look at that," he instructed, gesturing out across the world spreading out beneath them with his free hand. "Look at the beauty of this world and tell me that it's not worth my utmost effort. That my world is not worth even my dying breath. I've convinced dozens – hundreds! – of others of my cause. I think it's worthwhile to fight for it myself."

"And what if *you* don't come back?" she asked him softly.

"Then I will be missed, I think," he replied, equally quietly. "But I will have died in the cause I convinced others to take up. I can't... I can't think that isn't worth it, or everything I've done has been hypocrisy."

Amiri leaned against him.

"We'd better both come back, then," she told him. "Because you may be right, but I for one want to see the day *after* tomorrow, and what that brings."

"I can't say you're wrong," he admitted with a laugh, "though I'll admit to wondering what *tonight* is going to bring."

Amiri arched an eyebrow at him and smiled lasciviously.

"I don't think wondering is necessary."

#

The hangar was crowded with aircraft and empty of people when Damien returned to the hidden rebel base. All twelve of the Freedom Wing's aircraft were now stuffed into a facility designed to hold and service six of them.

The extra squadron had been armed at their southern base and had only needed to be refueled here, a necessity given that the lack of space meant the automated loaders built into the base couldn't actually equip *any* of the Phantoms.

Nonetheless, Brute neatly slotted the last gunship into the space left for it.

"Get some rest," Damien ordered the pilot. "We'll all need it tomorrow."

"*Que sera, sera,*" the pilot replied. "*Bonne nuit.*"

"*Bonne nuit,*" Damien returned, turning to glance around the hangar. Even with the hatch closed, the blast of cold air that had accompanied them into the hangar had chilled the entire space, and he shivered slightly.

With Brute gone, the cavern rapidly became eerily quiet, but he found himself unable to leave. He knew he wasn't going to be sleeping anytime soon – he was far too wound up.

Somehow, though, he wasn't surprised to find Lori Armstrong sitting on the ammunition crates exactly where he'd waited for Amiri the other day.

"Shouldn't you be sleeping?" he asked the rebel leader.

"It seems… unlikely to happen," she replied, her gaze fixed on the stealth aircraft filling the hangar. "Do you think this will work?"

"'He either fears his fate too much or his desserts are small, who dares not put it to the touch, to win or lose it all'," Damien quoted. "I don't know if the plan will work, such as it is," he admitted. "The Army will stay out of it, though, which just leaves us with the Scorpions."

"And most of them are cracking heads across the planet," Lori agreed with a sigh. "I hate that. People are *dying*, and we're using it as a distraction for our mission."

"If we succeed, it all stops, Lori," the Hand told her. "Vaughn goes down – arrested or dead. Ardennes rebuilds."

"It sounds so easy when you say it like that," she replied. "Was this what you expected when you came here?"

"This was supposed to be a cake-walk," Damien admitted. "An easy, if high level, arrest, with an entire Navy squadron for support if things went south. Then, Alaura died, and what was supposed to be a training opportunity turned into a trial by fire."

Lori snorted.

"Think you've passed?"

"These sorts of things are pass/fail from what I can tell," he said. "If Vaughn is dead or in chains by tomorrow night, and I'm still breathing, I'll call it a pass."

"What happens then?" she asked. "Part of me… was never quite sure. The other part expected a *coup d'état* that would leave me Governor."

"That won't happen," Damien warned softly. "Mars doesn't remove Governors lightly. We encourage civil wars… almost never. But it's happened. And we have a follow-up plan.

"An interim Governor is already preparing a Task Force on Mars," he continued. "He or she – I don't know who it is yet, other than 'not me' – will arrive with a force of Military Police, forensic auditors and political advisors. They'll take over governance and law enforcement until they can rebuild the institutions of democracy on Ardennes, one piece at a time."

"So, what?" she demanded. "We trade a local dictator for a Mars-picked one?!"

"No," he disagreed. "The interim Governor has a fixed term – a few years at most. You'll have a new assembly as soon as possible. But... it will be months under direct rule from Mars. Years before we pull the MPs off the streets – and we'll probably *never* fully withdraw our troops.

"'Regime change' leaves us with a responsibility we can't throw aside," he continued. "Mars will *not* permit Ardennes to descend into a chaos of factional strife, reprisal and counter-reprisal. History tells us what happens if you intervene in a country or a planet and don't stay the course.

"Mars has the resources and the will to stay that course," he finished. "We will. Ardennes will be rebuilt. There will come a day, soon I hope, when you'll be *proud* of your world again."

"It all sounds so easy," Lori repeated. "I don't know if everyone will be so accepting of an outside rule."

"It's a compromise, and compromises are never comfortable," Damien told her. "But, in the end, there's a reason Hands get away with forcing compromises: we find the compromise. The Navy *enforces* it.

"Mars has found we go a lot further with a compromise backed by firepower than with an unenforced compromise – or an entirely external decision imposed purely by firepower," he shrugged. "It sure as hell works better than forcing a change of government and walking away."

She sighed, shaking her head and looking back at the gunships.

"All of that presumes we win," she reminded him. "What happens if our plans fail?"

"Vaughn won't know what hit him either way," Damien said quietly. "He got a preview at Sunshine, but I don't think it sank home – no-one on this planet really knows what it means for a Hand to go to war."

#

The main conference room aboard the *Righteous Guardian of Liberty* was equipped to allow a mixed physical and electronic conference of every ship's captain in an entire fleet deployment. The Captains and Executive Officers of Jane Adamant's tiny task force rattled like peas in a pod.

"Thank you all for coming," the newly minted Mage-Commodore told them. Since she was still acting as Captain of the *Guardian* herself, there were only ten people in the room – six men and four women. "We've done a lot of electronic communication and preparation over the last two days, but I wanted to have everyone together face to face before we entered the Ardennes system."

A Mage could only safely jump every eight hours at most, and even the Navy had problems putting more than four on a warship – usually including the Captain. At a jump every three hours, her task force had been pushing to reach Ardennes.

They'd been floating at the last jump point for an hour, long enough to convene the Captains by shuttle and get them back before they made that final leap.

"Does anyone have any high level questions before we start going over the situation and potential operations plans?" she asked.

The other officers in the room exchanged a series of silent glances, until finally the senior-most of the women, Mage-Captain Nicole Isabel, spoke up.

"I think I have to ask what everyone is thinking," the dusky-skinned cruiser commander said softly. "Do we *really* believe we're going to have to fight our own cruiser squadron? I mean... this has *never* happened – not in two hundred years!"

"Two hundred and six," Adamant confirmed. "We have seen Navy vessels end up in criminal hands – the *Azure Gauntlet*, most recently. We have seen individual Navy Captains go rogue and have to be put down. But you are correct – in the two hundred and six years the Royal Martian Navy has existed, we have *never* had a major formation revolt.

"If the intelligence we have received is correct, we are about to participate in the single largest space battle since the Eugenicist Wars," she told them all bluntly. "Those battles may have had more *ships*, but the largest vessels were barely half the size of a modern destroyer.

"Unfortunately, the source of our evidence for Cor's treason is impeccable," Adamant reminded them. "I don't believe any of us makes a habit of doubting His Majesty's Hands?" she glanced around and smiled coldly.

"The best case situation is that only Cor's flagship is with her, and that the crew of the *Unchained Glory* mutiny when they realize she's been found out," she continued. "However, assuming the best is a good way to get our people killed.

"Make no mistake," Adamant told her people, glancing around the room. "Cor is *very* capable, and has demonstrated a ruthlessness I would not expect of *any* Navy officer. She blew up a *city*, people, and that's not an option I would expect anyone in His Majesty's uniform to embrace short of the worst scenario imaginable."

"Hope for the best, prepare for the worst?" Captain Kole Jakab, a pale-skinned Terran native, suggested softly. "If she surrenders, our preparations have at least tested and sharpened our crews. If she fights…"

"If she fights, Cor may prove a real threat," Adamant said grimly. "We have almost a hundred million tons of warship to her seventy-five, but if anyone can find a way to climb those odds, Adrianna Cor is one of the few who could."

"So yes, I intend to plan for the worst," she told them. "And, sadly, I really do believe we will have to fight her entire squadron and the ASDF. If there was even a chance of anything else, we would have known of her treason long before now."

#

Chapter 38

The alarm interrupted Cor's breakfast. The meal was the only time of the day she allowed herself to indulge her sweet tooth, and she glared at the communicator on the table in her quarters across the stack of waffles.

"What is it?" she demanded after swallowing.

"Commodore, we have a *massive* jump flare at the one light minute mark," Lieutenant Trevor Hamilton, *Unchained Glory*'s tactical officer, reported. "CIC is resolving further detail, but the Captain asked me to let you know."

"How many ships?" Cor demanded.

"Unsure, ma'am," the officer replied. "The flare was big enough to cause sensor interference. It'll be a few minutes before we can resolve detail."

"Any communications?"

"None yet. They may be blocked by the interference – I don't think I've ever seen a jump flare of this size."

The Mage-Commodore's blood ran cold. A jump flare that large had to be at least an entire squadron of cruisers. There was *no* reason for that kind of force to come to Ardennes – unless they had some idea of just what had *actually* been going on.

She gave her waffles a sad look.

"Inform Captain Ishtar I'm on my way to the bridge," she ordered. "Let me know *immediately* if anything changes."

#

Mage-Commodore Cor strode onto the bridge of her flagship with a storm cloud on her heels. Her quarters were only slightly further away than the Captain's, and there had been no time for anything to change before she made it from her uneaten breakfast to the central Simulacrum Chamber of the warship.

"We have a problem," Mage-Captain Devi Ishtar told her bluntly, and gestured at the section of the screens surrounding them zoomed in on the emerging ships.

Cor may not have understood the imagery and scans used for aerial and ground combat, but she knew the iconography the *Unchained Glory* used to identify starships perfectly. It still took her a minute to identify just what was at the center of the five-ship formation now dropping towards Ardennes.

"That is a *battleship*," she said aloud, her voice surprisingly calm.

"*Righteous Guardian of Liberty*," Ishtar confirmed. "Accompanied by four *Honorific* class cruisers. Last reports have all five ships in the Tau Ceti system."

"Have they communicated yet?" Cor asked. It was theoretically possible that they were here to refuel at the logistics base.

"Not yet... wait," Ishtar stopped as the communications officer held up his hand. "We've got something?"

"Incoming from *Righteous Guardian*," the officer confirmed. "I can forward it to your office?"

The battleship was still a full light minute away, ten hours travel to make a zero velocity intercept in orbit. Any message was a recording that could be played and replayed before responding.

Cor swallowed and glanced around the room. Everyone on the bridge had been there when they'd blown Karlsberg to hell. Everyone was in on the half-a-dozen dirty little deals she'd cut with Vaughn, and they'd all collected their own cuts of the 'special compensation packages'.

There was nothing she could hide from them.

"No," she answered slowly. "Put it on the screens."

The bridge of a warship was also its Simulacrum Chamber, centered on the small silver model that, magically at least, *was* the ship. All of its walls were covered with screens, with the bridge crew working on platforms suspended in the middle of the pyramid-shaped room.

A window opened on the screens ahead of them all, resolving into a familiar woman in the navy blue uniform of the Royal Martian Navy, and the same golden circle on her collar as Cor.

"Mage-Commodore Adrianna Cor, this is Mage-Commodore Jane Adamant aboard the *Righteous Guardian of Liberty*," the woman introduced herself. She would have known Cor would recognize her, but she was speaking for the record. Cor knew the tone.

"It is my duty to inform you that charges of the most grievous nature have been laid against you," she continued. "You stand accused of mass murder and grand treason. My orders from His Majesty are to take you into custody.

"You *will* stand down your ships. All of your vessels must power down their weapons and evacuate their Simulacrum Chambers.

"You have one hour to comply, or I will use whatever force is necessary to bring you in."

The transmission ended, and Cor stared at the screen, now showing the stylized rocket-and-red-planet logo of the Royal Martian Navy. The bridge was silent around her, and she realized *everyone* was looking at her.

"Ma'am," Captain Ishtar asked, her voice soft and slow. "What do we *do?*"

She swallowed and spoke as calmly as she was able.

"First, I think I need to talk to Governor Vaughn."

#

"What do you mean, there's a *battleship in my system*?" Mage-Governor Michael Vaughn demanded of the crew in the main command center. "Where did it come from?"

"IFF identifies it as the *Righteous Guardian of Liberty*, sir," Captain Duval reported. "Last Royal Navy listing we received reported it as being in Tau Ceti, preparing for a refit."

The newly promoted Captain swallowed hard as his Governor rounded on him.

"The cruisers are also from Tau Ceti," he said quietly. "All of them should be part of Mage-Admiral Segal's Tau Ceti Station."

"Why the hell are they *here*?"

"There was a transmission to Mage-Commodore Cor," Duval reported. "It was under a Navy encryption; we can crack it but it will take us some time."

"Fuck that," Vaughn snapped. "Get Cor on the private line in my office – *now*. And someone get Montoya – ASAP."

"He's in the Center," Duval confirmed quickly. "I'll have him join you in your office." The officer paused. "Mage-Commodore Cor has just opened a channel. She's requesting to speak with you in private."

"Connect it to my office," the Mage-Governor of Ardennes snapped. He left Duval, currently the shift commander, standing awkwardly at the edge of the command center's central pit.

Slamming his door behind him, Vaughn crossed the underground conference room he'd commandeered and hit the 'accept' key on his personal computer. The main wallscreen lit up with the image of Cor's personal office, a plate of waffles at the Commodore's elbow and a fork descending from her mouth as she swallowed.

"Governor Vaughn," she greeted him.

"Commodore Cor," he replied. "Would you mind telling me what the *hell* is going on?"

"I was planning on asking you the same thing," she said sharply. "You've noticed our new friends."

"Yes. I'm told they've communicated with you."

"They have," she confirmed. "Their commander is a Mage-Commodore Adamant – an old 'friend' of mine who has to be giggling in her shoes.

"I've been charged with mass murder and treason. They know, Michael. If they know enough to lay those charges on me, they know enough to hang you next to me.

"I *know* none of Stealey's people made it out of this system, Vaughn," she told him. "So tell me, how the *hell* do they know?"

Vaughn cursed as he remembered Montoya's fit of paranoia.

"It's... *possible*," he admitted, "that someone got access to the transceiver array. We had nothing confirmed," he pointed out, "but it's possible."

"I'd say it's *probable*, Michael," she snapped. "And now it's come home to roost. That battleship is going to settle into orbit and its Marines are going to arrest us both. They'll haul us back to Mars, give us a perfectly fair trial, and *shoot us*."

"Everything I have done was for Ardennes," Vaughn said stiffly. Much of what he'd done could be argued as criminal, but he was *the Governor*. It had been necessary.

"Martian courts won't care, Michael," Cor said softly, almost gently.

"I feel like we're missing something," he said after a moment. "A Hand falls, another rises..."

"What?" the Commodore looked at him like he was crazy.

"There's no Hand on Ardennes, Adrianna," he told her. "A Mage-Commodore with a warrant can arrest *you*, but she doesn't have the authority to arrest me. They need a Hand for that, and Stealey's dead."

The door behind him opened and closed and he glanced back to see Montoya enter the room. He gestured the General to a chair and turned back to Cor.

"It doesn't matter," he said with a shake of his head. "This Adamant needs to make orbit before she can do anything. What is your plan, Mage-Commodore?"

Cor paused for a long moment, her eyes falling to the half-eaten stack of waffles on her table. With a convulsive motion, she threw the entire plate into the garbage and looked back up to meet his gaze evenly.

"I intend to fight," she said flatly. "Adamant has us out-massed, but I have her outnumbered, and I have years more experience in squadron command than she has.

"What I need from *you* is the ASDF," she continued. "I want you to put Admiral Martine under my command. With those destroyers, we stand a chance!"

Vaughn considered. Admiral Delia Martine commanded the fifteen Tau Ceti-built destroyers of the Ardennes System Defense Force. They were modern, capable ships, if a generation behind the

Navy by Protectorate law. They'd been expensive as hell, but now they looked to be worth every penny.

"Done," he promised. "I will advise Admiral Martine immediately." He paused. "Don't fail me, Adrianna," he told her. "We can still get out of this."

The Mage-Commodore smiled thinly. "You mean *I* can still get us out of this," she told him. "We'll see what happens."

#

"They're here!"

The bellow that echoed across the main landing pad in the Freedom Wing's hidden airbase drew everyone's attention. They had a small 'sensor' station set up on one side of the cavern, though its data actually came from a hack into the planetary defense network.

The operator, who had been keeping an eye on the orbital scanners and watching for the Navy to arrive, was standing and pointing at the screen. A few keystrokes activated a hidden projector and threw the sensor return up on the smooth stone wall, highlighting the five signatures of the newly arrived Navy task force.

Damien whistled as he interpreted the data signatures. He'd suspected that Alexander would send Adamant and the *Righteous Guardian*, but it was still amazing to *see* that half-kilometer pyramid slicing through space.

The shorter and narrower spikes of the cruisers next to her were a welcome sight as well. His King had pulled out all of the stops – five ships might seem a bare handful against the twenty-one already in orbit, but there were only twelve battleships in the entirety of human space.

He watched, bemused, as everyone dropped what they were doing and started scrambling for preparation. A moment later, Brute – the pilot already half-into his flight-suit – stopped next to him in confusion.

"Shouldn't we be getting ready?"

"They're still ten hours out," Damien reminded him quietly. Glancing around, he realized that if he didn't put a hold on things, the Wing was going to fire off the operation with Cor still in orbit. That wasn't going to help anyone.

"Everybody calm down," he bellowed, loud enough for everyone to hear him, then hopped up on a box so they could all see him.

"That's Mage-Captain Adamant and the battleship *Righteous Guardian of Liberty*," he announced so everyone could hear him. "I promised you justice – I promised you Mars would come – and we sent our best. That is *fifty million tons* of long-overdue justice.

"*But*," he continued, "she's still a full light minute – *eighteen million kilometers* – away. It'll take the *Guardian* a little over ten hours to close that distance, and she won't maneuver faster than that unless something goes *damn* wrong down here.

"So, *breathe*," the Hand ordered. "Adamant will deal with Cor. It will fall to us to deal with Vaughn, but we won't do anyone any favors by rushing. Check and double check *everything*. We move into Nouveaux Versailles in six hours.

"Then our dear Governor Vaughn will learn the punishment for his many, many crimes."

The chaos slowed, a scattering of applause turning into cheers and waving fists. Every eye in the room was on Damien – was on the Hand of Mars.

Somehow, in kicking the Wing into gear, it appeared that he'd accidentally taken command.

#

Montoya had waited patiently while Vaughn informed Admiral Martine of her new orders. The Admiral, despite nominally being senior to 'Commodore' Cor, took the orders in stride. Any two of Cor's cruisers, after all, out-massed Martine's entire fleet.

"I'm assuming you didn't call me in here to have me listen to you talk to our naval commanders, such as they are," Montoya observed dryly after the call ended. "I take it that someone definitely did get to the RTA?"

"Most likely Montgomery," Vaughn conceded, agreeing aloud with what his chief General had said days before. "Alexander wouldn't have listened to anyone less – at least, not enough to send a fucking battleship."

"So, what happens now? We watch and pray that Cor wins the day?"

"Cor is going to get her ass blown out of the sky," Vaughn said bluntly. "I know it and she knows it. She probably knows it with more certainty – I'm guessing because I can't see Alexander sending a fleet that couldn't take out what he *knew* was here."

"Shit."

"So, my question for *you*, General, is where does that leave us?"

"In trouble," Montoya said dryly. "We have enough missile launchers and other defenses that any assault on Nouveaux Versailles will be messy as hell. There are definitely ways they can *get* troops here – if nothing else, they can fly down the Fault a hell of a lot more easily than we can get missiles or interceptors over it.

"Planetary assaults are an ugly, ugly business though," he continued. "Faced with that, they may be willing to negotiate. *If* we can rely on our troops."

"Your Scorpions?"

"Utterly reliable," Montoya replied. "They're already in control of Versailles' defenses. But we're pretty spread out, any defense of this city will fall primarily on the Army."

"If we're attacked, they will do their duty," Vaughn snapped. "Or they'll regret it.

"But you said you were working on an insurance policy, Montoya. Is it ready to be activated?"

"It is," the Scorpion's commander confirmed. "But... it's a last-ditch option, Governor. It should suffice to get you and me off the planet, but it won't save your government."

"Then we'll hold off for now," Vaughn told him, wondering at his friend's vagueness. The only option they'd really discussed was a fast ship, after all.

"I'll be ready if everything else fails, my friend. We *will* get out of this," Montoya promised.

#

Chapter 39

"Here they come," announced Commander Kayin Breisacher, the *Righteous Guardian of Liberty's* Tactical Officer. "Six *Hammer* class cruisers, fifteen *Lancer* class destroyers – looks like the entire ASDF is coming out to play too."

Adamant nodded, reviewing the tactical data herself. Cor's squadron mustered six identical ships, and the *Hammer* class were older ships but still serviceable. According to the Fleet List, all six ships had been fully updated with the latest electronics and missiles, too, so she had no range advantage.

The *Lancers* were a different matter. Tau Ceti built them for export, and the Charter limited what could be sold to another system's defense forces. Their missiles would be at least a generation behind the Navy vessels, with almost eight light seconds' less range given the current geometry.

Unfortunately, the people who'd designed the *Lancers* had expected that weakness. Despite being barely a tenth of the size of the *Hammer* class, each of the *Lancers* actually carried seventy percent of the *Hammer*'s missile defense lasers.

Those fifteen ships almost tripled Cor's missile defenses, and as long as she held her formation together they'd be a tough nut to crack.

"What about the logistics depot?" she asked aloud. "Shouldn't there be ships out there?"

"Negative, ma'am," Breisacher replied. "Looks like everybody was in Ardennes orbit."

Adamant nodded slowly. That made sense, she supposed – the planet was in civil turmoil, the Navy was expected to help. It did ignore the fact that Cor's squadron was supposedly here to defend the logistics depot orbiting the gas giant – a logistics depot that contained enough modern missiles to allow a smart and brave pirate to carve out a new empire.

"Any verbal response from Cor?" she asked.

"Negative, ma'am," her com officer replied. "But..." he gestured to the screen showing the slow advance of the twenty-one warships.

"Oh, her message is perfectly clear, Lieutenant," the Mage-Commodore replied with a small smile. "I was wondering if she'd bothered to try to make excuses. For that matter, her acceleration is damned low."

Her own task force was driving in at five gravities, an acceleration easily absorbed by the rune matrix that provided the ships with artificial gravity. Cor's force was only coming out to meet them at a single gravity. All of her ships *should* have gravity runes, but they were playing it safe anyway.

"Re-send the recording, Lieutenant Fiero," she ordered her com officer. "Let's take away any chance for the Commodore to pretend she didn't know what we're here for." She turned to Breisacher. "Commander – please have the squadron prepare to clear for action in…"

She checked her math. Her missiles had over twenty-five hundred times her own current acceleration – and no need to decelerate to a rendezvous with their targets. She'd be in weapons range of Cor's formation over ninety minutes before she'd hit turnover.

"We'll clear for action in three hours," she told the Tactical Officer. "Charles, pass the word to the task force to go to General Quarters at the same time."

That would be roughly twenty minutes before they reached missile range. If Cor was going to do anything clever, she'd have to do it before then.

#

Cor glared at the sallow-faced image of Admiral Delia Martine on her screen. She'd engaged a privacy bubble around her command chair on the *Unchained Glory*'s bridge to avoid blatantly dressing down another flag officer in front of her crew. The odds were that her long-term relationship with Martine was irrelevant, but it rarely hurt to observe the niceties.

"What do you *mean*, your ships can't make more than two gravities?" she demanded. The current acceleration of her task force felt like they were limping along – and they were! Most of the pirates in the galaxy would regard a Navy vessel traveling at one gee as blood in the water. "Your ships come from Tau Ceti with a full gravity rune matrix, don't they?"

"They had full rune matrices upon arrival, *oui*," Martine said precisely. "However, *Mage*-Commodore, there are only six Mages in the entire Ardennes Self Defense Force. Providing full and proper maintenance for the gravity matrices is not their top priority, *nes pas*?

"We made certain the runes worked enough to provide daily gravity, but I do not believe that the matrices would be able to safely provide more than a single gravity of inertial compensation."

The prissy little woman seemed completely unbothered by her announcement, as if the fact that her ships could *maybe* achieve twenty percent of their rated acceleration wasn't an issue. Cor carefully did *not* tell the stupid mundane playing at being an officer what she thought of the woman's little fleet.

"We will have to adjust our tactics," she said finally, through gritted teeth. "Given the reduced range of your weapons, we'll need to use your ships primarily as missile defense in any case."

And that would keep them out in *front* of Cor's ships, where they were unlikely to accidentally shoot her cruisers. If one of Martine's tin cans ate a missile from her ships, she wasn't going to be heart-broken, either.

She dropped the privacy shield and returned her attention to her bridge crew. They were, at least, *competent*.

"We will maintain one gravity of acceleration," she said calmly. "The ASDF units cannot safely maintain a higher speed."

If their rune matrices were in such bad shape, she wasn't sure about the rest of their equipment either. With fifteen fully functional *Lancers*, this wasn't a completely lost cause, but if Martine's ships were as incapable as it appeared...

"Ma'am, the *Righteous Guardian* has repeated their earlier transmission," her com officer informed her. "Shall we reply?"

"No," she said flatly. "There's nothing worth saying at this point – either we surrender or we fight. Surrender will only buy any of us," she gestured around the bridge, "a noose or a firing squad. I am uninclined to accept His Majesty's idea of mercy."

She glanced around at them. None of her crew looked *happy*, but they all seemed to be on board. Hamilton returned her gaze calmly, and then softly said what they'd all been thinking.

"Ma'am, we can't win this fight. Especially not if the ASDF ships aren't worth the scrap they're built of."

Cor sighed and glanced at the screen showing the fifteen destroyers formed up in front of her squadron. Their missile defense could make all the difference – if it worked. If it didn't, they were all going to die.

Dying was not something Cor intended to try just yet.

"You're right," she finally confessed. "Set up a squadron-level, maximum acceleration, course to the nearest location we can jump from, and keep it updated. We'll use the ASDF's missile defenses to get as far as they can, and then make a run for it.

"We've got a better chance to blast our way past that battleship than to fight it."

#

Space battles were slow, almost stately, affairs. Hiding the massive heat signature of a million or fifty million ton warship's matter-antimatter engines was nearly impossible, even for magic. Once two ships or fleets had decided to accept the engagement, everything after that was simple linear arithmetic.

Nonetheless, Adamant remained on the bridge of the *Righteous Guardian of Liberty*. Her experience was that her crew needed to see her – needed to know she was watching for tricks and traps to keep them safe.

Of course, 'her experience' was exactly two space battles, with vastly inferior opponents flying cobbled together pirate ships.

She could count the number of battles the Royal Martian Navy had fought in the last three years on her fingers. Given the restrictions in the Charter and the lack of availability of warships to anyone except star system governments, to her knowledge the RMN had *never* fought as even a battle as she was about to face.

"How long to missile range?" she asked softly.

"A little less than an hour," Breisacher replied. "About thirty minutes after that for the ASDF if Cor hasn't upgraded their weapons."

"Any change in their vectors?"

"Negative, ma'am," the Tactical Officer replied. They'd repeated the exchange every twenty or thirty minutes for over two hours now, but the little ritual and confirmation seemed to re-assure everything around them.

"Wait," Breisacher suddenly stated sharply, looking down at his screens. "I have an aspect change!"

"What are they *doing?*" Adamant asked, looking to the screens and seeing the icons shift.

"The Seventh Cruisers have broken off – they pulled a ninety degree course change perpendicular to the ecliptic and went to ten gravities acceleration!"

"What about the destroyers?"

"Still on course," her Tactical Officer reported. "… I think Cor just cut and ran."

"Agreed," the Mage-Commodore replied, scanning the screen and display as she judged distances and vectors in her head. "But the timing… can the ASDF evade us at this point?"

"Negative, ma'am," Breisacher replied. "Unless they managed to come up with ten times the accel they've shown so far and break in the opposite direction from Cor, anyway. At their current accel, they can only add maybe ten minutes to the time to range."

"Understood," Adamant acknowledged, and came to a decision.

"Signal to the Task Force," she ordered, glancing at her communications officer. "Mage-Captains Isabel and Jakab are to maintain their current course. They will intercept the ASDF destroyers and neutralize them. Accept surrenders if offered, but they *will* be in Ardennes orbit in eight hours to support Hand Montgomery."

"Mage-Captains Dionysios and Duane are to form on *Righteous Guardian*. They have five minutes to secure the ships for subjective acceleration, then we will fire one time-delayed salvo at the ASDF and break off to pursue Mage-Commodore Cor."

Adamant glanced at her Executive Officer, who nodded and started to give the orders for the *Righteous Guardian of Liberty* to prepare for the orders she was giving.

"We will pursue at fifteen gravities," she finished, ignoring the several sharp breaths taken around her. "Send, and have them acknowledge receipt," she ordered the officer, then turned back to Breisacher.

"Prep that time-delay salvo, Kayin," she told him. "We'll feed the timing and telemetry data to the *Master of Wisdom* and the *Esquire of Glorious Conflict*." For the first time in her life, she realized that the Protectorate Navy's taste in ship names added an unnecessary delay in combat. Something to point out to the higher-ups after this was done.

"Strap in people," she ordered the rest of her bridge crew. "The rune matrix *should* be able to compensate up to twelve gravities, but that'll still let three gees through, and none of us are used to that."

Settling herself in her chair in the middle of the bridge, next to the simulacrum that controlled the battleship's magic, Mage-Commodore Adamant followed her own advice as her crew sprang into motion around her.

"What about Ardennes, ma'am?" Kayin asked quietly. "Isabel and Jakab don't have the Marines to launch any significant ground attack."

"I know," she admitted, equally quietly. "But *my* job is to make sure that the woman who blew away a city doesn't escape to the Fringe with an entire squadron of Protectorate Cruisers.

"Hand Montgomery will need to deal with Governor Vaughn on his own for a little while longer."

#

For a few precious minutes, Adrianna Cor was certain she was going to get away. All Navy ships had the same gravity runes to reduce acceleration, and the battleship actually had less total delta-v stored aboard than her cruisers.

Their speed would bring them to a safe zone to jump well before Adamant's task force could bring them to bay.

Then the immense mass of the battleship shifted. Three of the five Martian ships flared to life with new energy, their heat signatures expanding exponentially as the warships turned to pursue her.

The *Unchained Glory*'s computer churned the numbers – and then informed her that the Martian warships would be in range in forty minutes. The massive increase in their acceleration needed to allow them to catch her ships meant they'd be in range *sooner*.

"How the *hell* can they *do* that?" she demanded aloud, glaring at the Captain of her flagship.

Devi Ishtar winced and glanced down at the screens.

"The *Guardian* is huge," she said quietly. "Everything on her is over-engineered – her thrust nozzles can withstand temperatures and pressures ours cannot. The *Honorific* class... was designed with similar criteria. They can't sustain this acceleration forever, but..."

"They can sustain it long enough," Cor said grimly. She needed roughly seventy minutes to make empty space with a low enough gravity to safely jump. Even with the seven minute flight time of Adamant's missiles, they would now be under fire for almost twenty-five minutes.

"Can we go any faster?" the Mage-Commodore demanded.

"We could," Ishtar said slowly, "but our engines are not over-engineered. We could gain perhaps another two, *maybe* three, gravities, but we could easily lose several ships to engine failure – potentially including *this* one – and still be under fire for at least ten minutes."

"I see," the Mage-Commodore said grimly, looking at the screen. The destroyers she'd abandoned were doing the only smart thing left to them – they were running. They'd pulled another two gravities out of their back pockets to do it too, she noted.

It wasn't going to save them. Two of Adamant's cruisers were still on vector to intercept them and reach Ardennes. Those two ships alone outmassed Martine's entire command by three to two, and Cor couldn't bring herself to feel sorry for the prissy bitch's now inevitable fate.

"Pull us ahead of the rest of the squadron," she ordered calmly. "Interface all missiles defenses through our primary computer net.

"Adamant *knows* which ship is the flagship," she continued as Ishtar started to object. "She'll focus fire on us, which will allow us to use the entire squadron's missile defenses against her attacks."

Cor turned her gaze grimly back to the screens, watching the three warships come thundering along on their intercept vector. With a battleship on the other side, she was going to need every edge she could get!

#

The minutes ticked by and the range slowly shrank. For all of the unimaginable acceleration of the missiles the Protectorate fielded for the Martian Navy, the ships themselves were still mostly limited by the tolerance of their crews and the ability of the magic to protect them.

Adamant had very quickly realized that she'd overestimated just how much acceleration the rune matrix would absorb. Every member of her crew was being pressed into their acceleration couches at four times their Earth-normal weight and it was wearing them down, fast.

After an hour of this, her crew wouldn't be worth much, and it would take several *more* hours for her to reach Ardennes' orbit. But Cor would *not* escape.

"All systems are armed," Breisacher told her quietly. "We are co-ordinating salvos across all three ships." He paused. "Ma'am, what is our target?"

The new Mage-Commodore studied her opponent's formation. She saw Breisacher's point – by pulling the *Unchained Glory* ahead of the rest of her squadron, Cor had given her a choice between making her salvo more vulnerable or working her way through the squadron ship by ship – and potentially letting Cor get away.

"We cut the head off the snake, Kayin," Adamant said quietly. "Everything we've got on the *Unchained Glory*. Once Cor's gone, the rest may surrender. And if they don't..." she shrugged. "I'm less concerned about hunting down a few rogue captains than an entire rogue squadron. Cor dies."

"Yes ma'am. I'll set up the fire plan."

Adamant left him to it and focused on the screens surrounding her. At this point, there was nothing she could do. Everything was set, and the only real question was whether Cor's people's *will* would hold up under fire.

How prepared were they to die for a traitor?

#

The geometry of pursuit allowed Cor to fire first. The traitor Mage-Commodore caught herself holding her breath as her squadron ceased acceleration to rotate in space. The Martian Navy had long ago optimized their warships for pursuit. It made Cor's position more tenuous than she liked – she had to rotate to fire, and when Adamant's salvos began arriving, she'd have to be facing them to use most of her defenses.

It would slow down her escape, but the alternative was fiery death.

Rotated and facing their enemies, the mighty ten million ton warships shivered from the recoil of their missiles, and then rotated again to blast forward once more.

Her tactical display lit up with first dozens, then *hundreds* of tiny lights. Three hundred and sixty missiles blasted into space, took a moment to orient themselves with their sisters, and then blasted back along her squadron's path at twelve and a half thousand gravities.

Thirty seconds passed in silence, her entire bridge frozen around her as they watched the suicidal little spacecraft charge backwards.

Then their pursuers launched. *They* had no need to rotate, and the three warships threw four hundred and sixty missiles back at Cor. Each cruiser threw twenty more missiles than her own warships, and the battleship carried *three hundred* launchers.

Then her own ships rotated again to fire their second salvo, exactly sixty-five seconds after the first. Thirty seconds after that, the pursuers launched again.

Both forces were using the same missiles. The same launchers. Every system on all nine ships was perfectly matched.

Cor glared at Adamant's task force on the screens. The weapons systems were exactly the same, but Adamant had more of them. At General Quarters, both were locked out of each other's systems, there was no way to abuse the similarities.

It was down to luck and formation. In less than six minutes, she'd find out if Adamant had fallen for her bait – and if her trick was enough to save her ship.

#

Cor's missiles came in first. They hit the outer defense zone of the three loyalist warships at a fifth of the speed of light, and lasers began lighting them up. Hundreds of invisible beams were marked on the screens with their patterns of energy, and missiles began to detonate.

Antimatter explosions formed their own kind of electronic jamming, and each explosion made it harder to track the missiles remaining.

Adamant was still the Captain of the *Righteous Guardian*, and as the missiles hit the outer perimeter she had already forced herself up against the force of the battleship's acceleration and laid the runes tattooed onto her palms on the floating silver simulacrum of her warship.

With an almost unfelt exhalation, she *became* the ship. Every rune carved into the fifty million ton hull told her their story in an inrush of data, and the screens around her became her eyes as she looked deep into space.

Mage-Commodore Jane Adamant saw the missiles coming and called her magic to her. Fire and lightning danced in her mind – and then danced in the empty void around her. She met the missiles with her will and training, and they died in their dozens.

The Mage-Captains of the two escorting cruisers lashed out with their magic as well. The space around the three warships was overwhelmed with antimatter explosions, invisible laser beams, and the plasma and lightning of human magic.

The first missile swarm was annihilated well short of the task force, and Adamant spared a moment to judge the success of their strike on Cor's fleet. A similar cataclysm of artifice and magic surrounded the Seventh Cruisers, making it difficult to make out much, but it seemed they'd successfully weathered the storm.

The second missile salvo burst into the cloud of radioactive debris in front of the *Righteous Guardian*, and Adamant turned her power back to the threat. More missiles disintegrated under the defensive laser turrets, and even more were shattered beneath the amplified power of the three starship captains.

Dionysios missed one. A missile slipped under the Mage-Captain's guard, diving towards the battlecruiser at twenty percent of the speed of light.

Adamant saw it and lashed out with her magic, summing a wall of force a kilometer across between the missile and the *Master of Wisdom*. The missile slammed into her magic with an explosion and impact that made her physically cringe backwards before regaining control of herself.

Another few moments of peace. They were gaining rapidly on Cor's ships now, the cruisers unable to accelerate away as their design forced them to face the incoming fire. Adamant's second salvo burned in hot on the heels of her first, and the debris cloud of five hundred missiles was worse than that of four hundred.

Adamant couldn't help but feel a stir of pride as she watched them fight for their lives – in the end, her enemies remained *Martian* warships, trained in the same school as her. They fought hard, but it wasn't enough.

A dozen missiles broke through the center of the formation, diving for the *Unchained Glory* with deadly speed – and then reality *shifted*. With a huge jerk of power, whoever was at *Glory's* amplifier *yanked* one of the other cruisers into the missiles' path.

The ten million ton ship slammed into the missiles from the side, crushing their containment fields and detonating their warheads. Moments later, the cruiser's own antimatter storage lit up – and a new, if momentary, star lit up of the Ardennes system.

#

The sound of a safety being clicked off echoed resoundingly in the sudden dead silence of the *Unchained Glory's* bridge.

It was enough to yank Cor away from the simulacrum she'd just seized from Mage-Captain Ishtar and draw her attention to Lieutenant Trevor Hamilton, who had drawn his sidearm and pointed it at her.

"Put that down," she snapped. "What are you *doing*?"

"What am *I* doing?" the young officer – the *boy* – demanded. "You killed the Captain!"

Cor glanced away from the automatic pistol at Ishtar and swallowed. She'd flung the Mage-Captain away from the simulacrum with magic in her rush to reach it and save them all. Now, the pale-skinned Ishtar lay slumped in a corner of the pyramid-shaped central chamber, her neck at a clearly impossible angle. She would never be getting back up.

"I saved us!" she snapped at Hamilton. "I did what I had to!"

"You've killed us," the young man told her flatly, gesturing to the screens with the pistol. "We could have held – could have stopped those last few missiles. But now you've shown your true colors – and no-one's going to die for a coward."

Mage-Commodore Adrianna Cor followed the line of her Tactical Officer's gesture and saw that the remaining other four ships of her squadron had decided they'd had enough. Each had taken off on a different vector, perpendicular to the *Unchained Glory's* course. None of them were firing on the remaining missile salvos, and *thousands* of weapons blasted their way towards the *Glory*.

"Cowards!" she snapped. "Traitors!"

"I think… I think we all know who the coward and the traitor here is," Hamilton said quietly. "We're all going to die anyway, Commodore, but I think the poor innocent youth I was when I met you deserves this satisfaction."

She turned back to him, staring down the barrel of the gun she *knew* the boy would never fire.

"We can still…" she began.

He fired.

#

Adamant watched as the Seventh Cruiser Squadron's neat formation came apart. Four ships blasted away to opposite corners, and the thousands of remaining missiles swarmed the *Unchained Glory*.

The missiles bearing in on the *Righteous Guardian* began to detonate on their own. First in tens, then in hundreds as the cruisers detonated all of their missiles as a token of surrender. Sweeping laser turrets cut down the remaining missiles, presumably launched by the *Unchained Glory* herself.

"Ma'am, we're getting surrender transmission from the remaining ships," Breisacher reported. Further reports were cut off when the first of *their* salvos struck home.

Whoever was running the *Unchained Glory's* defenses had done better than anyone could have reasonably hoped. With a single cruiser's laser turrets – not even the amplifier, as not a single spell fired in the cruiser's defense – they shot down nearly a hundred missiles.

Which had left over *three* hundred in the third salvo.

The screens surrounding Mage-Commodore Adamant blanked to block out the flash as a half-*teraton* explosion lit up the sky, overwhelming every sensor, every camera.

It lasted moments. Moments in which Adamant smiled grimly at her victory.

The blast faded to reveal the last trickling salvo from the traitor cruiser. Lacking control from their mothership, the sixty missiles threw themselves at the closest target – Mage-Captain Dionysios' *Master of Wisdom*.

The self-detonations of their sisters and the cataclysmic destruction of the *Unchained Glory* had hidden half of the salvo until it was far too late. They ripped across the last five light seconds in what seemed like moments. The Mages at their simulacrums lashed out with power, and the laser turrets from all three warships flashed their invisible energies.

Three missiles survived – guided by their suicidal computers, they slammed into the *Master of Wisdom* fractions of a second apart. Her armor was huge and magic guarded her core, but massive chunks of the cruiser vanished in plumes of vaporized metals.

Moments later, the crippled warship was back-lit by the detonation of her antimatter cores – *outside* the ship. The *Master* drifted, her engines gone, her weapons crippled, and her power source abandoned – but enough left for there to be survivors.

"Get me Dionysios," Adamant ordered. "I need a status report!"

It took a moment to establish a channel, but the response was not from Mage-Captain Dionysios.

"This is Mage-Commander Caliver," the voice of Dionysios's XO told her. "Mage-Captain Dionysios... is dead. He... teleported the antimatter cores outside the ship – far enough to be safe. It... was too much for him."

Adamant had seen the wreckage left when an amplified Mage over-exerted him or herself. *Master of Wisdom's* bridge had to be a preview of Hell.

"We'll deploy engineers and medical teams immediately," she told Caliver. "We'll have shuttles to you in ten minutes."

"Understood," the Mage-Commander said quietly, coughing against unseen smoke. "Thank you."

Grimly, Mage-Commodore Jane Adamant turned back to her screen. For the first time since closing with the Seventh Cruiser Squadron, she had time to look at the overall situation.

The remnants of the Seventh were still running. She'd deal with that in a moment. The Ardennes System Defense Force was in even worse shape. Six of their ships were gone – either destroyed in the mass salvo she'd launched or taken out by Isabel and Jakab.

The remainder had ceased accelerating, and were accompanied by data codes notifying her that they'd surrendered and Marine boarding shuttles were on their way. That battle had begun and ended while they'd fought Cor.

"All right," she said aloud. "Record for transmission to the remaining Seventh Cruiser ships:

"This is Mage-Commodore Jane Adamant. Your surrenders are accepted if you do the following immediately upon receipt of this transmission: you will stand down your engines and weapons and evacuate your amplifier chambers. Once this is complete, you will stand down from General Quarters and re-activate the external command access to your internal systems."

She looked at the wrecked hulk of the *Master of Wisdom*. They'd been lucky, but there were still going to be hundreds – possibly thousands – of dead aboard the cruiser.

"These terms are not negotiable. Failure to comply will be met with the destruction of your vessels."

#

Chapter 40

Even in daylight the deaths of starships were visible from the world below. Damien was grateful for the auto-darkening windows of the gunship as the sky above them lit up with white fire, and he checked the relay from the Ardennes military scanners.

"That's it then," he said quietly as he studied the vectors and positions of the warships. "Four of Cor's ships have surrendered, as has what's left of the ASDF. The Protectorate controls Ardennes space."

"Shouldn't that basically end this whole game?" Amiri asked from beside him. Her voice was also pitched quietly – he could hear her over the interior noise of the helicopter, but the Freedom Wing fighters in the rest of the passenger compartment probably couldn't.

"In a logical world, yes," Damien told her. "But the main advantage of the high ground is the ability to drop rocks, and we want to keep everything down here intact.

"So a ground assault becomes the only way, and Versailles' missile defenses…" he shrugged. "I don't expect Vaughn to tamely roll over. That's why we're moving."

The two cruisers that had taken out the ASDF were still on his original estimated time-table and had just made turnover. That put them five hours out. The Wing was moving into position, ready to deploy well in advance of their arrival – before Vaughn would, hopefully, expect any attack.

"Montgomery, we've got a problem," Leclair's voice cut into their conversation. She was transmitting over his headset, *very* careful to be sure no-one could hear it. "Take a listen to this."

The cyborg pilot relayed the voice clip into his headset.

"All pilots be advised, this is Nouveaux Versailles Air Traffic Control. Due to the attack currently taking place above us, a no-exemptions no-fly zone has been established above Nouveaux Versailles. All flights are to divert to Atterrissage. Any aircraft entering Nouveaux Versailles airspace will be shot down without warning.

"I repeat…"

Leclair cut off the transmission.

"The Phantoms can't hide their signatures enough to fly into the city without being detected," she warned him. "We were relying on being able to look like civilian aircraft."

"I know," Damien reminded her. "We're going to need to re-assess. Do we have any vehicles in position near the city?"

"Everything we had has already been commandeered for the ground teams we already have in place," Leclair told him. "Looks like they're drawing the no-fly line ten kilometers outside even the suburbs. That's a hell of a long way to walk, Montgomery."

"I don't care where Vaughn's people draw the line," Damien said dryly. "Assuming they'll shoot at us when they *see* us, how close *can* you get us?"

The pilot considered for a long moment as the gunships swept closer.

"We can get into the suburbs," she finally said. "We'll still have ten, fifteen, kilometers to go, but we can rendezvous with some of our existing people and, well, commandeer vehicles if needed."

"All right," Damien considered, glancing at the map. That would still be pushing the timing. "Next question. How close can *you* get *me?*"

He wasn't entirely sure *which* package of augments Leclair had received from her Legatan masters, but even the basic set would give her faster reaction times and better perception than the rest of the pilots. Presumably, since the Augment had been sent to train pilots and fly gunships, she had a piloting-oriented suite that should make her *much* better.

"That depends," she admitted. "How comfortable are you with them seeing us, and with them shooting at us?"

"The gloves are off, Miss Leclair," Damien told her. For him, the statement was as literal as figurative – the long black gloves he normally covered the runes on his hands with had been left behind at the base. "I am *perfectly* comfortable with both being seen and being shot at. They may be surprised at the results of the latter."

That managed to surprise a sharp chuckle from the pilot.

"I don't think I can get us all the way to the Command Center," she told him. "The Center has its own defenses, and I'm not sure we want to play with surface-to-air *lasers*. But the Central District's towers impede its line of sight. I can get us... a kilometer or so away?"

"Pass the orders for everyone else to land safely and move on the missile defenses," Damien instructed after a moment's thought. "Then take us all the way in."

#

Damien moved forward as they approached the city, displacing the co-pilot into the passenger compartment as he took the only seat available next to Leclair. The Augment spared him a quick look, nodded for her co-pilot to leave, and then returned her attention to the air outside them.

Nouveaux Versailles, with its glittering glass skyscrapers and crude concrete apartment buildings, was a solid block on the horizon, rapidly growing in front of them. The other gunships were barely visible blurs, speed and chameleon coatings helping to render them indistinct if you didn't know what to look for.

The Hand *did* know what to look for, so he caught the moment when the other eleven aircraft broke off, diving down to disgorge their cargo of Freedom Wing assault squads into the city's suburbs without detection.

From here, Damien could spot the 'apartment buildings' on the exterior of the Central District that housed Nouveaux Versailles' concealed anti-air defenses. In the current environment, much of the pretense built into the structures was gone. Radar dishes had emerged from the roofs, and panels that had appeared to be apartments had slid aside to expose the racks of surface-to-air missiles.

"Everybody hold on," Leclair said over the PA. "We're going in low, we're going in fast, and if you lose your lunch, you're fucking cleaning it up!"

Damien had enough time to check that he was fully buckled in and to swallow hard before the Legatan pilot demonstrated why she was the only one going any further.

She started by turning *off* the helicopter rotors. For a heart-stopping several seconds, the Phantom dropped like a stone, plummeting towards the ground.

Then she re-engaged the engines and shot forward. They were, at most, twenty meters above the ground. The Hand in her co-pilot seat could *see* the people on the streets taking cover as the gunship ripped forward, the wind kicked up by their motion sending objects flying and shaking trees apart.

"And they've got us," she said aloud, a tiny gesture of her head pointing out an icon on the dashboard flashing red – the radar had passed the detection threshold.

"You fly," Damien told her. "Leave the missiles to me."

He'd barely finished speaking before the first set launched. The four 'concealed' SAM sites in their line of sight fired simultaneously. Two missiles launched into the air from each site, sonic booms echoing out from their hulls as their engines flashed to full life.

Their speed saved none of them. For only the second time since arriving on the planet, Damien triggered *all* of his runes. His entire body lit up with a gentle warmth as energy channeled through the five Runes of Power on his torso and arms, doubling and redoubling, again and again.

With a smile, he reached out with his power and snuffed the missiles out. Each pair died together, moments after each other, their crumpled remnants falling harmlessly to the ground.

"*Son of a...*" Leclair cursed as the threats disappeared from the radar. "How did you...?"

"Magic," he replied calmly. "Watch your flying," he ordered, and turned his attention back to the exterior of the aircraft as the SAM sites launched again.

This time, each site launched *six* missiles – and he didn't let them get nearly as far. With a sweep of power, he flung the first set *back* into its launchers. The others made it further out, and he crushed them into harmless debris a second time.

There were fail-safes built into the missiles to stop them detonating too close to their launchers. Fail-safes meant to keep them from triggering in any circumstance except hitting their target. They worked perfectly – on five of the six missiles.

The sixth slammed head-on into the rack of missiles it had launched from and detonated. Sixty more SAMs followed a moment later, gutting the concealed launch site as a dozen tons of high density chemical explosives went off.

"One down," he said grimly. "Are we clear?"

Leclair ducked them into between two apartment buildings, diving them down a side street half a dozen meters off the ground.

"I am *so* glad I didn't push my luck with you earlier," she told him, then pulled the aircraft to a sudden halt that left him gasping for breath against his restraints.

"And yes, we're clear," she finished. "This is our stop."

#

Stepping outside of the gunship onto thankfully solid ground, Damien made sure his wrist computer was online, and linked into the Freedom Wing's communications network.

"Alpha, status report," he requested.

"You rang the doorbell nice and loud," Armstrong replied. "We're moving against the surface-to- space and surface-to-air sites now. They may not have been expecting us, but everyone was on edge – they're dug in and fighting hard.

"They're also under-equipped and outnumbered," she continued. "Zu kept his word – Iota confirms orders have gone out for the military to stay in their barracks. We've been identified as 'Mars-sanctioned special operatives'."

"That's what you are now," Damien reminded her. "Keep your people playing nice – let's do this cleanly."

"I get it, Montgomery," the Freedom Wing's leader replied. "No atrocities, no reprisals. Just... bring down Vaughn."

"We'll all do our jobs," the Hand promised, glancing around the empty streets. "Keep me in the loop, we're going in."

Amiri and Leclair had been extracting and organizing the half-dozen troopers with them as he spoke to Alpha, and he now had a small, eight person, squad in medium armor and all packing various degrees of heavy weapons.

Two of the troopers had backpack-powered battle lasers matching Amiri's, and the other four were armed with Legatus' finest multi-purpose firearm, a heavy battle rifle with a magazine-fed under-barrel grenade launcher.

Leclair was apparently following a similar 'gloves-off' approach as Damien was. She was carrying a drum-magazine-fed, fully-automatic, thirty millimeter grenade launcher. It was a weapon the Legatans made exclusively for the use of Augments. For anyone else, it was a belt fed tripod-mounted weapon.

Damien smiled grimly as he looked over his team. He wore the same body armor as them, but wasn't visibly armed.

"What do you need us to do?" Leclair asked. Unlike her men, she clearly knew who the most dangerous person on that street corner was.

"Keep up," he ordered flatly, and took off.

#

Whoever was in command of security for the Command Center hadn't taken the chance that Damien's team had landed so close to them by accident. They came around the corner to find a pair of armored personnel carriers rolling straight towards them – and the heavy machine guns mounted on the vehicles opened fire immediately.

The bullets ran into the shield of solidified air Damien was maintaining in front of them, ricocheting away as if they'd hit a solid wall. They intensified the fire, but he barely felt the impacts.

"On my count," he told his squad. Understanding his intention, Amiri hefted her laser and took aim. The Freedom Wing fighters followed suit a moment. "One, two… three."

On three, he shattered the air shield and threw its pieces at the APCs. The machine guns stuttered and jammed. He knew from his training that with the lack of anything actually *physical* blocking the barrels, the modern weapons would clear themselves in moments – but they had a few seconds of silence.

Three battle lasers and five grenade launchers fired into that silence. Full power shots from the battle lasers required a full minute to cool – but also applied a level of force equal to several kilograms of TNT.

The modern, Legatus-built, armor-piercing grenades, on the other hand, simply went clean through the APCs armor before detonating *inside* their crew and passenger compartments.

One vehicle was, to all intents and purposes, *gone* – ripped to pieces by the laser hits. The second was still intact... but an empty hulk, its crew and interior electronics shattered by explosions inside the armor.

"Move," Damien ordered, leading the way past the burned-out wreckage towards the Command Center. Every second they delayed was time for the defenders to get ready for them.

Past the APCs, they rounded another corner to see the slightly larger than usual office tower built on top of the Ardennes Planetary Command Center. Today, any pretense had been abandoned. Planters and glass had disappeared behind thick metal barricades that had risen from the ground, and heavy fixed weapons – mini-guns and automatic grenade launchers – had emerged from hiding places to join them.

A hail of fire greeted them, and Damien used his magic to physically *yank* the entire team back behind cover.

"Well, *that* is going to be a headache," Leclair said quietly.

"We'll deal," Damien replied, but a buzz on his wrist distracted him. Tapping a key, he linked his headset back into the Freedom Wing's net. "What is it?" he demanded.

"We're receiving an encrypted transmission from the incoming cruisers," Riordan told him. Despite his determination to be involved, the demagogue had been quietly shuffled into running their central field communications. "I don't have the code, but I can relay it to you."

The Hand glanced at the scarred street where he'd almost been shot.

"There's no such thing as a good time today, is there?" he asked rhetorically. "Put them through."

#

It took a few seconds for his personal computer to analyze the encrypted transmission and decrypt it. Once it did so, he told it to start with the current location in the message.

"... to reach Hand Damien Montgomery. Hand Montgomery, please come in. This is Mage-Captain Kole Jakab of the *Duke of Magnificence*, attempting to reach Hand Damien Montgomery. Message repeats. This is Mage-Captain Jakab of the..."

"This is Montgomery," Damien interrupted, sending the message back through the Freedom Wing's relay. The recording continued for a few seconds more – if nothing else, the *Duke of Magnificence* was still several light seconds out – then cut out.

"Hand Montgomery, thank God I could reach you," Jakab's interrupted himself. "We have a problem, and it's one I am supremely grateful to dump on higher authority."

"What's going on, Captain?"

"We received a transmission from the surface," the starship commander said grimly. "Tight-beamed to us, but we were clearly expected to relay to whoever was in command. You... you need to hear this, Lord Montgomery."

A different voice replaced Jakab's – not one that Damien was expecting to hear.

"Approaching Protectorate Forces, this is General James Montoya," a calm, even voice sounded in his ears. "Mage-Governor Vaughn has placed me in command of Ardennes's defenses against your un-provoked attack.

"I will not mince words or pretend our innocence against whatever charges you have decided to lay against my governor," he continued. "The destruction of our naval forces has made clear that you are determined to carry this fallacy through to its final conclusion.

"Therefore, you have left me with no choice. As a security measure, thermonuclear charges have been planted in the center of each of Ardennes' six largest cities. Should you attempt to land troops or intervene in our little rebel issue, you will force me to start detonating warheads. I estimate each will kill a minimum of seven million people. Their blood will be on your hands.

"Once we have dealt with our local issues, we can continue this discussion," Montoya continued pleasantly, as if he hadn't just threatened to murder forty-plus million people. "You may enter orbit, but any attempt to act from there will result in unfortunate consequences."

The transmission ended, and Jakab's voice returned.

"What do we *do*?" the Mage-Captain demanded, his voice torn. "We can't let him kill those people, but..."

Father, if you are willing, take away this cup from me, Damien prayed silently, the words coming unbidden to his thoughts and lips. How could he give orders to face *that* threat? Did he have the right – did *anyone* have the right – to risk all of those lives to remove one man from power?

"Vaughn is insane," he whispered, and Amiri and Leclair looked at him. He shook his head at them and slowly straightened, considering the situation.

"Captain, how long until you reach orbit?"

"Ninety-four minutes and counting," Jakab replied, clearly relieved to face an easy question.

He didn't even know what level of the Command Center Montoya would be on. Presumably, Vaughn would also be able to detonate the warheads. If they were together, he could neutralize them both – but all he could count on was that they were both in the Command Center.

Yet not my will, but yours be done, he finished the quote in his head. Regardless of what he wanted, he'd taken the damn Hand, and he'd led everybody this far. No-one would take this particular cup of poison from him.

"Mage-Captain Jakab," he said quietly, firmly, "these are your orders: if by the time you reach orbit you have received no countermanding orders from me, you will initiate a sustained heavy kinetic bombardment of the Ardennes Planetary Command Center. I see no other way to save the *other* cities but to accept collateral damage in Nouveaux Versailles."

Amiri and Leclair were staring at him in shock, and Jakab was silent.

"These orders are non-discretionary, Captain, and should be recorded in the records as such," Damien told Jakab gently. "If I fail, the fault will be mine alone."

"If you fail?" Jakab questioned. "What are you going to be doing?"

Damien sighed and glanced back at the scarred roadway.

"I'm going to be assaulting the Command Center."

#

As soon as he was clearly off the line, Amiri started to speak, but Damien waved her to wait as he triggered another communication code he'd saved in his personal computer.

The little wrist computer hummed for a moment, and then a very young-sounding cheerful voice answered.

"Lieutenant Chau, Ardennes Army Command," the young man introduced himself. "I'm sorry, General Zu is occupied, can I take a message?"

"Tell Zu that it's Montgomery," Damien told the cheerful young aide, "and I need to speak to him now."

He could *hear* the young junior officer swallow. Zu had apparently given the aide answering his phone enough information to at least recognize Damien's name.

The aide was also clearly screening the General's calls, as Zu was on the line *immediately*.

"What's going on, Montgomery?" he demanded. "It's taking everything I've got to keep some of Vaughn's loyalists bottled up, so this better be important."

"It is," Damien told him. "Listen to this." He forwarded Zu Montoya's message.

Zu listened to the message, and Damien could hear the muttered mix of curse words in at least three languages.

"I might be able to swing a few of the fence-sitters with this," he admitted. "Hell, I might even get some of Vaughn's appointees on board, but..."

"I don't need you to go into battle, Zu," the Hand said quietly. "What I *need* are evacuations. Starting *yesterday*. Can you get your men to do that?"

The General was silent for a long moment.

"Fifty million lives," he said finally, his tone suddenly utterly matter of fact. "Yes, My Lord Hand. For fifty million lives, I will get you your evacuations. One way or another."

#

Chapter 41

"My Lord, can I have a moment of your time?"

The last thing Mage-Governor Michael Vaughn expected as he stood in his office, watching the tactical display of the warships sweeping in to end his regime and the terrorists ripping apart his defenses, was Captain Duval's quietly calm voice.

Montoya was the only other person in the office, and he ignored the officer. The General's attention was on his wrist computer's holographic display as he attempted to co-ordinate more forces to help defend the Command Center – at least one Freedom Wing team was supposedly right at their doorstep.

There wasn't much for the Governor of the planet to do at this point, so Vaughn sighed and stepped out of his office, looking at the young officer he'd promoted so recently.

"What is it?" he demanded crossly.

Duval glanced at the other officers and techs in the room. They were all focused on their screens, all three shifts of staff trying desperately to co-ordinate the defense of a planet that was falling apart at the seams. Most of the terrorist attacks seemed to be in Nouveaux Versailles, but entire cities had erupted into rioting and the Army was refusing to respond to Vaughn's orders.

"You need to see something," Duval told the Governor and led him out of the Command Center into a side room. "Montoya ordered us not to tell you," he said softly, once they were out of sight and hearing of the others. "He made a transmission to the Protectorate fleet in your name."

"In *my* name?" Vaughn demanded. "I did not authorize any such thing."

"I know," Duval admitted. "We... weren't supposed to listen in. But I'm running the com network, and it didn't make sense for you to not know if he spoke in your name." He shrugged helplessly. "I can't... you have to see for yourself."

The young officer flipped a voice recording to the Governor's personal computer, and Vaughn eyed it for a moment. This could be some kind of plot, but Duval seemed to have taken his promotion to heart and tied his star even more tightly to the Governor than the rest of the Scorpions.

He hit play, and listened to Montoya's transmission with ever-growing horror. His heart collapsed in his chest as he realized just what his oldest friend's 'insurance policy' actually was.

"Son…" he stopped and cleared his throat, swallowing several times as he tried to understand just what was going on. "Captain Duval," he continued.

Then an alarm klaxon triggered, and both of them charged back into the command center as the main screens lit up with the image of the front entrance.

Vaughn had seen the same camera footage moments before, and the sight of the dozens of Scorpions with their heavy weapons and thick metal barricades had provided a reassurance that Montoya's transmission had turned to ash.

Now, the last remnants of that reassurance slipped away. The barricades were gone, ripped apart by some unimaginable force. Red and black uniformed bodies lay everywhere and even the *concrete* seemed to be burning. A single figure walked forward, slowly, implacably.

One of the soldiers managed to get a grenade launcher working again. A burst of three grenades flashed out at the figure, only to stop in midair and fling themselves back at their launcher. Even as they hit, a tiny white spark flashed into existence underneath the gun – and then exploded with a brilliant flash.

The attacker had just turned a tiny portion of the ground into antimatter. It was a trick many Mages – any decent Ship's Mage, for example – could do. The conversion was the key to the Protectorate's antimatter-driven economy.

It was normally done in vacuum, in sealed environments, and with a touch. Vaughn wasn't aware of *anyone* who could do it at a distance as a *weapon*.

"That's not possible," he whispered. "The Hand is *dead*."

"A Hand falls… another rises," Duval replied, staring at the image. "My Lord… what do we do?"

If Montoya realized the Command Center itself was breached… he would trigger his bombs. Tens of millions of people would die – the very people of Ardennes that Michael Vaughn had sacrificed so much, twisted so much, to uplift.

"Get out of here," he ordered aloud. "All of you – evacuate the Command Center. Let our friend come to *me*."

The duty supervisor glanced towards the closed door of his office, where Montoya was waiting, focusing on the scenes far away from the Command Center.

"I AM YOUR GOVERNOR!" Vaughn bellowed. "This Mage – this Hand, if that is what he is – will face *me*. Get out!"

He kept a careful eye on his office door as Duval ushered the rest out – and made *damned* sure the Scorpion officer in charge didn't get to Montoya.

In all things, in all ways, this was now Michael Vaughn's fight.

#

General James Montoya was still focused on his tablet when Vaughn walked back into his office. He looked up at his Governor and paused. Something about Vaughn's face clearly gave *something* away.

"What is it?" the General demanded.

"The outer defenses have been breached," Vaughn told him calmly. Something about knowing that he was doomed made it... very easy to decide what to do now. "I've ordered everyone to evacuate. It appears we have a Hand on their way."

Montoya held up the arm with his wrist computer. "Then we should access the PA system," he suggested. "I think it's time to discuss our insurance policy."

"The one where you blow up *my* cities and kill *my* people to save your sorry ass?" Vaughn asked conversationally and watched Montoya recoil as if struck.

"If it was about *my* sorry ass, I'd have been on a fast ship a week ago," Montoya snapped. "If this was about *self-preservation*, I'd have run when you *killed a fucking Hand*. This was to get *you* out. It's the only leverage big enough to even get you a head start.

"Besides, this all started when you blew up Karlsberg," the General continued, his voice suddenly calm, silky. "A little hypocritical to be arguing now?"

"Karlsberg was a necessary sacrifice," Vaughn told him gently, shaking his head as he removed his gloves. "Their deaths were a sad necessity to maintain order. Everything we did, James, was done to improve Ardennes and the lot of her people! A few broken skulls, a few rigged elections – these were nothing against what we could do for our planet!

"But to slaughter the very people we set out to uplift? These are *my* people, James. Everything I have done is for them."

"Because the luxuries and the money and the power were nothing?" Montoya asked sardonically. "I'm afraid I don't buy your bullshit, old friend. And I won't let you die for your bullshit, either!"

"And I won't let you blow up my cities," the Mage-Governor replied, channeling power into his runes and preparing to fight his oldest friend.

That moment of preparation, of steeling himself for what he had to do, was a moment he didn't have. He wasn't sure *where* the gun had come from, but it was in Montoya's hand and trained on him.

"I'm sorry, old friend," Montoya said calmly. "I'm with you to the end of the line, but I won't hang with you."

Vaughn hesitated. Montoya didn't.

#

Chapter 42

Damien had just finished ripping the doors off of the elevator shaft when his computer buzzed again.

"What is it?" he demanded harshly, looking at the wreckage of the building.

"It's Zu," the Ardennes Army General told him bluntly. "Are you okay?"

"I just killed thirty-four men for no reason other than that they were between me and Vaughn," Damien replied. "No. What do you want?"

"Trying to help you," Zu said. "Do you have *any* idea where you're going?"

"I have the building schematics from my download," Damien answered, glancing at the holographic display. "Command Center is buried beneath me, accessed via a secure elevator."

A somewhat less secure elevator now.

"Right," the General sighed. "You want the seventh level of the Center, third from the bottom. The elevator opens into a lobby, directly through that lobby is the main Operations Center. Vaughn has set up in an office just off the Center."

"Thank you, General," Damien said after taking a deep breath. "I apologize."

"Don't," Zu said calmly. "I'd rather you be aware of who you kill. There are a lot of people in that Center."

"The fewer of them who end up in my way, the more live," the Hand replied bluntly. "Not having to search helps."

"Good luck, My Lord Hand," Zu finished after a long moment of silence.

Damien cut the channel and stepped into the elevator shaft.

One of the first things a Ship's Mage learned was controlling gravity. In space, it allowed them to walk on ships lacking gravity runes or centrifugal gravity. On a planet, it allowed Damien to control his fall as he plummeted.

The ten floor Command Center was buried five hundred and twenty meters below the office building, and the elevator was locked at the very bottom as a security measure. Control of his speed and local gravity allowed Damien to plunge down the unlit elevator shaft fearlessly.

His personal computer's holographic display was the only light as he dropped, a tiny icon showing how far he'd fallen down the half-kilometer shaft and how close he was to Level Seven.

With trained practice, he slowed his fall and brought himself to a halt outside the sealed doors for the floor Zu directed him to. The doors were heavily reinforced, a multi-layered steel and titanium barrier.

It took him slightly more than ten seconds to burn a man-sized hole through them and step into the underground nerve center of Ardennes planetary defense.

He'd been expecting guards. Soldiers, Enforcers, some kind of defense. Instead, the lobby was empty. A set of high security doors blocked further access into the facility, but they immediately yielded to the overrides in his Hand, allowing him to follow Zu's direction.

When he reached the Operations Center, he knew something was wrong. The room was a series of concentric circles, each equipped with computer consoles and holographic displays. Communication channels linked out across the planet from here. This was the place from which Vaughn had run the planet since burning down his own palace.

It was empty.

There were a handful of doors leading from the room. Most were closed, but one was slightly ajar and Damien could see a light through it. Cautiously, carefully, he approached the door and threw it open.

"Ah, My Lord Hand," the smooth tones of General Montoya greeted him. "I've been waiting for you."

#

The scene inside the office was *nothing* like what Damien had been expecting. He'd expected to find and challenge Vaughn – known to be a powerful Mage, but no match for a Rune Wright with the Runes of Power in his skin.

He'd known General Montoya would likely be there, but the mundane soldier had barely registered in his plans.

Instead, Montoya stood on the opposite side of a mid-sized conference table. *Vaughn* lay crumpled against the wall, apparently having been shot in the stomach. The Mage-Governor appeared to be *breathing*, but not much else.

"Uh-uh," Montoya told Damien as he took a step forward. The Scorpion General held up his arm, showing the holographic display of his personal computer. It was filled with seven flashing red buttons. Even from across the room, Damien could see they were names.

"Take another step forward, and I blow up a city," Montoya said calmly. "Each step, I push a button. How many people are you willing to kill to reach me, My Lord Montgomery?"

"You know you can't escape," Damien told him quietly. "I can't *permit* you to escape."

"Do you really think Ardennes will thank you for overthrowing their tyrant if you kill half a dozen cities along the way?" the mad man on the other side of the room asked. "And it's on a dead man's switch, by the way," he added as Damien shifted in place. "Kill me, and all seven bombs go off. Fifty million people or so. Do you really want to have that much blood on your hands?"

"What do you *want*?" Damien asked. He was playing for time, trying to see an option. It was possible Montoya was lying about the dead man's switch – in which case, killing the man would save them. If not... even his orders to Jakab could still see the charges detonate.

"I want a shuttle and a fast ship," Montoya told him calmly. He glanced over at Vaughn. "Oh, and a doctor on said ship for our dear Governor here. In the end, it seems he lacked the fortitude for what needed to be done. He'll live, though. I'll save him before his wounds get too bad," he continued cheerfully. "That's what friends are for, isn't it?"

"I can't let you or Vaughn walk," the Hand told him quietly. "De-activate the detonators and hand over your PC, and I'll guarantee your lives."

As he spoke, he was tapping on his own PC behind his back, trying to feel his way through control menus by memory.

"I don't think my friend here or I have any interest in being paraded through the streets of Olympus Mons for the edification of the common rabble," Montoya snapped. "Keep your hands where I can see them," he added, gesturing with the computer – now the deadliest weapon on the planet. "You've a reputation for trickery – one well deserved, I see. We didn't even know you were a Hand."

"That was your first mistake," Damien told him, bringing his computer out in front. He'd apparently made it most of the way through the menus he was seeking, the ones only a Hand would have. It looked... possible.

"No, our mistake was killing Stealey rather than just running," Montoya told him. "A Hand falls, another rises. I should have known one of you would have come out the woodwork. No more stalling! Either call a ship, or I start pushing buttons."

The Scorpion's finger drifted towards one of the holographic buttons, and Damien cursed.

"Fine!" he snapped. "I'll have to call the Fleet, I don't know what ships are in system."

"Play nice now," Montoya said mockingly, but gestured for Damien to proceed.

Before he could do *anything*, a third voice bellowed: "No!"

Both of them had forgotten about Vaughn. The extent of the Governor's wounds were such that *any* exertion would likely be fatal –

probably why he'd been lying quiescent against the wall. Faced with Montoya's vicious threat *working*, the Mage-Governor acted anyway.

He lunged to his feet and across the room, a blade of force flashing from his hand to slash across Montoya's upper arm. Blood spurted as the two friends stared at each other in shock, and then a second blade of force flashed out to remove Montoya's head.

Even as the personal computer, still wrapped around half of Montoya's arm, fell to the ground, Damien was back into his own computer, digging for the command he knew was there, hoping – praying – he found it before being severed from the body triggered whatever criteria the dead man's switch needed.

The holographic screen started to flash – and then suddenly shut off as a Hand's override hit the tiny computer and shut it completely down.

For a long, seemingly eternal, moment they waited. Nothing happened. No earthquakes from buried warheads. No disturbances. Not even dust from the ceiling.

Finally, Damien turned his attention back to the two men in the room with him. Montoya was dead. Vaughn had chopped his General and friend into several pieces.

Vaughn himself had collapsed back to the floor. Whatever rough first aid Montoya had done before Damien arrived had been ripped open, and blood was *pulsing* from the gut wound. He looked up at Damien, gritting his teeth against the pain.

"He was right," Mage-Governor Michael Vaughn said harshly. "I have no interest in being paraded through the streets like a common criminal." He coughed, spattering blood all over himself. "Don't think you're taking me alive."

"It was never a priority," Damien said calmly, looking down at the man who bent an entire world to his twisted will. "You'd done too much harm, even before you killed Stealey."

Vaughn coughed up more blood. "You may judge me," he said, his voice clogged, "but everything I did... I did for Ard..."

The Mage-Governor and Tyrant of Ardennes stopped in mid-sentence, doubling over with more coughing, more blood. He convulsed once, and then was still.

#

Walking back out into the Operations Center to get away from the blood, Damien tapped back into the communications network, linking himself to Zu, Armstrong, and Jakab.

"The detonator is disarmed," he reported to them all. "Vaughn and Montoya are dead. What's our status?"

"Most of the surface-to-space defenses are offline," Armstrong told him. "The Wing is in control of most of Versailles, but we could use some help."

"I have the Army evacuating most of the major cities other than Versailles," Zu reported, "but there is unrest. No-one is sure what is happening, everyone is afraid."

"We'll be entering orbit in twenty minutes," Jakab reported in turn. "I'll have Marine boots on the ground shortly after that, but we won't have many until Adamant gets here. That'll be several hours, but she's got two thousand Marines on that battleship."

"Marines will help," Zu confirmed. "Mars has removed their Governor, people will look to Mars for answers. It would perhaps be best if we... got ahead of the rumors."

"What do you suggest?" Armstrong asked.

"From the Operations Center, Lord Montgomery can access the Governor's emergency override channel," the old General told them all. "That will allow him to speak to everyone. They need to see what has happened – they need to know a steady hand is at the tiller. The people of Ardennes need to see the Hand of Mars."

Damien nodded, taking a deep breath as he glanced around the abandoned room.

"Let's be about it."

#

Epilogue

There was an austere beauty to Olympus Mons in winter.

Damien shivered under his heavy black coat as he and Amiri caught up to the funeral entourage making its way up the mountain. He hadn't been sure they would make it on time, and he was reasonably sure Mage-Captain Jakab had pushed the course into Mars rather more than he should have.

This wasn't a funeral he had wanted to miss.

Kiera, perhaps inevitably, spotted them first. The Princess of Mars, Second in line for the Throne under the Mountain, yanked on her father's hand and pointed. Damien met his King's eyes as Alexander glanced back and bowed his head.

Alexander acknowledged him with a nod, and then turned his head back forwards, saying something quiet to his daughter. Damien knew he and the Mage-King needed to talk, but now was not the time.

Above the tiny, barely thirty strong, procession spread the Fields of Sorrow. Marked on the edges by unmarked black basalt obelisks half-buried in the snow, the mass grave of the Eugenicists' young victims stretched for kilometers upon kilometers. No-one knew how many bodies were buried there. No-one even knew their designations – for the children of the Olympus Project had never been given names. They were numberless, and nameless.

At the base of the Fields was a single low-slung structure carved of the same black basalt as the markers. The snow had been cleared from the front of the Black Mausoleum that morning, Damien presumed, but already several inches had gathered again.

Two hundred and fifty crypts had been built at the base of the Fields. The first men and women buried there were those who had died liberating the survivors of the Olympus Project. Since then, only a select handful of souls had ever been interred here.

Here lay the Mage-Kings.

Here lay their Hands.

At the front of the procession, Alaura Stealey's two nieces, both in their mid-teens, stoically carried their aunt's coffin. The entire crowd was silent as they followed, the only noise the crunching of feet on snow.

The two girls carried the coffin forward, past the first one hundred and sixty two crypts, each marked with a name etched forever into the basalt by magic.

Alaura was lucky in a strange way, Damien reflected as he walked past the graves of those who had worn the symbol he now bore. Of those hundred and sixty two crypts, only ninety-three actually contained bodies.

Hands did not always die in places or ways that allowed their family and their King to inter a body.

Finally, they reached the one hundred and sixty-third crypt. The slab of rock that would form its door was laid to the side, leaning against the wall of the Mausoleum. No name had yet been carved into the stone.

Silently, under the eyes of strangers they likely had never met – strangers who were the leaders of their government! – the two teenagers slid the coffin into the waiting crypt. If a tiny flash of magic helped catch a corner that slipped on chilled fingers, no-one present judged.

They stepped back. The Mage-King stepped forward, standing next to the black hole for a long moment, and then glanced back.

"Damien, I'm glad you could make it," he said quietly, but loudly enough to be heard. "You were with her closest to the end. Will you help me?"

Swallowing, Damien walked forward. The tiny crowd parted for him and he could hear the murmuring. He wore the Hand openly on his chest – and spotted two others in the procession. He met the gaze of Desmond's other Hands, and saw only support and sympathy there.

Somehow, that was enough.

He joined his King at the crypt of his teacher and met Alexander's eyes.

"There isn't much to it," Alexander whispered. "Just follow my lead."

Then the Mage-King raised his hand, and with a small flash of power, black basalt began to turn white. He started at the beginning of the name – Damien started at the end.

When they met in the middle, 'Alaura Stealey' was carved into the crypt. That was it. No dates of birth or death – the first few dozen burials here had been of men and women who didn't *know* when they'd been born, and the tradition continued.

With her name forever marked for the world to see, Damien and Desmond each took ahold of part of the basalt plinth with their magic, lifting it gently into place to forever seal off Alaura Stealey from the world she had served.

#

Later, there was food and drink. Warships ran on Olympus Mons Time, so Damien had re-adjusted to the time of his home before arriving, but none of the food appealed to him. With a single glass of half-drunk wine, he propped up a smoothed stone wall and watched the quiet, low-key, party.

"I'm glad you made it back in time," Desmond Alexander told him. Damien turned to find his King watching him, the older Mage's eyes unreadable. "We had to wait for Alaura's family to arrive, but we couldn't hold off much longer."

"I... wasn't sure I should leave," Damien admitted. "Watts seemed to have things in hand, but..." he shrugged. "Jakab is still in orbit, I should be able to return relatively quickly."

"That won't be necessary, Damien," Alexander said dryly. "With Zu and Armstrong both on side with Watts, the situation seems well under control. You did good work. Better than I dared to hope for."

"We came too close to disaster," the Hand whispered.

"Get used to it," his King advised. "You won't often find situations that aren't on the edge of disaster in my service. With the resources Watts has at his command now, you aren't needed on Ardennes. You delivered him the planet with Vaughn removed and the civil war ended – what more did you think you needed to do?

"No," the Mage-King of Mars said firmly, "your mission to Ardennes is complete. It was far more difficult than any of us expected, and you rose to the challenge with flying colors. You have earned that trinket." He tapped the golden hand on Damien's chest.

"Now," he continued, "you will rest. In the morning, you will report to Doctor Andreas – he's the Mountain's new chief psychiatrist.

"Once Andreas has cleared you for duty, I have another mission for you," Desmond Michael Alexander told his Hand softly. "You know the reward for a job well done, after all."

#

If you enjoyed the novel, please leave a review!

To be notified of future releases, join my mailing list at
www.faolanspen.com

Other books by Glynn Stewart

Starship's Mage
Starship's Mage: Omnibus
Hand of Mars
Voice of Mars (upcoming, see www.faolanspen.com for latest estimated launch date)

Space Carrier Avalon
Space Carrier Avalon
The Stellar Fox (upcoming, see www.faolanspen.com for latest estimated launch date)

Stand Alone Novels
Children of Prophecy
City in the Sky

Made in the USA
Middletown, DE
26 November 2015